SINS OF OUR BLOOD

Thunder Moon

R. Nicholas Pohtos

Copyright © 2020 Robert Nicholas Pohtos

All rights reserved.

ISBN: 979-8-9854842-0-5

DEDICATION

Dedicated to sound serial moviemakers like William Whitney and all the others who crafted cliffhanger endings that made us have to come back in a week to see the next episode as well as for the popcorn and candy.

CONTENTS

ACKNOWLEDGMENTS

NOTE TO READERS

THE STAGE

THE LIST OF PLAYERS

PROLOGUE – 1986   1

1   SINS OF THE FATHERS -1986   2

2   WAGES OF SIN - 2016   13

3   LETHAL LIQUOR   21

4   FALLING TO THE END OF HERSELF   26

5   ANY LANDING YOU WALK AWAY FROM   32

6   THROUGH THE LOOKING GLASS   42

7   THE PLANNER AND PAINT   54

8   ASSAULT IN AN OLD WOUND   60

9   EXPLOSIVE MEMORIAL   72

10   LAST WILL AND BAY CRUISE   80

11   A FAMILY FALLING OUT   90

12   RECKLESS PASSING   98

13   IN THE CROSSHAIRS   109

14   SHE'S STILL A KNOCKOUT   116

15   PRESSING MATTERS   122

16	CRUSHING DEFEAT	132
17	A CHEATING HEART	144
18	DEADLY OPENER	153
19	TROUBLED WATERS	162
20	A ROCKY FINISH	174
21	R.I.P. TIDE	183
22	A SHOT IN THE DARK	192
23	FIREWORKS AND MOONLIGHT	202
24	DEADLY TOUGH LOVE	209
25	A FALL DOESN'T KILL – A SUDDEN STOP DOES	217
26	THE FATAL SHOT	227
27	HEART ATTACK AND HEARTBREAK	238
28	BOMBS AND BULLETS	246
29	HEAD FAKE	255
	EPILOGUE - 2019	260

ACKNOWLEDGMENTS

Several people deserve acknowledgement and thanks for their encouragement, review of, edits proposed for, and comments on the many drafts before publication.

Journalism professor, Tom Bowers, provided a much needed and thorough edit of the first draft. His contributions are much appreciated.

Historian and educator, Rachel Thompson, provided chapter-by-chapter specific comments, suggested changes and critique. Her feedback regarding writing style and storytelling - scene setting, pace and tone – were invaluable in completing a quality final draft.

Navy shipmate and fellow writer, Bill Rohm, provided a storyteller instinct that compelled a revision to the opening chapters. This greatly improved the telling of the tale as well as a better reader hook.

Fellow author, Joel Pannebaker, provided comments that refined dialogue and proved once again how invaluable another set of reader/author eyes is in polishing a manuscript.

Aviator extraordinaire, Skipp Maiden, provided invaluable technical feedback that made for a more realistic crash landing in Chapter 5.

Likewise, Rich Zaia, Ernie Terril, Teri Cassias, Susan Collins and Paul Gappa provided suggestions and observations that helped to better mold character actions and reactions.

My sister, Judy Harris, provided encouragement and comments on the very rough original manuscript. The first to express a 'ladies' take on the original ending - echoed by several others - compelled a revision that I hope satisfies.

Pastor John Woodall, graciously granted permission to use his personal boyhood tale of confronting a bully. This gave a principal antagonist a needed depth of character that would otherwise have been noticeably absent.

Last, but not least, my wife, Samantha, provided love, encouragement, support, patience and understanding. This was especially true on those days when I was very much caught up in the imaginary world of Driftwood Cove, making her feel I was missing in action.

If I have missed someone, my apologies.

NOTE TO READERS

Sins of Our Blood was written to tell a tale along the lines of the 1930s-1940s American movie matinee sound serials. Popular in the pre-TV first half of the 20th century, the serials are prototypical of later television shows and akin to TV mini-series. They consist of twelve or fifteen chapters or episodes, each fifteen to twenty minutes long. Chapters were shown sequentially over as many weekends in local, single-screen theaters prior to the afternoon's main feature.

Chapters generally follow a set pattern. Each begins with a resolution to the prior week's cliffhanger ending in which one or all heroes appeared to suffer a fatal injury. The chapter's middle contains action sequences; fist and gun fights and high-speed chases are the norm along with enough dialogue to move the story along as well as set up a cliffhanger ending. Such an ending usually includes a devilish peril contrived by the villains to kill the hero. The final scene is staged such that it appears they succeed.

Sound serials have a typical cast of characters. Protagonists - good guys - include at least one clean-cut young woman and man. Good guys, motivated by just the desire to do good, are courageous and self-sacrificing. Antagonists - bad guys - are, well ... bad, greedy for wealth, power or both. Directors and screenwriters referred to the object of their greed as 'the weenie.' Good guys also pursue the weenie, but for good and not the evil the bad guys intend. Good and bad guys and the weenie are introduced in the first episode, but each chapter's story is told such that an episode can be missed with minimal loss of entertainment value.

The sound serial's target audience was adolescent. So, there is little character arc. Rarely included is any depth, development or explanation of why a character is good or bad. Given a juvenile audience, there is little romance beyond a suggestion of developing affection between the lead good guy and gal. Noteworthy exceptions are found in the 1930s serials. For instance, in the three Flash Gordon serials Flash and Dale Arden fall in love and are demonstratively affectionate.

Though the sound serial construct is the inspiration and adopted for *Sins of Our Blood*, it doesn't translate quite as easily into a novel as it does into a screenplay. Written using the close third person, character arcs were inevitable. Still, a three-part structure in each chapter is sustained: start with the cliffhanger resolution, include middle action and the cliffhanger setup, and conclude with an apparent lethal event. Also, I included a slow simmer, developing romance between the good guy and gal as well as a boy-gets-girl ending – with a cliffhanger like twist of course!

R. Nicholas (Bob) Pohtos
Ashburn, Virginia, USA

THE STAGE

THE LIST OF PLAYERS

Moses Martin .... Founder GASMAX Industries

Corbin Schwartz .... Martin Family Doctor

Niles Tannerson .... Moses' Silent Partner & Chemical Engineer

Melody Tannerson .... Niles' Daughter

Justice (J) Martin .... Moses' Oldest Son & GASMAX Chief Engineer

Joan Johnson Martin .... J's Wife

Sylvia Martin .. J's & Joan's Oldest Daughter & J's Executive Assistant

Clint Martin... J's & Joan's Middle Child & J's Special Projects Assistant

Dannell (Danny) Martin ...... J's & Joan's Youngest & Plant Operator

Jacob (Jake) Martin .... Moses' Middle Son & Paramedic

Mary Marks Martin .... Jake's Wife

Cynthia Jones ...... Jake's & Mary's Daughter & GASMAX Executive

Joel Martin .... Moses' Youngest Son & GASMAX CEO & President

Tanner Strong .... GASMAX Corporate Pilot, Driver & Security

Julie Simpson .... Private Investigator

Buck Wilson .... Danny's Boyfriend

Louis Belmont .... Martin Family Lawyer

Brian Smith .... Driftwood Cove Chief of Police

R. NICHOLAS POHTOS

PROLOGUE

1986

Handwritten note on a flyleaf page torn from the Martin family Bible

Niles and Melody Tannerson were my other family. They and their home, the Tannerson House, were a haven and tonic for my mind, body and soul. The old house was firmly anchored on the rural, rocky outskirts of the Village of Sand Dollar. The two-story, wood framed home and five generations of Niles' family survived over a century and a half of nature's numerous assaults as well as Tannerson family eccentricities and dysfunction. Nature's frequent invaders - blizzards, tornadoes, earthquakes and hurricanes – pitilessly assailed the rugged four walls and roof. Still, the old house survived to shelter and protect Niles and Melody as it had their ancestors. According to Niles, over a dozen times the house was pummeled by hail that holed shingles and broke windows, near ten times ice collapsed tree limbs and crushed its roof, and, more than a handful of times, thunderbolts overwhelmed and bypassed the lightning rods arrayed along the peak of the black shingled roof. Unbeknownst to any Tannerson was that an early lightning strike likely initiated a crack in the loadbearing beam above the living room ceiling. Undetected, it's speculated, the crack grew with subsequent decades of battering, but, over the many decades, the beam held and the house stood – until that fateful night, just weeks ago, during the hurricane of 86. In the thick of that tempest, I was made all too painfully aware of that fractured beam. Worst yet, I fear my iniquity and deceit, though well-intended, joined ranks with Niles' and the storm to finally crush the Tannerson house and family and dump retribution for my sins into the laps of my children and of theirs after them. Can my wife or they or God forgive me?

Do what's necessary, love God and do good in keeping with repentance.
GASMAX Industries Company & Martin Family Maxim

CHAPTER 1

Sins of the Fathers - 1986

Village of Sand Dollar Tannerson House

DOCTOR CORBIN SCHWARTZ STEPPED INTO the Tannerson House's living room. After his eyes adjusted to the dim light cast by a single candle, he sighed and announced, "It's done." His voice, laced with regret and fatigue, possessed an accent betraying Southern origins. Regret because two patients had died despite his best efforts. Fatigue because of, in addition to a duo of complicated deliveries, driving for over two hours in what the citizens of Sand Dollar dubbed 'the storm of the century.'

Three times he had traveled the motorway running between the village's hospital and the Tannerson home. The twenty-mile stretch of road ran due west from the coastal community, and it was more dirt and gravel than asphalt. Rain had reduced its mixed surface to mud and, several times, the visibly to near zero. This night it was partially obstructed by trees knocked down by powerful winds swirling about the hurricane's eye. As he completed the third trek, the eye of the storm passed over the Village of Driftwood Cove another hundred miles farther south along the Atlantic's rocky northeast coast.

The tempest's track had compelled an emergency evacuation from Driftwood Cove's hospital to Sand Dollar's of all its many patients and, what was proving to be too few, physicians and nurses. As a result, though only a first-year intern, Dr. Schwartz had completed the two complicated, emotionally and physically draining deliveries.

The midwife for the planned natural birth at Tannerson House was absent due to the storm. So, Schwartz had been dispatched. Despite four-wheel drive and a young man's reflexes and determination, by the time he reached the mother-to-be, Melody Tannerson, she had lost too much blood. Despite just twenty-plus years of age, she didn't survive, but she delivered a healthy baby girl. Corbin rushed the newborn to the hospital.

Upon the doctor's arrival at the hospital, Mary Martin, an expectant mother evacuated from Driftwood, went into premature labor. Due to the storm, her husband wasn't present and couldn't be contacted. Since the doctor knew her father-in-law, he called Moses Martin. He wasn't surprised when the Martin family patriarch requested that he deliver Mary's child. Sadly, the infant female was stillborn due to placental abruption.

With no other family to inform, he immediately notified Moses. That sad conversation necessitated his last journey to the Tannerson house. Upon arrival, with Mary's dead child in a swaddled bundle and cradled in the crux of his arm, he hurried up the front steps. Since power was out, he slowly made his way to the living room. Water running off his raincoat puddled around his feet. The exhausted physician made his two-word announcement of completion and handed a sealed plastic file folder to the house's sole living inhabitant, Moses Martin.

Bathed in the pale-yellow candlelight, Moses Martin looked up and set a book with gilt-edged pages on the coffee table. He stood and clasped a large hand on the doctor's shoulder. Martin's grip was firm but with a gentleness that surprised Corbin and belied Moses' large, lean six-and-a-half-foot frame. He was a head taller and almost three decades older than the stocky young doctor who was dressed in scrubs beneath a dripping yellow rain slicker.

"Well done, Corbin," Moses said in a strong baritone that easily rose above the sound of heavy rain on the walls and windows. "Is ... was that my granddaughter?"

Lightening flashed, and the room briefly filled with vivid white light before a crack and boom of thunder rattled the house. Unbeknownst to either man, an unseen crack in the living room ceiling beam grew another inch.

Corbin nodded. In the brief illuminated instant, he saw that the older man's face was etched with sorrow, regret and a fatigue of its own.

Moses tentatively extended his hand toward the bundle, but, choking back a sob, withdrew it suddenly.

Schwartz nodded toward the folder. "It's all there."

"Original birth and death certificates?" Moses asked, having regained his composure and thumbing through the folder's contents. "Copies too?"

"Yes. Elizabeth Tannerson's and Cynthia Martin's as well as copies of the ... ah ... revised documents," the doctor replied.

"Very good," Moses said sadly. He smiled and handed Corbin an unsealed envelope. "You more than earned this."

Corbin accepted the open envelope. He glanced at the check inside. "Wow," he managed after a pause, realizing what the money represented. "Mr. Martin, you've been more than generous financing my education. Thank you. This lifts a great weight, but ... what we did tonight. It is ... feels ... wrong."

"Never mind that, just put her with ... with Mel ... the mother," Moses said, shaking his head slowly.

The doctor crammed the envelope in his coat pocket and carried out Moses' command. He laid the stillborn body next to Melody Tannerson's remains in the bed in an upstairs room and rejoined Martin.

"It's done," he said. "Mr. Martin, I ... I've got to go. We're shorthanded at the hospital. You can go with me. This old house sounds like it's about to collapse."

"I understand, Corbin, but you look like you're about to collapse. Stay and wait out the storm." Moses pointed at the couch. "My years in the merchant marine tells me that the recent barometer change and wind shift means there's only another hour of a really hard blow. And don't worry. The coroner's probably slammed at the hospital and won't be here until tomorrow. I'll take care of the paperwork. Now sit with me, and, please, call me Moses."

Amplifying Martin's commanding presence and bolstering his assertion, another flash of lightning and a clap of thunder rattled the windows. That and weariness compelled Corbin to shrug off the raincoat and sit. "What ... what was that!" he asked. "I heard a crack." Still unseen, the living room ceiling beam's fissure widened.

Driftwood Cove Wilkes Tavern

"ONE MORE SHOULD do it," Joel Martin, youngest of Moses Martin's three sons, declared loudly. His young boyish features glistened with sweat as he drained the beer bottle that made an even dozen for the night. He tossed it over his shoulder and hefted a fire extinguisher above his head. The oldest sibling, Justice Martin, 'J' to family and close acquaintances, and the middle child, Jacob Martin, were only a few bottles behind. Despite their natural skepticism of most of their little brother's claims, they tapped their bottles' long necks and cheered him on. The metal cylinder came down fast and hard, causing a loud collision of metal-on-metal easily audible above the howl of hurricane winds and the creaking timbers of the century old Wilkes Tavern. The lock held fast.

"Okay, little bro," J, tallest of the Martin boys, slurred, elbowing Joel aside, "you almost got it. This is no job for a business major, let the family engineer have a go at it."

"Hey," Joel protested, rolling aside and laughing as J took his place. "Some hurricane parteee, huh guys?" Joel asserted as he sat. He rearranged his wiry frame and plunged his hand into the plastic cooler. "Too bad sweet Joan had to go."

"Not bad at all. I'm glad my bride got out of here with our car," J countered, looking up before examining the lock and testing his grip on the fire extinguisher. "And, Joel, you are a bit too handsy with the ladies – any lady - when you've had a few. Most importantly, Hurricane Rob or Bob is a killer, one of the top five worst in Atlantic history. It may yet shake this old tavern down on our heads. Jake, move that light a bit to the right."

"Sure," Jacob replied and rotated one of the three high intensity military grade flashlights which illuminated the lock. He told his brothers he had "borrowed" them from the fire and rescue station where he worked as a fire fighter and paramedic. They were his contribution to Joel's hastily arranged hurricane party at the old tavern perched just barely one hundred yards inland of the cliff that dropped over five stories to Driftwood Cove's Smugglers Cove Beach. "I'm just glad Mary's too far along in her pregnancy to join this insanity. Joel, next time the company builds a hydroelectric plant, please pick a part of the East Coast out of the likely path of hurricanes."

"That's 'tidal hydroelectric plant,' my man," Joel corrected his stout but muscular sibling, pointing to where he thought north was. "Don't diss my brainchild. I brought this concept to dear old Dad, CEO and boss of all at GAS-ELECTRIC-MAX. That tidal basin a few miles up da coast will be a gold mine someday. Mark my words. I see a future with GEM plants all up and down the Coast and around the globe."

Jacob snorted. "I see an immediate future with a hangover up and down your drunken butt."

"That's if we live to see either future," J added flatly, as he pushed his glasses back up his long narrow nose and raised the extinguisher over his head. "Don't let it go to your head, Jake, but for once I agree with you. We should have left with Joan and our company colleagues when the cops showed to break up this parteee. You shouldn't be in this tavern's cellar, but at home with your expecting wife."

"Oh, she's weeks away from delivery," Jake said. "Besides Joan said ..."

"Justice, my big brother and fearless leader of Old man Moses Martin's boys," Joel said, cutting off Jake, "don't be so true to your name and such a party pooper like our papa. We'll be fine. I scouted out this burg for months. According to locals, there's a tunnel below that trapdoor that runs to the beach. We'll be safe down there even if this old tavern collapses."

"Hope you're right. Just pray they don't have to dig us out," J said and brought the metal cylinder down with a grunt. The lock snapped open.

"Thank God!" Jacob shouted and downed his beer's dregs.

Joel stared at the open lock with wide eyes. He slapped J's back. "That's why I'm so glad Dad hired you on as chief engineer. You're a man who knows how to get done what needs ... what's necessary. Let's get below, boys. J, give me a hand." He and J, with great effort lifted and heaved open the wooden door. Joel swung one leg over the opening.

"Whoa," Jacob ordered, grabbing his little brother's arm. "Let me check it out first." He looked from Joel to J and shook his head. "You two wouldn't last a minute at a fire."

Despite the alcohol, Jacob nimbly grabbed a flashlight, dropped flat on his stomach and stuck his head and the light through the trapdoor. "Looks okay. There's a metal ladder and lots of head room," he reported. "But man, does it smell of rotted fish or something."

A crash shook the cellar roof. "Whatever, it may soon be much better than staying put. Let's go, men," J commanded, picked up his light and lowered himself until his foot found the first ladder rung. "Come on." His brothers followed.

Jacob was last down the ladder. "What the ..." he started when he didn't find J and Joel waiting for him and before he saw the glow of their flashlights beyond a bend further down the passage. He tested his footing and checked overhead. He grimaced and wiped his eyes. In addition to odor of blackish, standing water, the smell of fish, saltwater and something more pungent assailed his senses. The sandy floor was firm enough for a brisk walk. Joining Joel and J, he noted that the tunnel overhead was heavily timbered and high enough to accommodate the upright stride of even J's six-foot plus frame.

"It's a hidey hole," Joel said as Jacob stood next to J. Joel shined his light down and into a six-by-six-foot framed hole in the side of the tunnel. Its wooden door was broken off rusted hinges and leaned against the tunnel wall. "Smugglers would hide or store their contraband here until they could safely remove it. One of the old timers told me Wilkes Tavern was a speakeasy during Prohibition. You can almost see crates of bootleg whiskey stacked in there. Come on, let's see what else."

Joel flashed his light down the tunnel and followed the path it illuminated. J shrugged and nudged Jacob to follow. "This looks pretty solidly built," Jacob said, continuing to examine the sides and overhead, "but if just one or two key timbers let go ..."

Suddenly air rushed through the tunnel. The hairs on J's arms stood on end. "I don't like the feel of that. Joel, wait up," he shouted. When he and Jacob turned the next bend, the airflow in the tunnel suddenly reversed. They found Joel at an apparent dead-end. His flashlight lay on the ground casting enough light so that his brothers could see that Joel had his back pressed against wooden planks blocking the way. Pushing with his legs, his heels slipped, and the barrier didn't move.

Joel looked up. "Great. Get in here guys," he directed, nodding to the empty space on either side of him.

"Is that wise?" Jacob asked as J bunched in next to Joel. With his flashlight's beam, he traced the boundaries of the wooden barrier of boards nailed to a frame of logs anchored to a massive overhead beam. "That thing could be holding this end of the tunnel up. Or, maybe, that'll open right onto the beach and into the storm."

"Oh man up, my brother. Where's your sense of adventure?" Joel motioned again for Jacob to get on his other side. Shaking his head, Jacob joined them. "Okay, now push." The wooden barrier moved suddenly, broke free of the overhead beam and collapsed. The three men fell. "The beam!" J shouted, crossing his arms in front of him.

Village of Sand Dollar Tannerson House

"RELAX, DOCTOR," MOSES said. The older man sat next to Corbin. He placed the folder in the briefcase set on the coffee table next to the book that Corbin now recognized to be a Bible. "This old house is like me. It has good bones. We both tend to rattle and creak in a storm, but we don't break."

"You reading the Bible isn't a confidence builder," Schwartz said and sat back. "Still, I'll defer to your judgement in the matter of storms and houses, but what about the babies?"

"Look, I'm as good a judge of character as of the weather. You're a good man, Corbin, and you're becoming an excellent physician. My continued generosity in funding your education is selfish. I consider it a retainer. I knew I could trust you tonight when circumstances presented this ... opportunity." He patted Corbin's knee. "You deserve to finish your internship without all that student loan debt, but, most importantly, you did a good thing tonight. You gave an orphan a good home and spared a new mom the heartache of stillbirth. Also, you have my family's gratitude for life. You'll appreciate that someday soon."

Which family? Corbin wondered silently. "But what about Melody's dad? We didn't spare him heartache," Schwartz countered aloud. Another lightning flash and thunder clap rattled the wood-framed structure already creaking due to high and gusting wind. The crack in the ceiling beam at the inside wall grew to span the entire beam's width. "By the way, where is Niles Tannerson?"

"Mel's father is out of town on business," Moses said. "My eccentric and silent business partner and his daughter are my ... friends ... close friends like family. Since I was in Sand Dollar on business, he asked me to look in on Mel. I'm glad I did."

"Won't he be devastated by ...?" Corbin started, pointing above.

"No," Moses said, cutting him off. "Corbin, Niles wasn't happy or excited about the pregnancy, and he despised the father. He was a twenty-something punk who abandoned Mel before wrapping his car around a tree."

"But, Niles' daughter and, he'll believe, his granddaughter died tonight."

Moses shook his head. "He had a very strained and distant relationship with Mel," he said sadly. "Niles is brilliant but ... not given to traditional family values or sentiment."

"Uh, Mr. Martin ... Moses, I'm sorry," Corbin said, sensing some deeper connection between Martin and Tannerson that was none of his business. He sought to change the topic. "Where's Mary's husband? Her sister-in-law, Joan, and your wife showed up right after I made the switch."

"Jake's out with his brothers at some damn fool hurricane party in Driftwood Cove." Moses snorted. "The Driftwood Police said my boys left when they broke up the party at the tavern, but I couldn't reach him when I heard that Mary was in the hospital or when she was evacuated up here. So, I phoned Joan and Rose after your call. Besides, Jake's absence made our swap possible."

"I see," Schwartz said.

"Conveniently, Niles and Jake were both out of the way for the evening, making possible this act of family justice or compassion, for lack of a better term. And, doctor."

"Yes?"

"That's just the Martin family now, me, Rose, and my boys and their children. We're the only family you need to concern yourself with. Understood?"

Schwartz looked at Moses and nodded slowly. "Understood," he said finally, wondering if the envelope in his pocket was worth this understanding.

Driftwood Cove Smugglers Cove Beach

AFTER BREAKING FREE of the overhead beam, the wooden barrier crashed back onto a pile of driftwood. The three brothers fell with it and rolled onto the beach.

"You guys, okay?" J shouted as they staggered to their feet. Brushing sand off his arms, he looked back. The light from their flashlights outlined the tunnel entrance. "Thank God. That beam, only one end came loose. It just dropped a foot or so. Jake, you were right. That beam and the whole end of the tunnel could have killed us."

"Whoa!" Joel gasped, eyeing the sagging timber. He knocked sand out of his black hair. "Jake, are you alright, man?"

"Yeah, yeah I'm okay," Jacob replied. "Hey, who turned off the storm?" Lightening flashed with distant thunder, revealing a wide but sharply curving beach that sloped down to a vague surf line. Shortly after a crash of thunder, another bolt of far-off lightning backlit the high bluffs that completely encompassed the unseen waters of the circular cove except for where they ended and defined a narrow seaward entrance to the cove's sheltered waters.

"Turned off the ..." J started, shook his head and held his hand out. "You're right! The wind and rain have stopped!"

"No, no, not stopped!" Joel shouted and danced about his brothers. "This is so cool. That old guy told me about this. You see this cove is some kind of rare geographic-hydraulic formation. With the right wind, seas and pressure, this cove is an acoustic and hydraulic shadow zone."

"Joel, did you hit your head?" J asked, grabbing Joel by the shoulders and examining his scalp.

"I'm okay, really," Joel asserted and shook free of J's grasp. He pointed seaward. "The storm's still out there beyond the entrance. But in here the wind is a whisper and the rain this mist. Look now. Wait for it ..." Lightening flashed. Before the thunder Joel continued, "See dead calm waters and ... crap! Did you see that?"

"Yeah, I did," J stammered. His next words were drowned out in a clap of thunder.

"What was it?" Jacob shouted. "I didn't see anything ..." Another flash of lightning revealed the answer. Just before where the beach disappeared into the darkness, a large sailboat was beached and heeled over. The brothers briefly saw that its mainmast was bent forward and what little sail it had up was shredded.

"Jake, get the flashlights," J ordered.

"One step ahead of you, bro," Jacob said and handed out the flashlights. "Let's go. There may be survivors."

"How did that happen if this is a shadow zone?" J asked as the three approached the boat. He still couldn't get over how quiet it was. It was possible to hear the sound of their steps in the wet sand. He swept his light up and over the boat's topside and broken rigging.

Joel's shoulders sagged as the beam of his light followed J's. "That's the rest of it. The local guy said that when conditions create the shadow zone, they also make it possible for very large waves to form tsunami-like in the cove. The water level can rise without warning to flood and flush this beach. If there was anyone onboard, they may already have been swept out to sea. I don't ..."

"Look!" Jacob broke in. "There in the sand." The oval patch of light cast by Jacob's flashlight illuminated a man face down and spread-eagled just forward of the boat's midsection. The three men ran to his side. Jacob knelt beside him and rolled him over. He felt along his throat and then pressed his ear to his chest. "No pulse. No breath," he stated flatly, and rolled him on his side and pried open his mouth. Some water came out. Rolling him flat again, he started CPR. After several tries, Jacob sat back and sighed. "It's no use. We're too late. He's gone."

"Hey, look at this," Joel said as he raised the man's right arm. Though the dead man was dressed in the expected yellow rain suit of a mariner caught in a storm, clutched in his right hand was a briefcase. Joel looked closer at the man's face. "Looks more like some egghead college prof than a sailor. Tall lanky dude too. Like you, J."

"Okay you two, drag the professor up to the tunnel," Jacob directed and pulled himself up onto the boat's deck. "I'll check to see if there is anyone else."

"Jake, no!" Joel shouted, raising a hand in protest. "It's not necessary ... I mean there's no one else ..."

"You can't know that. Gotta make sure," Jake countered before he disappeared below decks. "Now get him to the tunnel."

J and Joel dragged the dead man to the tunnel. Having laid the body outside the tunnel's entrance, J lifted his head and sniffed. "Did you feel that?"

"Yeah, that wind shift like when we first got in the tunnel," Joel answered, finally prying the briefcase loose. "Now let's see what's so important ..."

"Hey, Joel, did that local guy say anything about any indicators of those big waves?"

"Ah, something about ... my God! There's a sudden wind shift!" Both men ran back down the beach in time to see a monster wave flood the beach, lift the sailboat and propel a towering wall of white water toward them.

Village of Sand Dollar Tannerson House

LISTENING TO THE storm batter the house, Moses and Corbin sat in silence for a while. Moses leaned back and closed his eyes. Corbin stared at the candle. "Moses, do you believe in the Bible?" he asked, nodding toward the coffee table.

Moses opened his eyes and sat up before he said, "Do you?"

"Yes, of course, but do you?"

"So much so I've read it front to back," he replied, picking up the Bible and facing the doctor, "and I run my family and business on Biblical principles."

"Then you may recall some verse that says something like don't bow down to or serve idols because I am a jealous God, "visiting the iniquity of the fathers upon the children unto the third and fourth generation of them that hate me." I assume you don't hate God, but given what we've done, doesn't that passage bother ... worry you?"

"No. Why should it?" Martin replied instantly in a strong voice, but softened his tone before adding, "No, I don't hate God, but ..."

"But?" Corbin asked, forgetting the storm and the bodies upstairs.

"But I worry about possible idols – my company, family, possessions and wealth and so on. Without a doubt, I have sins and iniquities, the sins of my blood, I must answer for. However, I fear I've created an inherited sin debt, making it the sins of our blood? I'm willing to pay my debt, but I can't bear to witness payment extracted from my wife and three boys and their families."

"So, in that context, what we did tonight does bother you?"

"In that sense, yes, as well as the fallout for the Tannersones," Moses said sadly but brightened before adding, "However, I've found a work around."

"Work around?"

Moses frowned briefly and tapped the Bible before setting it in the briefcase. "Perhaps 'work around' is not the right term. 'Biblical out' may be closer to it. You see, in a few places God contradicts himself. In one place he says, "The fathers shall not be put to death for the children, nor the children be put to death for the fathers; but every man shall be put to death for his own sin."

"So, only you have to pay. You're punished and your family dodges the bullet, is that it?"

Martin sighed before replying, "I thought so. But, a little later a verse again asserts that punishment for the parents' sins is dumped into their children's laps."

"I'm no theologian," Corbin said quietly, "but, your contradictions are resolved in the New Testament."

"Yes," Moses said after a pause. "A blind man who Jesus healed was not blind because he'd sinned or his parents had, but so that "the works of God should be made manifest in him." That means that good works and repentance are the out."

"Moses, I don't think ..."

"No," Martin said, cutting him off and placing a hand on the doctor's arm. "Hear me out. For every wrong, there is a related good work of God that offsets. Jesus said to produce fruit – good works – in keeping with repentance. See, what we did tonight is a good work since I genuinely repent the wrong done to my friend, Tannerson."

"But, Moses, I don't ..."

"No, listen. It follows that if I and my boys can manifest God's good works and a repentant heart, we can still do what business, family, and healthy ambition dictates."

"Do your sons subscribe to this theology of walking such a spiritual tightrope?" Corbin ventured after a pause.

Martin sighed, touching the Bible. "They will, but one or two of the next generations of the Martins - Justice, Jacob and Joel and my grandchildren - may still have to pay the wages of the sins of our blood," he said. "However, a few or more will do good works in keeping with repentance, setting things right." He snapped the briefcase shut and faced the doctor. "Trust me,

Corbin, at home and at the office, I will ensure that they never stray from doing what's necessary, loving God and doing good that bears fruit in keeping with repentance."

"Moses, I think using the Bible is sound, but I don't agree with your Biblical out," Schwartz said, sitting up as a sharp gust of wind shook the windows. The crack in the beam above their heads widened, and the beam sagged.

"Why is that, doctor?" Moses asked.

"Martin, it is possible God's hand was in tonight's events, but just as important as loving God you must love ..." Schwartz started, but the thirteenth lightning strike to hit Tannerson House in one hundred and fifty years struck the roof, cutting off his reply. The strike violently shook the house. Fires started in the attic and in the walls of the second floor, and the slender candle flickered and went out. In the dark and relative silence following the thunder, both men raised their arms above their heads when the living room ceiling collapsed.

Driftwood Cove, Smugglers Cove Beach

"JAKE!" J SCREAMED as the wall of water swept towards Joel and him. Joel grabbed J's arm and pushed him toward the tunnel entrance. They ran. J leaped over the dead man, but Joel tripped over his arm and fell facedown. He pushed himself up and scooped up the briefcase. He ran to catch up with J.

The wave filled the tunnel and raced after the fleeing men. J was a step or two ahead of Joel when the water caught up with them. The ladder to the cellar and safety above was visible in J's light when the water swallowed them. After Joel was engulfed in the seawater, he opened his eyes. Though he'd dropped his flashlight, it briefly lit up the water around him. He reached out. *Odd, like glass, very dark glass*, he thought.

CHAPTER 2

Wages of Sin - 2016

Central City, GASMAX Industries Headquarters

JOEL MARTIN LOWERED HIS HAND from the surface of the large smoked plate-glass window that defined his corner office's west side. *Odd, like glass, very dark glass*, he thought, rubbing his fingers together. He sniffed and pursed his lips. *I can still smell ... taste seawater.* "To J and Jake and trapdoors," he whispered and raised his scotch on the rocks in salute. *What a ride but what a cost*, he concluded silently.

Three decades later the memories of his brothers and the events of the Driftwood Cove hurricane party had dimmed only slightly and were never far removed from his thoughts. They were foundational to his rise from the junior business associate job gained largely through nepotism. Proving himself uniquely capable and beyond his father's expectations in the company's transformation from GAS-ELECTRIC-MAX to GASMAX Industries and its rapid growth, he gained favored-son status, surpassing J to replace the old man as CEO and President.

Yeah, what a ride, he thought. This evening he allowed the memories to run their course. He flexed his right hand as he recalled clinging to the briefcase as he was tossed head over heels in that wave-swamped tunnel. The fingers on his left hand jerked, as he remembered flailing with his free hand as the water receded, dragging him back down the tunnel.

After several failed grasps, he was finally able to latch on and not lose his grip. Though he couldn't see J, he realized he had wrapped his legs around him. Likewise, he maintained a vice grip on the briefcase while his other hand was white knuckled about a vertical timber framing the smuggler's hidey hole. Slowly the wall of the water's inky black gave way to dim light, *like through glass, very dark glass.* "Justice ... J, are you alright?" Joel remembered asking when the water lost its grip. Unlike the present, he was genuinely panicked by the possibility of the loss of both brothers.

Clearly etched in his memory was J's cough when he rolled out of his legs' saving embrace. After coughing and several deep breaths, he replied, "Yeah ... I'm okay. How ... ouch, I hit my head on that damn ladder. There's already a knot and a gash in my scalp. Think I'm bleeding. How bout you?"

"Okay ... I think," Joel replied and sat. Setting the briefcase in the hidey hole, he checked for injuries. "Nothing broke."

"Thanks, Joel, you saved my butt." That was the last time that J had genuinely thanked him for anything. *Of course, that was the last time I ever was concerned about anyone but myself.*

Joel frowned as the memory continued. "Don't mention ... I ... hey, look, a light."

Indistinct light came from farther down the tunnel where it outlined the bend not far from the ladder. "Flashlight! Let's go," J said as he got to his feet. He staggered two steps before Joel reached out and steadied him.

"Hang on," Joel directed as they made their way toward the light. Rounding the bend, they found one of the three 'borrowed' flashlights wedged between two tunnel timbers. J pulled it free.

"Let's go see if Jake made it," J said after testing the light.

"J, you're bleeding," Joel said when the flashlight shone on his brother's face.

J patted his scalp and examined his hand. "It's nothing. Move it."

When they reached the beach, they noted that the dead man's body was gone. Flashes of lightning and what they could see with the flashlight revealed no trace of the sailboat or their brother.

"One more look around," Joel pleaded when J motioned with the light toward the tunnel entrance.

J looked up at the sky. He grabbed Joel's arm. "No, Joel, we've got to get off this beach before another big one hits."

"But, Jake ... what if he's ..." Joel protested, pulling his arm free.

"He's gone," J said flatly, his own grief was obvious on his face and in his voice. "The cellar's our best bet."

After thirty years, Joel still opened and closed his mouth when he recalled how he'd not objected. *I should have said something ... made him ...*, he thought. That sole genuine instance of remorse for doing what was necessary haunted him. Then as today, he embraced selfish, common sense. Despite the sorrow in J's eyes, he finally agreed, "Yeah, you're right. Let's get off this damn beach."

They retraced their steps, stopping only to retrieve the briefcase left in the hidey hole. They climbed the ladder, and they shut the trapdoor.

Despite the wool suit he now wore, Joel shuddered when he recalled the chill when adrenaline rush ended abruptly and they collapsed on the cellar floor. After some minutes, Joel sat and shined the flashlight to look around. J, sitting and moaning held his head in his hands. Joel opened the cooler. He took off his tee shirt and dipped it in the ice and water caressing two bottles of beer. After wrapping a few cubes in the shirt, he handed it to J. "Here, put this on it," he said.

J took the jury-rigged ice pack. "Thanks," he muttered before applying it and lying down.

Joel fished a beer out of the cooler. He sat cross legged, opened the bottle and took a deep drink to wash away the taste of saltwater. He pulled the briefcase in front of him. Positioning the light, he snapped the latches and swung the case open. "Let's see what's worth two men dying," he whispered grimly and lifted out a clear plastic pouch. Joel placed the flashlight under his chin, and he pulled open the pouch's press-tight seal.

"What's in there?" J asked.

"There's four ... no, five journal notebooks like the ones you use, some file folders and a computer disk."

"What's in them?"

"The disk isn't labeled," Joel said as he thumbed through some pages of the journals and examined the contents of the folders. "Wow."

"What is it?"

"A trapdoor to fortune," his brother whistled finally and kicked Justice's foot. "J, you gotta see this."

Joel returned to his desk and sat. A copy of the latest *Driftwood Weekly*, the Village of Driftwood Cove's sole newspaper, lay on his desk blotter. "Justice Martin Dies in Climbing Accident," the headline of the special edition declared. In a recent meeting with J, Joel used the "A trapdoor to fortune" line. J laughed and said, "I clearly remembered that moment. Mostly because my head pounded something awful when I sat up and asked, "See what?" Joel smiled briefly at that memory and frowned. J concluded the remembrance, declaring, "Lately, more and more, I wish I'd been the third casualty of that Driftwood Cove hurricane party."

"I guess in some ways you were, big brother, just thirty years later," he said in a low, sad voice. "Your delayed demise is without doubt connected to that night, that briefcase and where they both took us. If only you had been reasonable."

Joel sighed and spun his chair to look out the window. Central City's skyline was broken by several construction cranes. Each was a testimony to the city's growth and prosperity due to the success of GASMAX Industries made possible by the Martin brothers. Leaning back in his chair, he laced his hands behind his head and closed his eyes. *It was so perfect, J, you idiot*, he thought as his thoughts returned to the events in Wilkes Tavern cellar three decades earlier.

As he and Justice waited out the storm, they studied the contents of the briefcase. They went through each of the loose papers and the five journals.

"J this guy was a chemical engineer like you," Joel said. "You know him?"

"No. His name isn't familiar, but he was a genius," J said after looking at the name on the cover of one journal. "These four journals detail a significantly improved methane gas production process and an associated business plan."

"That so?" Joel looked up from the fifth journal. "Can we, GAS-ELECTRIC-MAX, use it?"

"Yeah, yeah, we can do this," J said. "It's amazing. The process would evolve with increasing efficiency in four phases over decades. There's one journal for each phase. A preliminary phase of three to four years involves a demonstration plant for proof of concept and time to raise the necessary capital for subsequent phases. Each phase anticipates likely material strength and computer capacity and capability advances, making the next phase possible and increasingly more profitable. The level of automation envisioned in the fourth phase reads like science fiction, but he makes its sound very possible. But there's a problem."

"That is?"

"He probably patented his work."

"That may not be a problem," Joel said. "This journal is a personal log. Your new engineering hero was a retired college professor, a long-time widow and essentially a hermit. In an entry a few days ago, he stated he was just about to apply for the patent, go public and implement the business plan. He and an unnamed business partner were soon going to seek investors."

"Did he mention any family?"

"No mention of family except a brief entry about an estranged daughter."

"So, we'd still have to find her and the business partner." J sighed. "And, even if we did, we'd be looked at more as investors and/or contractors than partners. Besides, how do we know he's the dead sailor or that the patent isn't pending?"

"I'm certain the dead man is our guy and that the patent isn't pending," Joel said.

"How's that?"

"Read the pages I dog-eared," Joel said and passed J the journal. "Those entries portray a man highly suspicious of others. His personal record rambles at times with delusions and fears. Some are centered on the business partner. Not trusting the phone or postal service, according to one of the last entry he was the victim of his fears. He'd decided to solo sail to Central City to file the patent."

J looked up from the journal. "He got caught in the storm."

"Right, and unaware of Smugglers Cove's propensity for storm-driven tidal waves, mistakenly sought refuge from the hurricane in the cove instead of Driftwood Bay. See, we've gone through a trapdoor to fortune, big brother." Noting J's excitement about the engineering and science behind the four-phase process, Joel invited him to consider a life-changing proposal.

J laid down the journal and looked at his brother. "Joel, even if we can rule out the business partner and the daughter, what your suggesting is still illegal. We'd be stealing another man's work."

"True," Joel said and smiled. "Not illegal so much. As Dad says, in business, you've got to do what's necessary even if a few rules are stretched. You and I know the tidal hydroelectric plant was along shot to save the company. This is a sure deal and big money, right?"

"True."

"Besides, this will be the something good that comes out of Jake's death."

J nodded. "Yeah ... but the business partner and daughter?"

"Look, you tend to the engineering and I'll rule them out and nail down the patent. That new lawyer Dad hired, Louis something, offered to do some legal work for me on the side."

Joel opened his eyes and considered the city skyline. In the last thirty years he and J had become very rich and quite influential. Joel was a big deal in Central City, and J had achieved near royalty status in the Village of Driftwood Cove where they built the demonstration plant.

At J's insistence, except for the Driftwood Cove facility, GASMAX abandoned the tidal hydroelectric business plan and shifted solely to methane gas. He and Joel had implemented the four-phase process over the last three decades. J oversaw the building and operation of the demonstration processing plant inland and just south of the Driftwood Cove's abandoned rock quarry. Joel, with great success and demonstrating exceptional business acumen, marketed process licenses to a vast global market.

With the old man's blessing and J's surprising though begrudging acquiescence, Joel ultimately replaced his father as the CEO and President of GASMAX Industries. J, quickly became senior vice-president in charge of research and development. Despite living a lie and becoming his little brother's subordinate, he found contentment with the engineering and science. He was hailed in the power industry as the chemical engineer who had developed the new process. He reveled in that and enjoyed the monetary fruits of their labors.

Joel shook his head. *You had it made, J.* He looked at the photograph of J on the front page. He and the lawyer ruled out the daughter and business partner and nailed down the patents, locking away J's one skeleton in the family closet. *Trust me brother, I am caretaker of a closet full of skeletons. As Dad knew, it's more my style, and you were much better with the gas, nuts, bolts and pipes.*

Joel considered the portrait of his father on the wall opposite his desk. "Do what's necessary, love God and do good, bearing fruit in keeping with repentance," asserted the old man's Biblical aphorism in black, bold letters on a shiny brass plate below the frame. So, only J, not Joel, was surprised how readily their father embraced the process idea and the new direction for the company.

Joel knew it was Moses' mantra and Jacob's death on the day of his daughter's premature birth as well as the old man's near-death experience on that fateful stormy night that made him eager to shift the burden of the business vision and direction to his sons. The roof of the house where he and the doctor took refuge collapsed. Incredibly, a briefcase containing the family Bible bore just enough of the weight of the split end of a falling ceiling beam to prevent it from crushing them to death. They escaped with their lives and the briefcase before fire destroyed the house and all that was in it. Declaring it a sign of God's blessing on the family enterprise's new direction, Moses told Joel privately, "I wrote Plan A for this company, but I always knew it would have to give way to a better Plan B. This is it."

The unwritten codicil to the 'better Plan' was how the brothers concealed the theft of intellectual property. They agreed that J would go public with the science and engineering for each phase only when material and computer advances dictated by the journals supported the implementation. Consequently, J's research and development branch devoted most of its time to monitoring and leveraging scientific, engineering and computer innovation. J alone integrated their findings with the next phase's process, orchestrating the next innovative rollout. With the Internet and computer advances, J eventually moved his family to Driftwood Cove a few hundred or so miles to the north. From his beach house study, he ran the research and development.

As a hedge against public disclosure of their deception or either one of the brother's striking out on his own, J and Joel secured the original four process phase journals, the personal journal and other papers in a dual-lock safe in a secure location in Driftwood Cove. Each brother held one of the keys. They periodically accessed the safe and its contents and planned the rollout of the next phase.

At the end of the demonstration phase and the successful implementation of each of the next two phases, the GASMAX board of directors voted very large bonuses and stock shares for J and Joel. Before the elder Martin died, Joel's accession to CEO and President made sense to all including J but with unstated reservations. Despite J's cautions about hurrying the launch of Phase Four with its greater reliance on AI - artificial intelligence - Joel made the company's major stockholders another quick fortune by advance sales of Phase Four process licenses.

Joel looked at the two large envelopes on his desk. *If only you had kept your end of the deal, this would not be necessary*, he thought, eyeing the first words of

Moses' edict. He pulled the papers out of one envelope and, for a second time, read the report's first page.

The report had been prompted when J announced in a private meeting six months ago that he had obtained evidence of Joel's deceit in ruling out the business partner and the daughter. For this reason, "as well as significant AI safety concerns, regardless of advance sales, we're not going to do the next phase." He threatened, "I've made provisions to protect Jacob's family and mine if you try anything." His provisions included a complete written confession of their thirty-plus-year deception.

"Damn!" Joel declared to his empty office. *J, you left me no choice*, he concluded silently as he read the portion of the report which stated that the third and fourth journals and some of the other documents were no longer in the dual-lock safe. *I'm more surprised that he did circumvent both locks than by the fact that he could.* Joel tapped the envelope, comforted somewhat by the fact that the safe in his office now held the first two journals and some of the other documents. However, not surprisingly, the report stated conclusively that the written confession of their deceit as well as the final two technical journals and personal log were not in the safe.

The conscience driven, written confession was, J warned, "the heart of the provision made for my family in the case of my death before yours, Joel." He knew that J was a clever planner as well as an engineer. *No doubt your 'provision' has all sorts of safeguards and contingencies, dear brother, but I have a few contingency plans of my own. As Dad often said, "You must always have a Plan B."*

He put the report away, grabbed his cell phone and called a contact named BW.

"Lo," a sleepy voice said.

"You get the clothes and package?" Joel asked.

"Yeah," BW replied. "We doing this?"

"You see your hometown rag?" Joel asked, glancing once more at the photograph of his brother beneath the headline.

"Sure did. Sorry for your loss," BW said. "Such a tragic accident, wasn't it?"

"The other documents I seek are not in the safe," Joel said, ignoring the question. "They're likely still in Driftwood Cove, and ..."

"Wait. How'd you know that?"

"Let's just say that our cohorts and an unknowingly cooperative source confirmed this week that the key to my brother's plan is Cynthia Jones and what's in his will."

"I see, you can't let Princess get out of Dodge here without a private chit-chat," BW chuckled. "So, we're doing this tonight, right?"

Joel hesitated as he looked at the silver-framed photograph on his desk of J, his wife and three children and the pretty young blonde lady who was their late brother Jake's, daughter, Cynthia Jones. Her last name was a legacy from her mother's alcohol-soaked and short-lived second marriage. Though he'd watched his niece grow up and worked with her over the last five years, each time they met he was still taken with what an intelligent and strikingly good-looking woman she was. At her graduate school commencement ceremony, Joel remembered J correctly observing that if it weren't for the obvious Martin chin, there would be no way that Jacob and Mary Martin had sired a daughter with such classic blonde, blue-eyed good looks. He cleared his throat and said, "Yes, she's the key. If I can't get the information from her, be ready for Plan B."

"Yeah, Plan B." BW chuckled. "The other boys and girls on our team know we're doing this?" he asked without mirth.

"They do," Joel replied, considering once more J's wife, Joan, his two daughters, Sylvia and Danny, and the middle child, Clint, a son who looked very much like his father. He pressed the phone face, terminating the call.

Picking up the framed photo, he stated grimly, "This is all on you, J."

"Sir, Ms. Jones is here," Joel's executive assistant announced over the intercom. He flinched, set the frame face down and downed the rest of his drink. Finding his reflection in the chrome framing the office's large plate glass windows, he straightened his tie. Despite the stress of and toll taken by success, the years had worn gently on his physical appearance and well-being. The developing pouch of middle age had yet to force a suit-size change. Clean jaw and cheek lines, a few wrinkles and a full head of dark hair grayed only at the temples suggested a man in his prime and not one on the verge of retirement.

After stacking the large brown envelopes, he placed the framed photograph upright. "Well, J, you bastard, here's another bill to be paid for climbing through that trapdoor to fortune," he hissed. Taking a deep breath, he pushed the intercom button. "She's early," he said. "Oh well, send her in." He released the button. "As the lamb to the slaughter," he finished softly.

CHAPTER 3

Lethal Liquor

Central City, GASMAX Industries Headquarters

THIS IS IT, CYNTHIA JONES thought, knocked and opened the door. "Uncle, is this a good time?" she asked.

"Ah, Cynthia, there you are," Joel said, looking up from the photograph, and smiled at Jake and Mary Martin's daughter. "You look especially stunning for your big day. The black dress and pearls - perfect. I do believe your cheeks are flushed with victory."

"I'm a little early," Cynthia said after a brief grin. Pushing a strand of blonde hair off her forehead, she stepped into the room. "I can come back." Even though her uncle appeared distracted, she concluded to herself, *this may not be so bad.*

"No. No need. Please, have a seat." Joel waved at the lone chair that fronted his wide, dark and glass-topped desk. He sat back, folded his hands in his lap. "I'm ready for you."

Cynthia smiled, sat, crossed her legs and, out of habit, tugged at the hem of her dress. Though she knew she had the upper hand in this meeting, she held Joel in affectionate high regard. He had been a mentor long before he and Uncle J hired her on and groomed her for company leadership. Also, since she had concluded long ago that Joel was a sly old fox and J the bulldog, she let her smile linger. "Uncle, out of deference to you, I thought that you should decide how we should proceed this evening."

"That is very considerate," Joel smiled and searched her blue eyes. "It does seem somewhat out of character though. Are you sure you want me to call the beat here?"

"I'd welcome it," Cynthia responded in a friendly confident voice.

"Nervous, huh?"

"A little ... Yes, you call the beat."

"Very well. I say we'll have this conversation a year from today. Thanks for stopping by." Joel Martin chuckled. The slightly lined face, once sharply handsome but now slightly blurred by age and the few gray hairs, relaxed. "Also, I'll have HR pack your golden parachute."

Cynthia laughed. "I wish, but you and I know that's not an option since..."

"...you have this locked up," Joel finished for her and frowned.

The mirth left her face before Cynthia replied. "Uncle, I know this must be hard for you," she said. She sat up straighter and again pulled at the hem. "I am so grateful ... rest assured that HR has packed 'your' golden chute, but it will never be enough." Noticing the newspaper on Joel's desk, she added, "I just wish Uncle J ..."

"No! This is not about J," Joel said, leaning forward and waving a hand. He tapped the brown envelope on his desk and sighed. "It ... it's just necessary."

Cynthia sat back.

"You know, I can see how you bested the young bucks who competed so unsuccessfully with you for corporate ladder rungs."

"What ... what are you talking about?" she sputtered.

"One of your annual performance evaluations said it best," he continued. "Cynthia Jones is smart, hardnosed when necessary, and beautiful. The last word was underlined. Times really haven't changed too much. Sleeping your way to the top is about the same, isn't it?"

"What?" Cynthia snapped back, her mouth agape and her cheeks flush. She gripped the armrests tightly and fought an urge to scream. She took a deep breath and leaned forward.

Joel didn't shrink back as a straight line now separated her red lips and anger filled her eyes. "You are so much like me when pushed by a sudden sea change," he said calmly.

"What is this? What's happened? You can't be serious."

"Oh, but I am," Joel replied evenly.

"Is this about Uncle J being gone?" Cynthia asked, releasing some of the tension in her posture and voice, relaxing her hands and sitting back. "We've had that conversation."

"No, it's ... it's just necessary."

Cynthia shook her head. "I've tried civil ... loving, and that doesn't work. You are a bullheaded corporate relic, and somewhere along the way you lost the edge as well as the good sense that got you into this office. You don't even know when you're beat. It's over."

"Now that's sounds like your Uncle J when he thought I was off base," Joel said. "In this case, I'm not. You are ... well, you're almost right that it's over. See, you're use to always being right. You have the game ... this game all figured out. You believe the contest is won. I'm out and you're in. Game-set-point as they say in tennis. The board has voted you in and I'm out, right?"

"Not exactly how I'd put it, but yes," Cynthia replied flatly.

"Now you help me lug a banker box full of mementos out the office door, and the staff and some other company minions will clap, and a few will shake my hand on the way to the first floor," he said flatly. "No doubt you've got the company limo waiting to whisk us to the farewell reception that is more of a coronation for you and a memorial for J than a celebration of my going. That's about it, right?" He sat back and donned the poker face that Cynthia had witnessed win numerous piles of chips and close multiple deals.

Cynthia relaxed and thought, *Uncle is coming to grips with his situation*. Her combative stance melted. Her best, practiced smile, with which she closed many a deal, graced her face. "Yeah, that's about it. We play our parts and do what's necessary, right? You taught me that," she finished with a sigh and frowned.

"I also taught you to expect the unexpected," Joel replied. "Flip over all the stones. You never know what will crawl out. You may want to look at this before we waltz out of here arm-in-arm." After a brief hesitation, he pushed one of the brown envelopes across the desk.

Cynthia sighed and took the envelope. It was an unremarkable inner-office memo envelope with the sole stop boldly annotated 'Joel Martin - Eyes Only.' "What's this?" she asked as she opened it and slid the contents into her lap. "Nothing will..." Her voice faded to a whisper and her eyes widened.

"You never know ... what ... will ... crawl ... out," Joel said and frowned. "The flush of victory is fading."

Cynthia quickly flipped through the half dozen or so photographs and fingered a handful of bank and credit card statements. *Oh my God*, she thought. "What the ... how ...?" she stammered.

"Game and set, my dear," Joel said, leaning forward and pushing the intercom button. "Margret, please tell Tanner to bring the limo around. We'll be down shortly."

"Uncle, why?" Cynthia asked, looking up at her uncle, her face contorted by a mixture of disbelief, sorrow and betrayal.

Joel, looking once more at his brother's newspaper photograph, shook his head.

―

Central City Carlton Plaza Hotel

THE NEAR SILENCE in the banquet room was about the same as that during the limo ride. The muted exception was the dinner music played softly for GASMAX's small, no-matter-what dance crowd. The evening's celebratory spirit collapsed early and very shortly after Cynthia stepped to the rostrum at the head table occupied by GASMAX board members and their guests. Her brief memorial remarks for her Uncle J were solemnly received, quieting the room. But her announcement of her resignation and Joel's agreement to stay on as CEO was like a pin-prick to the festive balloon of what should have been the best night of her life. Cobbling together fragments of several farewell remarks she had heard over the last five years given by various departing GASMAX senior executives and other old-time employees, she fashioned a bittersweet expression of gratitude and leave taking. She sat down to polite but muted and hesitant applause.

Before, during and after the usual banquet fare, Cynthia fortified herself with and drowned a gnawing sorrow in alcohol. With each drink she cared less about figuring out which was worse, the insincere well-wishing for future success by board members who had not supported her accession to CEO or the masked accusation of betrayal by those who had been in her corner. Cutting through the gathering alcoholic haze was the genuine lament of her longtime executive assistant, confidant and closest thing to a friend at GASMAX, Connie Barnes. True to form, Connie rescued her from the head table and parked her at the now vacant table where Connie and other support staff had sat. Setting a cup of coffee in front of her former boss, Connie left to find Tanner Strong, the limo driver, to take Cynthia home. Pushing the cup aside, the almost-CEO crossed her wrists and rested her head on her forearms. Her hair fell in a careless golden cascade over her face and arms. "Just need to rest my eyes a few ..." she muttered.

The scrape of a chair pulled out and the clank of an ice bucket on the tabled roused her. As she sat up and pushed hair out of her face, the face of a compact man in an ill-fitting tuxedo came into focus. He set two fluted glasses next to the silver container wet with condensation. A smile broke his ruddy features that were at odds with his slick dark hair and shadowlike cast of a half-grown beard. *I know this guy*, she thought. ... *but I don't. That's weird.*

Cynthia's new companion leaned forward. "Last call, darling, and you look like you could use a nightcap," he cooed and filled the glasses.

I know that voice, Cynthia thought. "Have we met before?"

The man laughed and pushed aside the last strand of hair obscuring her face. "That's supposed to be my line. You really need to do something about this hair." Cynthia looked away, shook her head, and pushed her tresses into some semblance of order. While she did so the man dropped a pair of small white tablets into her glass. They dissolved quickly in a small cloud of the sparkling wine's bubbles before Cynthia again devoted her attention to figuring out, *who is this guy?*

She picked up the drink and studied his face. "Who did you say you were?" she asked and set the glass down without drinking.

"It would be no fun if I didn't let you figure it out," he replied and guided the glass to her mouth. "Now drink up." The rim of the glass touched

Cynthia's lips, she titled her head back slightly, narrowed her eyes and the pale white fluid flowed toward her parted lips. She knew she'd had too much to drink, but the heightened carbonated lure and anticipation of the champagne passing beneath her nose made her eager for more and, now, she felt it would aid her in solving the puzzle of ...

CHAPTER 4

Falling to the End of Herself

Central City Carlton Plaza Hotel

"THE LADY HAS HAD ENOUGH," a clear male voice announced as a hand firmly, but with surprising gentleness, enveloped Cynthia's wrist and prevented her from drinking.

"What the ...?" Cynthia and her companion both sputtered. They followed the restraining hand up its arm to the face of Tanner Strong, the corporate chauffeur and pilot. His square jaw and dimpled chin were attractively arrayed beneath lips pressed thin in a grimace and crowned by a thin black mustache. Green eyes were narrow slits focused not on the woman but locked on the man next to her.

Cynthia set her glass down, knocking the other into her table companion's lap. "Hey," he fumed and stood. "Who the hell ...," he said and pulled his tux jacket open, revealing a holstered gun. He went for it. Still restraining Cynthia's hand, Tanner beat him to it. Grasping the pistol grip, he swung it up in a back-hand motion, connecting the gun butt to its owner's chin and laying him out flat. Releasing his hold on Cynthia, he ejected the clip, checked the chamber empty and threw the empty pistol on the floor between the unconscious man's legs.

"Tanner, what have you done?" Cynthia asked after looking at the fallen man and back at Tanner. She pushed herself up with difficulty. Tanner steadied her, but she fell into him and she placed her arms about his neck. She relaxed as he held her. "Why'd you do that? We're only having a drink."

"He put something in your drink," Tanner said softly and looked to see if the altercation had drawn any attention. It had. Joel Martin, standing next to a table across the room, was pointing in their direction. "We need to go."

Cynthia smiled. "So, you've been spying on me?"

"Let's just say you still have people here who care about you," he answered, looking over to where Connie held a door open.

"My hero," she cooed and leaned in to kiss him. Before their lips met, her eyes fluttered and she passed out. Picking her up, Tanner carried her to the door, nodded to Connie and took her to the waiting limo.

Two blocks later, after a careful search of the side and rearview mirrors to insure no one was following the GASMAX limo, Tanner briefly examined his charge. She lay sideways in the passenger seat very much dead to the world. *You'll have a major hangover, but it's better than whatever that clown had in mind for you*, he thought and returned his attention to the road. Taking the next right turn, he thumbed the car phone switch on the steering wheel. "Dial 688-692-7334," he commanded.

"Dialing," the car's computer-generated female voice announced. As the phone rang, Tanner checked to see if the exchange had roused Cynthia from her slumber. It had not.

"Hello, Tanner?" a female voice inquired.

"Hi. Yeah, it's me," he replied. "I have her, but she's in no shape to talk to anyone."

"Well ... news like this doesn't age well," she replied, but after a pause and a sigh, "I guess it'll keep til tomorrow."

"It'll have to," Tanner agreed. "Nothing new, huh?"

"No. Gotta go." The connection broke and the car's computer hung up. Tanner tapped the steering wheel. *Not good*, he thought and checked again for a tail. There was none. "Time to get you home," he whispered to his slumbering passenger and turned at the next light.

Central City Carlton Plaza Hotel

BW, BUCK WILSON, came to and was helped to his feet by a waiter and a hotel security guard. After showing his concealed carry permit, he went to the men's room to relieve himself and mop up some of the champagne soaking his trousers. He was at the sink drying his trousers as best he could when Joel Martin entered. Martin looked to ensure the stalls were empty and stepped to a urinal.

"I take it she didn't drink it," he said, facing the wall.

Wilson looked up at Martin's backside reflected in the restroom mirror. "No. If that guy had been a few seconds later, she would've. Hey, who was that anyway?"

"Tanner Strong. He's the corporate chauffer and pilot as well as security. He's a Marine vet who my brother hired."

"Figures." Buck snorted and turned his attention to combing his hair. "That's the type the old man liked, huh?"

Joel stood next to Wilson at the other sink. He turned the water on and washed his hands. "Yes, he is. It's not too surprising Strong stepped in," he said thoughtfully, *Strong probably had a standing order from J to keep an eye on our niece. I was right keeping her close all these years. So, Big Brother, as loving uncle and mentor, I kept an eye on her also. And, she was right where I needed her when she went from being an asset to a liability.*

Drying his hands, he considered his reflection in the mirror. Wilson's failed attempt to sideline Cynthia for the next three days and the reports from J's children confirmed that Cynthia in Driftwood Cove, CEO or not, was the agent, knowingly or not, of J's plan to expose their decades' long deception. How so, no one could figure. No matter, all he knew was Cynthia in Driftwood Cove over the next seventy-two hours would bring down GASMAX and ruin Joel's and J's family fortunes. Thankfully he was able to convince enough of J's family that they faced financial collapse unless they aided him in taking very immediate and drastic action concerning their loose-cannon relative.

If only you had got her, he thought. Drying his hands, he faced his accomplice in what was now a lethal business. "Well, on to the next Plan B." He sighed. "You understand what to do?"

"Yeah," Wilson replied pulling a key and an index card from his pocket. "Hanger fourteen at the airport, right?"

"Correct. Any questions about what's on the card?"

"Not a one." Wilson smiled, returning the key and card to his pocket. "You sure she'll be on that plane tomorrow?"

"Positive," Joel said. "My sources tell me that the flight plan and manifest already exist. Strong's the pilot and the only passenger is Cynthia Jones."

Wilson rubbed his chin where Tanner hit him and recalled the bitter memory of how Cynthia Jones ruined his life. "Good, they'll both crash and burn."

Central City Cynthia Jones' House - The Next Morning

"CYNTHIA, HI," Stan Carter said softly and brushed away her hair covering the one eye not pushed deep into the deckchair pillow. "Good morning, I guess."

"Stan!" Cynthia Jones cried and sat upright. She felt her heart race and was briefly disoriented. Lowering her voice and covering her eyes with one hand, she placed the other firmly on Stan's chest. "Oh, it doesn't feel so good."

"I suspect not," Stan agreed, and he pointed to an abandoned bottle of champagne on the floor in her boudoir, just visible from the pool deck through the sliding glass doors to the bedroom. "Tanner Strong spent a good half hour last night getting you on your feet when he dropped you off. He hadn't been gone ten minutes before you popped another cork."

"I wish that wasn't so. I ... please stop the spin and turn down the sunlight," she pleaded and fell back on the deckchair, pulling an oversize beach towel over her head. *I couldn't feel any worse*, she thought as the events of yesterday came to mind. "Tanner ... Strong ... did he tell you what happened?" she asked, pulling down the towel and venturing a look at Stan.

"Yeah," he nodded, sitting down next to her on the double wide wooden recliner.

"Everything?"

"Yes. The CEO thing as well as that joker he laid out," Stan answered softly. From the small matching redwood table next to the chair, he thrusted a coffee mug towards her. "Now, here, drink this," he ordered quietly but firmly.

Opening her eyes briefly, Cynthia gasped, "Forget it. This is beyond coffee." *Just leave me alone to die*, she screamed silently.

"It's not coffee." Stan chuckled. "It's hair of the dog that bit ... no that ripped you last night."

"That sounds worse than coffee," Cynthia declared and sniffed, but she sat up and took the cup hoping Stan would stop speaking.

"It isn't," Stan insisted. "It's the hangover drink I introduced you to four birthdays ago. Drink ... all of it, big gulp it."

For unknown reasons a years-old memory rose above the sea of her confused and troubled thoughts as a beacon of hope. So, she chugged. "Ugh," she managed, wiping off some of Stan's potion that escaped her mouth. She set the cup on the table next to her cell phone.

"Better?" Stan asked tenderly after a few moments and again brushed the hair out of her face. Their eyes met.

"Some," she muttered before adding more strongly, "thank you." *How can he always be so nice?* she wondered silently. Stan's clean-cut look had a soft edge in the morning light that made him so damn attractive.

"You're welcome," Stan smiled.

"What's this?" Cynthia inquired as her vision cleared and took in the luggage and cardboard boxes set next to the gate in the pool deck fence that opened onto a stepping stone path to the front of the house and the driveway.

"It's what I wanted to talk about last night before you ordered me to "Shut up! Get your clothes off.""

"You could have refused," she responded after a pause and realizing she was naked except for her bra that was entangled by one strap around her left arm. *What the hell happened*, she speculated inaudibly. "Did you ... refuse ...?"

"Both times," Stan sighed and looked away, "but you were all 'I got fired,' and 'hold me' and then you used your Cynthia-in-charge voice salted with tears to demand ..."

"Oh Stan, I'm ..." Cynthia gently put her hand to his cheek, but she felt more shame than compassion because she took some pride in the triumph of her seductive powers despite way too much alcohol.

"Save it," he said sharply, pushed her hand aside and stood. Then, taking the edge off his voice, he went on, "It's lousy timing but I can't take this anymore. Sorry about your Uncle J. He was a good man. Also, the job thing sucks, but I packed yesterday morning. See, it wasn't a client meeting that kept me away from your promotion celebration, I was picking up the keys to my new place."

"Stan, don't," Cynthia begged as she pulled the towel around her and put her feet on the pool deck. The tile was moist with morning dew. Panic seized her. "I need you now more than ever."

"I wish that was true and didn't sound like some line from a country song." Stan turned and took a step toward his belongings. "Besides, you crying out 'Tanner!' in the midst of 'our' passion last night kind of put a period to us."

"Don't make me laugh. It hurts with this hangover, and I'm sober enough to see this is serious." Cynthia let the towel drop and put her hands on his shoulders. *Maybe sex and the 'I got fired' ploy would work again*, she thought desperately. "Let's go inside and ... talk." She took his hand and pulled him, without success, toward the sliding glass doors. "Come on, you are important to me ... beyond words."

"I always liked your laugh. I ...," Stan said warmly, pulling her to him. He embraced her but quickly pushed her away. Cynthia's unstable legs gave way and she sat down hard on the deck chair. "I ... forget it. We both know that Cynthia Jones doesn't really need anyone beyond their part in her fan club. I need ... my need ... is something more, deeper."

"Stan, no ... look ... ow," Cynthia protested as she got to her feet and once more wrapped the towel about her. *That didn't work. Why should it? I'm a mess*, she concluded to herself. "I'm ready for some coffee now. That gunk you gave me is working. Please let me run through a shower and we can talk this out over ..."

"No, Cynthia. It's over," Stan said firmly, unlatched the gate and hefted the two suitcases. "I'm sorry this comes on the heels of Joel's screw job, but I need out. Besides, I know Cynthia Jones always lands on her feet. She does what's necessary in true Martin fashion. Joel Martin will be Cynthia-roadkill this time next year."

"Stan, please," Cynthia cried and, knocking over the long pole of the pool skimmer, followed him through the gate. The morning sun brightening that side of the house was at odds with her crumbling world as well as the hangover and the stones beneath her bare feet. The latter finally made her stop and cringe.

"This is tough. So, so tough," Stan said sadly and turned to face her. "I'll come by tomorrow to get the boxes. Oh, Sylvia called. The message is on your phone."

"But ... but we're in love," Cynthia sobbed as warm tears drew dark lines of mascara down her cheeks. "I love you." Though true sorrow made her weep, the 'love card' was played with calculation.

"Yeah, I love you too 'as part of us'," Stan replied without warmth and adjusted his grip on his bags. After two more steps down the path, he again faced her. "You love 'you' more 'apart from us' in your steel and glass corporate castle." He laughed and shook his head. "You even insisted that you had to bring that damn company cell phone with you last night when we went quote out to be by the pool to be alone unquote."

"No, I ..." Cynthia's voice failed and heartache never before experienced gripped her as she stumbled back against a gate post.

"Goodbye, Cynthia. I truly wish you well," Stan declared sincerely and made his way to the driveway. The sound of his car starting, backing out of the garage and driving away was drowned out by Cynthia's ragged weeping. Considering her near nakedness as well as the barefooted walk across rocks, she resisted the urge to run after him. Instead, she made her way to the bedroom. Tracing the trail made by her black dress, pearl necklace and high heels, she sat and then lay on the unmade bed. Even though she felt like she was drowning in the depths of sorrow, yesterday's events joined ranks with the morning break up with Stan and she realized this was the worst she'd ever felt. *I couldn't feel worse, but maybe I've hit bottom*, she thought and closed her eyes.

The ringing of a phone woke her. The clock on the wall told her that she had been asleep for over an hour. Patting around on the bed for the phone, she remembered it was outside by the deck chair. Hoping the call was from Stan, calling to express second thoughts about the breakup, she smiled and ignored the sudden headache and nausea when she rose. Wrapping the towel snug about her, tucking the corner in tight over her left breast, she ran out the door onto the pool deck.

Failing in her attempt to high step over the fallen pool skimmer pole, she slipped, tripped and fell sideways into the pool. Before hitting the water, she struck her head on the diving board. Floating face down, as she lost consciousness, she thought, *I was wrong. I haven't hit bottom yet.*

CHAPTER 5

Any Landing You Walk Away From

Central City Cynthia Jones' House

TANNER STRONG PARKED THE GASMAX SUV in the driveway of Cynthia Jones' ranch style house. Her three-bedroom home with an attached two-car garage was fronted by a well-manicured yard and tucked away on a cul-de-sac. It was part of one of Central City's newer housing developments. As the company's executive chauffeur and pilot for five years, Tanner knew that if enough layers of incorporation and investments were peeled back, they would reveal that GASMAX and some of Joel Martin's personal funds had bankrolled the construction of his niece's house.

From previous visits to Cynthia's home and driving for her uncles, he was familiar with the house's interior as well as her living arrangements with her longtime boyfriend, Stan Carter. *Odd, the garage is open, and Stan's BMW is not parked next to hers,* he observed. Ignoring the path to the front door, he knocked on the door from the garage to the house. Getting no answer, he tried the doorknob. It turned.

"Hello. Cynthia, it's me, Tanner," he said loudly and walked to the kitchen. The counter lights were on. He noted that a can of tomato juice, several bottles and cans of spices and more than a few eggshells cluttered the island countertop.

"Cynthia, your ride's here," he shouted, making his way into the family room just off the kitchen. A sectional couch, matching chairs and two end tables and a coffee table as well as a gray shale-faced fireplace defined the room. It also allowed access through sliding glass doors to the pool deck. Vertical blinds obstructed his view of the deck. Pushing them aside, Strong looked out. His eyes widened, and he yanked the door open.

"Cynthia!" he yelled as he ran across the deck and dove into the water. Though he normally sank like a rock, two powerful strokes closed the distance to the woman floating face down. He soon had her on the tile deck.

After making sure that her throat was clear he started CPR.

His lips were on hers when her eyes fluttered open and she coughed. "Tanner! What are you ...?" she sputtered, pushing him away. "What do you think you're doing?" Tanner rocked back and sat on his heels. She sat up and put a hand to her head. "Ow!"

"Saving your butt," Tanner said and smiled.

"Once again," she said and smiled briefly.

Tanner chuckled. "Sounds like you're okay. Looks like you fell in and hit your head." He frowned, remembering Stan's absent car. "Or did someone hit you?"

"No. No," Cynthia replied. She looked around and then back at Tanner. Running one hand through her wet hair and using the other to ensure that the soaked beach towel covered her, she continued, "I tripped running to answer my cell." She pointed in the general direction of the deckchair.

"And where was Stan when you took this header into the pool?" Tanner asked with an edge to his voice.

"He ... he had to leave this morning ... he left ... Look, I was just trying to answer the phone."

Tanner glanced over his shoulder at the small table as he stood up. "Stay put," he ordered. He pushed the pool skimmer pole upright before retrieving the phone. "Can you stand?" he asked, extending a hand. She nodded and he helped her up.

Cynthia leaned against him for a moment before testing her ability to stand alone. "Not that I'm not grateful, because I am," she said finally, looking up at Strong and keeping a hand on his chest, "but what are you doing here?"

"The phone call was no doubt from your cousin, Sylvia," he replied, offering her the cell phone. "She left a message. You better listen."

Tanner found a dry towel and draped it around Cynthia's shoulders. He guided her to a chair as she opened her voicemail. "Thank you," she whispered, then smiled and pressed the phone to her ear.

"Cynthia, this is Sylvia in Driftwood. I ..."

Cynthia's smile evaporated. The image of the serious countenance of her Uncle J's eldest adult child, Sylvia, readily came to mind.

"I know you don't need any more problems, but you need to get up here ASAP. Dad's lawyer showed us a letter that he left with him to show to me in case of his death. It says a lot, but the short version is the memorial and will reading must take place sooner than we planned, like in the next seventy-two hours. And he specifically said you must be present."

How awful for Aunt Joan, Cynthia thought.

"We're all pretty crushed, but Mom is the worst," the voicemail continued as if Sylvia knew what her cousin's reaction would be. "She's been asking for you."

Yeah, I'll come right away, Cynthia declared silently. Forgetting Tanner, she stood and walked into the bedroom. Her mind raced, calculating how long it would take her to get cleaned up, pack a bag and drive to Driftwood Cove. Strong followed her, but stopped at the door to her bedroom.

"Just get yourself packed and ready to go," Sylvia's recorded voice ordered. "Pack something appropriate for a memorial service. Don't worry about driving. When I called Uncle Joel and Stan, they told me about last night. Sorry to hear about the CEO thing, I ... and well, Stan said you're in no shape to drive. So, Joel has put the company plane at your disposal. The pilot, Tanner Strong, will be by in an hour to pick you up. Little brother Clint will fetch you from Driftwood Regional."

Damn decent of Joel and Stan, Cynthia thought and waved Tanner into the room.

The voice mail recording went silent when Sylvia took a deep breath to keep her voice from breaking before she continued. "Let's have a good cry and all that when you get here. Goodbye."

After the message ended, Cynthia stared at the phone for a few seconds. Then looking at Tanner and realizing that he was as soaked as she was, she pointed at the bedroom door. "Out that way and across the family room is a guest bedroom and bath. You may shower, and Stan may have left some clothes that'll probably fit you. Give me thirty minutes."

"Yes ma'am," Tanner said and headed to the door.

"Tanner," Cynthia said. "I'm sorry. That wasn't meant to be an order."

"Didn't take it as one." He smiled. "See you in thirty,"

"Tanner," she said softly and smiled.

"Yeah?"

"I am very grateful. I owe you one."

Tanner smiled and said, "You're welcome."

Corporate Airplane En Route Central City to Driftwood Cove

TANNER STRONG PUSHED forward on the Beechcraft G36 Bonanza's yoke and returned the GASMAX corporate aircraft to level flight. Satisfied after a scan of cockpit indicators, he flipped a switch, enabling the autopilot. Though he could have employed the avionics to climb to the new cruising altitude, years of military flying had instilled the need to fly a plane to truly know how it handled. It also fostered a respect for and a healthy suspicion of electronics. The single engine plane now sailed smoothly above a layer of clouds spanning from horizon to horizon without a break.

"That better?" he asked, donning a pair of gold wire-rimmed sunglasses. "The air is better up here, less bumpy."

Strong's voice crackled in Cynthia's headset that reduced engine noise to an acceptable drone for her hangover. However, bright sunlight now flooded the six–seater cabin, easily penetrating large sunglasses shielding obvious bloodshot eyes that no amount of makeup could conceal. Neither did the dark lenses mitigate the extra jab of pain the sun and the knot on her head added to her headache. "Ow, my head!" Cynthia gasped, activating the headset microphone and briefly holding a hand to her forehead before gently probing the lump above the scalp line. "Yeah, that's better, but who turned on the lights?"

Tanner and Cynthia occupied the pilot's and copilot's seats. The four passenger seats in the rear of the cabin were empty. He glanced at her and suppressed a chuckle. "Nothing I can do about that. It's the price of smoother air. You need something for that headache?"

"No, no thanks. I swallowed a near toxic dose of aspirin before we left." Cynthia shifted in her seat and looked at the cloud cover below. "It's not too bad. Maybe I can nap it off now that you stopped throwing my stomach around."

"Hope so," Tanner said. "Hey, it's been kind of crazy. I meant to tell you how sorry I am about your uncle. He was a good man. He took a chance on me when no one else would. Your cousin Sylvia reminds me a lot of him."

"Took a chance on you?" Cynthia frowned and considered Tanner's square jaw, chiseled looks and physique. "He always spoke of you as a cross between a super soldier, a race car driver and a flying ace. And, if I didn't imagine you laying out that guy last night with one backhanded blow and, as you said, "saving my butt this morning," it doesn't seem like Uncle J took much of a chance."

"Hand me that screwdriver in the door pocket," Tanner ordered, pointing to the door on Cynthia's side of the cabin.

He took the screwdriver by the handle and raised the blade over his right shin just below the kneecap. With obvious force he slammed it into his leg. Cynthia eyes widened and she cried, "No!" but she still heard the clang of metal-on-metal. Mouth agape, she looked at Tanner who was smiling broadly.

"Metal prosthetic," he said flatly and handed her the screwdriver. "It's the enduring souvenir of an aborted career as a Marine Corps pilot."

"I never knew ... you can't tell. What happened?" Cynthia asked. Her piqued interest eased her headache.

"The short unclassified version is I crashed and burned," Tanner said, scanning the avionics and making an adjustment. "The Corps said it was pilot error - my fault – but I didn't agree. That's usually true in any crash, but in this case ... well, even with my squadron commander on my side, I wasn't going to win that argument. So, after a very long rehab learning how to do almost everything with a peg leg, including flying and driving, I took the disability compensation. That pilot error thing is pretty hefty black mark on a résumé though. I met your uncle at a bar in Central City. I should say I picked him up at a bar. I was driving a cab. I think he had one too many and wanted to talk."

Cynthia nodded and smiled. "That's sounds like him. You probably got an ear full, and he pumped you for your life story."

"Sure did. I heard all about his three kids, Sylvia, Clint and Danny as well as ... you."

Cynthia raised an eyebrow, a facial movement that reminded her that the hangover still held sway. "Ow. All good, I hope," she managed weakly when she relaxed her face.

"Oh, yeah. You and Sylvia most of all. Clint he was worried about." Tanner paused.

"And Danny?"

"Danny ... he was ... perplexed. Yes, that was the word he used, perplexed. You know, I hear a lot in this job."

"I bet you do," Cynthia nodded and frowned. "And see a lot too, huh?"

Tanner glanced at his passenger briefly. He had been her driver on a number of occasions, but this was the first time their conversation went beyond greetings, shallow comments on the weather and directions. *Does that frown mean she suspects that in all her years at GASMAX I was under orders from J to keep an eye on her?*

"Met Sylvia once or twice," he said. "She seems to be a lot like her dad. You I've chauffeured and heard others talk about. J's pride was well-placed. Clint I never met. If J worried about him, I'm sure it was compassionate concern."

"Yes, Sylvia is very much like J, but she's organized and regimented to a fault."

"Clint?"

"He's picking me up at the airport. You can judge for yourself," Cynthia said with a sad grin, "but he fruitlessly spent too much time striving to gain his father's attention, respect and approval."

"How so?"

"He ... Well, he just has a near-constant melancholy that was alien and off-putting to J." Cynthia sighed. "It only got worse when he changed majors in college from engineering to philosophy."

"I could see that."

"You ever meet Danny?"

"No, but if she perplexed J Martin, I'd like to. J was never puzzled or confounded by anyone. And I overheard several, let's say, heated and challenging conversations he had with the cast of characters that work for and do business with this company. He was many things with people but never perplexed."

"Yeah, that is true and so much ..." Cynthia's voice broke. She took a deep breath and sighed. "Danny, the baby, never cared what her father, mother or anyone else for that matter thought of her. She was always getting into trouble with Uncle J and Aunt Joan and ... well, yeah, she was and probably still is perplexing. We're estranged."

"Cynthia, I'm sorry. This is personal stuff, none of my business." Tanner looked at his passenger. "You've got a lot on your plate. What with J's death and the job thing, and I also noted there wasn't much of Stan's stuff at the house. I'm sorry. That was out of line too."

"Okay. It's okay, Tanner. Thanks," she said, patted his shoulder and yawned. "Look, how much longer til we land?"

"About an hour," Tanner replied after checking the geographic presentation on the navigation display.

"I'm going to take a nap and see if I can get rid of what's left of this headache."

"Sure. I'll wake you when we descend. You warm enough?"

"I'm fine," she answered, adjusting the vent next to her seat. "This warm air is just right, relaxing. And, Tanner, I appreciate this. Driving two hundred and fifty miles with this hangover would have been miserable."

"At your service," Tanner said making a two-finger mock salute. He glanced at Cynthia as she turned in her seat and put her head back.

HER EYES CLOSED immediately. *Just hope I don't have the dream*, was her last thought before the drone of the plane's engine and the warm dry air lulled her to sleep.

In the depths of her slumber, the plane's drone became the surf on the beach heard through doors opening onto a small balcony. The plane's cabin became her room on the second floor of Uncle J's Driftwood Cove beach house, the Eye of the Storm. The dry air heated by the plane's engine became the moist, yet warm night air scented by the ocean. Her dark slacks, brown slip-ons, white blouse and modest undergarments became a pair of immodest panties matching the ripped and tattered remains of a black negligee. The dull fading pain of a hangover became the constant sharp pain of a deep scratch in her side. Her assailant inflicted the wound when he tore away her flimsy night attire.

She was no longer contorted in an aircraft's passenger seat. Her slumber-induced imagining had propelled her sprawled across a bed. She had landed on her back when she had struggled free of the unwanted embrace of the attacker. There was a full moon out, but by the time she freed herself, clouds covered the silver orb, casting the room into a deep inky, darkness. Her pulse raced and heart pounded as she frantically worked her feet and hands to reach the other side of the bed. Though her breath was rapid and shallow, and her ears pounded from the effort, she heard the man laugh and say, "So that's the way you want it. Just stay put and I'll find you."

———

"I KNOW THAT voice," Cynthia's voice crackled in Tanner's headset. He glanced at his passenger. Her eyes were shut. "Talks in her sleep," he whispered. "Must be dreaming." A marked change in the sound of the plane's engine drew his attention immediately back to the panel in front of him.

———

CYNTHIA'S RIGHT HAND pushed once more on her bedding and closed on a hard metal object. Realizing it was her assailant's gun, she grasped it. He had tossed it on the bed to allow the full use of both hands in carrying out his lust-fueled assault. Finally, able to draw her legs beneath her, she swung them and pivoted off the bed. Based on what she saw before the moonlight was lost, the full-sized bed was between her and the attacker. Drawing on some vague memories of Uncle J's tutelage in using small arms one summer, she cocked the pistol. Pointing it in the direction of where she estimated the target, her finger found the trigger. "I ... I got your gun! Stay away ...," she cried.

"I can't see you, so you can't see me," the man said and laughed just as clouds parted. Moonlight flooded the room. Silver light and charcoal shadows clearly etched the bed separating them, the near-naked woman grasping his handgun in a two-handed grip and the fear on her face. "You wouldn't dare."

"Stop! I swear, Buck Wilson, I'll kill you!" she threatened. Desperately she fought the shakes to hold the barrel steady and tightened her finger on the trigger.

———

THE SOUND OF the surf and the warm air ceased and the pain returned to Cynthia's head. Silence in the plane's cockpit yanked her awake.

"Tanner, what's happened?" Cynthia shouted.

"Lost the engine," he replied calmly, nodding at the slowly spinning three-bladed propeller visible through the front windows. "No need to shout, we still have electrical and radio. I've notified air control and declared an emergency."

"What happened? Why'd we ..."

"Don't know," he said, cutting her off. "Not sure. Could be a fuel pump. Or we're out of fuel even though both primary and backup indicators say we aren't. In any case, I can't restart the engine. That's the bad news."

"So, there's good news?" Cynthia asked, sitting up straight and looking out the side window. "We're going to crash, aren't we?"

"Maybe," Tanner replied as he attempted once more to start the engine. "The little good news is we may not. We can glide to a landing, if we can make it to the Driftwood airport."

"But why not put it down in an open field or on a road?" Cynthia asked.

"I will if we find one. We'll be back in the clouds shortly and by the time we get below the ceiling we'll have precious little altitude and time left to find one. Besides, most of this side of Driftwood Cove is hills and forest."

"Damn," Cynthia said and nodded. She locked her eyes on the view out the front cockpit window.

"Couldn't have said it better myself," Tanner said as calmly as he could, sensing her growing distress and masking his rising anxiety. To keep her mounting fear in check, he asked, "Who's Buck Wilson?"

"Who?" She looked at him wide eyed. "This is no time to ..."

"Just before you woke up, you cried out "I swear, Buck Wilson, I'll kill you"."

Cynthia visibly relaxed and thought for a moment. "Buck ... Buck Wilson, Tanner, that's the guy you punched out last night."

"You obviously didn't kill him. An old friend?"

Despite their predicament, Cynthia chuckled. "No, no I didn't." She paused and sighed. "He ... he was a guy who ... I'll tell you later. Just fly!"

"Ten thousand feet," Tanner announced as the plane broke out of the clouds. Once the cabin windows cleared it was obvious to the pilot and his passenger that a near continuous forest blanketed the rolling hills this side of Driftwood Cove. He shook his head. "The airport is our best bet."

Cynthia scanned the landscape bathed in the gray sunlight penetrating the clouds. She spotted a few cabins whose access roads were not visible even from the decreasing altitude. Her gaze locked on an even discontinuity in the trees on the right side of the airplane. "What about that break in the trees over there?" she asked, pointing out the side window.

"That's the B&O Central railroad. It's not a good option," Tanner replied as he punched a few buttons on the avionics display. "Likewise, we'll soon see the open track for the power lines, another poor choice. We're going to the airport ... if we can."

Giving up her search for the hoped-for farm field or straight stretch of road, Cynthia sat back and sighed. "That doesn't sound very confident. What are our chances?"

"Not great, but not bad," Tanner stated positively. "This bird will glide about two miles for every one thousand feet of altitude we lose. We broke through the clouds at ten thousand and, if this electronic navigator isn't screwed up like the fuel tank indicators, the apron of the runway is twenty miles. So do the math."

"So, we just make it," Cynthia said after a brief pause.

"Yeah, but since the ten thousand feet is above sea level and the airfield at Driftwood is four hundred and fifty or so, we're cutting it close," he answered with slightly less confidence. "And, on the approach, there's a tree line and service road to clear, then a security fence and finally an open patch of ground with field lights before we reach the runway."

A recorded female voice sounded in her headset, "Landing gear, landing gear, landing gear." She looked at Tanner as he lifted a switch cover and pushed a button, silencing the warning voice.

"Hey! Aren't you going to lower the gear?" Cynthia asked, sitting up.

"In this case, not until I know we'll make the runway."

"Oh," she said and sank back into her seat. "What can I do?"

"First, tighten that seatbelt and harness. Nap time is over," he replied, tugging at his belt and harness straps. "Now help me find the airfield. We should see it soon. We're crossing the railroad which runs up the west boundary of the field. We're making about one hundred and fifty knots, so we're going to be on the ground – somewhere - in five minutes or so."

"There!" Cynthia shouted and pointed.

Tanner had already picked up the row of three hangers on the east side of the runway when he'd asked her help. *It may keep her mind off crashing. The last thing I need is a panicky passenger.* "Thanks. I got the runway," he said and studied the ground from directly below to the concrete apron. Experience boosted by adrenaline kicked in. He rapidly assessed the glide path over the trees, the access road, the chain linked fence and the patch of grass before the runway. He quickly dismissed putting the gear down and setting ten degrees of flaps before concluding, "No good. We're going in wheels up."

"What the ...?" Cynthia hissed as she stared round-eyed at the pilot.

"Brace," Tanner ordered. "Gonna leave the nose down to clear everything." The plane shook violently and the nosed pitched down when the tail wings broke off the tops of two trees. Tanner fought the controls to pull the nose up. It was enough to clear the fence but not before the bottom of the fuselage scraped the barbed wire topping the fence. Though they cleared the fence, the contact twisted the plane to the right. It sailed over the grass and field lights and pancaked onto the end of the runway, going into a sideway skid. A stream of sparks sprayed out both sides of the plane as it completed a long slide down the runway. It finally stopped, but not before it had rotated a full ninety degrees to the right. The already battered aircraft would have rolled onto its left side if not for the wing. The fuselage lifted up enough to bend the left wing before the bent part and the main body's weight slammed it back upright on the runway.

Because they were held in their seats by the belts and harnesses, the pancake landing, skid and near wingover tossed pilot and passenger first one way forward, then another sideways and finally and abruptly down and to the other side. In the first gyration Cynthia struck her head on the window frame, knocking her unconscious. Despite his shoulder harness, Tanner was thrown forward, striking his forehead on the glare shield, dazing him. He fought to remain conscious as the aircraft came to a stop. He smelled aviation fuel and saw flame outside the pilot side of the cabin. *That shouldn't be. We were empty ... great another crash and burn*, he thought, just before he slipped into darkness.

CHAPTER 6

Through the Looking Glass

—

Runway Driftwood Cove Regional Airport

CYNTHIA'S HANGOVER MADE HER PAINFULLY sensitive to pungent odors as well as the usual bright light and loud noises. Hence the whiff of aviation gas wrenched her back to full consciousness. Pulling off her headset and pushing hair out of her face, she saw the flames outside the pilot's window.

Quickly associating fire with the aviation gas odor, she realized their peril. Though she recognized that dire circumstances warranted prompt action, with great calm she undid her seatbelt and shoulder harness. After shoving Strong upright, she unfastened his belt and harness and pulled his arm free. "Tanner, wake up!" she shouted after pushing off his headset.

There was no response.

She slapped him.

Tanner grunted.

She worked the cabin door latch and opened it. "Come on, big guy," she said, pulling him forward and wrapping her arms around him beneath his arms. Locking her hands behind his back, she planted both feet against the center floor console. Hearing what sounded like "What ..." from Tanner, she took a deep breath and pushed with her feet while pulling him and throwing her upper body at the open door. Still firmly entwined, they landed on the wing. His weight on top knocked the wind out of her, and the impact caused him to moan. Fighting for breath, she held on tight and rolled them off the wing onto the tarmac.

"Cynthia," Tanner said as his eyes opened and found her face within an inch of his. "What happened?"

"We ..." she started as he pushed himself off her.

He sat up and surveyed the crumbled remains of the plane and smelled the leaking aviation fuel. "Avgas! Come on! We gotta move!" he shouted, cutting her off. Driving himself upright on his good leg and pulling her arm to follow, he ordered, "Run!" Taking the first step, he stumbled, but Cynthia got under his right arm in time to steady him. With his arm around her shoulders and hers around his waist, they hobbled away from the doomed Beechcraft.

When they were well clear of the wreckage, fire found the fuel tanks. Staggered by a heat blast, they fell hard on the grass that abutted the tarmac. Sitting up, they stared back at the wreck now engulfed in flames. Once their hearts stopped racing, they became aware of the approaching emergency vehicles.

"You okay?" Tanner gasped, looking his passenger over for signs of injury.

"Yes, I'm fine," she answered after she gave him the once over and completed a quick personal inventory. Her right hand rested briefly on the right side of her head. "Just a new bump, but there's nothing else except my hangover headache is gone." She placed her hand on his shoulder. "How about you?"

"Yeah, me too. I'm okay, but I still have a hangover peg leg," he said and chuckled. "Thank you for hauling me out of there."

Cynthia smiled. "Don't mention it. I owed you." Two paramedics approached and told them not to move.

Cynthia's cousin Clint arrived as the paramedics pronounced that she and Tanner required no further medical care. After a hurried introduction to Clint, Tanner departed with the airport's manager, the Driftwood Cove fire chief, and a police officer to make the initial call to the National Transportation Safety Board.

Though she was no longer a GASMAX executive, Tanner promised to call her later with an update on the crash as well as to see how she was doing. "I'll call corporate HQ to likewise report and assure them we survived the crash unharmed. I'm sure they'll be relieved," he finished. He nodded to Clint and frowned before stepping away to join the three men.

"Yeah, thanks," she said after a brief smile. *Some of them might, but I'm not so sure Uncle Joel will be that happy*, she thought, turning to leave with her cousin. "Clint, I need coffee and something to eat."

"Your boyfriend doesn't like me," Clint stated as they climbed into his dark silver pickup. The fenders and sides were splattered with mud and the bed crammed with camping supplies as well as other outdoor gear.

"He's not my boyfriend," Cynthia protested. "He's the GASMAX corporate pilot. Sylvia got Uncle Joel to have him fly me here even though I got ... I don't work there anymore."

"Yeah, I heard. Sorry about that," he said flatly. "Tough break."

Cynthia glanced at him. *That sounded just like something Uncle J would say when you told him bad news*, she observed silently. In profile, she saw that Clint had grown to look very much like a younger version of her uncle. *Maybe he's matured.*

They said little else during the drive to Driftwood Cove's sole coffee shop. What seemed to come from forced politeness and some familial concern, Clint inquired about the crash and how she survived. Dismissing his apparent lack of genuine distress as a result of grief over the recent loss of his father, she briefly recited what she remembered. She noted that Clint's interest peaked briefly when she described the engine loss, but it waned as she articulated what she considered the most harrowing parts.

"Wow, really a tough break," he said flatly after she described the white-knuckle moments just prior to and after the pancake crash and the in-nick-of-time escape from a fiery death. As if having read her thoughts, he said, "Boy, I sounded just like dear old Dad then, didn't I?"

Driftwood Coffee Shop

AFTER BEING SERVED cups of coffee, a carafe for refills and two ham sandwiches with tourist-oriented names, Cynthia took a large bite. She washed it down with a deep drink from her white mug. Chewing the next bite, she studied her cousin. Slouched in his chair, he looked very much like his father. Like Justice Martin, he was tall and lanky. Except for the day's growth of black beard that her uncle would never have tolerated, the blue jeans and flannel shirt with rolled up sleeves was similar to what J Martin favored on even the hottest Driftwood Cove summer days. "Clint, what did you mean when you said you "sounded just like dear old Dad"?" she asked. "You mean what you said or how you said it?"

"More what than how," he replied, sitting up and raising his right index finger. "You see, Princess C, Dad would have given you little sympathy since you survived, and, more important to him, he would've quizzed you about what 'life lessons' you'd learn. 'What doesn't kill you makes you stronger,' 'You just did what's necessary,' or some baloney like that would be the only solace he'd offer." He dropped his hand and sat back before taking a long drink of coffee and raising his eyebrows.

He's not entirely wrong, she admitted silently. However, suppressing her partial accord, she smiled and said, "Clint, that's not true. Your dad was a good and caring man." Despite her desire to be entirely serious, she laughed. "And you know when we were kids, I hated it when you and Danny teased me with that 'Princess C' thing. I still don't care for it."

"Yeah, sorry about that." He chuckled. "But you gotta admit that Dad treated you like royalty when you were here. Danny and I also resented how you and Sylvia ganged up on us so that, though we all were getting into trouble, he'd assume we were to blame and never 'Princess C' or 'Lady S.'"

Cynthia joined his laughter. "Clint, you're so right. We were awful to you two at times. I don't know if I ever apologized, but I should have."

"Thanks for saying that." Clint nodded while still grinning at the memory. "I forgive you, but I don't know about Danny."

"How's she doing since ...," Cynthia began.

"She got out of the joint?" Clint finished. "Actually, pretty good. Uncle Joel got her a job as a shift operator at the plant. Been doing it for six months now. From what I hear, she's doing quite well. She completed the training program, including the phase four enhancements, in record time and with flying colors."

"Good for her. I knew she was out and working at the plant but not much else."

"I guess prison got her attention. There's true remorse and a desire to do better," Clint observed, rubbing his chin briefly. "You know, she's actually doing good works in keeping with repentance as Grandpa would say. In some ways, she has you to thank for all that."

"How so? I'm the last person she'd thank."

"Well, Mom and Dad believed it. One of the many times they thought that I couldn't hear them, they said that if it hadn't been for the attempted robbery, Buck Wilson's assault on you and prison, she'd have gone completely off the rails. They believed she would've killed herself with drugs or something else."

Cynthia flinched at Wilson's name.

"You still have Buck Wilson nightmares, huh?" Clint asked quietly, leaning forward with his hands crossed. "I thought Doc Schwartz's hypnotherapy fixed all that."

"It did, but, on rare occasions, there still are some," Cynthia replied and frowned. Then she brightened to change the subject. "But back to you sounding like Uncle J. I'll admit that he could be more analytical and practical than compassionate at times, but he was a good man. He loved us all."

"Well, Cuz, you didn't have to live with him year-round," Clint replied bitterly, and he grimaced briefly.

"How can you say that? Ever since I was seven or eight, I spent most every summer with you guys." The memory of J Martin's grin and lean, tanned face sustained her smile. "During those four-month stays I got to be with and to see a lot of him. I considered him to be more like a father than an uncle."

"Summer ... yeah that was his fun and the best-side-on-display time." Clint sighed, and, after a deep breath, he said, "Cyn, you should have been around for the off season."

"Come on," she retorted and grinned. "My mom said he was always helping others. He even found a place for a philosophy major in the family business, right?"

"Yeah, Clint Martin, GASMAX 'Special Projects Assistant.' A tribute to nepotism if ever there was one," Clint sneered.

"No, Clint. Look at what GASMAX's done for Driftwood. The hospital, the condos and, as I understand, the campgrounds north of the plant will open to the public before the season's out. You and he have made all that happen."

"Maybe." Clint sighed. "It'd have been nice to hear him say that now and then."

"Perhaps, but I can't believe he wasn't all that more invested, three-sixty-five, twenty-four, seven, in your mom, you, Sylvia and even Danny."

"Believe it," he countered, clenching and relaxing his fists. "Even if we ignore the faint or absent praise, the man could be a bastard to his own flesh and blood. Ask Sylvia. Though she shares your high opinion, she'll eventually admit the same."

"Hey, I'm sure he was just being a parent," Cynthia shot back, not retreating, and smiled. "You know, doing what's necessary. Spare the rod and all that."

"Yeah, he may have been well-intended, but ..." Clint's voice faded to a whisper, and a faraway look etched his face.

Cynthia swallowed another bite of sandwich and some coffee. She slowly set the mug down as she thought of the best reply. "Look, Clint, all I know is your father helped me so much. It was more than just paying my college and grad school tuition and helping me land a job ... that I recently lost." Taking her voice down a notch, she continued, "He took real good care of Mom when Dad was killed. And after that thing with Danny and Wilson ..."

"You're probably right," Clint conceded quietly, cutting her off before taking another drink from his cup.

"And, after ... what happened, he was there for me all the way. He made sure I had the best shrink and therapy so I could get on with life," Cynthia continued, sensing she was helping him to see his father in the proper light. "Even the martial arts and small arms training he insisted we all go through was a godsend."

"Yeah." Clint chuckled. "He did make sure we could all take better care of ourselves. Even Sylvia suffered through it. She became a pretty good shot. Still keeps a pistol in her nightstand and occasionally packs heat in public. You carrying?"

"No. The gun was a casualty in the crash."

"I can fix you up. I have an extra." He smiled.

"No thanks. I packed it out of habit." Cynthia smiled back. "Can't imagine a safer place than Driftwood Cove surrounded by family."

"Even unarmed, your fists-of-fury black belt still makes you pretty formidable, Cuz," Clint said and laughed.

"Yeah. So does yours." Cynthia chuckled. "I take it Sylvia never finished."

"No, she was okay learning how to shoot, but I guess she figured the hand-to-hand messed up her hair or something. Also, I think she believes she can counter any threat with her puzzle-solving prowess."

"Yeah, she's still into that, is she?"

"You bet." He snorted. "From a daily crossword, in ink of course, to Internet gaming and the logic challenges, she does it all. Now Danny would have out done us all if ... sorry."

"Hey, that's okay," she waved him off. "You can talk about Danny and Buck Wilson and what happened." She shifted in her seat and frowned briefly. "I've put that all behind me. You're right, if she'd applied herself, according to Uncle Joel at least, she could have been a world-class biathlete like he almost was. She had the athletic ability for the skiing and the steady hand for the rifle."

"So, I can talk about Wilson?"

Cynthia nodded. "Sure."

"Well then ... okay. On the whole dear old Dad was good as the world judges good, and he certainly strove to live up to Grandpa's code, 'Do what's necessary, love God and do good, bearing fruit in keeping with repentance,'" Clint said. He waved a finger in a circle. "No doubt we'll get an earful of Saint Justice tales tomorrow at the memorial. But, let me tell you one you won't hear. I got to warn ya, it includes Buck Wilson."

"As I said, it's okay. Go ahead," Cynthia said, and she figured there just might be another side, a darker facet, to Uncle J. "But then you've got to take me somewhere I can buy a replacement wardrobe and accessories for what went up in flames. Deal?"

"Sure," Clint replied.

"Also, I need a lift to the car rental place. Now tell your tale. I'm all ears."

"Okay," Clint said and nodded. "You may recall that while Dad built most of his GASMAX fortune, despite all the eventual family wealth, the Eye of the Storm beach house that you enjoyed in the summer was in sad shape. Most of those early years, he kept us in near-minimum wage circumstances. Any surplus profit he poured into the business and making minimal repairs and upgrades to a drafty old summer home that was not yet renovated for year-round living."

"But his fortune grew like crazy," Cynthia observed with a measured but genuine enthusiasm developed over her five years as a GASMAX executive. "It can't have been all that bad for too long."

"Yeah, yeah and don't get me wrong. He didn't force us to live in any danger or real poverty," Clint conceded with a smile and body language that told Cynthia that not all his memories of J Martin were bad. "At least I never felt we were deprived or in any jeopardy. Heck, I didn't know any better. I was a kid. I pretty much enjoyed the village and never really realized how well the old man could have lived until much later."

"So later you felt he cheated your mom, Sylvia, Danny and you out of a better quality of life?"

"No, that wasn't it. Matter of fact, Dad was my hero, bigger than life, until ... well, here's the tale. You be the judge." Clint sat up a bit straighter and took a deep breath.

"Do we really have time?" Cynthia inquired, glancing at her watch and recalling the earlier phone conversation with Sylvia shortly before they got coffee and sandwiches. "We've got that thing with Sylvia and the lawyer, right? And I need to pick up the rental car and want some clothes that don't smell like smoke and aviation gas."

"Yeah. The thing with the lawyer is just Sylvia ... you know, planning for the memorial and will reading," Clint said quickly. "Also, the car rental place is now part of Wilkes General Store. Remember Rick Wilkes? He and his sister, Brenda, own and operate it now."

Cynthia remembered the Wilkes. They had hung out with Clint and Danny one summer. "Vaguely. Bet they've changed," she said finally.

"They sure did. They're all growed up like all of us." Clint laughed. "Anyway, they bought out the car rental business last winter and moved it into the store. Its one-stop shopping, and the store is just up the block from here. So, it's walkable and there's plenty of time. Besides it's a short but pointed story."

Cynthia nodded. "Okay, continue."

"See, I was eight or nine. Buck Wilson lived in the village in one of those houses across from the courthouse. Even though he wasn't yet a teenager, he was big for his age and a first-class bully. He seemed to especially enjoy terrorizing me and my friends after school." Clint carved the air with his hands to demonstrate the David-and-Goliath disparity between his younger self and Buck.

"I know the type," Cynthia whispered. Her last encounter with Joel Martin and the Buck Wilson dream on the plane came to mind. "Bullies come in all sizes and shapes."

"What, yeah ...," her cousin said and paused. "Anyway, one terror-filled day I finally had enough. I told Buck off and called him something I knew would piss him off, and I questioned his manhood. Needless to say, I immediately beat feet, and he chased after me. Oh, did I run. I was fast then. It was before that incident with Danny." He pointed to his left leg. "Dad was just up the block from the school waiting in his car – that old double cab truck - to pick me up. So, I figured I could get to the pickup and get inside before Buck grabbed me. Well, I got close. You remember that old truck?"

"Yes." Cynthia nodded, recalling rides in the back of the pickup.

"Well, I not only got three steps on Wilson and was almost within arm's reach of the truck, but I saw Dad sitting inside. Now I felt like I'm really home free." Clint's voice was filled with excitement, and he raised a hand above his head. "Remember, Dad was six-three or so and broad-shouldered. So, I figured I'd not only get inside, but my dad would scare off Buck if need be. So, all was good, right?"

"Right. Uncle J to the rescue," Cynthia replied heartily, anticipating a happy ending.

"Wrong!" The air went out of Clint's voice and his shoulders drooped. "I almost got my hand on the rear cab door when I saw Dad reach back and lock the door."

"What!" Cynthia laid both hands flat on the table.

"Yeah. So, Buck grabbed me, and, as he's drug me to the ground, I shouted "Dad, Dad, please help me!"" Clint clawed at the air in front of him.

"Did he?" Cynthia asked, but anticipated a negative reply.

"No. Wilson beat the crap out of me," Clint replied flatly. He pointed to a faint white line above his right eyebrow. "See this scar? It's a reminder. I see it every time I shave."

"How awful," Cynthia declared and sat back. The story fanned the embers of her bitter memories of Buck Wilson.

"Yeah, it sucked big time. So, after Buck finished and skedaddled, Dad rolled down his window and said ... I'll never forget, "That will teach you a lesson.""

"I'm sure it did. I bet that was the last bully you ever trash-talked," Cynthia concluded with faint conviction.

"Yeah, I got that," Clint admitted. He tilted his head to the left and narrowed his eyes as he studied his cousin's face. "You know something, Cynthia, I just realized that unlike Sylvia, who wishes she was cut from the same cloth as Dad, you are."

"I'll take that as a compliment," Cynthia said with some pride, "but I suspect it wasn't intended to be one."

Clint scowled. "Anyhow, here are the other lessons the eight-year-old me learned: 'Dad, you won't always protect me,' and 'Dad, I can't always trust you.'"

Cynthia sat up. *All these years and Clint didn't get it*, she thought. "But he was teaching you a life lesson, Clint, an important one. You have to choose your battles wisely."

Clint chuckled. "Cynthia, that's so very Dad of you. Right, learn to do what is necessary, but don't you see that I didn't need a teaching moment. I needed affirmation and protection. I stood up to a bully, figuring that was worth something and Dad in his truck should have been a safe place," Clint countered passionately, and sadness or regret carved his face. Cynthia wasn't sure which. Then, with less passion and more sympathy, he concluded, "I ...

look I know you loved the old man. After all, he got you through that ... that incident the summer you spent with us while you were going to Yale."

Besides the clothes on her back, Cynthia's cell phone was the only thing that survived the crash. It now rang sharply, cutting off her cousin. "Okay. Let's stop. I gotta take this. It's the car rental place. Besides, Clint, it's not that I don't want to talk about it, but I ... well, not now, please."

Cynthia answered the phone. While she forced herself to pay attention to the young woman on the other end, her eyes moistened. Starting with the dream on the plane, a door to the distant painful past, which she believed had been shut long ago by therapy and time, had opened. All those trips to Driftwood Cove during her time with GASMAX had never resurrected these memories. For whatever reasons, she soon realized that door could not remain completely closed during this visit. *My God, that night ... and this feels just like when Stan dumped me.*

"The car is ready," the woman's voice on the phone broke her anxious reverie.

"We'll be right over," she said and, after a pause, "I also need a complete wardrobe." After another brief silence she finished, "Great. Goodbye."

"Cuz, I'm sorry," Clint said and gestured at the phone.

The door to the past closed a little. "Thanks, Clint."

"Car ready?"

"Yes, it is," Cynthia smiled.

"Let's roll, Princess C," Clint ordered with a wide grin, rose and bowed deeply. "I'm going to skip the thing with Sylvia. I've heard it already. See, I'm not staying at the house this summer. I'm working on the cabin, and I've got a contractor coming by shortly."

Cynthia stood and they walked to his truck. "I thought the cabin was beyond repair."

"Yeah, most everyone told Dad that, but, well, you don't tell Justice Martin it can't be fixed. He and I've been ... had been working on it off and on this last year. He spent many weekends on it. It's far enough along to live in, and I figured I'd finish it this summer."

"Uncle would like that, Clint," Cynthia said softly.

"Well, tell Lady S I said hi," he said and laughed, climbing behind the wheel.

Wilkes General Store

WILKES GENERAL STORE, or 'WGS' as its signage declared, was indeed a one-stop shopping experience. Rick and Brenda Wilkes had transformed their great-grandfather's bait and notions shop into a small-scale general merchandise store. It was no longer the weather and tourist-worn, dark, stark and limited selection shop that Cynthia remembered from her childhood summers in Driftwood Cove. It now featured groceries, clothing, sundries and other services demanded by a seasonal tourist population and the year-round locals.

Clint was right, Cynthia thought. *Rick Wilkes is indeed 'all growed up.' Some college and obvious time in a gym has fleshed him out nicely.* The gangly, negative boy who stuttered was now a mature, poised, well-spoken and dark-featured young man. As he processed the paperwork for Cynthia's dark blue sedan, he explained how they had finally bought out their father the prior fall, and then they closed, gutted and made over the store before reopening in the spring.

Incorporating the latest retail technology and small business practices, the Wilkes siblings saved the family trade. Rick described how the general store Cynthia remembered had financial roots in Prohibition in the nineteen-twenties. Their grandfather and his dad ran a robust bootlegging operation and a popular speakeasy at Wilkes Tavern and Inn, located just north of the Driftwood Cove village center. The tavern's north property line, he reminded her, was the south line of the property on which J Martin had restored his beloved family beach house, Eye of the Storm.

Before she asked, Rick stated that the old tavern and the tunnel from its basement to Smugglers Cove were still there. The tavern was condemned and the tunnel boarded up. Cynthia had fond memories of the beach at Smugglers Cove. She, Sylvia and some of their teenage summer buddies went there to underage drink and for the privacy to do other things teen girls and boys enjoyed.

When he handed her the car keys and paperwork, Rick expressed his condolences for her loss. He added that he and Brenda owed the family business' salvation largely to J Martin. The funding for the business upgrade and to care for their father, suffering from early dementia, was realized from the sale of the Wilkes Tavern property to her uncle the prior summer. She hid her surprise. Even though Sylvia faithfully kept her informed regarding 'big' family news, this was the first she had heard of it.

Brenda Wilkes was a half a head taller than Cynthia and her brother. As an adolescent she was all knees and elbows, chubby, freckles and hay-colored and straw-styled hair. Like her younger brother she'd matured well. She was slender in a willowy way most men noticed, compelling a quick second look. Her hair, though still worn short, was styled, a light brown now, and framed a face still blessed with a hint of freckles on high cheeks, engaging eyes and a friendly smile.

Considering Brenda's shorts, a polo shirt with the WGS logo and sandals as well as her slightly tanned complexion, Cynthia concluded that she was the public face of the business. She had greeted Cynthia when she entered. Her brother appeared to have less customer interaction and more behind the counter duties. They were a perfect team.

After expressing her condolences for J, she said, "And thank God you survived the crash."

"You heard, huh?"

"News still travels fast in Driftwood. One of the village's finest, Officer Harper, was in the store a while ago. He told Rick all about it."

"You're right. News like that would travel fast in this burg," Cynthia said with a knowing smile.

Brenda brightened. "But WGS has everything for the woman who has lost everything in a plane crash." She laughed. "I've already selected clothing, toiletries and other travel items for your consideration once you're finished seeing Rick about the rental."

Concluding the rental agreement, she found Brenda in the back of the store putting items on a shelf. The sign on a door behind her said, "Employees Only." "I'm ready to see what you picked out," she said, tapping her on the shoulder.

Brenda smiled, grimaced, sniffed the air and shook her head. "Smelling like a gas station, you aren't." She pulled a key from her shorts pocket and gave it to Cynthia. "I live in the apartment just through that door and down the hall," she said, pointing over her shoulder with her thumb. "Get in there and bathe. You'll find fresh towels in the closet just outside the bathroom. These should fit you." She handed her a WGS store bag with a tan skirt, a white blouse, undergarments and sandals.

"Brenda, thanks, and that's kind of you but not necessary ..."

"No arguing," Brenda cut her off, raising a hand, signaling "stop," and smiled. "You're not trying on my clean clothes like that. Go."

Sometime later, after a much welcomed, long, hot shower and attired in the new clothes, Cynthia stood in front of the full-length mirror in the clothing section of the store. Brenda stood behind her and held up the various pieces she had selected, either under Cynthia's chin or at her waist. The small suitcase Cynthia was purchasing was soon filled with clothing as well as the toiletries and makeup. Not one item was the wrong size or rejected. "You have a real knack for this, Brenda," she said as she held a dark gray sun dress under her chin.

"Despite the low cut, I thought this would work for the memorial and reading of the will," Brenda said, smoothing out the material over Cynthia's breasts, waist, hips and legs.

"Perfect," her customer commented and grinned. "This is even better than what I'd packed."

Brenda put the dress back on a hanger and draped it across the open suitcase. She picked up another garment. "One more, this nightgown should do nicely." It was a knee-length dark silver nightgown with a satin finish.

As with each other selection, standing behind her and, with the left hand, she held the top under Cynthia's chin. Using her right, she smoothed the rest of the garment into place. "What do you think?"

———

FEELING THE PRESSURE of Brenda's hands, Cynthia's vision blurred. She closed her eyes. The store and its bright lights faded into her room and the moonlight at the beach house. Brenda's hands became Buck Wilson's. As Brenda was, he had stood behind her but with one hand on her throat and the other on her stomach, pressing her body into his.

His breath, smelling of alcohol and tobacco, was warm and rapid on her neck. He slid his hand further across her waist to turn her into his embrace. "What do you think, baby?" he leered. Cynthia, with her hands on his forearms, pulled to escape. This caused his right hand to slip. He grabbed a fist full of her nightie. He ripped it, scratching her side.

"No!" she screamed. With a final pull and twisting her body, she escaped his hold and fell backwards on the bed.

CHAPTER 7

The Planner and Paint

———

Wilkes General Store

AFTER CYNTHIA APPROVED THE GRAY dress, Brenda draped it across the suitcase. Brenda smiled and picked up a short, dark silver garment with a satin finish. "One more, this nightgown should do nicely," she said.

With her left hand, Brenda pressed the top under Cynthia's chin. Using the other, she smoothed the gown into place. "What do you think?" she asked, pressing the hem in place.

Cynthia's eyes rolled shut, and she fell against Brenda who instinctively caught her. "No!" Cynthia screamed, grabbing Brenda's forearms before pushing and twisting herself free. She fell on the suitcase and her eyes opened wide. "Brenda? What ... happened," she stammered.

"You suddenly collapsed," Brenda replied, extending her hand. "Cynthia, are you alright?"

"Yeah, I'm fine. Just got a little dizzy," Cynthia said as she regained her feet and weakly smiled. "Sorry about that."

"Damn, girl, you scared the daylights out of me." Brenda placed hands on Cynthia's shoulders. "You need to sit down?"

"No, I'm fine really." Cynthia smiled as she smoothed her hair back into place. "Maybe the day is catching up to me."

"That's right. It's not every day you survive a plane crash."

After being fired, almost drowned, dumped, nearly poisoned and passed-out drunk, Cynthia thought but said, "That's true. It's not been my typical day. I just need to rest. Let's settle up."

Brenda picked the nightgown off the floor. "I take it you didn't care for the nightie?"

"No, no it's perfect, like everything else. Just ... it reminded me of something I didn't like, but it's fine."

R. NICHOLAS POHTOS

Driftwood Coffee Shop

A SINGLE DING sounded on the personal computer speakers. "Perfect," Sylvia Martin said, and, without looking, laid her hand upon the PC's mouse. She sat up straight in her usual chair at the same coffee shop table she'd staked out years ago. Informally the wait staff reserved it for her daily use and served her custom coffee promptly upon arrival. She tipped liberally, and her entry was hard to miss. She was one of the very few customers dressed in business attire in a small tourist town whose dress code was seasonal but always casual.

Planner Plus software was already opened in anticipation of the day's five o'clock alert to layout the next week's activities in detail. As she had done most of her adult life, Sylvia looked forward to this personal, self-imposed weekly planning session as a religious zealot anticipates a church service or a daily time of prayer.

As she pushed dark-framed glasses up a slim nose and thinking of her younger brother Clint, her full pink lips broke into a smile. As a child and as an adult, his planning was short-term and too reactive. Though Clint's approach to life was alien to Sylvia's, she at least understood her sibling's approach. *Unlike Danny, at least he plans*, she mused, her grin fading to a frown. Her oval face fell further as she reflected on the youngest Martin child's chaotic and undisciplined slant on living. *Grandpa must roll over in his grave each time she's done what's not necessary.*

With a well-manicured index finger, Sylvia clicked on the month tab, and the current month's calendar opened. Her brown eyes, a shade darker than her brunette hair styled along short lines, beamed again as she noted that each day was rich with black-letter detail. However, red lettering for the current week and part of the last indicated several incomplete action items. She winced. "Well, dear father, your death sure threw a monkey wrench into things," she hissed. Since the coffee shop was crowded and abundant with conversation white noise, she knew that talking aloud to herself would go unnoticed. It was just one more reason that she felt compelled to carry out the weekly planning ritual there. "Oh well." She sighed and grinned briefly. "Let's begin."

The first red letter items appeared early in the last week on the day J Martin's body was discovered. After cancelling the dailies and rescheduling some weeklies, monthlies and a quarterly, Sylvia changed the entry, 'Dad Out' to 'Dad found Dead at Quarry.' She paused and frowned. That day she and her mother had identified his battered, broken body at the morgue. He was found in a rappelling harness at the base of the highest rock wall in the abandoned quarry.

It surprised them all that an experienced climber like her father should die in such a fall. That he was alone was not a shock. He was known to, without any more notice than announcing "I'll be gone for a while," walk out the beach house front door, hop in his pickup truck, hastily loaded with camping equipment and supplies, and drop out of sight. These periods Sylvia labeled 'Dad Out' in her planner. He'd do this a couple of times each summer, solo hiking and camping. Both she and her mom were frustrated when he'd leave without his cell phone or even specifying a general destination.

J had been 'out' four times last summer instead of his usual two or three. This year, only a month into the summer, he'd already been 'out' twice. As he had the year before, he stayed away longer, ten to twelve days each time, instead of five to seven. Sylvia had confirmed and quantified this conclusion by reviewing the detailed record of events that her planning software archived. Her weekly entries included making the digital plan reflect, as accurate and detailed as possible, how events had actually unfolded.

Sylvia sipped her coffee. Not captured in her digital log was what had been different the last time her father departed. Though it was his typical abrupt exit, in addition to the one-liner announcement, he hugged each of his children. He told each, even Danny, much to their surprise and delight, how proud he was of them and how much he loved them. Also, she felt dread and sensed finality in how her father embraced and kissed her mother. Oddly, her father's profession of pride in his oldest child was followed by a reminder to her to keep an eye on her cousin, Cynthia, via his driver Tanner Strong. Her trepidation deepened when her father whispered something in Joan Martin's ear, and Sylvia saw grief briefly crease her mom's face before she nodded and kissed him back. Sitting up straight, and recalling her father's last words, she forced her fingers to dance across the keyboard, adding a new entry to last week's schedule: 'Called Tanner Strong and Cynthia.'

Sylvia cleaned up the last few subsequent days. Several more frequent 'Cynthia Jones' entries joined a cadre of routine items that colored most of Sylvia Martin's life. Except for the phone calls to notify her cousin of J Martin's death and the fast-track memorial and will reading, the other 'Cynthia' entries were from telephone and text exchanges with Tanner Strong and inquiries from Joel Martin.

Cynthia was the perplexing relative. Sylvia had her brother and baby sister figured out. Cynthia, however, was more akin to the enigma that was her father. She sighed. *As with Dad, she will remain a puzzle.* "No, Cynthia can still be figured out," she protested aloud. "Maybe with Dad's passing and her recent troubles at work and in her love life, I can finally solve the riddle of what makes Cynthia Jones tick and why I care. It's more than I just love solving puzzles."

Sylvia stopped typing. Long ago she recognized that her dad and Cynthia Jones were alike. She liked her cousin very much. Being the oldest could be exhausting since her father expected her to lead and guide the other two. When Cynthia joined the family for the summer, without anyone saying it, the burden of sibling leadership fell to their blonde cousin.

While Clint had inherited his tall and lanky frame from their dad, Uncle Joel and Grandpa Moses, Sylvia had Danny's and her mom's smaller compact but still attractive stature. She was at peace with that as well as the fact that she lacked their ease in drawing others to them and compelling their compliance. In appearance and temperament, Cynthia fell somewhere in between.

When Cynthia arrived, Sylvia would gladly defer to her relative's lead. She admired and was impressed by the way Cynthia easily led the Martin kid pack. Clint and Danny were eager, but at times rebellious and jealous, cohorts and followers. That was okay with her. Cynthia also received J Martin's negative attention when the pack strayed. However, she noted with envy that his rebukes of Cynthia were less severe than they were when his other children strayed off the Martin path.

She sat back and sipped some neglected and now lukewarm coffee. *I really don't care about that*, she thought. *Cynthia always treated me as an equal, a sister, and made me feel like we were both becoming women together.*

Sylvia resumed pointing, clicking and typing. The current week was much easier to sort into a new and manageable set of action items. Even those associated with her father's death were integrated with great ease from years of planning practice and experience. The only tough one was the meeting later at the beach house with Cynthia, Clint and Danny. Though the relationship with Danny was still tense, Cynthia claimed to hold no grudge for the part Danny played in the assault she suffered at the hands of Danny's loser boyfriend. "Time heals all wounds?" Sylvia wondered aloud. "If not, hopefully the scars will remain covered."

The time display in a corner of the laptop screen declared '5:25 PM.' *On track*, she thought with a smile. *Plenty of time left before the six-thirty meeting.* After reviewing once more the events of the coming weeks, she opened the daily display for the next seven days. *Now for the fun part.* The recurring daily, weekly, monthly and annual items had been automatically populated into each day's schedule by the software. She opened each day of the coming week and massaged times, duration and start dates to accommodate and factor in what the software could not. The point-click-type pace slackened only as she wrestled with tomorrow's memorial and the subsequent reading of the will.

Adding 'Smugglers Cove' as the location for the memorial reminded Sylvia that she would be expected to say something – give some kind of eulogy. Backing up to the current day's schedule with a click, she blocked off some time to write. *One hour, will that be enough time?* she wondered, filling in the event's end time. With all the other arrangements and action her father's sudden exit had spawned, this was the first time she thought about what the world - her world - would be like without Justice Martin. She knew that she should be sadder and more reflective ... *weep and grieve a little maybe? No, no time for that now*, she sniffed and stayed with one hour. *I'll come up with something.* She brightened as she remembered today's call from Driftwood Cove's mayor, requesting that she give the Justice Martin testimonial remarks at the Founder's Day opening ceremony next week. *I can kill two birds with one stone*, she thought. J Martin was to be recognized this year for his numerous civic and community contributions. *He was, after all, the face of GASMAX Industries that floated the village's economic boat. Will that fall to me now?*

Sylvia considered herself to be like her father in at least one aspect; they both disliked lawyers. The one exception was the family lawyer, Louis Belmont of Logan, Logan and Belmont. He was more like family than a hired professional legal expert. J and Joel Martin retained Louis in the years before her birth. She always felt that there was something suspect or forced in the deep and long-lived relationship between the three men. She speculated that it involved some secret shared by Belmont and her dad and uncle. *One hour should do it to read the will and answer questions. No, better make it two,"* she decided silently for the session one day hence. *Maybe Uncle Louis,* as her father always referred to Belmont*, will reveal the big secret and there's no telling what its fallout will require in time for dialogue and family angst and drama.* "Also," she sighed aloud, "No matter what Cynthia claims, extra time may be very necessary with the Cynthia - Danny elephant in the room."

'5:55 PM,' the white letters in the screen's lower corner declared. Sylvia smiled. "Five minutes to spare." She powered off the computer after verifying that the planner had already updated on her cell phone. After slipping the computer into its case, she placed her phone in her purse. It rang. *No time, let it go to voicemail.*

The coffee shop was located on the ground floor of one of eight buildings arrayed four on each side of the village center's main street. Except for one, all were two-story wooden structures with brick facing on the ground floor. The cobbled main drag was one block off the Driftwood Bay waterfront and its extensive collection of docks, slips and shack-like affairs that catered to the fishing and pleasure vessels which found shelter and seasonal dockage in Driftwood Bay. Each year, property owners and the town split the cost of power washing and any needed painting for the main street storefronts. As a consequence, one of the coffee shop's two outdoor sitting areas was temporarily closed. Tables and chairs were pushed aside to make room for painters' scaffolding, and they were covered in splattered and various-sized drop cloths.

Sylvia stopped a few steps outside the coffee shop's door, having second thoughts about the phone call. Stepping just inside the open sitting area, she dropped her computer case and purse onto an empty table. She retrieved the phone from the purse and checked the caller ID. *Damn, it's Uncle Joel again. Third call today, and it's weird. He's been asking more about Cynthia than Dad.* Noting that there was no voicemail, she shook her head. On the GASMAX payroll she was J Martin's executive assistant. With her father's death, Joel Martin was technically her boss, so, she initiated a call back.

ONE STORY ABOVE, the two painters, Jasper Carpenter and his teenaged son, Pete, were working quickly to finish applying the last coat on the second floor before losing the late afternoon sunlight. Jasper, noting that they were about out of paint in the opened bucket, directed young Pete to open the five-gallon bucket set on the scaffold's end near the ladder. "If you can't get the lid off, roll it down here on its side like you did with this one, and I'll do it."

Pete nodded. "No probs, Pop. I can do it." He smiled confidently, but he soon found he couldn't get the lid off the fifty-pound bucket of paint.

"Put it on its side and roll it here," Jasper ordered. He looked at the sun now low in the western sky over the building across the street. "We're losing daylight, son."

"I can ... okay I'll roll it," Pete conceded finally and tipped the can. It landed on its side, and he lost control of it. It didn't roll toward his father but, it rolled quickly off the end of the scaffold.

"Damn!" Pete cried, wide-eyed as he lunged after the bucket. He failed to reach it. Hanging out from the end of the scaffolding, he shouted, "Look out below!"

Hearing the warning cry from above, Sylvia, with the cell phone pressed to her ear and listening to Joel Martin, looked up. In a split second the falling bucket and Pete's wide-eyed face registered. Concluding there was no time to jump clear, she dropped the phone, raised both arms above her head and lowered her chin. *This really screws up the schedule*, she thought.

CHAPTER 8

Assault In an Old Wound

Driftwood Coffee Shop

JULIE HARRIET SIMPSON OCCUPIED ONE of the coffee shop's sidewalk tables. One of a handful of licensed private investigators in Carlton County who serviced the Village of Driftwood Cove she was on assignment. The majority of the county's private investigators resided and made a living in Central City over two hundred miles to the south. This job was a second homecoming of sorts. Though she had gained several years of law enforcement experience as a Central City uniformed cop, she was born and raised in Driftwood Cove. She jumped at the opportunity when the village, infused with GASMAX money, expanded its small police force and lured her home the first time to serve as one of two detectives.

She worked two years in plainclothes partnered with a veteran investigator, Brian Smith. The old pro was a good teacher and mentor. However, she eventually learned that his nerve and moral compass were bent. He'd crossed a line in her book when he pressured her into suppressing evidence in one of the village's very few high-profile cases that included felony charges and prominent locals. She quit, turned in her badge and gun and set herself up as a PI in the city. She had to hustle, but she made a decent and honest living. Smith was rewarded by being made the Driftwood Cove Chief of Police. Though this still rankled her, as a PI she had to rely on a certain amount of Driftwood Cove PD cooperation. Accordingly, several years ago she sought out Chief Smith and made peace with him.

Julie sat up and lowered her newspaper when her assignment, Sylvia Martin, emerged from the coffee shop. She checked her floppy tourist hat in place over the careless array of dark red shoulder-length hair. Pushing up the large-framed sunglasses that hid her green eyes, she shoved the final bite of bagel into her mouth, chased it with some coffee and stood. She slowly lowered her five-foot five-inch frame back down when Sylvia stopped to make a phone call.

Julie's latest client had engaged her to surveil Ms. Martin, reporting any unusual activity. Julie knew Sylvia and her family well because the Martin's oldest child was a classmate in grade, middle and high school. That made covert surveillance of her school chum challenging. The trick was to get close enough but not be recognized.

To Julie's advantage, time, and years of it away in the big city, had worked significant changes in her appearance. She was no longer the short-haired, plus-sized public-school student or plump police detective who later dealt with the Martin family in the wake of robbery and assault. She was now much slimmer. Setting up as a private investigator, she grew out her hair, adding a number of ways to arrange it with varied hats, glasses and clothing to very much minimize the chance of recognition. Julie also knew that Sylvia was a slave to schedules and routine. Even with her father's death last week, tracking her whereabouts and recognizing unusual activity was still easily done at a distance.

Julie was close enough this time to hear Sylvia say "Joel" and "Yes sir." *Must be talking to Joel Martin*, she thought, averting her gaze so that Sylvia would not think anyone was eavesdropping. She looked away in time to see Pete Carpenter on the scaffolding wrestling with a bucket of paint. She realized he had no success in prying its top loose and watched as his father gestured impatiently for Pete to roll it to him on the narrow scaffold. *Bad idea*, she thought and stood.

When Pete shouted, "Look out below," Julie already recognized the immediate danger to Sylvia. The PI took two steps towards her and wrapped her arms around the woman as Martin raised her arms. Julie tackled Sylvia, and they fell and rolled away from the plummeting paint bucket. The thick plastic container hit with a thud, smashing Sylvia's cell phone but missing the two women. As Julie pushed herself into a sitting position and realized that Sylvia was unharmed, she was surprised to note that they were not covered in paint. The bucket's lid had held. The container was dented but otherwise intact.

Jasper and Pete Carpenter descended to the sidewalk quickly, and they helped the two women to their feet. After verifying there were no injuries or damages other than Sylvia's phone, they profusely apologized and promised Sylvia a new phone before turning their attention to the paint bucket.

"That was a close one," Julie said and smiled. She frowned when Sylvia didn't even grin briefly, and it appeared that she was near to tears. "You're okay, right?"

"Yes," Sylvia replied. "It's just that my phone. I ... I'm sorry. Thank you so much. I know that bucket could have hit me."

"You're welcome."

"What time do you have?" Sylvia asked as she gathered her computer case and purse.

"Ten after six. You want me to take you to the ER? Sometimes injuries are masked by an adrenaline rush."

"No thanks. I'm fine," Sylvia replied, patting her hair and tugging her collar into place. When she looked up, her lips broke into what Julie called the Martin smile. "Julie Simpson, is that you? I almost didn't recognize you. You look great. It's been forever. Perhaps we can catch up over coffee some time, but right now I'm late for a meeting."

"Sure. Okay, later then." Julie chuckled as Sylvia quickly walked away. *The Martins*, she thought, sighed and shook her head. *I'll let her get a head start and see where she goes.*

Eye of the Storm Beach House

SYLVIA TURNED OFF the two-lane Highway 733 onto the packed gravel driveway leading to the Martin family home of twenty plus years. Her dad had christened it 'Eye of the Storm' in a solemn ceremony that also memorialized his brother Jacob. Uncle Jake's loss during the hurricane party was a sad event mentioned by her parents only in the sketchiest detail and usually as the sole cause of Aunt Mary's drinking problem. She and her siblings shortened the name to 'The Eye' and lately, in text messages, to 'EOS.'

Sylvia's imported sedan's tires crunched the loose gravel as it came around a sharp tree-and-bush-lined bend. This afforded a better view of the landward side of EOS' wood and stone structure. Beyond the roundabout drive that fronted wide steps to the landing and front door she recognized her mother's car. She speculated that the blue sedan next to it was Cynthia's rental.

The Driftwood Cove beach house was more of a large beach cottage. However, her father, as well as realtors who occasionally inquired if J Martin was interested in selling the hundred-plus-year-old edifice, felt comfortable in calling its rambling twenty-five hundred square feet a house. Sylvia agreed. As a little girl, she believed her family lived in a mansion on an enchanted rocky ocean coastline with a beach in the backyard. Passing into her adulthood and after college, the grandeur of the slate sides and gabled roof topped with a widow's walk had faded as had the magic and mysteries of rocks and sand.

Though she still found joy in spending time here away from her Driftwood Cove apartment as well as the one she kept in Central City, she came increasingly to view it as just another family asset. Its potential value continued to skyrocket in Driftwood Cove's limited-inventory real estate market. Even the active adult community of luxury condos under construction just up the beach would do little to dent the sales value when her parents' eventual passing would likely compel Sylvia and her siblings to sell. This reality was driven home by her dad's early and accidental demise.

Sylvia glanced at the reflection in the rearview mirror of her brother and sister in the back seat. Clint, gazing out the side window, had the same sad, faraway look in his eyes as she had seen in her father's more often in the months before his death. Danny was engrossed in her cell phone.

Sylvia figured it would naturally fall to her to take the lead in the eventual sale of the beach house. Clint would be too sentimental, and Danny would be concerned only about how fast she would obtain her share of the profits. "How are you two doing back there?"

"Good," Clint instinctively replied to Sylvia's pro forma big-sister inquiry about his well-being. She accepted the likelihood that years of practice had taught him to put enough sincerity in his one-word reply to ward off further questions and, heaven forbid, a deeper conversation.

When Sylvia made the turn, she took in the beach house at once. *Nothing's changed*, she thought. A broad, beaten path of packed gravel and sand led to the three steps ascending to the worn front door landing flanked by white columns and topped with a square canopy roof. The widow's walk crowning the two-story house well complemented the home's weather-beaten peaked gables. Externally, the Martin family home appeared small since it had been built into and not on the rocky hill facing the ocean. Visitors usually drew this conclusion before they entered the spacious three-floor interior that included a finished cellar. Likewise, the structure's broad back sundeck that overlooked a wide stretch of sandy seashore added to the open look and feel. The EOS private beach was fringed with dunes and tall grass parted by the dozen steps and raised wooden walk from the deck to the beach and the expanse of the ocean beyond.

She glanced at Clint. He was smiling. Only a vestige of the prior gloom remained. The sight of EOS and/or the smell of sea air, she figured, must have triggered the change. "Clint, you thinking of those frequent, long solitary morning walks on the beach?" she asked. "How'd you always put it? Yeah, "soothing contemplation of the ocean...""

"And its many facets," he said and laughed.

Danny glanced up from her phone. Her raven hair was parted in a bob, revealed warm gray eyes, a ski-jump nose and full lips attractively arranged over the unique Martin chin. She gave her sister a thumbs-up.

Sylvia's frowned.

Danny, looking past her brother at the beach house, said, "This place never changes, does it?" Though no one answered, Sylvia knew that her sister was confident that Clint was thinking the same thing and about long walks on the beach.

Despite their falling out, those two are still nearly telepathic, Sylvia thought. She also knew that Danny had spent little time at the beach house since getting out of jail. Before that long-ago night of surprises with Buck Wilson, Cynthia and the cops, she and Clint were thick as thieves and shared a love of the beach house. It afforded a little girl many places to hide from her siblings. Much later, its nooks and crannies, including a creepy cellar and wine press, provided the cover in which a rebellious teen could take refuge from, as she put it, a demanding father, a too-often worried mother and an uptight princess cousin and her sycophant lady-in-waiting.

Sylvia pulled into her usual parking spot next to her mother's car, climbed out and looked at the front door. *I almost expect the front door to open and Dad to step out with Mom in his wake,* she thought sadly.

Once the Martin children were out of the car, Danny grabbed her bag from the trunk. Clint pulled his bike off the roof rack and set it on its kickstand. Despite Sylvia's pleading, he persisted in his plan to stay at the cabin. He shrugged a worn backpack onto one shoulder.

Sylvia retrieved a small suitcase, purse and briefcase from the empty front passenger seat. Reaching for her cell phone, usually placed on a pad on the dashboard, she recalled its earlier demise. Eyeing with some envy Danny holding her cell phone in her free hand, she thought, *Somehow tomorrow I must make room on the schedule to get a replacement.* With the other hand, her little sister clutched the handle of the worn tote containing her work clothes as she waited for her brother and Sylvia to lead the way.

The setting sun broke through the clouds and front-lit the house's entrance. Somewhat unsettling to all three Martin siblings, the screen door swung open. However, Cynthia Jones, not their father, stepped out with their mother close behind. Sylvia forced a smile. Clint pursed his lips and shook his head. "Ah, Princess Cynthia is in the house," Danny quipped and bowed briefly from the waist.

Clint smiled. "This should be great fun," he said.

———

AFTER REQUISITE BUT strained hugs and kisses, Joan Martin directed her children to the dinner table. The dining room was softly lit by the setting sun and a corner lamp bought long ago at a flea market. The table was informally set with a large wooden bowl of salad, two boxes containing pizza and paper napkins and silverware arrayed on five woven placemats. Despite her grief-creased features, Joan managed a genuine mother's smile. "Sit. It isn't fancy. Cynthia put it together."

"That's iced tea," Cynthia said, pointing at a dark blue pitcher next to the salad. "There's beer and wine in the fridge," she added after she sat and poured tea into her ice-filled glass. "Help yourself."

Joan took her seat at one end of the table. She was still a compact, trim and fair skinned blonde. Gravity and time had only begun to blur and deepen the once clean and sharp lines of youth. A few gray streaks were evident if her blue eyes didn't captivate too much attention. Some new unwanted creases and pounds were stylishly concealed by a loose-fitting gray dress.

Cynthia and Sylvia took chairs on one side of the table while Clint and Danny filled the two on the opposite side. "Just like old …" Danny started brightly, but abruptly stopped when Clint elbowed her. They all stared at the empty chair with the high back at the head of the table.

Cynthia recalled from a college psychology course that how families processed grief and loss was an aggregate of the clan members' roles and their relationship at the time of such misfortune. If true, she wasn't surprised that, in the initial gathering of the Justice Martin family in the wake of Uncle J's death, the pizza and salad were consumed with only polite, superficial and utilitarian conversation. The patriarch's demise, Cynthia's near-death experience and personal and professional travails, and the Danny-Cynthia stress fracture were all topics avoided but never far from mind.

They discussed Sylvia's brush with injury and the loss of her phone. "Julie Simpson saved me. It could have been much worse. I do feel naked, however, sans cell phone," Sylvia lamented.

Her remark brought polite smiles and expressions of gratitude that she was okay. Danny only frowned.

"Julie Simpson, how's she doing?" Clint asked. "I heard she quit the police."

"That's true," Sylvia said and ate the last bite of her second slice of pizza.

"Yeah, I heard she's one of the few city private eyes who work in Driftwood," Clint remarked, nodding his head toward Danny and Cynthia.

"That's right. I have her card somewhere. Dad used her for some investigations for new hires at the plant," Sylvia replied before she caught Clint's nod and added, "She looks great. She's lost a good deal of weight."

"Yeah, I've seen her around town," Clint said and looked at his mother. "Mom, I've got to get going soon. I'm staying out at the cabin."

"I see," Joan said without emotion. She then recited the others' sleeping arrangements.

"Oh, before I forget," Sylvia said, raising her index finger. She quickly shared what she and the family lawyer discussed. This included the schedule for the memorial the next day and the reading of the will after.

Cynthia hadn't seen her closest cousin in many months. Sometime in the last year, as she navigated the shoal waters of GASMAX board politics and Sylvia spent more time in Driftwood as J's assistant, they ceased their weekly meetings for drinks at a favorite Central City watering hole. She observed that Sylvia was becoming more and more like a younger brunette version of her still attractive mother. Her hair and makeup were infrequently out of place and not arranged to complement stylish clothing. Intellectually and in professional temperate she was like her father. However, she lacked his, and Clint's, passion for periodic escape from business to the great outdoors. As a result, being casual and relaxing were tasks for Sylvia, and her face showed the early onset of frown lines just now forming on her mother's face. Clint and Cynthia locked eyes, smiled and nodded when Sylvia announced, "Uncle Louis and I plan to meet after the memorial tomorrow to complete planning for the reading of the will."

Clint, in brief detail, reported his progress in the family cabin renovation. Mostly he covered what work remained. He looked down at his plate and dropped his voice when he again reminded everyone he was staying at the cabin.

"It's okay, Clint," his mother said quietly. "I get it. Your father loved that place, too."

Danny, also in short order, stated that work at the GASMAX plant was going well. "Mom, I can get off my shift tonight if you'd like. The backup operator already offered."

Joan shook her head. She then looked at her niece. "How about you, dear?"

Cynthia laid a hand on her aunt's. "I'm just a little tired after all that's ... but I'm good, Auntie, right where I need to be."

"No doubt," Joan said warmly and patted her hand. "Now, that nice young man, Tanner Strong, will be at the memorial tomorrow, right? J thought highly of him."

"Not sure," Cynthia replied. "He called before everyone got here and said he may be late or unable to attend. It's something to do with the plane crash. Sorry."

Joan frowned briefly and smiled. "That's fine. Perhaps he can join us later. Now, children, excuse me," Joan said and rose. "I'm going to retire early."

Grief over J's loss had taken its toll on his widow. Cynthia and her cousins had never seen Joan Martin act and appear so deflated. They stood. "Auntie ... you need ... want ... anything?" Cynthia asked.

"No, dear," Joan said quietly, waving her away. "You all stay and visit. Not too late. Tomorrow will be long and ... trying." She kissed each one on the cheek and left the room.

THE POST-DINNER VISIT on the sundeck began cordially enough, and the initial conversation well complemented the cooling sea breezes. Clint had agreed to stay a bit longer to join the conversation without Joan in the room. However, the geniality abruptly ended in acrimony, at odds with the ocean's fresh scent and the evening silence usually broken only by the sound of the surf.

After Danny casually claimed that her father's death was the result of murder, Clint stood, clinched both fists and said, "You're nuts, Danny! It was an accident, plain and simple. Sure, Dad was an experienced climber, but he was getting older and he persisted in going on those fool solo out-and-abouts. It was just a matter of time."

"You're the one who's nuts!" Danny retorted. She swung her legs sideways off the armrest to sit upright on the deck chair. Despite the dim light cast by the house lights inside, her face was obviously flushed with anger.

Years in prison aged her, Cynthia observed. Danny's bobbed and flat dark black hair had once been long, shiny and flowing. The tattoos on each arm exposed by her tee shirt were far from a stylish fashion statement. Her face was still more appealing than attractive with gray almost hazel eyes and the clean Martin jaw and cheek lines. Her grooming and fashion choices as well as lacking the blue or brown-eyed cast of her parents and siblings, made Danny appear less vertically constructed than the rest the Martin clan.

"Dad was too good a climber to fall like that. It was no accident!" She stood, raising her voice, as the flush deepened. "Something is fishy here. I think ..."

Sylvia, raising her hands to separate her brother and sister, stood between them. "Enough," she commanded. Danny and Clint both looked like they had something else to say, but they fell silent. "I think it is time to say goodnight."

"Amen to that," Cynthia said flatly. "Clint, you have a bike ride in the dark to the cabin, don't you?"

"Yeah," he sighed, dropping his open hands to his side. "Guess I better get going."

"Danny, you've got to get to work soon, right?"

Danny nodded. The color left her cheeks. She caught Clint's eye. "Sorry, bro," she said and looked at her phone. "Wow, I'll just make it. Syl, Mom said I could use her car."

"Okay." Sylvia said.

"Sylvia, the memorial starts at ten sharp, correct?" Cynthia asked.

Sylvia nodded.

Cynthia stood and placed a hand on her shoulder. "I bet that except for Sylvia, I'm not the only one who hasn't thought out, let alone written, what they're going to say."

Clint and Danny exchanged guilty glances.

"I'll just change into my work clothes and be off," Danny said and walked to the door. Over her shoulder she quickly added, "I'll write something on my lunch break."

Clint followed her. "I get up early. I'll put something on paper in the morning."

After Clint and Danny left, Sylvia and Cynthia looked at each other and laughed. "Well, Lady Sylvia, just like old times," Cynthia said and sighed.

"True, Princess C. Keeping those two in line took both of us. That's for sure. Somethings never change."

"Syl, I'm going to follow Clint's plan. I need some sleep." Cynthia turned to go inside. Sylvia joined her. "Your mom insisted on taking my bag up. I just need to do a little unpacking and get settled."

They crossed the family room with the large plate glass windows and chairs and couch that afforded a million-dollar view of the beach and ocean. At the foot of the stairs to the second-floor Sylvia placed her hand on Cynthia's shoulder. "Look, if you want, I'll stay in your old room and you can have mine."

"I appreciate that," Cynthia replied with a weak smile as they climbed the steps and paused outside her room. She opened the door, looked in, flipped on the light and looked down the hall to the next door leading to her uncle's study. "I'm too tired to let old ghosts and bad memories rob me of sleep."

Sylvia nodded. "Okay, I'll make sure you're awake in time for breakfast and have time to write something."

"Thanks, Cuz. Good night," Cynthia said, closing the door. She opened the French doors leading to the small balcony overlooking the beach. After changing into her new nightgown, she brushed her teeth and washed her face, before falling into the double bed. Though she wasn't too tired for nightmares, fatigue and demands of the last two days easily propelled her into a deep well of sleep.

AT THE BOTTOM of the well a voice and a thud woke Cynthia. She sat up. Her room was now bathed in moonlight coming through the open balcony doors. She quickly determined she was alone in her room. A voice again, but this time she realized it came from through the wall. It was a man's voice and it was familiar, but she could not place it. *Someone is in Uncle J's study*, she concluded.

Throwing off her covers, she got up. "Stan!" she whispered with excitement and smiled broadly. "He made it up after all." She smoothed her hair into place. They both had final exams that week, but, though they took their last final the same day, she was done in the morning and he finished in the late afternoon. They agreed she would drive up to her uncle's beach house and settle in before his later arrival in the evening. Since Uncle J had emailed her the prior week that no one would be home until the next day, they'd have at least one night of passion before Aunt Joan arrived and imposed segregated, boy-girl sleeping arrangements.

I guess packing this little number wasn't a wasted effort, she cheerfully thought. Pulling the hem of her short black nightie into place and pushing the spaghetti straps up her shoulders, she stepped out into the hall. *He must have gone into the wrong room*, she thought. Sure enough, the door to the study was open, but dim light as if from a lantern lit up the green runner that passed outside the door.

Odd, she thought as she swung the door open and stepped into the study. Out of habit she flicked on the room light. Instead of a lost and tardy boyfriend with romance on his mind, she was startled to see her youngest cousin, Danny, seated at her uncle's desk. Her long, shiny black hair was pulled into a ponytail that cascaded over her left shoulder. The wall safe behind the desk was open. Two large stacks of wrapped paper money sat on the desk. Next to them lay a small opened journal. Ignoring the cash and journal, Danny's attention was focused on a single page document. "Danny!" Cynthia exclaimed. "What are you doing here?"

"Cynthia!" Danny replied with equal surprise, looking up when the overhead light came on. "What the ...?" She set down the flashlight that she had held over the document while she read.

Despite her surprise, Cynthia noticed that Danny's eye makeup was running down her cheeks. *She's been crying*, she thought as she tried to make sense of her discovery. "What are you doing here? That's Uncle J's money and stuff."

"Grab her," Danny ordered as she gathered the stacks of bills into a black leather bag.

A man's arms encircled Cynthia and rough hands grasped her shoulder and waist, pressing her into his taller frame. "Well, well, well if it isn't Princess Cynthia," Buck Wilson leered. His tobacco-scented breath was warm on her neck.

"Buck, Buck Wilson, what ...Let go!" Cynthia cried and struggled to no avail.

"No one was supposed to be here, Danny," Buck hissed.

"Mom and Dad and the rest of the family don't show until tomorrow," Danny said. She pulled a handgun from her bag and stood. She came around the desk and leveled the gun at her cousin. "Let her go."

Buck released Cynthia. After shaking herself free of Wilson, she raised her hands and watched Danny as she walked behind her. "By the looks of things, I'd say Princess here and her boyfriend figured on one night together before Mom showed up. Is that right, Cuz?"

"Danny, a gun? You're robbing your father ..."

Danny pressed the gun into Cynthia's back. "Is Stan here?"

"No, but you're right. Stan finished finals late this afternoon. Mine were over in the morning. He was going to drive up and ..."

"You figured lover boy had wandered into the wrong room," Danny finished for her and laughed. "Kind of funny, ain't it, Buck?"

Buck stepped forward and lifted the hem of Cynthia's nightie and dropped it. "Yeah, pretty funny and interesting, but we've got a problem."

"Yeah. We said no witnesses," Danny said and handed the pistol to Buck. She returned to the desk and picked up the journal and the document.

"Danny, don't do this," Cynthia pleaded, keeping her voice low and steady. "Put everything back in the safe. Uncle J doesn't need to know. It'll be our secret."

"It'll be our secret, huh?" Danny replied as she considered the journal and document through narrowed moist eyes. "Yeah, this family is big on secrets, ain't it? Buck, take her back to her room. It's next door. Sit on her until I finish with this journal and ... and think ..."

Buck pushed Cynthia toward the door with his free hand. "With pleasure," he said with a smile that revealed crooked teeth and was flanked by a day's growth of dark beard. "Move it, sweetheart."

"Buck, you've got to stop her," Cynthia said before they entered her room and he turned on the light. Cynthia, with her hands still up, turned to face him. "Buck, no good comes of this for either of you."

Buck stuck the pistol in his belt. "You're right, but not completely," he said and stepped towards her. "There's some good. For instance, you and I get to pick up where we left off. It would be a shame for that nightie to go to waste." He slipped his left hand up under her raised right arm and grasped her neck. He slipped his right behind her waist. "Remember two summers ago at that beach party?" he asked as he pulled her into him. Slipping his right hand below the small of her back, he pressed into her and forced her lips to his.

"What the ... no! Let go of me!" Cynthia protested, pushing herself away but not free of his embrace. "Ow, that gun."

"Yeah, right," Buck chuckled and flipped the pistol onto the bed before pulling her back. "Remember how we got it on that night in the tall grass?"

"Buck, that was ... was just way too much alcohol, and we didn't 'get it on.' It was just some kissing and drunken groping." Cynthia struggled but managed only to roll them into the door. Letting go the one hand that was pulling at Buck's wrist, she slapped it flat against the wall, preventing them from falling but also switching off the lights. Moonlight flooded the room.

"Maybe that's all it was for you, honey," Buck hissed as he ran his hand up her back. "But I figured it was the start of some unfinished business." Locking her in his arms, he maneuvered her toward the bed. Cynthia pressed and pulled when he eased his grip to move his right hand up to her breast. She broke free and fell onto the bed. Buck staggered back, and, as he did, he grabbed her nightie, ripping it and scratching her side.

Just as she freed herself, clouds covered the moon, and the room was cast into inky darkness. Her pulse raced as she frantically worked her feet and hands to reach the other side of the bed.

"That's right where I want you, baby, and how I want you." Buck laughed, holding the tattered silk close enough to his face to realize what he'd done. "Just stay put and I'll join you,"

Though she couldn't see him, and her breath was shallow and fast, and her ears pounded from the effort, she heard him. "The hell you will!" she said as her hand closed on the pistol that he'd thrown on the bed.

"Cynthia, honey," a dark form that towered over the bed said softly.

A hand grabbed her shoulder. "Don't touch me!" Cynthia cried, aiming at the form.

"I'll kill you," she screamed and pulled the trigger.

CHAPTER 9

Explosive Memorial

Eye of the Storm Beach House

SYLVIA MARTIN KNOCKED AND SLOWLY opened the door to her cousin's room. Though a cool morning breeze blew in through the open balcony doors behind partially drawn drapes, the room was still cast more in shadows than light. Noticing motion beneath the bedcovers, she walked to the balcony doors and fully opened the drapes. Sunlight now held sway over shadow. "Cynthia, as promised, I'm here to wake you," she announced.

"The hell you will!" Cynthia snarled as her hand closed on her cell phone where she'd dropped it on the bed when she fell asleep. Eyes closed, she sat part way up and grasped the phone in both hands, extending it in front of her.

Initially startled by the angry outburst and bizarre action, Sylvia recognized that her cousin's eyes were shut. "She's asleep and dreaming," she said and crossed quickly to the bed. Towering over the bedside, she touched Cynthia's arm gently. "Cynthia, honey."

"Don't touch me!" Cynthia cried, aiming the phone at Sylvia.

Nightmare. Gotta wake her, she thought. Firmly grasping both shoulders, Sylvia shook her.

"I'll kill you!" Cynthia screamed, pulling on the phone with her index finger.

Sylvia let go of her arms and stooped to see if Cynthia was truly awake. Both women stared at each other. Satisfied that she was awake, Sylvia stood and placed her hands on her hips.

Cynthia sat up fully. She placed the cell phone on the nightstand and slid a hand over her nightgown. It was not torn, and she was not scratched. "Syl, I ... Thank God, it was just a dream," she said, smiling weakly.

Grinning and partially amused but mostly concerned, Sylvia helped her cousin to her feet. "Sounded more like a nightmare. What was it, bad memories or old ghosts?" she asked.

"Both."

Smugglers Cove Beach

DANNY MARTIN INHALED deeply and exhaled slowly. If nothing else, sea air and sunlight at Smugglers Cove beach was a tonic for the ill effects of the family gathering the night before. *Not to mention the little rest coming off a night shift*, she admitted silently. She sat up in the folding chair. It was surprisingly steady. It sat in beach sand as one of fifty in a five-by-ten array with an aisle between each half.

The chairs were mercifully arranged by her big sister and cousin so as to face away from the sun. They faced north of the cove's opening that ran one hundred yards to the Atlantic Ocean through a deep channel flanked by steep rocky bluffs. She allowed her eyes to follow the semi-circular ridge running from the north bluff to the cliff upon which Wilkes Tavern sat. Atop the ridge, she knew, was a beaten and broad path that ended at a walk leading to the tavern. Just as worn and wide was the trail atop the southern semi-circle's ridgetop. It ended, however, at a raised wooden platform bleached gray by the sea air and affording a clear view to the ocean beyond the bowl-shaped cove below.

From the platform a long flight of wooden steps permitted access to the flat crescent expanse of sand on the cove's west side. The beach was edged by rocks, tall grass and two small dunes split by a path to the smugglers tunnel leading to the tavern's basement via a trap door. *Had some good times and adventures in there*, she recalled with a smile.

From the platform a wide gravel path led to the two-story tavern building, sitting a few hundred feet back from the cliff's edge. The path's breadth permitted early arrivals to the Justice Martin memorial service to park near the platform instead of in the parking lot on the other side of the defunct tavern and inn. She had not been surprised to see Lady Sylvia's sedan and Princess Cynthia's rental car parked end-to-end at the head of the stairs. Clint's truck was wedged in next in line. *Good*, she had thought, eyeing Cynthia's rental, *that means he took care of business.*

Danny, sitting at the end of the family's front row of chairs next to Louis Belmont, the family lawyer, considered the urn and framed photograph of J Martin atop a table draped in black. A metal podium with a portable sound system was set next to the table, and they faced few empty seats. *Dad could always draw a crowd in this burg*, she mused. *Of course, it helps when your company is the number one part of the local economy and you and other GASMAX execs belong to every community civic and charitable organization you can join or sponsor.*

Sylvia Martin, serving as emcee, occupied the single chair behind the podium. Despite early summer warm weather, she wore a black dress with long sleeves. Danny noted without surprise that she frequently glanced at her watch and frowned if any non-family eulogist exceeded their allotted five minutes. *She would have elected to arrange deck chairs on the Titanic instead of getting in a lifeboat,* Danny thought and shook her head.

She sat up as the president of the chamber of commerce concluded the last non-family eulogy. *Almost show time,* she thought, sticking her hand in the pocket of her black slacks. She felt for the crumbled sheet of GASMAX memo stationery that contained her remarks. *Yep, still there.* After straightening her gray polo shirt, she pulled out and unfolded the single page. *Not bad,* she concluded after skimming what she'd written. *Just what they expect, and there won't be a dry eye in the house. I guess it's my gift. I can pitch the bull with the best of 'em.*

During his last visit with her before she was paroled, her dad had asked her what she planned to do to get her life back on track. She effortlessly pitched some high-quality manure that day, telling him what she knew he wanted to hear. *Just like those clowns on the parole board, he bought it,* Danny recalled smugly.

Let's face it, a lie is as good as the truth if you say it right, she affirmed silently. Growing up she discovered that even Dad could be fooled if she said something containing some truth, used a sincere tone, and did a certain thing with her mouth and eyes. It was especially effective if you recited some part or all of Grandpa Moses' motto, 'Do what's necessary, Love God and Do good, bearing fruit in keeping with repentance.' *It's a gift alright. I can convince any audience, like this crowd here, that my words are sincere, plain truth-speak and the song of a repentant heart. Just to survive, it's a gift that I had to hone in prison. I learned from pros.*

Danny paused her bout of self-congratulation when Sylvia introduced their mother. Joan Martin sat between Clint and Cynthia, who escorted her to the podium. Head down, Joan gripped the sides of the podium, and her knuckles were white. "Hang in there, Mom. Don't fall," Danny whispered.

She looks like hell, Danny thought when her mother finally raised her head and faced the crowd. Despite the sunglasses she appeared exhausted from grief and a lack of sleep. Joan removed the glasses, dried her eyes and cleared her throat. "J ... my husband was a ... he was the best ...," she managed before she choked and shook with a sob that Danny was sure was heard in the back row. Sylvia and Cynthia rose simultaneously and went to the grief-stricken woman. Joan, sobbing, shook off Sylvia's hand and leaned on Cynthia who walked her back to her chair.

Sylvia, visibly perturbed at her mother's preference for Cynthia's comforting touch, promptly regained her composure. Desiring to keep the memorial moving along, remain civil and reflect well upon the Martins' good name in the community, she launched into her testimonial. Her voice was clear and strong, and not shaken by grief like her mother's.

Extolling her father's many positive attributes, which she claimed he had instilled in all his children, she briefly glared at her mother and Cynthia. She quickly returned to her upbeat delivery, describing J Martin's deep love for their mother and family. Locking eyes with Driftwood Cove's part-time mayor and fulltime dentist, she declared that J's passions and familial ties were heightened by working in and mostly by residing in the ocean village. Forcing a smile, she described his deep affection for their Driftwood Cove home and the nearby Smugglers Cove beach. She continued with supporting anecdotes, including tales of J's solo hikes and exploration of the old quarry where he met his end.

I'm not my sister, Sylvia, Danny reflected as her sibling continued. *She's an organization freak as well as too sold out to the J Martin line of baloney. She hasn't had an impromptu day of fun in her life. It's what she deserves.* Still, she felt rare sympathy for her sister. She too was taken aback by the thing with her mom and Cynthia.

But I'm not surprised by Mom's preference for Princess C. Danny observed silently. She had spent many hours in prison trying to make sense of the Martin family's dysfunctions. *I'm the baby, right, but I never went along with Dad's program like Sylvia and Clint,* she thought, recalling the jailhouse conclusions. *I'll admit I fought Mom and Dad at every turn. Yeah, and it was kind of fun. If I could get Dad's vein in his forehead to bulge, I knew I'd won no matter what punishment the old man dished out. Later, Dad, without great sincerity, forgave me. Mom, on the other hand, held a grudge that ... well, it created a void between our parents and the three of us.*

For reasons still unclear and beyond the obvious fallout of her arrest and jail time, her mom and dad remained her greatest critics. They were only slightly less critical of Sylvia and Clint. Cynthia, however, seemed to fill some kind of proud parent void. No matter how hard Sylvia and Clint had tried to please them, Cynthia's accomplishments were the gold standard for Joan's and J's parental pride. *I gave up trying.*

Danny frowned as the events of her arrest and trial suddenly loomed large in her remembrances. *Why dear Dad didn't drop the robbery charges I can't figure. Legally, I'm flesh and blood, his kid, after all. He should have bailed me out. He always had before. It was a Buck Wilson thing. Dad never liked him, and precious Cynthia remained Dad's princess pure. That was incredible,* she seethed. *Even though she was in a skimpy nightie that night, anticipating her lover's arrival, and her history with Buck came out at the trial, in Dad's eyes she was ... no, couldn't be without blemish. So, I guess he figured Buck had to be solely to blame and suffer the consequences. Even if that meant that I had to serve time so Cynthia's honor would remain intact.*

Danny, shaking off the bad memories, glanced at her written notes and smiled. *Yeah, I could have spun a much better tale if I had had that trial today. What I learned in jail was that the trick is in the tale and its telling. Let's face it, most guilty people like Buck and me are heroes in some sense. And, yeah, most innocent people like Cynthia are the true villains in a larger sense.* Her satisfied smile dropped into a frown. *But I must confess, at times, I find it hard to remember what the larger sense is that condemns Cynthia as a villain and exonerates me as the hero. Sometimes this bothers me, because I get confused and stop being the hero of my own story. The trick, I guess, is not to overthink it.* The frown disappeared and she brightened. *Yep, gotta live from my instincts and I can't go wrong ... I don't think.*

Clint tapped his sister's knee on his way to the podium. His touch brought her back to the present from another stroll, too often taken recently, down crime and punishment memory lane. *More like hell's highway*, she thought, sitting up and anticipating a Justice Martin tribute closer to the truth of J the man, Joan's husband and their father.

In his only and ill-fitting suit, Clint had not gone too far into his eulogy before he too disappointed his little sister. He started well, countering one of Sylvia's key points that elicited a classic big sister frown, a startled look from Cynthia and another backrow sob from her mother. Then he backed off into a rambling, melancholy and bitter tinged testimonial that listeners would interpret as deep grief, respect and love for a loving father and family man as well as the great outdoorsman Clint wished most to emulate. However, Danny did think it odd that he shared a story of Dad's growing aversion to Smugglers Cove and a deepening gloom following one of J's solo hikes around the quarry over a year ago.

I'm not my brother, either, Danny observed in silent disappointment. *As usual he just goes along to get along, his idea of a Martin doing what's necessary.* Though closer to Clint than anyone else in their dysfunctional clan, she long ago recognized he just talked a good talk in their private brother-sister family bashing sessions. *He's a nice guy, and yet, he hasn't had a day of living that was any better than okay. I often tried to get him to push back against Dad, but he never would. How sad for him. Just hope he had the spine for today.*

Clint finished abruptly with a mumbled, "Thank you." Waving Sylvia back to her chair with one hand, he motioned with the other at Danny. "You're up, sis," he said.

Danny resisted the urge to smile and high-five him as she took his place at the podium. After patting her memo paper flat on the lectern, Danny launched into her eulogy. It was a cross between an angry rant born of father issues and a film critic's one-star movie review. After one particularly unflattering remark concerning J's dark obsession with Smugglers Cove, many of the non-family members left. By the conclusion of her left-handed tribute, only Joan, now sobbing heavily, Sylvia, white with anger, Clint, slouched and covering his mouth and her cousin, visibly astounded, remained.

"They're all yours, Cuz," she said, looking at Cynthia.

Cynthia nodded at Danny as she stepped forward. Danny sat next to

Clint and whispered in his ear. Sylvia took the seat next to her mother and placed an arm around her. Cynthia, seeing it was only her aunt, cousins and Louis Belmont who remained, shrugged. Clearing her throat and setting her notes on the podium, she sighed and started.

And I'm certainly not cousin Cynthia, Danny thought, amazed that she made a gray sleeveless sundress work as proper attire for a memorial, despite the cleavage it revealed. Looking at Clint and Sylvia, she concluded to herself, *she's better than the other two, but not much. When we were all kids, she could be fun, and she did push back against Dad with respect and effect when necessary. Unlike my resistance for the hell of it, hers was for a purpose, sometimes selfless and other times self-serving. Despite her going on about fair play, she surprisingly caved in to Dad about that supposed assault by Buck. If anything happened ... well, Buck is just a man and she had a thing for him. I think that's really why she backed off from the assault charges, and, fortunately, Buck and I were only charged with robbery. Prison confirmed that I am tough and that only saps like Cynthia will waste their lives in corporate ambitions and pursuing someone else's idea of love, family and all that crap. Real living involves risk, cunning, taking what you want and winning no matter what it takes – or who gets hurt. Now that's doing what's necessary.*

Cynthia's testimonial was truly a tribute and obviously heartfelt. She cited many instances which substantiated her claim that Justice Martin was an exemplary man, father, husband, mentor and friend. The joke about their mandatory ethics, martial arts and small arms training got a chuckle even from Danny. Joan stopped sobbing. Sylvia lost her composure and cried. Danny and Clint both moved to sit behind their mom and laid a hand on her shoulder as Cynthia sang J's praises for the role he played in her life as a stand-in father, sharing his home and family with the effectively orphaned daughter of a single, alcoholic mom.

Cynthia paused to wipe away a tear as well as to marvel and relish in, despite the circumstances, the first warm family moment since the crash landing in Driftwood Cove. Her final remarks collapsed the moment when she expressed her deep gratitude to J and Joel Martin for the part they played in her education and, regardless of recent events, in her subsequent work experience and rapid advancement at GASMAX.

At the mention of Joel Martin's name, Joan sobbed. Danny and Clint nervously locked eyes, stood and whispered in their mother's ear. Joan nodded, and her youngest children abruptly left. Joan's sobbing increased, and Sylvia looked at Cynthia with disdain.

Cynthia, her mouth forming a silent oh, surveyed the aftermath of her expression of gratitude to Joel Martin. Though crushed by Uncle J's death, Joel's betrayal and her sudden job loss, being dumped and Danny's presence and anger, she still recognized the good in her living uncle despite any failings he may have. Her cousins' exit and Joan's sobs ended her remarks. She sat down next to Louis Belmont.

"Don't let them bother you," he said, leaning in and patting her arm. "That was well said and from the heart. Besides, it may have laid some groundwork for family damage control in the wake of Danny's comments."

"Thanks. I hope your right," she said.

"I best look after your, aunt," he said. He moved and sat next to Joan as Sylvia gathered her father's urn and photograph.

Belmont, Joan and Sylvia departed. *What father wounds did you inflict on your children, Uncle J?* Cynthia wondered and looked around the beach. Noting that the event caterer who provided the chairs, podium and table was descending the steps to the beach, she retrieved her purse and hefted the banker box containing the unused memorial flyers. Placing it on the table, she looked around for anything else she needed to schlep out. *And what is at the quarry and here at Smugglers Cove that lured you and caused such family sorrow?* she pondered as her eyes found the break in the dunes leading to the smugglers' tunnel.

AS CYNTHIA TOOK the platform's top step, the sun blinded her. Raising a hand to shield her eyes and shifting the box onto her hip, she fumbled to find the dress pocket holding her sunglasses. Donning the glasses, she saw that her car was the only one left parked on the gravel path and Tanner Strong was leaning on its passenger side. He waved and walked quickly toward her.

Stepping off the platform she waved back. "Tanner, hi," she shouted and smiled. *At last, someone who I haven't offended*, she thought and shifted the box to her other hip and found the key fob for the rental car.

"Hi yourself," Tanner answered. "You need a hand?" Though still some steps away he raised his arms to accept the box.

Cynthia squeezed the button on the key fob that she believed opened the trunk remotely. Instead, she pressed the simultaneous key combo that started the sedan remotely. The engine rumbled to life. "I sure could. Let me ..." Her next words were cut off when the car exploded. The force of the detonation first staggered her and caused her to stumble back toward the edge of the cliff and the drop to the beach below. Then like a giant fist to the gut it lifted and propelled her.

As she realized her own dilemma, the explosive force threw Tanner toward her. Though quickly grasping the likelihood of her own demise or at least serious injury, she found some comfort when he landed face down, slid and appeared that he would stop just before going over the edge. Then a sense of falling filled her with panicked fear. Wide-eyed and with her mouth contorted in a scream, she locked eyes with Tanner, who had managed to grasp one post of the platform's rail and was hanging feet first over the cliff. *He'll make it*, she thought as her arms flailed above her head and the sundress blossomed and then collapsed like a failed parachute unable to break her fall to the rocks three stories below. *But I won't.*

CHAPTER 10

Last Will and Bay Cruise

Smugglers Cove Beach

TANNER STRONG LEANED AGAINST THE fender of what he assumed was Cynthia's rental car and glanced at his watch. He knew that the memorial had ended when he waved to Sylvia and Joan Martin and the family lawyer. *Maybe I missed her*, he thought just before Cynthia took the final step on to the wood platform.

Watching her raise a hand to shield her eyes and shift a banker box to be carried on her hip, he smiled for the first time in a day spent answering FAA and GASMAX inquiries. Scrubbing off the smell of aviation gas, donning new clothes and getting some sleep last night did little to prepare him for this day. The terse and lengthy conversation with Joel Martin that morning was particularly onerous. When he had hung up, Tanner felt that the GASMAX head man was disappointed that he and Cynthia had walked away from the crash. Now, watching his fellow survivor fumble for her sunglasses somehow buoyed his sagging spirits. He waved and walked toward her.

Stepping off the platform, she waved back. "Tanner, hi," she shouted.

Looks like her day after hasn't been much better, he thought, noting the frown that had vanished just before she saw him. She shifted the box to her other hip and found the keys for the rental car. "Hi yourself," he answered. "You need a hand?" Though still some steps away, he raised his arms to accept the box. She pointed the fob at the car and squeezed it to open the trunk. Instead, he heard the engine start.

"I sure could. Let me ...," she said, but her next words were cut off by an explosion. The force of the detonation behind him lifted and propelled him toward the cliff's edge. As he flew toward her, he saw that as Cynthia absorbed the impact of the blast she staggered backward. Suddenly, as it had with him, she was lifted and thrown toward the cliff's edge. The box and sunglasses flew away and she flailed her arms, grasping for anything that would stop her fall.

He landed face down and slid. Though the fall momentarily stunned and winded him, his vision cleared quickly enough for him to see that one of the platform rail posts was within arm's reach. He closed his right hand on the post as he went over the edge. At the same time, using an experienced pilot's instinctive ability to visualize in space and time, he grabbed at where he thought the falling woman's flailing arms would be. His left hand closed on her wrist. The force of stopping her fall nearly wrenched his right hand free from its grip on the post. Despite the pain in his shoulders and arms, he managed a tight grin when he saw Cynthia looking up at him wide eyed and her mouth still contorted by a scream.

They both hung feet first on the cliff face that fortunately was not a complete vertical drop. After a deep breath, she found a hand hold and a foot hold. With his support and encouragement, she climbed up and on to the cliff. Tanner, with a hand from her, likewise extradited himself from the cliff face. They staggered to their feet and collapsed on the platform.

Tanner's heart pounded and his pulse raced. With shaking hands, he pushed himself up to sit. He fought to catch his breath and to form words, barely keeping at bay an adrenalin-induced scream. Extending the hand that shook the least, between ragged breaths, he finally managed, "Cynthia ... you ... oh ... kay?"

Cynthia sat up with difficulty. Nodding, she grabbed his hand and pulled herself into his embrace. Tanner felt her labored breath on his neck and her shaking body next to his. Once her breath was more even and the convulsions dissipated, she finally replied, "I'm ... okay. You?"

"Yeah," he gasped, and held her tightly. "Just need a minute to ..."

"Me too," she said, slipping her hands behind his back.

After several minutes, Tanner asked with a forced smile, "I'd say we're even for yesterday, wouldn't you?"

Cynthia looked up at him. "I'd say," she nodded and grinned before laying her head back on his shoulder. "Need just a few more minutes before I can walk."

"Take all the minutes you want," he said softly, stroking her hair.

Louis Belmont Law Offices

THE LAW OFFICES of the Martin family lawyer, Louis Belmont, occupied the ground floor of a modest two-story structure planted atop the hill overlooking the double row of village shops and businesses, and the docks, slips and waters of Driftwood Bay just beyond. His residence was on the second floor. The home was one of several built with the GASMAX funding and J Martin backing that had made most all village development and improvement possible. Across the street, this included the civic center containing the village's bank, the court house, police station, town hall and public schools. All had been renovated or built as a result of Justice Martin's commitment to the community. That made Belmont's office an appropriate setting for the reading of his last will and testament.

Joan Martin glanced at her watch and frowned. *Five past seven. We've got to get started*, she thought. Seated in the chair at one end of Louis Belmont's conference room table, she looked at the lawyer seated at the other end. He smiled, showing no concern as he nudged the portfolio containing J's will. She knew, however, that he too was unhappy that they had missed the 7PM start. J's emphatic last wishes which put the memorial and estate settlement on an exact and fast track included that requirement. *I can almost hear J say "7PM means 7PM."*

To her right Sylvia fidgeted in her chair. Her eldest child repeatedly tapped the table top with her pen when the clock over Louis' head reached the hour. Her eyes went frequently to the room's door.

No doubt Cynthia's been delayed by the police investigation of the car explosion, Joan reasoned, *but J's instructions were specific that she must be present.*

Opposite Sylvia, Danny and Clint focused on their cell phones.

"Louis, perhaps we should start," Joan suggested in a calm clear voice. She was pleased that she had regained control of herself following the memorial. The nap Sylvia had insisted on helped, and, she was certain, so did the two shots of very fine bourbon Belmont served before her children arrived.

Before the lawyer replied, the door behind him opened. Cynthia, escorted by Tanner Strong entered. Everyone at the table rose. Joan hugged her niece. "Thank God, you're alive," she said, gently touched Cynthia's cheek before turning to Tanner and embracing him. Startled and visibly embarrassed, Tanner returned her hug. "And you, young man, thank you so much for saving my girl. It's a miracle. You are a hero." Sylvia, whom Cynthia had called as soon as she could, had relayed to her family and Belmont the story of how they had escaped death. Sylvia also convinced her mother that Cynthia was insistent that the reading of the will proceed on schedule per J Martin's instruction.

Tanner untangled himself from Joan's embrace, mumbling "You're welcome." He looked at Cynthia.

"Auntie, sorry I'm late," she said, taking the empty seat next to Sylvia. Everyone sat and Tanner opened the door.

"Tanner, please stay," Joan insisted.

Cynthia tilted her head toward the door. He stepped out. "Tanner will wait outside. He understands this is a family only thing. He insisted," she said and smiled warmly at her aunt. "Mr. Belmont, please get on with it.

Uncle J was such a stickler for starting on time."

Joan nodded. Belmont opened the folder and began. As he read the boilerplate opening paragraphs, she focused her attention on her niece. *She's so much like her father*, she mused. *You'd never know she had twice escaped death and now knew for certain that someone was out to murder her. Get on with the mission. Yeah, Moses, J and Jake would all be proud.*

Joan knew that the contents of J's will would spark family acrimony. He had even predicted how each would react. She shifted her attention to the three siblings. Their facial expressions revealed the reactions he foretold. J split his estate six ways – Sylvia, Clint, Danny and Cynthia each got one sixth and Joan two. Additionally, the terms specified that Danny was to receive her inheritance in quarters, one now and one each at ages thirty, thirty-five and forty. Each installment was contingent upon her demonstrating successful accomplishment of his stipulated tasks to Cynthia's satisfaction.

Belmont looked at Cynthia. "The specific tasks and measures of success are contained in a codicil," he said. "I'm to provide it to you in a separate meeting." He returned his attention to the folder and read J's instructions for the disposition of specific personal possessions.

Sylvia's facial expression told her mother that the amount didn't bother her too much. However, as her husband claimed it would, what really irked and hurt was that her father's preference, even from beyond the grave, was for his niece's judgement and not that of his dutiful eldest child and trusted executive assistant. He and Joan had had several arguments on his obvious favoritism for his niece over his oldest daughter.

Clint's dark glare at his cousin and his sisters told Joan the amount did matter. Again, J called it. His son's anger was somewhat mollified by the bequest of the family cabin they were renovating. Joan saw that he had something to say, but J had long since worked almost all active rebellion and fight out of his son.

Danny's eyes flared wide and then narrowed on Sylvia and Cynthia. *She's going to explode*, Joan thought, recognizing tell-tale signs of her youngest child's volatile and ill temper. J had said it would light her fuse. Though Danny's bad humor had been reined in with age and time in prison, J and Joan knew she was still volcanic.

When Cynthia's inheritance was announced, Joan couldn't read her. *That poker face is more Joel's than J's*, she observed silently. *There's not a bit of her alcoholic mom's passive nature in this one.*

Louis finished reading and closed the folder. Before he could speak, Danny stood and erupted. "Mom, how could you?" she shouted. Her face turned a deeper red as she faced her sister and cousin. "And you two!" She glared, and her eyes darted back and forth between Sylvia and Cynthia. "This is not the end of this!" she declared and slammed the door on the way out.

"Sylvia, we need to do something about this," Clint said, leaning across the table and taking his sister's hand. He squeezed hard to convey the words that always eluded him when he was angry and hurt.

"There's nothing to be done, Clint. The will can't be changed," she answered. She pulled her hand free and looked to the lawyer.

"She's quite right, Clint. I'm sorry," Belmont added sadly, seeing what the children's reaction was doing to their mother. He went to her. "There are no grounds to contest it. Perhaps this is not a good time to have this discussion. Come by tomorrow and see me."

Clint shook his head and stood. "Maybe we all should have a sit down with you later, counselor," he said, stepping to the door. He looked at Sylvia and Cynthia. "I'll see if I can reel in Danny to join us."

Ignoring her cousin, Sylvia nodded, stood, and turned to her mother. "Mom, let's get you home."

Though the will had had the anticipated effect, Joan was no less shaken by the family rancor and discord. Likewise, she now understood the machinations behind one likely and one confirmed attempt on her niece's life. Realizing that they were part of or a reaction to some J Martin contrivance, she was sick in spirit as well as heartbroken. She stood with the aid of Louis and Sylvia. She was now very unsure of her ability to hold it together over the next one to two days as J, from beyond the grave, would attempt to clear the family conscience in addition to his own. *J, you cowardly bastard, why did you leave me to deal with your fallout?* she thought as she agreed to Belmont's urging to go home, have one more stiff drink, and get a good night's sleep.

As another family gathering fell apart, Cynthia for the second time that day found she was last to leave. After Sylvia, Joan and Belmont left the room, she stood. "At least it wasn't anything I said," she said. "Maybe Tanner will buy me a stiff drink. Or I can buy him one now that I have a few extra dollars."

Martin Family Cabin

SEATED AT THE family cabin's sole table, Clint positioned a smart tablet so he'd not be backlit during the video chat. The table in reality was a large piece of paint splattered and marred plywood propped up by two saw horses. A stove and sink as well as a table saw covered with sawdust were on the opposite side of the two-room cabin's front room. Power tools, paint cans and lumber were scattered about the room with drop-cloths here and there to safeguard the few pieces of furniture that still filled what was now Clint's rustic home.

Clint stretched, yawned, and slouched. It had been a long day. Although the bedroom and bath in the back rooms were far enough along to make habitation possible, they did not yet promote a good night's rest. "But there's no way I'd stay at EOS with Princess C and Lady S in the house," he whispered to himself. Also, he was nervous about what would be a contentious phone call with his uncle. As if cued by his anxiety, the tablet came to life with a new-age ring tone. He cringed and sat up.

"Well?" Joel Martin said as soon as his image filled the screen.

Clint saw that his uncle was in his Central City office. "Hello to you too, Uncle," he started with forced bravado. Since his uncle, like his father, could humble and silence with a look, he dropped the bluster. "Yeah, it went down just as you said."

"Cynthia got her marching orders?"

"That she has Danny by the short hairs for the rest of her foreseeable life," Clint affirmed and shifted in his chair. "There's some codicil to the will that she's to get from the lawyer in a separate meeting."

"Hmm, that it?" Joel asked, and Clint could see that he reached toward the screen. "That's too bad."

"Well, you know what's in the codicil, right?"

"That's one of the gaps in my knowledge of J's plan." Joel paused, and Clint knew he was mulling something over. "Too bad you missed with the car, Clint."

"Yeah. Tough break," Clint sighed and sank in his chair. "If it hadn't been for Strong ..."

"I've heard that one before. Haven't I, Buck?" Joel said, cutting him off.

"Yes sir," Buck Wilson's voice but not his image joined the conversation.

"I asked Buck to join us, Clint." Joel smiled.

"Great," Clint said, sitting lower in the chair.

"He's driving your way. Where are you, Wilson?"

"Just passed the airport. Wow, what a wreck we made. They've pushed it off the runway."

"Joel, look, I'll be with Cynthia tomorrow. I can take her out, I promise," Clint pleaded.

"Appreciate your enthusiasm, but, as I've said before, Plan B is dynamic. It now must evolve with circumstances as they develop. So, Buck's up. You just let him and me know when she gets the codicil. Buck, you be ready to roll on short notice."

"Roger, boss."

"Gentlemen, Tanner Strong has now got to go. I suspect that soon, if not already, Cynthia has told him too much. So, I've made arrangements for him to be like white on rice with her. Whatever means you employ, they both must be in your crosshairs. Understood?"

"Got it," Buck said with an obvious relish. "Already planning on it. I've got a score to settle with both of 'em."

Clint was not surprised by Wilson's enthusiastic reply. However, even though this was the second time that he had heard Uncle Joel order the murder of his cousin, he was still taken aback by Joel's cold-hearted tone. *Just like dear old Dad and Grandpa. Blood wasn't always thicker than water, the old man used to say, and Gramps would nod*, he recalled, but meekly and with barely suppressed regret he replied, "Understood. But I have a question."

"Yes," Joel said impatiently. "You getting weak knees, boy?"

"No, but what ... what if Wilson fails? He's struck out once already?"

"Hey, that wasn't my fault!" Buck protested with anger.

"No more than it was mine!" Clint retorted and sat up.

"Enough," Joel commanded. "If Buck isn't successful, I've got someone else on deck. Remember Plan B is dynamic. Got to always have a backup plan. Now get some rest. Tomorrow is a big day."

The screen went black. Clint slumped in his seat. "Crap," he sighed and searched his feelings. "Maybe I'm more like Uncle Joel than Dad. Why can't I just be like me?"

Bait and Switch Bar and Grill

THE VILLAGE LOCALS and repeat tourist and summer sailors called the Bait and Switch Bar and Grill the "B and S." Like most Driftwood businesses, it no longer reflected the anemic pre-GASMAX economy. The dark hole-in-the-wall saloon, serving beer, whiskey and hotplate sliders, was now an open, bright and airy restaurant boasting an extensive and varied menu of drinks and social media praised cuisine, ranging from traditional bar favorites to fine dining selections.

Tanner pushed aside the glasses containing their second round of drinks. He slid a gray seven-by-seven-inch case across the table.

"What's this?" Cynthia asked.

Not for the first time since they had sat down at the back-corner open air veranda table, Strong gaze went to the front door. He quickly glanced at the steps leading from the veranda's wooden deck to the boardwalk and docks and boat slips lining the west side of Driftwood Bay. "Yours if you want it. Here's the key," he replied after checking that the nearby table was still empty.

Cynthia pulled the case onto her lap and worked the lock. Hefting the pistol from its dunnage, she ensured that the chamber was clear and returned it to the case. "Ruger LC9," she said and nodded as she verified that the clip was full. "Nice." She looked at Tanner after locking the case. "But why?"

"In addition to my gun case, they found one in what was left of your luggage. I took the liberty of having Connie Barnes fax me your permit. So, when I drew a replacement XD-M from the plant's security armory, I got that for you and figured it would be more portable for a lady."

"Very efficient, Mr. Strong, and thoughtful." Cynthia grinned, sliding the case into her purse. "You're right. It just fits. How'd you know I had a permit?"

"Funny, about six months ago your Uncle J made a point to brag to me about the small arms and martial arts training he made your cousins and you go through. So, when they found the case, I assumed you felt it necessary to pack a weapon."

"Makes sense," Cynthia said and nodded. "Bet J's bragging didn't include Danny."

"Yeah, but he made it clear to me that she was a crack shot with a rifle. It sounded more like a warning than bragging."

Cynthia nodded. "So, you really are my bodyguard?" she asked.

"Your Uncle Joel insisted," he replied. "I'm to, and I quote, stick to Jones like white on rice, unquote."

Cynthia arched her eyebrows.

"Yeah, it surprised me too." Tanner leaned in. "But I'm glad he did. Someone is trying to kill you, me or maybe both of us. Though the FAA team gave me the usual 'can't say anything conclusively until all the data is analyzed' answer, the lead guy more than hinted it was no accident. Someone, somehow, short-fueled us. They hacked the avionics so that the fuel pumps shut down with plenty of gas left in the tank."

"So, there was plenty left to burn after the crash."

"Yeah, it was no accident."

"After the car bomb I'm not surprised," Cynthia said flatly. "But it seems like the police would do something proactive if they thought we were in immediate danger."

"Like protective custody?"

"Something along those lines," Cynthia said with a shrug, "and maybe they'd have the house watched."

"Maybe I overstepped, but, after I explained my role, I talked the police chief out of protective custody. He is, however, going to have a patrol car make frequent visits out to the house."

"Great," Cynthia said. "Besides I think you realize by now that I can look out for myself ... when I'm sober. And I know you have skills."

Tanner chuckled. "Seems Chief Smith has a history with you and your family. He was acquainted with your self-protection training." Tanner grinned. "He is eager to ensure that you are kept alive. He seemed indifferent about my well-being though."

"No doubt. He was 'Detective Brian Smith' when he investigated the assault ..." Cynthia looked past Tanner at the boats berthed in the slips nearest the restaurant. She lowered her voice, "He investigated a crime against my family. He's a good and fair man."

"Seems like it. When I told him that Joel Martin had assigned me to be your security during the rest of your visit, he quickly backed off. But what was this assault or crime all about? Maybe we should share some history to see if we can sort out who and why someone is trying to kill you, me or both of us."

Cynthia bit her lower lip, swallowed the last of her drink and glanced about to see that no one was nearby. "Okay, but not here. I'd like to have this conversation in private."

After throwing some bills on the table, Tanner stood and offered her his hand. "No problem. I have just the place. Let's go."

Offshore Near Smugglers Cove

ONCE CLEAR OF the channel connecting Driftwood Bay to the open ocean and well offshore, Tanner killed the V8 Mercruiser engine of the GASMAX Chris-Craft Launch 27. It was one of two that the company used to run people and, occasionally, special deliveries to the tidal hydroelectric plant or to the gas plant. It was slack water, and the craft slowed to a stop about one hundred yards off the narrow entrance to Smugglers Cove. A slight swell gently rocked the boat.

"This private enough?" he asked as he swiveled the captain's chair to face Cynthia in the one next to him.

"Yes. Perfect," she sighed. "You first or me? Not sure where to start."

"You," he said softly. "Let's start with who's Buck Wilson."

Cynthia started slowly and struggled to put into words her life in the context of Driftwood Cove, but soon the tale came fast and with little effort.

"That's some story," Tanner said when she finished. "Wilson could be the culprit, but, if you don't mind a blunt observation, the Martin part of your family is not without its suspects."

"True." Cynthia chuckled darkly. "How about you, Mr. Strong? Is the stoic, heroic and much-wronged peg-legged vet a facade? Did you really just run into Uncle J while driving a cab?"

"Not completely true. He poured me into a cab that night that we met at the bar," he replied, scanning the horizon, out of habit as well as buying time to sort out how to explain himself. "Your uncle helped me in some ways like you. He even sent me to the same shrink, Corbin Schwartz, whom he had you see after the assault. The doc's hypno-therapy put to rest a number of the lethal demons and helped me cope with the others sans alcohol. Best of all, J even got me back into a cockpit."

"You an alcoholic? I have some experience there," she said and frowned. "My mom was."

"No, but I was heading there."

"Other than the ones from the crash and burn, what are the other demons?" Cynthia asked, visibly holding back a yawn.

"Some are like yours. I was an only child but functionally an orphan," Tanner said. "My mom died when I was young. Instead of abusing alcohol my dad indulged in harsh corporal punishment. To his credit he slavishly worked long hours to ensure we didn't want for anything, but the 'his way or the highway' beatings was his parenting strategy to 'toughen you up, kid'." He cleared his throat and continued. For the first time in a very long time, he told another person about his brief failed marriage, the brush with alcoholism and painkiller addiction as he adjusted to the prosthetic during very painful physical therapy and mostly the fact that his career-ending crash killed a close friend and fellow Marine.

"Wow," Cynthia whispered when he finished. Stifling a yawn, she placed a hand on his forearm. "Doctor Schwartz, your close relationship with Uncle J and working for GASAMAX may have painted the target on your back. It could be guilt by association with me, Uncle J and the company. I'm starting to think we're both someone's loose end."

"Yeah, that's kind of my thought," he said, looking at his watch after seeing her eyes go shut. "Getting late. I better get you back to EOS. Rest your eyes if you'd like."

Cynthia nodded and yawned. "Okay, I will," she said softly as the gentle rocking of the boat lulled her asleep. Tanner swiveled forward and started the engine, and she woke up just before the aft end of the boat exploded and burst into flames. "Tanner, no!" she screamed as the flames engulfed them both.

CHAPTER 11

A Family Falling Out

Eye of the Storm Beach House

"Cynthia, this is getting old," a voice said from within the flames engulfing her and Tanner.

"Tanner, no!" Cynthia screamed again and sat up. The sound of her own screams and the realization that the fire's bright light was from the morning sun flooding the bedroom pulled her fully awake. "Thank God. It was a dream." She fell back on the bed, wide-eyed and stared at the ceiling.

"Cuz, over here," Sylvia barked, standing next to the bed with her arms folded across her chest.

"Sylvia," Cynthia cried. She sat up slowly and put her feet on the floor. "Sorry, just another bad dream. Tanner and I were in a boat, and there was an explosion and fire."

"I guessed another nightmare. Must have been a doozy. I was about to knock when you first shrieked "Tanner, no!" So, I figured I'd better come in and wake you. Before you yelled "Tanner no!" again, you mumbled something about "Doctor Schwartz, close relationship with J and GASAMAX painted a target on your back." The rest was garbled, but it sounded like you muttered something about "'guilt by association" and being "somebody's loose end"."

"Tanner?" Cynthia rose and grabbed Sylvia by the shoulders. "Is he okay?"

"I guess," she answered and shook herself free. "He dropped you off late last night. You went straight up to your room. He and I chatted for a while."

"About me?"

"He told me he took you out on one of the company boats for an open-ocean heart-to-heart," Sylvia replied, nodding. "That chit-chat must have been the stuff of dreams."

"So, that part was true. Good," Cynthia said with obvious relief. She picked up her purse that lay on the floor. She patted it and felt the gun case. "Great, did he say anything else?"

"Yes. He told me about Uncle Joel's orders that he's to be your bodyguard and about the periodic patrol car drive-by. Oh, he said he'd be back later this morning," Sylvia answered. "What's in the purse ... Cyn, you okay?"

"Yeah, yeah. It's just the dream gave me the shakes. It was so real." Cynthia sighed, as the actual memories of the night before emerged and the fog of nocturnal hallucinations completely cleared. She sat back on the bed. "Sorry for the ruckus. Am I late for something today?"

"No, but Clint called. He said that he and Danny buried the hatchet, not in each other, and they no longer wanted to bury it in us. My brother has a way with words. Anyway, he wants us all to meet this morning to discuss the estate."

"Well, I guess that's some kind of good news. When and where?"

"He suggested the wine cellar for the family powwow. He said it would be less likely Mom would walk in on us."

"So, Auntie's not going to be there?" Cynthia asked as she stood to sort out what to wear. "How's she doing today?"

"She went sailing. That's a good sign that she's better than last night. I've never seen her so far from herself, except when your mom died."

"Yeah, she took that about as hard," Cynthia recalled sadly. She wasn't surprised that her aunt had gone sailing. Joan was a very capable day sailor, and she routinely went out alone in the small boat to collect herself. *Lord knows she needed some time alone to clear her head and to grieve.* Needing to change the subject, she asked, "So, the wine cellar. What time?"

"Though it's roomy with a Gothic kind of charm, I nixed the wine cellar idea. We agreed on the widow's walk at 10AM," Sylvia said, pointing to the ceiling. Above them sat the wooden platform atop the roof with a picnic table overlooking the house's stretch of private beach and the ocean beyond. "He liked the change. I think Clint wants to show off his refurbishment of the widow's walk. Also, as you recall, Dad loved to have family meetings there."

"Over hot chocolate and doughnuts," Cynthia said, smiling at the memory. "That was fun."

"Humph. Well, we've matured and are more health conscious," Sylvia commented. "It'll be coffee and bagels. I picked some up this morning while you were sleeping in." She frowned.

"Why so glum, Cuz?" Cynthia asked.

"The widow's walk refurbishment and the cabin were the last home improvements Dad started. Clint worked with him, and he threw himself into finishing the widow's walk before the memorial. Also, it's just as well Mom's not there. We all need to talk and make some tough decisions regarding her."

"Without killing each other," Cynthia added and smiled.

"I'm sure we can talk without bloodletting. Martins are good at doing what's necessary, present company included." Sylvia chuckled and turned to leave. "You've time for a shower. After a car explosion and another in your dreams you need it. Pew, you stink."

"Get out of here." Cynthia laughed and threw a pillow at her cousin. It hit the door as it swung shut.

Eye of the Storm Widow's Walk

DESPITE HER BEST efforts to focus on what Clint was saying, Cynthia's thoughts wandered. They were the first to ascend the iron staircase to the eight-by-ten-foot widow's walk atop the beach house. The white picketed and railed enclosure kindled precious childhood memories. Her recollections were dimmed only by less expansive adult imagination and whatever dulling in the aging process that had caused Sylvia's maturing from doughnuts to bagels.

Clint sounds just like Uncle J the first time he brought us kids up here to show off his handiwork, Cynthia observed silently. She recalled fondly her uncle's obvious excitement as he described his restoration project. Even as an adolescent, she had appreciated the remarkable transformation of the wood platform, and the additions of a sturdy table and benches. Subsequent harsh winters and neglect had beaten the platform into disrepair.

"It looks great, Clint. I knew it was just a matter of time before Uncle J would again work his magic," she said, breaking in on his excited recitation. "You've done a superb job. Uncle J would be most pleased and very impressed by how you finished the work. Looks like just some white paint and you're all done."

"Thanks," he replied and smiled broadly. "I'd like to think that the old man would be impressed," he continued as they sat at the table. "I'm not done yet. Work got put on hold for a while when we heard about Dad. But I wanted to get it done before yesterday. There are a few final touches. So be careful because the back railing isn't fully secure. It's just set with a few finishing nails. I ran out of screws and rail brackets. Also, I've replaced the decking and supports with composite lumber. So, there's no painting."

"Beautiful work. You have a real knack for this, just like Uncle."

"Hey, I ... thanks, Cynthia," Clint said. He shook his head and smiled before he continued in an affectionate tone, "I'd be glad to show you the cabin when it's a bit farther along."

"I'd like ...," Cynthia started, briefly seeing something alarmingly dark in her cousin's eyes.

"How about some help here," Sylvia barked, cutting off further contemplation of the glimpse of Clint's dark side.

Clint and Cynthia rose and relieved Sylvia of bags of bagels, cups, napkins and tubs of cream cheese. Reaching back into the stairwell, she retrieved a large silver carafe of coffee and put it on the table as they sat down. "Clint going on and on about his refurbishment project?" she asked, setting out cups and pouring coffee. "Looks great, huh?"

"Yes, and yes," Cynthia answered brightly, glad for the aromatic brew. "The ghost of old lady Holland must be happy."

"That's what I was going for." Clint and Sylvia laughed.

Cynthia joined in the laughter, remembering her uncle's claim that the ghost of the wife of the whaling ship captain, Horace Holland, could be seen on nights when the moon was full pacing and scanning the horizon for her husband. Captain Holland built the Eye of the Storm in the nineteenth century, shortly before he and his ship had been lost at sea. Until the day she died, Sally Holland never gave her husband up for dead. Daily, she climbed the thirteen steps to the widow's walk and paced, scanning the horizon.

Pointing at the back railing, Clint said "It really creeped me out when Dad told us she died right there."

"Not to be a wet blanket," Sylvia said once her laughter and smile disappeared into the business at hand, "but we should have a few words before Danny shows. She called and said she was running late."

"Agreed," Cynthia said. "This morning I called Louis Belmont and asked him to join us around eleven. There'll likely be legal questions, and he can advise us of our options."

"Is he going to deliver the codicil?" Clint asked.

"Yes. Also, I had him give me the highlights so I can think of how best to mollify Danny."

"Super," Sylvia said, placing her hands palm down on the table. "But let's talk about Mom first."

Sylvia's brother and cousin both nodded.

"It may not be my place to speak first," Cynthia began, looking at Sylvia for permission to go on, "but I have a proposal regarding Auntie that may save a lot of discussion."

"Sure, shoot," Clint said after Sylvia nodded. "As far as Mom goes, Danny would be onboard with anything that helps her. As far as the codicil goes, that may be a harder sell."

"No argument there, but I have a proposal that should win her over." Cynthia sipped her coffee, took a deep breath and continued. "Uncle J parceled out the estate in one-sixth shares. The four of us got one each, and Auntie two along with the house. Since the liquid assets of Uncle's estate are substantial, our shares are multiple-seven-figure cuts. So, I propose the three of us each give Auntie one-third of our cut. This gives her one half. In compensation, Sylvia, you take the title to Wilkes Tavern and Clint you already get the family cabin and the large property it sits on."

"Hmm," Sylvia paused. "What do you get?"

"Just enough of each of your GASMAX shares to get back on the board."

"And Danny gets to keep her full share because ...?" Clint asked quietly.

"Wait, I gotta hear this," Danny declared after she opened the stairwell door fully. "Also, the family lawyer may have something to add."

Danny and Louis Belmont joined the gathering. Danny poured coffee for herself and grabbed a bagel. Sylvia served the lawyer and poured refills. "I assume, instead of immediately joining us, you were eavesdropping and heard everything Cynthia said, correct?" she asked her sister in icy tones.

Danny swallowed hard and gulped coffee to wash down the bagel. "Sorry about that, but yes. It's a habit I picked up in prison."

"You also understand that Mom is out sailing and doesn't know anything about this family meeting?" she added, looking at Belmont. "We all need to be on the same page and ensure we're on sound legal footing before we tell her anything."

"You are," Belmont injected quickly. "Also, I swung by the docks and verified Joan is still out to sea. Cynthia, while I briefly have the floor, Mr. Strong is waiting downstairs. He's standing guard and will let us know if your aunt returns unexpectedly."

"Great, Louis," Cynthia said.

"Yeah, great," Danny said. "And yeah, yeah, Cynthia, I'm all onboard with Mom getting a third of your cuts."

"And the stock and real estate allocations?" Cynthia asked.

"Sure, no probs, Cuz," Danny replied with a smile. "But since dear Dad put the bulk of my financial future in your hands, I'd like some relief from the doling out process of my share. The silent Mr. Belmont tells me the codicil gives you great latitude."

"Danny, I hope you know I was just as surprised by that as you were?"

"Yes. And I owe you an apology for yesterday. I'm sorry," Danny answered, doing that thing with her voice and eyes that always worked so well with J Martin.

All eyes were now on Cynthia. "Of course, Danny, apology accepted and very much appreciated. You guys and Auntie are the only family I have left," she said warmly.

The youngest Martin child was now the center of attention. "Cynthia, I ... I ..." Danny began, her voice breaking, as an emotion seized her that she had not felt since before that night in her father's study. "Like Grandpa always said, we must actually bear some fruit in keeping with repentance."

Cynthia smiled warmly. "We certainly are."

Danny cleared her throat and said, "Cuz, as always, I trust you to do the right thing. Matter of fact, I'm counting on it."

"Thank you for the vote of confidence, Danny. Here's what I propose."

Eye of the Storm Front Porch

BRIAN SMITH, VILLAGE of Driftwood Cove Police Chief, rapped three times on the beach house front door before letting the screen door swing shut. Tanner Strong opened the door. Smith saw that he had a drawn pistol held against his pant leg. "Good morning, Mr. Strong." He chuckled. "Good to see you're on duty."

Tanner nodded and waved him in. "Hi, Chief," he said after a quick glance outside, shutting the door and holstering his weapon.

"My patrolman said you'd arrived. So, I sent him home," he declared as he walked down the entry hall toward the living room. "Where's everyone?"

"On the roof in a family meeting," Strong replied, pointing toward the staircase. "Anything I can do for you, Chief?"

"A visit with Sally Holland on the widow's walk." Smith chuckled as he stopped and straightened a framed recent Martin family photograph. The smiling faces included Cynthia Jones'.

"Who?"

Smith laughed. "Oh, it's a joke. It's just an old Driftwood Cove ghost story about this house's original owners. No, there's nothing you can do. I need a few minutes with Ms. Jones."

"Related to the car bombing?" Tanner asked as he followed Smith into the living room. "Maybe I can help."

"No, this is on an unrelated matter," he replied and opened the sliding glass door to the deck. "You stay put, on guard. I'm going to wait out on the deck and enjoy one of Driftwood Cove's million-dollar views."

Eye of the Storm Widow's Walk

"THAT'S VERY REASONABLE and gracious, Cynthia," Danny said quietly after Cynthia explained her proposed plan to execute the terms of the codicil. "Uncle Louis, can she do that?"

"Yes, she can. Your father gave her great leeway in the codicil," the lawyer answered. "I'll prepare the papers if you so direct, Cynthia."

She nodded, and the remaining tension among siblings and their cousin evaporated when Danny rose, went to Cynthia and hugged her. "Not to spoil the moment, but may I ask a sensitive question?" Cynthia asked.

Everyone nodded, but Sylvia frowned and said, "Sure, about what?"

"Actually, it's about who - Uncle Joel."

"Yeah, go ahead, Cuz," Danny said, breaking the awkward silence that followed Cynthia's clarification, accompanied by what was now a trio of scowls.

"I can see this is still a sore spot, but why wasn't he there yesterday?" she asked and stated the obvious. "He's Uncle J's brother as well as long-time business associate."

"Uncle Joel called me with his condolences and his regrets that he would not attend the memorial due to an emergency board meeting called in the wake of your ... sudden departure," Sylvia said as Danny and Clint nodded their heads. All three gave Cynthia a dark look.

Sylvia seems to relish reminding me of my recent misfortune, Cynthia thought with dismay, but said flatly, "I see."

"It was probably best he wasn't there," Sylvia added. "After the will was read, Mom had a heated phone conversation with him. I couldn't hear what was said, but she was pretty pissed."

"I'm not surprised given that blow-up he and Dad had just before Dad's last solo hike," Danny injected. "Is there any cream cheese left?"

"That's right," Sylvia explained, passing the last tub of cheese to Danny. "Clint and Danny were downstairs in the living room, and they heard them shouting. I was upstairs in my room, and I came into the hall when I heard them. But I heard only bits and pieces."

"What were they fighting about?" Cynthia asked.

"Well, I just heard a few words and parts of some sentences, but there was a clear reference to the quarry and something about 'that night.'"

"Not surprising," Danny said as she spread another bagel with the white topping. "I ran into him downstairs after Uncle Joel left. He was upset like Mom had been on the phone. He didn't say about what when I asked, "What's wrong." He just snarled, "Nothing," and muttered something about the quarry. It's just a hunch, but I think something or someone at the quarry worried him."

"You have anything more than a hunch to base that on?" Sylvia asked.

"Not really, unless you count my expertise and practice at making him angry and knowing when I succeeded," Danny answered and quickly added, "Can't say I'm proud of that like I used to be. Anyway, it was that look and the fact he left shortly on that last solo hike with the weird extended goodbyes."

"That has some substance," Clint added. "Dad visited me at the cabin later that day to borrow, without explanation, some rappelling equipment. He also took one of the old 45 cals we kept at the cabin. He never took a gun on a hike before."

"So, that and your hunch are why you say your father's death was not accidental?" Cynthia asked.

Danny nodded. "It was too much like fights I saw in prison that resulted in some nasty 'accident'."

"That so?"

"Hey, Cuz, don't get me wrong," Danny said quickly. "I don't suspect Uncle Joel or anything like that. He and Dad were brothers and all. They both got me the job in plant ops. Also, Uncle Joel was the one who encouraged me in the biathlon. I haven't forgotten that. Wish I hadn't blown that opportunity."

"Don't forget the visits in prison, Sis," Clint mentioned.

"That, too," Danny responded. "Saw more of him than I did any of you guys and the parents."

"I see," Cynthia said and smiled at Danny. "Clint, could you meet me at the quarry tomorrow morning and show me where they found Uncle?"

"Sure," Clint said slowly, looking at Danny. "I assume your bodyguard will be with you?"

Cynthia nodded as Sylvia rose and said, "Unless there's something more, I think we're done here."

"Cynthia, may I speak with you in private?" Louis Belmont asked as they crowded the back of the platform.

Cynthia nodded.

"Hey, everyone," Sylvia shouted and handed the lawyer her new cell phone. "Family photo. I don't know when we'll all be together again. Uncle Louis, will you?"

"Sure, everyone, please line up against the back rail," Belmont directed.

"Ah, the photo of Princess Cynthia and her court," Clint added with a laugh.

"Clint, cut that out," Cynthia commanded, twisting to glare at him. The motion and crowding in threw her off balance. She stumbled backward into the railing. The finishing nails gave way instantly and she fell off the platform.

CHAPTER 12

Reckless Passing

Eye of the Storm Beach House

CHIEF SMITH TOSSED HIS HAT onto a deck chair. This house, this deck and his interaction with the Martin family just before and after Justice Martin's death not only rekindled old memories but also an old addiction ritual. As he patted the breast pocket of his uniform shirt, but not really expecting to find a cigarette pack, he recalled the investigation seven years ago. It had shocked the village and rocked the Martin family. He sighed and wished that he knew only the J Martin from those days rather than the one who he met on this spot just before his death. *Something was really off in that last meeting. Justice Martin wasn't himself,* he thought. The consistently practical, upbeat village benefactor was uncharacteristically emotional and morose during their last conversation that included him saying several times how he was "failing to bear fruit in keeping with repentance." *That was the only time I had ever talked with J that made me feel down.*

Smith considered his reflection in one of the living room's plate glass windows. Memories of the Martins during their first encounter seven years ago in conjunction with the robbery and assault came to mind as well as the last meeting with J Martin. Then there was yesterday's interaction related to the attempt on the Jones girl's life. These memories sparked an anxiety he'd not felt in years. Unlike other times, his vain-consideration of the thirty-pound lighter, fit, ex-boozer and former smoker's reflected image did not lessen his angst.

He heard laughter and looked up. On the widow's walk, he could easily see Sylvia Martin and her cousin. The one male he could see was likely Clint. Based on his patrolman's report, he was certain that the sister, Danny, and the family lawyer, Belmont, were present.

He walked to the deck's edge and considered the clean line of the horizon, dividing a deep blue sea from a lighter blue sky marred only by a few scattered clouds. A single white sail broke the horizon. The tranquil scene reminded him of the news he was here to deliver. It would still the family's laughter as much as the first reports of J Martin's death.

For the third time since leaving the station he patted his pocket, verifying that it still contained the number ten envelope Justice Martin had given him at their last meeting. That was the other reason for today's visit. Sealed with tape and, as he could best judge, containing no more than two or three sheets of paper, it was addressed 'To Cynthia Jones, Eyes Only.' J had called in a favor to get him to play messenger, a role he had protested as more appropriate for Louis Belmont. Martin assured him it was not, telling him to deliver it in private as soon as possible and as appropriate in the event of his death.

The meeting with Jones at the station regarding the car bombing didn't seem an appropriate time, so here he was today with some extra time to conjure up the past. The report by one of his officers that Buck Wilson was back in town further brought to mind the seven-year-ago investigation of the Martin robbery and assault. *I'll never forget the first encounter with that punk Wilson*, he thought with renewed disgust.

Driftwood Cove Police Station Seven Years Ago

DETECTIVE BRIAN SMITH banged open the interrogation room door and sat down. With a well-practiced move, he pressed the tape recorder's *Record* button, setting the device squarely on the metal table. In an instant he sized up the perp, deciding how to proceed. "Let's start with your name," he commanded the younger man.

Thinking of his younger female partner, Julie Simpson, Smith had decided he'd be bad cop. His salt and pepper hair and a face full of lines etched by experience suited him well to that role. Reading the suspect's face and body language, he concluded that the scary-cop persona was spot on. *This'll go well*, he concluded silently.

The shaggy-haired suspect cleared his throat. "Wilson, Buck Wilson," he replied slowly, looking Smith in the eye. "And you are?"

This punk must think his voice and eye contact sets the tone and gains some advantage. "I'm Detective Smith," he snapped back, thrust his chin out and leaned in. "And, Buck, I'm your worst nightmare unless I get the truth. Like your full real name, Reginald."

"Hey, I go by ..."

"Your name, boy."

"Okay, Reginald Buchanan Wilson. Sheeze. I go by Buck."

"Okay, Buck, why did you assault the Jones girl and burgle the safe?"

Buck cleared his throat and smiled. "Whoa, detective. You don't waste any time, do you? But aren't you forgetting something? What about my rights?" Buck leaned forward until Smith smelled the odor of cigarettes and Wilson's cheap aftershave.

Not retreating, Smith replied calmly, "Didn't the arresting officer read you your rights?"

"Yeah, but where's my attorney?" Buck spread his palms up even though they were shackled to the table. "Are these really necessary?" he asked, nodding at the handcuffs.

"Didn't you just tell my partner you'd talk without a lawyer?" What passed for a smile creased Smith's thin lips. "You want your rights read again?"

"No, but I thought your partner would be doing the talking," Buck replied and smiled. "She didn't say anything 'bout you. No offense."

"None taken, but she's busy with your girlfriend." The detective sat back and sighed. *Time to ease up*, he thought. "Hey, if you want to wait for a lawyer, we'll do that. Besides, Danny Martin is giving you up. Kid, things will go better for you in court if you fess up."

Buck was silent. He appeared to mull over Smith's claim about Danny selling out her boyfriend.

"Wilson, don't be a sap. Dannell Martin essentially sold out her father. Blood, especially a boyfriend's, is no thicker than water with her and the rest of the Martin family. Just think about what she was doing last night. She was helping you to break into her old man's safe to get his emergency cash and her mom's jewels."

Nodding, Wilson's replied, "Okay ... okay, I'll talk."

"Smart." Smith leaned in. "So, why did you assault the Jones girl and burgle the safe?"

"Is that what Danny told you?" Buck asked.

He's fishing. He wants to see if I'll slip up and reveal that Danny hadn't said a thing against him ... yet. He's a cagey little bastard, Smith thought suppressing a chuckle. "Danny and Cynthia both." Smith pulled a dog-eared notebook from his suit pocket and flipped a few pages. "Danny says the robbery was your idea." Turning to another page, he continued, "And Cynthia Jones says that after she walked in on the robbery, you took her at gunpoint back to her bedroom and assaulted her."

"Both are lies," Buck stated with, what Smith concluded, was forced confidence. The accompanying hand gestures intended to make his answer more sincere were truncated by the handcuffs. "Detective, are these really necessary?"

"Yeah, they are." Smith said, looking up from his notes. "So, they're both lying, huh?"

"Yes, I had no idea what Danny was up to until we got to the beach house and she opened the safe. That's when Cynthia walked in. You see, they're cousins. Cynthia always spends the summer at the beach house."

"What about the gun? You don't have a permit to carry." Smith studied Wilson closely.

"Yeah, but the gun ..." Buck's voice rose and faltered. He took a deep breath and dialed it down a few decibels. "The pistol is Danny's. She pulled it when Cynthia barged in."

"So how come it ended up in the bedroom and Jones used it to shoot you?" Smith nodded toward the bandage on Buck's arm.

Smith knew that the bullet had passed clean through Buck's right bicep. He noted that talking about the gunshot made Wilson wince. The young man's face was briefly etched with anger and maybe something darker. "Well, Danny gave it to me when she told me to get Cynthia out of the study. I gotta say, detective, I felt safer with it than knowing Danny had it. Danny's ... well, she's unpredictable at times."

"So, I understand," Smith admitted, glancing at a prior page in his notebook. He knew the Martin family well enough to know that Dannell was the wild child. "And you didn't try to rape Cynthia Jones?"

"No," Buck stated, again using what Smith now knew to be a false confident voice.

Smith's face revealed nothing, but the detective now considered it likely that Danny had the leading role in the crime. However, explaining away the rape charge was something else.

Smith pulled a stack of photographs from his suit pocket. He rifled through them, selected two and slapped the pair in front of Buck. "So, Cynthia ripped her nightgown and scratched herself? We're waiting for the DNA results, but something tells me it's her skin we scraped off your fingernails."

In one photo, the ripped and torn parts of Cynthia black nightgown were arrayed on a white background. In the other, Cynthia's bare back was exposed to the camera and three diagonal scratches were evident. "Yeah, but ..." Buck sat back, sighed and his shoulders slumped.

Smith's heartless countenance broke with a satisfied grin. "Look, Buck, you may have been in the wrong place at the wrong time for the robbery, but I don't see any wiggle-room on the sexual assault charge." Smith leaned in. "Just admit it, kid, and everything will go easier for you." He laced his voice with concern even though he knew Buck didn't believe it for a second.

Buck sat back up and took a deep breath. "Okay, I know this looks bad, but it's like I said. Danny and I have been going together for some time. We hang out at the beach house a lot. So, I didn't think anything was up when she said she wanted to hang out there before the whole family got back the next day. Honest, I didn't know bout the safe until we got there."

"We covered that, but what about the assault?" Smith asked without emotion and with the determination of a dog clamped onto a new bone.

"That's not what it looks like," Buck replied calmly.

"Well, what's it like?" Smith rapped the table with his pen.

"You see Cynthia and I ... well, we have a history."

Smith rolled his eyes.

"I'm not kidding, we met last summer," Buck continued quickly. "We dated for a while. Ask her."

"I'll do that, but if so, that doesn't excuse assault." Smith pursed his lips. "Are you with Danny now?"

"Yeah. I met Dannell – Danny - at the beach house when I was still seeing Cynthia, and ... well we have more in common. Danny is not so intense. She's got her problems, but we're more alike. Cynthia wants to be king of the world or something. She can be ... well, demanding in everything including love-making," Buck said, leaning forward and spreading his palms as best as he could in the handcuffs. "Look, Cynthia and I were together last summer. We had sex. Sometimes in that room. And she liked it rough at times. She's used to getting her way, so ..."

"So?"

"So, when we went to the room, she came on to me," Buck said, mustering up his best sad smile. "You saw what she was wearing? I'm only human."

Smith silently agreed that Cynthia Jones was very attractive. "She wanted it, huh?"

Buck nodded and Smith grunted. "So, why'd she shoot you?"

"It was like this. The gun was tucked into my waist. We kissed, and she complained it was poking her. So, I tossed it on the bed. Then she was on me, and we got on the bed. I started to undo her nightie, but she told me to rip it off. That's how it got torn and I scratched her in the process."

Smith shook his head. "Bullshit. Again, if this was consensual why did she shoot you?" he asked with a skepticism mitigated only slightly by Buck's explanation.

"I don't know exactly, but when I touched her ... you know, there ... she went all, "Get off me" and hit me."

"Did you get off her?" Smith asked, cutting him off.

"You bet I did, and I got off the bed. I knew from past experience I'd crossed some 'she's-gotta-be-in-control' line," Buck replied, heaping fault on Cynthia. "But the next thing I know she's got the gun, and she ..."

"She shot you?"

"Not right away. She first ranted something about some boyfriend at college who was supposed to come up and then started talking about Danny's feelings. I raised a hand to calm her, but that spooked her or something and she shot." Buck sat back. "My arm didn't hurt right away. Next thing I know she's got a cell phone and is calling 911. Danny came in and ... well, we had no choice but to do what the crazy lady with the gun said. We all waited for the cops."

Smith stood and put his notebook away. He snorted and left the room. He noted that Buck smiled. *It won't hurt to let him think he's convinced me, for a while*, he thought. Later that day and seven years later he'd know ...

Eye of the Storm Beach House

SYLVIA MARTIN'S VOICE pulled Smith back to the present. He turned and saw that the rooftop meeting was breaking up. He crossed the deck to retrieve his hat and noticed that Jones and the Martin kids had lined up against the widow's walk back rail. *Family photo time*, he concluded as he put his hat on and tightened his tie. *Hate to be the bearer of these bad tidings.*

He was sure he heard Clint Martin's voice say something about "Princess" before he heard Cynthia Jones laugh and reply. Her retort turned into a startled cry as she stumbled and fell back and through the widow's walk's railing. She hit the roof, falling flat and rolling off. Instinctively he rushed to catch her. He did, but the added weight of the woman buckled his knees. They fell to the deck in a pile.

The fall knocked the wind out of him, but he managed to keep Cynthia cradled in his arms. He sat up and took a deep breath. *Nothing broken*, he concluded after a silent body inventory. "Jones, you okay?" he managed after two deep breaths.

Cynthia face went from fear to surprise. "Chief ... yes, I'm okay," she managed finally, sitting up and standing with the police chief's assistance. "How ... how are you?"

"Good," he said and guided her to a nearby deck chair. "Here, sit for a minute to collect yourself."

Cynthia nodded and sat.

As he retrieved his hat, he saw the faces of Tanner Strong and the Martins at the sliding glass door leading to the deck. Realizing their time alone was about to end, he stated, "Look, I need a moment of your time in private."

"Sir, you can have all the moments you'd like." She smiled. "Thank you for catching me."

"Were you pushed?"

"No, we crowded together and, I tripped over my own feet," she answered, shaking her head. "My fault. Clint warned me earlier that the back rail wasn't yet fully secure."

"Humph," Smith replied and helped her stand. "I'll believe that for now. I have some news for the whole family, but then we need to chat in private."

Cynthia nodded just before Sylvia hugged her cousin, and Tanner and the rest gathered around them.

Eye of the Storm Beach

CYNTHIA CURLED HER toes into the sand as she accepted the sealed envelope from Louis Belmont. Just as when she was a child playing on this beach, that gesture, the moist sand, and the sun calmed her spirit, now set back into turmoil. Before walking the beach with the lawyer, the gruff police chief with as much sympathy as he could muster delivered an emotional gut punch to a family already reeling from the loss of a father and the resulting swirling cauldron of family dysfunction.

Chief Smith, cutting short any demonstration of gratitude for Cynthia's rescue, herded Louis Belmont, Tanner Strong, Cynthia and her family into the living room. Obviously ill at ease, he reported that the Martins' sailboat was found adrift about two miles out to sea from the tidal hydroelectric plant north of Driftwood Cove. The Coast Guard found a suicide note and a lot of blood. He told them that it was likely Joan Martin had slit her wrists and jumped overboard. The boat's anchor was missing, suggesting she jumped using the anchor to ensure the quickest watery demise. Her body was not yet found. The shocked silence that followed was broken by a sob from Danny, a curse from Clint and whispered "oh" from Sylvia.

Before Cynthia could react, the chief mumbled something like, "I'm sorry for your loss," and motioned for her to follow him into the hallway leading to the front door. There he delivered the envelope from her uncle and told her what little he knew of it. Torn between the desire to see what was in it and the need to get back to her cousins, she shoved it into her skirt pocket, and they returned to the living room.

Though stunned by the chief's news and the uncertainty of Uncle J's 'eyes only' message, Cynthia still noted that Louis Belmont was seemingly not surprised and callously indifferent to her family's shock and dismay. Before she could join her cousins, he brusquely took her by the arm and steered her away for a private shoreline chit chat.

After Belmont convinced Tanner Strong that he needed a moment with Cynthia in private, they all agreed that her new bodyguard would stand out of earshot but remain close enough for him to quickly come to her aid. Visibly not happy with this exposed arrangement, Tanner drew his firearm and now stood upwind about twelve paces away.

"Louis, what's the deal? This is more than rude and insensitive. You're taking Auntie's likely death rather calmly," Cynthia challenged the longtime family lawyer and friend. He handed her an envelope. She glanced at it briefly. Her name had been handwritten on it by her deceased uncle. *A second message from the grave*, she reflected, thinking about the unopened envelope in her pocket.

"Regrettably this takes precedence over any personal feelings," he replied, nodding at the envelope. "Please believe me, I'm as shocked and filled with grief by the news delivered by our less than diplomatic police chief as you are. However, my feelings and capacity for surprise regarding Joan have been badly blunted by events preceding and following the discovery of J's body."

"That so?" she said, arching her eyebrows.

"Joan's emotional well-being has been a rollercoaster ride." Belmont sighed. "She'd become very, very depressed prior to J's death, but, much to my relief, she bounced back to her usual stoic self shortly after they found his body. You saw for yourself how she's been all over the emotional landscape since you arrived and as we've marched down the lock-step path dictated by J."

"That's true," Cynthia admitted, recalling the rushed nature of the memorial service and reading of the will as well as Chief Smith's hurry to deliver his J Martin envelope and be gone.

"With great difficulty, I've stuffed my emotions as I've carried out your uncle's last wishes," he stated, placing a hand on her shoulder. "Losing your aunt as well as J is almost too much. They were more family than clients. But, thankfully, delivering this envelope to you is one of J's last biddings."

"What's in it, Louis?" she asked, her voice having lost its edge.

"Don't know." He shrugged. "I met with J about a week before he left on that last solo hike. He gave it to me and said you were to receive it directly and in private. He told me no one else knew its contents."

"Can I share what's in it," she asked, looking up the beach to where Tanner stood, gun at the ready and eyes never resting.

"He said that's up to you. Whatever is in there as well as anything else it leads to," he replied, following her glance. "I'm not violating any lawyer-client confidentiality by telling you I have a similar envelope with different contents for Mr. Strong, but with the same ground rules."

And the same rules Chief Smith told me, she added silently. "I see," she finally commented. "Anyone else get an envelope?"

"I don't believe so, but both J and Joel have always impressed me as men who never take anyone completely into their confidence. So, there may be others."

Interesting, unless he's lying, he doesn't know about the envelope from the chief, she thought. She nodded, recalling the same impression of her uncles that she formed after going to work at GASMAX. There was some secret they shared. No one else knew it, not her aunt, her cousins or anyone else in the family or at GASMAX. "Let's see," she said, slipping a finger under the flap to open the envelope.

"Wait," Belmont commanded, placing a hand on her forearm. "Justice said that you had to open it in private."

"I see." She stepped away, turned her back to the lawyer and opened it. A key, obviously to a safe deposit box, and a one-page handwritten note from her uncle were inside. Without removing the note, she read its few words. Eyes wide, she staggered back a step. Pulling the other envelope from her pocket, she examined its contents. "Oh my God!"

Stuffing both envelopes into her pocket, she turned to face Belmont. "We must go," she commanded, stepping past Louis and waving to Tanner to join them. They returned to the house. Though Cynthia's mind raced, she saw Danny sitting on one of the deck chairs lowering binoculars as she waved. She stood and waited for the trio to join her.

"Danny, hi. Where's everyone?" Cynthia asked, looking beyond her to the empty living room.

"Sylvia and Clint went with the police to look at the family sailboat. The cops think they may see something they've missed."

"Why didn't you go?"

"I've been a little out of the sailing game for a few years, Cuz," Danny replied with a brief grin. "Besides, I need to go to work for half a shift. We're doing system testing, and they need extra hands."

"Seriously," Tanner said. "I'm sure the company ..."

"Hey, it's okay," she said cutting him off. "I'm a Martin. Work helps us cope. Do what's necessary and all. Right, Cuz?"

"Right, I get it," Cynthia said, and stroked her cousin's upper arm. "Tanner and I need to go to the bank."

"Why's that?" Danny asked and thought, *Perfect*.

"I ... I don't know ... yet," Cynthia replied slowly. "I'll call you later to see how you're doing. Also, we need to talk. You may be right. Your dad's death might not have been an accident."

Danny smiled nervously and nodded. "Sure ... yeah, let's talk soon," she agreed. "I'll catch up with you in a minute. Gotta call the plant." After Cynthia stepped into the house, her cousin pulled her cell phone from her pocket, stabbed at the screen and pressed it to her ear. Following a brief one-sided call, she joined the lawyer, Tanner and Cynthia.

Cynthia saw her cousin off before asking Belmont, "Louis, would you please contact Chief Smith or whoever may know Julie Simpson's phone number?"

"Julie Simpson?" Belmont asked. "Oh, the detective who worked with the chief during the robbery investigation. I have that, but she's a PI now. She's done some work for me. So, I've got it. I'll text it. Anything else?"

"No, but I need to speak with all my cousins soon. As I said, Danny may be right. Uncle's death may not have been an accident. No time to explain nor am I sure I completely know why - yet."

Highway 733

TANNER TURNED THE GASMAX company vehicle onto Highway 733 as Cynthia put her cellphone into her purse. After noting that there was lighter than usual traffic for this time in the summer season, in the rearview mirror he saw that a black, double-cab pickup with tinted windows had turned off GASMAX Road onto the highway. GASMAX Road, formerly just a numbered, dirt rural route to the Martin family cabin, now was paved and provided access to the gas plant's southern parking lot. It intersected the highway at the same place as did the long driveway to the Martin house.

The truck closed the distance between them as Tanner steered into the approach to the dogleg portion of the road that skirted the rocky Wilkes Ridge. The crook in the highway defined the southwest side of the property upon which rested the old Wilkes Tavern. It also created a blind bend in the road that the locals, without much originality but with good cause, dubbed 'Dead Man's Curve.'

"You set up the meet with the PI?" he asked, noting with growing concern that the pickup had closed to a few car lengths.

"Yes," Cynthia said after closing her purse. "We're meeting tomorrow morning."

"Where?"

"Wilkes Tavern. She's doing some kind of surveillance. It's the only way she can fit me in."

"I'll plan on going unless you tell me otherwise."

"We'll see." Cynthia smiled. "Since she's a former cop, maybe you can sleep in."

"Great," he replied vaguely, pressing the accelerator. Both vehicles were now approaching Dead Man's Curve. They entered the banked curve marked by a yellow warning sign and another demanding a well-warranted twenty mile an hour speed limit. "This joker is riding my bumper," Tanner said sharply. "Hang on!"

Cynthia looked over her shoulder as the truck filled the entirety of the rearview mirror. "Damn!" she exclaimed, grabbing the armrests as they went into the bend at higher than prudent speed.

Before rear-ending them, the truck suddenly veered into the left lane. "Jesus!" Tanner, cried. He stomped the brake pedal, throwing them both into the embrace of their shoulder strap's inertial lock.

He risked a glance at the truck as it pulled even with them. Tinted glass and a quick look garnered only an impression of a male profile. Instead of passing, the pickup driver, with suddenness equal to his swerve into the left lane, turned into them. Despite Tanner's best efforts, the collision drove them into and over the guard rail. The pickup wobbled but regained the right lane, slowed briefly and then sped away.

Tanner instinctively worked the steering wheel to regain control but without effect. They flew one car length before hitting the ground and slamming into a car-size boulder. Cynthia's scream and Tanner's curse were cut off as they were thrown forward.

CHAPTER 13

In the Crosshairs

Harper Bluff

HARPER BLUFF RISES SHARPLY on the southern border of the Village of Driftwood Cove. A hiking trail runs roughly east-west along its crest. The north side drops steeply to the village center and the southern end of Driftwood Bay. The south side gently slopes away to thick forest. The promontory, like Wilkes Ridge, is an esker formed by a glacier that melted and retreated north several millennia ago. Both sides of the ridge and bluff are encrusted with car-sized or larger rocks that geologists call erratics, deposited by the same sheet of ice that scooped out Driftwood Bay and Smugglers Cove.

On the bluff's north side, behind one such boulder, Danny Martin sat well off and out of sight of the trail above. Sitting cross-legged, she enjoyed a bird's eye view of the village and civic center, including a clear line of sight to Cynthia's destination, the bank. The granite-faced structure with arched windows was less than a half mile away. *Perfect*, she thought, laying her guitar case flat. Before she could open it, her cell phone rang.

"How'd you do?" she asked after pressing the phone to her ear.

"That woman has nine lives," Buck Wilson declared.

"Do tell," she said, sitting back and pushing her sunglasses back on her nose. "Couldn't force 'em off the road, huh?"

"Oh, I did. They even smacked into one of those big freaking rocks. The front end was all smashed in."

"How'd you know that?"

"I parked around the bend and hiked back."

"And?"

"They both were already out of the wreck and walking around."

"Were they at least injured?"

"Nope, they looked okay. Guess the airbags and seatbelts did their thing."

"They see you?"

"No. They were too busy checking out the damage, and, get this, they both had guns pulled."

"So, Princess C is carrying," Danny said.

"Yeah, and they're coming your way."

"That so?" Danny said, sitting up and grinning. She ran her hand over the guitar case and chuckled. "Well, it was worth a try. So, on to Plan B's next part, me. I'm setting up. I'll be ready for them."

"Well, you don't have much time. That heap was still drivable."

"No problem. I'll be ready. Where are you?" she asked while she stood and searched the stretch of highway visible above the trees to the north and west.

"In the church parking lot behind the gas station. I'm going to wipe my prints off and hike back to my ride at the docks. This truck's probably been reported stolen by now."

"No doubt," Danny agreed, nodding.

"Look, I ... are you okay doing this? She's your cousin and all."

"Careful, lover," Danny said. "You're sounding like you have a heart or a conscience. Don't worry about my nerve. If anything, prison made me strong in that regard."

"I believe you," Buck replied and forced a nervous laugh. "Call me after and we'll meet to ... celebrate, I guess."

"You bet we will. I'm in the money now. Don't worry about me," Danny said. She smiled, warming to the task ahead. *I've been looking forward to ending her since I was locked up. Payback time, Princess,* she finished silently.

"I won't worry ... too much. Good luck," Buck said and ended the call.

After noting the time on the phone, she put it away and did another look around to ensure that she was out of sight from the trail above. She turned her attention to the guitar case and smiled. The top of the faux leather hard case was festooned with stickers. Flanked by flowers, one commanded, "Make Love Not War." Another declared, "No More Silence, End Gun Violence." The last simply proclaimed, "Ban Guns." With well-practiced ease she snapped open the five chrome latches and opened the case. Instead of the headstock, fingerboard and bridge of an acoustic guitar, the case contained foam dunnage caressing firmly in place her bolt-action sniper rifle, an H-S Precision Pro 2000 Heavy Tactical Rifle, and its accoutrements.

Putting the detachable telescopic sight to her eye, she found the front of the bank. "Damn," she hissed as she saw Cynthia enter the bank and Tanner Strong drive the battered vehicle away. "Well, she'll have to come out eventually," she whispered, hefting out the HTR 2000. "I'll be ready."

R. NICHOLAS POHTOS

Driftwood Cove Bank

CYNTHIA JONES SIGHED and slumped in one of two cushioned chairs facing the lone narrow table in Driftwood Cove Bank's cramped safe deposit box private room. The chair's comfort and the subdued lighting precipitated a catharsis. The adrenaline rush from the car crash, another likely attempt on her life, dissipated suddenly, leaving her drained, yet with a sense of security – for the moment.

After a glance at the wood-framed and opaque-glass door to ensure that it was locked, she sat upright. *I must have looked like a crazy lady to that bank clerk*, she thought, running a hand through her hair and straightening her clothes. She rubbed the hem of her khaki skirt between her thumb and forefinger. The black blemish from her roll off the roof refused to come out.

Taking a few deep breaths to hold at bay a wave of fatigue, she considered the long metal box that, until recently, had been locked behind the double-lock door of safe deposit box 687. Next to it she placed the envelopes delivered by Chief Smith and family lawyer Belmont. During the ride to the bank, she had studied their contents and shared them with Tanner.

Except for the key in Belmont's envelope, each contained a single piece of letter-size paper with one word handwritten by her uncle. Taking both sheets out, she laid them side by side. The one from Smith on the left was inscribed with 'SPOLETO' and the one from Belmont with 'PICCOLO.' Neither she nor Tanner could make sense of them. He was about to tell her what was in his envelope from J when the black pickup truck grabbed his attention.

Maybe it's the crash, these cryptic one-word messages from Uncle J or the other near-death experiences, dreamed or real, she thought. *They make this homecoming's surreal and illogical events near normal and expected. Also, there are the things I'd forgotten and I'm now remembering, making them more and more ordinary and familiar.*

For instance, she wasn't surprised when the bank clerk found her name and signature on the card for safe deposit box 687. The card, along with the key from Belmont's envelope, permitted access to the metal container now sitting unopened in front of her. Before today she would have sworn that she'd no memory of signing the card on the same day her uncle had five years ago, but seeing her signature sparked some vague recall. It was as if cracks and fissures were forming in a walled-off portion of her mind, freeing the nocturnal dreams and lost memories of the events of and after the assault.

Dr. Schwartz, her shrink, had warned her that this might happen. *But it's also things completely unrelated to and before the assault*, she thought, closing her eyes. *Like the boat dream and how I remember ... when Mom started drinking.*

Her eyes went wide. *Yeah, I was a freshman in high school. Uncle Joel came to visit one night right after dinner. Mom sent me to the living room to watch TV. She said they needed to talk in private. After about twenty minutes I heard my mom say something in a loud angry voice. A moment later Uncle Joel left after a quick "goodbye" to me. He said it with a forced smile. I clearly remember that look on his face. He was upset, mad and sad all at once.*

Cynthia put a hand to her mouth. "Oh my God." *Mom came out to the living room. Her eyes were red like she'd been crying. I asked her what was wrong, but she said nothing. Her thoughts, obvious even to the fourteen-year-old me, were elsewhere. Suddenly, she just said, "Go to your room! Bedtime!" After a peck on my cheek, she got the whiskey bottle from the rarely opened side server, and ... well I found her the next morning passed out on the couch and the empty bottle lay on the floor. She never completely sobered up after that night.* "Mom showed up, but she never was fully present again," she observed aloud. *That's exactly what I told Doc Schwartz in one of our first sessions,* she recalled. *I told him, "Things were never the same with Uncle Joel or even Uncle J or Aunt Joan either. It wasn't bad like Mom ... just ... different, very different."*

"Where's that memory been?" she asked aloud, swinging open the hinged lid of the gunmetal gray box. "Maybe an answer is in here." The box contained a letter-size file folder and two black and gray speckled composition journals. *Just like the ones Uncle J used,* she observed, nodding her head. Setting the three items on the tabletop, she closed the box and pushed it aside.

Flipping through a few pages of each journal, in the newer and less worn of the two, she recognized her uncle's untidy and right-leaning handwriting and style of scientific annotation. He had labeled the front 'Phase 3 of 4' and below that was a date of five years ago. This made sense because that was around the time when she had started work at GASMAX. The buzz was all about J's and Joel's planned launch of the next system upgrade, Phase 3, of the GASMAX industry-leading and proprietary natural gas process.

In her first year onboard, Cynthia had been essentially J's executive assistant, the position Sylvia now held. Serving as scribe, she sat in on the numerous meetings J held with his team of engineers and scientists. Scanning several pages, she saw very familiar equations, diagrams and calculations. *I may have even seen this journal,* she speculated, looking again at the cover. *He had many of these journals filled and sitting on a bookshelf in his office. So, why's this one locked up special like?*

Placing the other journal on the top of J's, she noted that it was different. Most notably, it was severely water marked and soiled, as if it had been out in the rain or in a coffee spill. It too was labeled '3 of 4,' but in a different hand with no date. Instead, a name, 'Niles Tannerson,' was handwritten below. "Niles Tannerson," Cynthia whispered, leafing through the journal. "Never heard of him, but something familiar ... what the ..." She found a piece of GASMAX memo paper stuck between two pages in the middle. It was a handwritten note from Joel Martin to his brother and dated six years ago. It read:

J-

Hi, big bro. Awesome work as always. I agree with the schedules you outlined as well as other implementation plans. Proceed. This includes bringing niece Cynthia onboard after graduation. I don't agree for the reasons of conscience or Dad's edict to do good that you stated. This is just business. Remember what the old man also said, "Do what's necessary and, in business, blood is no thicker than water." But I do agree we keep it in the family, and she's the brightest and smartest of the bunch – no offense, ha ha :) However, just remember I reserve the last word if we ever have to cut her free.

As you did with the other souvenirs from our trip through the trapdoor to fortune, deep six this one as soon as you can.

Joel

I guess you did have the last word, Uncle, Cynthia thought and frowned, recalling being fired on the eve of her promotion. *I must have failed to meet some unspecified 'family' expectation or need. So, while Uncle J was building me up, his little brother was gathering that crap in case he needed to force me out. What do ... wait."*

Setting the Tannerson journal next to her uncle's, Cynthia leafed through both, comparing them page-by-page. "My God!" she uttered suddenly and sat back. "It's a copy. J copied Tannerson's almost word for word, formulas, flow diagrams and all."

Pulling the file folder to cover the two journals, she sat up. Still pondering the implications of J's plagiarism, Joel's complicity and her apparent role as a family pawn in some corporate intrigue, she lifted one of the sheets contained in the folder. *What's this doing here?* she wondered silently. *Why would copies of my birth certificate be locked up with these journals?*

She quickly leafed through the other sheets. Only the last one was different. It was the death certificate for someone she didn't know. Before she could examine the certificates any further, her cell phone came to life. The familiar but sudden ring tone announcing a text shattered the silence, startling her. She worked the screen. The text was from Sylvia. She confirmed that she and Clint had gone with Chief Smith to identify and examine the sailboat that the Coast Guard towed back to the Driftwood Bay docks. The brief message also stated that Danny had called to get Cynthia's cell number to set a meeting. Sylvia ended, providing Danny's phone number, and advised her to call Danny since "she can be a little forgetful."

After checking that there was no missed call from her youngest cousin, she dialed Tanner's number. "Hi, I'm ready," she said after his hello and setting the cell down with the speaker phone enabled.

"Pick you up outside in about ten minutes," he replied and laughed. "I can't get a new ride until later today. So, look for the rolling wreck. It's still rolling but with an occasional backfire. Anything interesting at the bank?"

"Very much so. I'll fill you in on the way to the beach house," she answered, folding the birth and death certificates and putting them in her skirt pocket along with the two envelopes. "Until I study it more, I've still more questions than answers. See you out front."

"K, bye," Tanner said.

Cynthia put both journals in her purse. With the pistol's hard case inside, the bag was full. Tucking the purse under one arm, she opened the door. With some difficulty, she scooped up the safe deposit box without dropping the purse and, with the bank clerk's help, secured the box before leaving the building.

Harper Bluff

DANNY MARTIN TOOK her eye away from the sniper scope and looked at her watch. "What are you doing in there, Princess?" she asked, returning her right eye to the eyepiece. The double glass doors of the bank filled the scope. She'd use them to verify the range and adjust the elevation. The doors opened, and she slipped her finger inside the trigger guard. A stout local who looked vaguely familiar stepped out. She retracted her finger and tapped the guard.

Just like hunting deer with dear old Dad and Uncle Joel, she thought, smiling. Hunting was the only one of the many outdoors activities J Martin made all his children try at least once. *Joel's repeated "Don't rush the shot" is burned into my brain. He'd been some kind of big deal biathlon athlete in college, an alternate or something for the Olympics.* So, he was the family firearms expert and instructor. He took a special interest in Danny since she was the best shot of all the Martin kids including Cousin Cynthia. *He had some idea that I could compete in the Olympics,* she recalled with some pride. *But he was sure sore when I didn't share his enthusiasm or display any interest in cross country skiing and the ridiculous training regime. "Forget that," I told him. I was an idiot.*

The door opened and a dark-haired woman stepped onto the sunlit sidewalk. *Nope, not her, either,* Danny observed. Feeling a sudden breeze on her cheek, she looked up to check the flag on the pole atop the bank. No longer slack, it now fluttered steadily. She gave the scope's windage knob a slight twist. "That should do it," she whispered, placing her eye to the scope and centering the crosshairs on the doors.

Danny flexed her grip on the gunstock behind the trigger guard and smiled. *Uncle Joel became very generous after we came to our final 'understanding' regarding the contents of that Martin family who-is-who document I found in Daddy J's safe. If Princess C hadn't blown up Buck and my heist that night, I might have sorted out how to use it to stay out of jail. Still, Uncle made a present of this beauty right after I got out of the joint. More than the steady work at the plant, the practice sessions with my HTR has made life as an ex-con quite bearable. The double-pull trigger was his idea so I 'Don't rush the shot,' but the guitar case was my idea, and ... whoa, it's show time!"*

Cynthia Jones stepped into the crosshairs. Danny tracked her cousin as she walked to the curb, stopped and, after looking up and down the street, pressed her cell phone to her ear. *Calling Tanner, no doubt,* she surmised while placing her finger on the trigger, centering the weapon's sights on Cynthia's head and inhaling deeply. *Good. That's it, Princess, just hold it and say bye-bye,* she ordered silently, exhaled and squeezed the trigger to the first pull position.

CHAPTER 14

She's Still a Knockout

Harper Bluff

A<small>FTER</small> D<small>ANNY</small> E<small>XHALED AND</small> S<small>QUEEZED</small> the trigger to the first pull position, Joel's words, "Don't rush the shot" delayed her pull to the final position. In that delay's split second her cell phone lying next to her rang.

In her peripheral vision, she immediately saw the caller ID, 'The Princess,' and Cynthia's image, captured at Justice Martin's memorial service. The juxtaposition with the same image in the scope created the visual equivalent of audio feedback between a microphone and a speaker. This disoriented Danny briefly as her mind made sense of the dual input. She smiled and released the trigger. *Well, this should be fun. Let's play with the mouse before we kill it*, she purred silently. She pressed the speakerphone icon and returned her eye to the scope. "Hello, cousin," she said warmly and again lined up the shot.

"Hi, Danny. Sylvia said you wanted me to call. We must talk about J's murder."

"Murder?" Danny arched her left eyebrow. "So ... so you found something at the bank that ..."

"Yes," Cynthia replied, cutting her off. The rolling wreck of a car that Buck had described appeared in the lower portion of the scope. "I've got to run, but yes, I found some things that show Uncle J likely had someone or some people who may have wanted him dead. When can we meet?"

"I'm not surprised. Ah, I'm kind of busy right now," Danny replied, placing her finger on the trigger. "Can we meet later? My shift ends at six."

"Perfect," Cynthia said, as Danny saw her juggle the phone and her overloaded purse to free a hand to open the car door. "I'm heading back to EOS to clean up and take a nap. We can meet there later."

"Sounds like a plan, Cuz," Danny said softly, pulling the trigger to the first position. "Tanner be there too?"

"Not for a while. He ... he's got to get us a new car," Cynthia answered, as she finally quit moving, the phone tucked under her chin, the overloaded purse clutched in one hand and the other now free. Her forehead was dead center in the cross hairs. "So, call me when you're off, Danny. I gotta go. I'm dead on my feet."

"That you are, Princess. Goodbye," Danny hissed, exhaling and pulling the trigger.

The cell phone slipped from beneath Cynthia's chin, missing Danny's farewell. She instinctively stooped and caught it with her free hand. Danny saw that this had spoiled her shot when one of the bricks framing the bank's doors exploded. Over the still open phone connection Danny heard what sounded like a car backfire as she saw the brick shatter. "Damn!" she shouted, instinctively cycling the rifle's bolt action, but Cynthia had opened the car door and disappeared. *That wreck's backfire probably masked the shot,* Danny reasoned. *So maybe she doesn't know she was shot at.*

"Damn it all to hell," Danny cursed, rolling over on her back and grabbing her phone. She punched the screen twice. Buck Wilson's caller ID appeared.

"You get her?"

"No," Danny sighed. "She found another life. Look, get over to the beach house fast. She and Strong are headed there. But he'll leave shortly after dropping her, and Sylvia and Clint are gone for a while. So ..."

"Yes ma'am, 'nuff said," Buck replied, more pleased than Danny cared for. "I'll take care of her and place Joel's Plan B gadget."

"Buck, toss her room and get whatever she found at the bank. It looks like it's all in her purse, but she may have other stuff in the room. I saw Belmont slip her an envelope, and I think Smith did too."

"Will do. Where're you going?"

"Work."

"Okay. See ya."

"Yeah, see you," Danny said as the call ended. She momentarily stared at Buck's caller ID image before dialing another number.

"Yes?" a familiar voice inquired.

"Lo, I've some good news and bad news."

Eye of the Storm Beach House

"DAMN," BUCK WILSON cursed when he heard voices and the door downstairs opened. "Jones." The balcony doors through which he had entered were still jar. No longer encumbered by the back pack he'd carried in his climb, he was confident he'd quickly escape. Well ahead of Cynthia's arrival, he concealed Joel's Plan B device in the study and thoroughly searched her room. He found nothing. Since a clean exit was steps away, he conducted one last, quick search of the beach house's guest bedroom that Cynthia occupied. Nothing. *She must have everything with her*, he reasoned.

He pressed himself against the wall next to the room's door and opened it a crack, as he heard Cynthia say from below, "Goodbye, I'll see you later." The front door closed.

Good, Tanner isn't with her, he concluded silently, softly shutting the bedroom door.

"Sylvia? Clint?" he heard her shout.

No one's home, sweetheart, he silently declared and remembered that she had a gun and that he had left his in his truck when he decided to use the boat. *Damnation! Gotta hide and somehow get the drop on her.*

The sound of footsteps on the stairs drove him to yank open the closet door opposite the bed. The louvered-door's hinge creaked loudly. After stepping into the closet, he pulled the door shut slowly without making a sound.

Through the door's slats Wilson watched the room door open and Cynthia enter. He noted two journals sticking out the top of her purse. *That must be the stuff from the bank.*

Cynthia's eyes went wide as she took in the aftermath of Buck's search. Little had been spared being upended, opened, or knocked over. She set the purse down slowly. Her eyes darted back and forth as she pulled her cell phone from her skirt pocket. After pushing the black screen twice, she held the phone in front of her.

"Hello, Miss Jones, what do you need?" he heard the familiar voice of Chief Smith ask.

Great, she's got it on speaker phone, Buck observed silently, *but she's called the cops. I don't have much time. Just need some kind of weapon.* He looked around the closet.

"My room ... the house ... there's been a break in!" Cynthia shouted sharply, as he watched her continue to survey the upheaval.

"Okay, Cynthia, what's happened?" Smith's voice was steady and calm and Cynthia visibly relaxed. *She must find the old man's words comforting. He's still a charmer*, Wilson observed, remembering the interrogation that led to his imprisonment. *Like a snake.*

After seeing her take a deep breath, he heard her answer in a lower, calmer voice, "My bedroom ... the guest room has been ransacked."

"Cynthia, are you injured or in danger?"

Wilson followed her gaze to the open doors to the small deck and beach beyond. A strong breeze off the ocean beat the drapes against the door frame. "No ... not hurt. It looks like whoever did this is gone," she replied slowly, but Buck noted that she couldn't mask some residual anxiety.

Good. I need you a little on edge, he thought, finally seeing a baseball bat leaning against the back wall of the closet. *That's right. Danny said her old man put bats in all the closets after my last visit. This will do nicely.* He wrapped his right hand around the bat's grip.

"Okay, Cynthia, take a deep breath, sit down and stay on the line," he heard Smith command. "Is Tanner Strong there?"

"No, he had to ... we had car trouble and he's gone to get it fixed," Buck heard her answer slowly.

Hmm, she didn't mention their accident on Highway 733, he noted as he watched her sit on the one corner of the mattress still propped up by the box springs and frame. She appeared to focus on the mattress and easy chair cushions that he'd split open.

"What were they looking for? The journals?" he heard her speculate. Though they stuck out of the top of her purse, she patted them, evidently to verify that they were still there.

Bingo! Everything in one nice package, he concluded and hefted the bat.

"Okay Cynthia, patrolmen are on their way. Is anyone else home?"

Batter up, he thought, placing a hand on the door. *Just a quick hit and grab.*

"Damn," Buck hissed and pulled his hand back when he saw Cynthia pull a gun from her purse. *Gotta time this just right.*

She stood, went to the bedroom door and looked down the stairs to the landing below. Pausing, apparently to listen, she replied, "No. Just me ... I came straight up to my ... the guest bedroom. I didn't really look to see if anyone else was here." She crossed the room and stepped out onto the balcony. "There were no other cars out front. No one is out back on the beach. I think Sylvia and Clint are still not back from looking at the boat. Should I look around?"

No, no, sweetheart, just sit tight and wait for the cops, Buck ordered silently and grinned, thankful he had beached the GASMAX fast boat up the beach out of sight from the house.

"No, sit tight and stay calm. The cavalry is on the way," Smith said firmly, making Buck's smile widen. "My men will search the place when they arrive. I'll stay on the line until they get there. This is your cell phone, right?"

Buck placed his hand on the door as Cynthia stared at the phone before pressing it to her ear. She walked back inside. *Good, still a little rattled.*

"Yes ... yes, it is," she finally replied, stopping with her back to the closet. "Battery level okay?"

Smith is well practiced at settling others' nerves, Buck thought. *Just stay put.*

"Over fifty percent." The sound of a tire skidding on gravel briefly joined the rhythm of drapes and wind from the balcony doors. "Hey, I hear a car. It may be your officers." She didn't move.

Good, stay put, Buck commanded wordlessly.

"Good. I'll stay on the line until you give me an officer's name," he heard Smith direct as Buck pushed hard on the door.

The sound of the closet's squeaky hinge startled Cynthia as the door behind her swung open and slammed into the wall. "What the ...?" she cried, turning.

Buck stepped into the room, his arm and the bat upraised. "Time to hang up, bitch!" he cried. His arm came down.

"No!" Cynthia screamed, raising one arm, deflecting the blow but the bat still connected with the back of her head. She staggered, reaching out toward the bed to steady herself, before collapsing onto the floor. Her gun discharged harmlessly into the floor.

Wilson stood over her briefly. *She's out cold*, he concluded quickly. Except for the rise and fall of her chest, she lay motionless at his feet, both eyes closed. He kicked at her side. Satisfied she was out, he grabbed her purse. "Game over, sweetheart," he declared savagely and raised the bat to administer a fatal blow.

Cynthia eyes fluttered open, and she rolled away from the bed. The bat connected with the floor. Having put his weight behind the death blow, Buck was thrown off balance. Seizing this advantage, Cynthia swung her right leg and delivered a fierce kick to his shaky legs. He fell on his left side between her and the bed, dropping the bat.

Cynthia, visibly still shaken, got to her feet. At the same time Buck saw the gun and scooped it up as he rose. As she raised her fists to continue hand-to-hand combat, she realized that he had her pistol. "Buck, what the ..." she gasped, breathing deeply as she raised her hands.

"Well, well isn't this like old times," Wilson said and grinned. "If we had more time, I'd ..."

"Police," a loud voice announced from downstairs.

When Wilson looked at the door, Cynthia's leg shot out and up, connecting with his left leg. Though not a bone crusher, it still had the desired effect. Wilson staggered, and his one shot went wide of its mark. He fell onto the bed, dropping the gun. Cynthia rose and lurched toward him. As he balled his right hand into a fist, his left closed on her purse. She unwittily stepped into the punch that caught her on the chin. She collapsed at his feet not far from her phone.

"Police," he heard again as he searched for the gun.

"Damn," he said, eyeing the doors to both the bedroom and the balcony.

He heard footsteps on the stairs. "Well, this is it anyway," he said, hefting the purse and looking again at Cynthia. She moaned, clenching her fists. Her breathing was labored, and her eyes narrowed to slits of dark blue. "And now to end you," he hissed savagely. Hearing footsteps outside the door, he kicked at Cynthia's head while eyeing the door. The jolt that traveled up his leg convinced him he had connected with and broken her skull. With a quick glance he confirmed Cynthia Jones' demise. She was motionless, her eyes were shut, and her labored breathing had ceased.

"Good riddance," he shouted, bolting onto the balcony, before he dropped to the beach below. He was well out to sea before a police officer stepped on the beach.

CHAPTER 15

Pressing Matters

Eye of the Storm Beach House

B<small>UCK'S PUNCH CONNECTED SQUARELY WITH</small> Cynthia's chin, stunning her. The blow dropped her to the floor. Her vision blurred.

She heard, "Police," and what sounded like Wilson searching for the gun. Her fuzzy image of Wilson was distinct enough to see his eyes dart from the bedroom door to the open balcony entrance. *Unless he gives up on the gun, they'll catch him,* she thought hopefully, hearing footsteps on the stairs and struggling to focus on her assailant.

"Damn," she heard Buck curse, and, despite distorted vision, she saw him stand and heft the purse. "Well, this is it anyway."

She moaned, clenching her fists. Her breathing was difficult and her heart raced. *Playing possum again won't work,* she concluded. *Got to get up ... move.* She fought to open her eyes.

"And now to end you," she heard Buck hiss fiercely.

She heard footsteps outside the door, and, through fading vision, she saw Buck kick at her head. With great effort she forced her head out of the way. Fighting a losing battle with impending unconsciousness, she realized that he missed her head and kicked the bedframe. As darkness swallowed her, she went limp, her eyes fully shut and, after a sudden deep breath, she exhaled what felt like her last.

"Good riddance," she heard Wilson declare, but the words were garbled. Heavy footsteps and silence followed. *He must be gone*, she concluded with her last conscious thought.

T<small>ANNER STRONG WALKED</small> down a flight of stairs. *Nice basement*, he thought. The room was softly lit with a low, timbered beamed ceiling and wood paneled walls. *Great man cave.* Wooden casks and a bar with three stools and a brass rail filled one side. A floor-to-ceiling and wall-to-wall case with glass doors occupied the side across from the stairs. It was nearly filled with wine bottles resting neck-down on racks. *Lots of bottles with lots of dust*, he observed silently. The final wall grabbed his attention and the others faded.

What the ... he wondered as he realized that in the center was a large, very large, wooden tub. A blonde woman, with her back to him and wearing a white toga that clung to pleasing curves, stepped up and down on a deep purple mass of grapes. Her hair was pulled up and arrayed atop her head revealing a lovely neck. *A wine press*, he concluded silently, *but who is that? She's stunning.* Fascinated, he watched her work her legs up and down with great enthusiasm. Crushing grapes caused her to slowly turn and face him. *It's Cynthia*, he realized with a delight he hadn't felt since the war and the crash. "Very beautiful, she's a stunning beauty indeed," he whistled softly.

Her face lit up with a smile that exploded into her eyes. "Tanner," she said, waving and pointing. "It's in the wine press."

"What's in the wine press?" he asked, his mouth forming the words, but there was no sound.

"Tanner," she said again with a slight frown, pointing at her feet. "Right below you in the wine press. Just use Beth Togarmah's OT numbers."

"Where? What?" his mouth moved but again without an audible syllable.

"TANNER," CYNTHIA SAID, shaking his shoulder. "Wake up."

"What?" he said sharply and sat up before falling back onto the chair next to her bed. "Wow, it was a dream."

"Must have been," she said and sat back on the edge of the bed. "Sorry. I'm still a little shaky on my feet."

"Hey, you should be in bed," Tanner said, stood and guided her to lie down. He felt her forehead. "No fever. Any headache?"

"No, just this lump." She rubbed the back of her head. "I must have been out for some time. I have a few questions."

"I bet you do. Do you remember what happened?" he asked, smiling and sitting on the edge of the bed.

"Unfortunately, I do ... in great detail. Another great memory to attach to this room and ... hey, where am I?"

"Sylvia's bedroom," he said. "She took her mom's. Yours is still a crime scene as well as all torn up"

Cynthia sat up and ran her hand over her nightgown. "How'd I get in this?"

"Sylvia and I ... I mean I carried you in here after the medics finished with you." He blushed. "No, I didn't ... I mean Sylvia got you into the gown."

"I see. Thanks," she smiled and placed a hand on top of his. "How long have I been out?"

Tanner looked at his watch. "About four hours. It's 9PM."

"I guess I missed the meetup with Danny." She sighed and laid back.

"Yeah. She called and so did Clint, but Sylvia talked with them and told them what happened."

"They catch Wilson?"

"No. He got clean away. They think he used a boat."

"Damn," she hissed. "So that's why you're standing guard?"

"Something like that," Tanner said and pointed to the night stand. "Also, Wilson only got your purse. The stuff from your skirt pockets is in the drawer there."

"Damn, he got the journals, but what was in my pockets is probably the most important anyway," she said and told him about the journals and the certificates.

"Wow." Tanner whistled, and after a pause told her, "Your gun's in there along with your phone. The Chief wanted me to make sure you kept them both and me close by at all times. Otherwise, I'm sure he'd have you in the hospital with a cop at the door. Since the medics ruled out a concussion, I convinced him that with me on guard you were just as well off here."

"Hmm." Cynthia looked at the ceiling. "What's in the wine press?"

"What?" Tanner asked in a concerned voice. "That knock on your head ..."

"No. You were talking in your sleep. That's what woke me up." She rolled up on an elbow to look at him. "You said it clear and with great urgency."

"It was just a crazy dream."

"Tell me."

He did except for his thoughts regarding her beauty.

"That's not so crazy," she said. "It may be a memory of sorts."

"Huh?"

"Yes, after I saw the words in those envelopes, I've been remembering things long forgotten. And the dreams about the assault may be related. Could be your subconscious has been jarred by the words you found in your envelope or just being here."

"It could be both. My message from J was just 'Beth Togarmah'," he mused and shrugged. "But come on, a wine press. Besides, I don't know any Beth Togarmah, let alone her overtime numbers?"

"As I said, it's not so crazy," she commented, pulling the covers back and swinging her legs over the side of the bed. Tanner helped her stand.

"You good?" he asked and took his hand away.

"Yes," she replied and looked at the door. "Please hand me that robe."

"Where are we going?" Tanner asked, helping her into the robe.

"I'm going to show you the wine press," she said, smiling at his surprise as she knotted the robe. She opened the nightstand drawer and placed the gun in one pocket and the items from her skirt in the other. "Wait a minute. I need to call Clint, Danny and that PI. I want to see them all tomorrow."

After the calls, Cynthia led the way downstairs. "Shouldn't we get Sylvia up?" he asked as they walked down the entry hallway.

Cynthia held her index finger to her lips. "No, let her sleep. We may find something she's better off not knowing," she replied finally after they made their way to the kitchen. She opened the door to the basement, flipped a light switch, looked at Tanner and smiled. "Tell me something, Tanner."

"What?" he replied with a puzzled grin.

"Do you know that you talk in your sleep?"

"What ...?"

"Do you really think I'm a stunning beauty?" She laughed warmly and motioned him to follow her down the steps.

Martin Family Cabin

CLINT MARTIN SLUMPED in his chair. He half listened to his Uncle Joel and Buck Wilson seated across the table, devoting the rest of his attention to the cabin's state of renovation. Since the electrical system was torn apart, the front room was lit by a few lanterns. In their yellow light he studied the fruits of his labor. *Got to get the new windows in before the snow flies*, he decided as Wilson slid two journals in front of Joel.

In recent days, his thoughts were increasingly captivated by the incomplete cabin project that his father bequeathed him. *It's a form of pure escape*, he thought, *from circumstances now evolving way out of control and more than any I'd anticipated.* These included the sense of growing menace to his life from his little sister and her boyfriend, who was crowing about killing Cynthia.

After the windows I'll ... No, focus on what Buck's saying! he chided himself when he heard Wilson with pride and a smile boast of "finishing Jones for good." His uncle's eyes narrowed as he flipped through the pages of both journals before slamming the last one shut and slapping it on the table. The loud noise captured his full attention and collapsed Wilson's arrogant smile. *My butt's in a sling if there's another screw up*, he admitted silently. *Why'd I ever let 'Uncle' Joel drag me into all this? I'm not a murderer.*

"You finished her, eh?" Joel asked sharply and leaned forward. "How'd you know?"

Clint repressed a smile as Wilson squirmed in his chair. *Just like Dad, Uncle knows how to crush confidence with a word or two.*

"Yeah, I did," Wilson answered with waning assurance. "I ... I saw her take her last breath and her eyes went blank. You know, like they do."

I do believe Uncle does know how a murder victim's eyes look, Clint concluded, arching his eyebrows when his uncle's angry facial expression confirmed Buck's assumption. *Damn, he looked just like Danny did at the trial when I testified and ... and the other day when she showed me that guitar case.*

"Feel for a pulse?" Joel asked in a flat voice.

Buck shook his head and looked away momentarily as if searching his memory. "No time," he said finally. "I had to get out there with the cops and all. Besides, that jolt up my leg when I kicked her meant I broke her damn thick skull open."

Joel nodded, picked up a Tannerson journal and held it in front of Wilson. "This is good," he said. "This is a missing journal. Likewise, the other one is valuable ..."

"But?" Buck ventured.

"But these journals didn't come out of the envelopes she got from Belmont and Smith, and there's likely more that my dear brother would have left behind. There's another journal that remains unaccounted for. She got these at the bank and who knows what else."

"It was all that was in her purse," Buck protested. "There wasn't ..."

"Did you search her?" Joel pressed sharply, raising his voice.

Easy does it, Bucko, Clint cautioned silently, seeing his uncle's face flush a red he hadn't seen since that night Joel and his father had pressed him to testify against Danny.

"No ... I ... like I said there was no time," Wilson shrugged and looked at Clint who frowned. "What? What's going on?"

"Not only is this not all of it," Joel said, smacking the journal again on the table, "but Cynthia is still very much alive and kicking. She's back at the beach house resting."

"That's not possible," Wilson countered with some certainty. "She should be at least in a hospital if not in a morgue."

"Well, if so, it must have been her ghost who called him," he said, pointing at Clint, "and your girlfriend." Joel waved his hand when he referred to Danny who was absent from their meeting without any explanation.

"Really?"

"Really," Joel replied, eyeing Wilson as a cat might do when sizing up a mouse for the kill. I was with Clint when she called, and Danny called me right after she got off the phone with her."

Wilson slumped in his chair and shook his head. "More lives than a cat," he whispered.

"Seems they both have a meeting set with a ghost tomorrow," Joel said with a mixture of sarcasm, frustration, and a dash of disappointment. "You and Danny have had your shot without success, so Clint's up again."

Clint straightened in his chair, setting his face with a determined grin to project a calm and confidence he really did not possess. *I'm not a murderer, but I gotta admit I like the ingenuity of Joel's plan. Even Dad would have been proud of it, even if he'd hate the outcome.*

"We've got to assume she has the birth and death certificates, the missing journal and possibly the letters. Also, Strong now no doubt knows what she knows," he said, looking at Clint. "So, if you fail, we'll have to go through with the next progression of the backup plan, and you don't want that."

Clint nodded and said, "I won't, and I don't. The meet is set for early tomorrow morning at the quarry. I'll take care of both of them." He looked about the cabin. "I'm not keen on giving this up if we have to go to the next progression."

Joel shook his head slowly. "Neither am I, son, but, if Cynthia and Strong are alive tomorrow evening, we have no choice, understand?"

Clint nodded and said, "Yes."

"You, Buck?"

"Yeah, I get it," Wilson replied. "What do I do while Clint's at bat? I at least got things set up in the study like you wanted."

"That you did, Buck. Clint, you have the number in your phone?"

"Yes, sir. It's all set."

"Good," Joel said. "Buck, while Clint takes his swing, you get that package we discussed and lay low until I call you if it's needed."

"What about Danny?" Clint asked suddenly interested in where she'd be the next day.

"Danny has already been briefed," Joel replied, pulling the journals in front of him. "All depends on you, boy. She'll be ready either way."

Eye of the Storm Beach House Basement

CYNTHIA FLIPPED A light switch at the bottom of the basement stairs. Light flooded the room. *This is incredible,* Tanner thought and walked to the long table in the center. After slowly considering each wall, he said, "This is it."

"What is?" she asked, joining him.

"The wine press room from my dream. The bar, the oak casks, and the racks with dusty wine bottles." He pointed at the bar, casks, and bottles. "They're exactly like my dream."

"What about the wine press?" she asked, pointing at the wall across from the bar.

That's different, he thought with a disappointment that surprised him. *No scantily clad Cynthia here.* Instead, the wall was dominated by a near-ceiling high and cylindrical shaped wooden cask fronted by three, broad steps leading to its hinged door. Half of the large cask was sunk into the wall. It was flanked on one side by two deep sinks with a green rubber hose coiled beneath them and on the other side by two tubs on wheels. One tub was positioned under a spout protruding from the press at the height of the middle step.

"No, in my dream there was a wood tub shaped like half of one of those casks," he said pointing at the three casks alongside the bar. "And you aren't ... what is this anyway?"

"It's the wine press," Cynthia said and smiled as she led him to its door. After climbing the steps, she pushed a green button on the panel next to the wine press' access door, and it swung open. She threw a switch next to door and soft yellow light flooded the interior.

"I'll give you the tour," Cynthia said as he stepped up and looked in. "The interior is a ceramic tile-lined cylinder about four feet across and eight feet high. That shiny metal piston spanning the top engages those guide slots embedded in the wall with a tongue-in-groove arrangement on either side of the piston head. This permits it to travel to the bottom about level with the middle step. The large center drain dumps through the exterior spout."

"Not the first time you've given this tour, is it?"

"No, it's not. Each tile is four-by-four inches. See how flush and tightly grouted they are? J did that all himself."

"Nicely done. What about the column of tiles lettered 'A' through 'Z' from bottom to top and the 'M' row of tiles numbered '1' to '40'? Did he do that?"

"Sure did. He was quite the craftsman."

"This is a quite a bit more modern than what was in my dream," he said finally.

He looked at her when she laughed. "On top is the motor and gear assembly Uncle J designed to replace the hand crank arrangement of the original."

"Original?" Tanner asked, stepping back and studying the button panel on the door frame and the alpha-numeric keypad mounted next to it.

"Yes. This was originally a late nineteenth century French wine press," she replied with pride in her voice. "When I was a teen, Uncle J got on this wine kick. He imported this antique press from France and, like most things, the engineer in him demanded he make it modern and better. Likewise, that's when he finished the basement, dragging all of us kids into the project. Sylvia and I hated it. Danny was bored and snuck off whenever she could."

"Clint probably loved it, right?" he asked, glancing away from the alphanumeric keys.

"Yes," she said after a pause. "What ... how'd you know that?"

"Just like the dream," he answered, pulling from his pocket the envelope he had received and handed it to her. "Ever since I saw what was in here, I just know things I didn't before. Besides, Clint impresses me as the type craving daddy's attention and affirmation but not getting it."

"Well, Tanner Strong, I ..." Cynthia started, smiling broadly.

He laughed, cutting her off. "Yeah, surprises me, too, that I recognized that, let alone can say it out loud. Hey, do those letters and numbers on the tiles have anything to do with this keypad?"

"Yes, they do," she said while pulling the single sheet from his envelope. "Uncle installed pressure sensors in each tile. He was a nut about figuring out how to best crush grapes, spent hours on it. Letter-number combinations allowed him to monitor pressure. It actually helped him make some decent wine after some seasons of experimentation, and ..."

"And what?" he asked when she suddenly went silent.

"As you said, your message 'Beth Togarmah' just like in your dream," she commented after unfolding the paper and reading. "You have a chance to find anything online about Beth?"

"Yes. While you were sleeping, I did some online searches until my phone died. I didn't find a person named 'Beth Togarmah,' but I found a place. It was some town in the ancient Middle East. It's mentioned in the Bible."

"Old or New Testament?"

"In Zek ... Ezekiel a couple of times," he said after a pause. "That's Old Testament, right?"

"Yes, if my mandatory Sunday school memory serves," Cynthia replied, pulling her phone from her robe pocket and tapped its face to open an online Bible. She motioned him to the table. After sitting, she opened a drawer at the end of the table and shoved a pad of paper and pen in front of him. "Here it is. Twice in the Ezekiel. Write."

Cynthia Jones in Sunday school? Tanner mused silently and nodded.

"Ezekiel 27, 14 and Ezekiel 38, 6," she said, but, in Marine Corps phonetics, he wrote "Echo 27, 14, Echo 38, 6." He twisted the pad and they both stared at what he'd written.

Tanner broke the silence, quoting her from his dream, ""Right below you in the wine press. Just use Beth Togarmah OT numbers." That's what you said in my dream. These are the Beth Togarmah OT- Old Testament - numbers!"

"You're right," Cynthia agreed with excitement that visibly faded in an instant.

"But?"

"But how do we use them in the wine press?"

"That's it, 'in the wine press,'" he said pointing at the open door and standing. "Inside you said J installed pressure sensors in each tile, and obviously the letters and number define the sensor grid. I'm guessing that if we go in and press tiles 27, 14, 38 and 6 in the E row, we'll find out what J wanted us to find 'in the wine press'."

"It may be dangerous," she cautioned, placing a hand on his arm. "We'll have to power up the press so the sensors will work. Also, it will take both of us if the four tiles have to be pressed at the same time."

"Yeah, you're probably right," he agreed and sat down. "This looks like a dangerous setup for a house full of kids. Didn't J install some safety device that we can use?"

"Yes and no," Cynthia said quietly. "Uncle took a lot of pride and delight in making systems safe. Just like the safety interlocks and such at the GASMAX plant, J made it near impossible to get crushed, but not impossible."

"How so?"

"Well, first you'd have to go upstairs and pull the safety pin out of the drive shaft. It's behind a panel in the living room. Then you'd have to enter the operational code in the panel to power up the press and its controls. Also, the piston won't lower unless the door is shut. Then the piston lowers, crushes the grapes and, when a couple hundred pounds of pressure are sensed, it retracts and locks."

But no dead man device, Tanner wondered and nodded. "Clever. You guys ever go in there?"

Cynthia looked at him oddly. "More post-envelope knowledge? Anyway yes, but you needed a flashlight. The lights go out when you shut the door. Danny smoked pot in there. Clint looked at girly magazines."

"And the Princess and Lady Sylvia?" Tanner asked smiling.

Cynthia frowned and shook her head. "We would ... look, I can pull the pin and the code is Aunt Joan's birthday. Clint noddled it out one summer. We could leave the door open and rely on that one interlock."

"Though it goes against my grain as a pilot to rely on a single interlock, the Marine in me says, "I'm game"," Tanner said, standing and offering her his hand.

After returning from the living room, Cynthia joined him on the wine press steps. "The pin is pulled," she said and entered Joan's birthdate. The panel came to life and the backlight for the keyboard glowed green. The screen above the keypad announced, 'Power On.'

"Just to be safe, I'll go in alone and press the numbers in sequence. If that doesn't work, then we'll go in together."

Cynthia nodded, and Tanner touched her shoulder before entering the press. "Okay, read me the numbers," he directed after crouching to reach the E row and to see the line of numbers at the M row.

I've got a bad feeling about this, he thought, looking out the open door briefly. He saw fear or concern mixed with concentration on Cynthia's face. *She does too.*

He stooped and found the E row. "Ready," he said.

As they'd agreed, Cynthia read each number, pausing between each to allow him time to say back the number and find and press the appropriate tile. "Last number, six," he heard her say after they'd worked through the first three.

"Six," he echoed and traced his finger along the E row from the 38th to the 6th column. He pressed the tile at the same time that he realized he'd dropped to the D row. Damn!" he cursed as the door to the wine press door slammed shut. The lights went out and he heard the sound of the motor atop the press start. Totally in the dark, he stood and felt along the wall to where the door was and pushed. It didn't move.

He heard Cynthia's faint cry, as well as the sound of her yanking and pounding the door. He pushed it with more force and finally threw his shoulder into it without success. The motor noise increased, and the piston could be heard moving. He held his hands over his head and soon felt the piston head. Though he pressed with all his strength, the interior volume continued to shrink unabated. He kneeled, keeping his hands pressed against the piston head. "Well, at least I didn't crash and burn this time," he said and thought of Cynthia. *Just real sorry I'm leaving you alone*, he finished quietly to himself as he was forced to sit.

CHAPTER 16

Crushing Defeat

Eye of the Storm Basement

EVEN THOUGH IT MAKES SENSE, I've got a bad feeling about this, Cynthia thought as Tanner entered the wine press alone. *It sounds like he does too.*

"Ready," he said.

As agreed, she read the numbers distinctly, pausing between each to allow him the time to repeat it back and press the tile. "Last number, six," she said with relief, having worked through the first three without incident.

"Six," he repeated. She visualized him tracing his finger along the E row from the 38th to the 6th column. Her eyes went wide when he shouted, "Damn!" and the door slammed shut.

"No!" she screamed as the door locks engaged and the motor atop the press started. *He's in the dark*, she realized, pulling the door handle without effect. "Come on!" She yanked again and pounded the door with her fists. "Open!" The door locks creaked. *Tanner must be throwing his weight into the door*, she reasoned. It didn't move.

She smashed the open button without effect. The motor noise increased and she heard the piston moving. "No!" she yelled, visualizing Tanner being crushed from a standing position to kneeling, sitting and finally ... . "The breaker!" she shouted, recalling the breaker panel on the wall to the left of the press. She leapt off the steps and swung the panel door open. Before she could pull the breaker, the motor stopped. "Too late," she sobbed. *Tanner, you can't be gone*, she cried silently. As tears streaked her face, the motor started again, and from where she stood, she could see the piston rod gearing. The piston rose after completing its grizzly cycle.

The door had swung open by the time Cynthia had climbed the top step. Though the last thing she wanted to do was look at Tanner's crushed remains, she knew she had to. *Too many 'have-to's,'* she thought.

"Hey, how about a hand here," Tanner called out.

"Tanner!" Cynthia cried with relief and joy as she looked in.

As he held his prosthetic leg in one hand and extended the other to her, he smiled. "I told you it was Titanium." He chuckled as she pulled him upright and helped him out. "Glad I lost enough of my leg so that this contraption sensed it was done before I ran out of living space. If not, I'd ..."

"Tanner, shut up," Cynthia cried and pulled him into a long hug before looking him in the face. "Thank God you are alright. I don't know ..." What she didn't know was cut off when his lips met hers.

SYLVIA MARTIN, DRESSED in a nightgown and carrying a gun in one hand and the baseball bat from her mom's closet in the other, took the basement steps slowly. *What the ...*, she thought. Her pace quickened when she saw her cousin and Tanner Strong. A wine bottle rested on the table between them. A pile of letters and what looked like two of her father's journals lay just beyond two glasses from the bar, both half full. "What's this, a private party or can anyone join?" she asked, pocketing the gun and laying the bat aside before lifting the bottle. "One of Dad's better years."

"Oh ... Sylvia," Cynthia said and smiled, holding a hand to her chest. "You scared me."

"That contraption's motor woke me. From Mom's room it sounds like it's rattling the whole house," she stated flatly, pointing to the wine press. Her eyes went wide when she realized the door had been broken off. Before she remembered he was gone, she blurted, "Hey, Dad's going to ..."

"Syl, we can explain," Cynthia said.

"Mr. Strong, the fact that I could sneak up on my cousin doesn't reflect well on your bodyguard qualifications," Sylvia challenged.

Tanner raised his pistol from his lap and grinned briefly. "The safety was flipped off when I saw your feet on the upper steps." He lowered the weapon.

"Join us," Cynthia commanded, motioning to the seat at the head of the table. She looked across the table at Tanner, who nodded. "This stuff here will explain the door and a bunch of other things."

"Sounds like I need some of this," she said after reaching behind the bar, grabbing a glass and sitting next to Cynthia. "What's all this?"

"Letters, a lot of them, from Uncle Joel to your mom," Cynthia replied and picked up a journal. "This is one of Uncle J's personal journals, an old one, and the other is Niles Tannerson's Phase Four journal."

"Who?" Sylvia asked after taking a drink. Surprise and interest creased her face and stiffened her posture. "And, where'd you get these?"

"From that drawer behind a panel in back of the fuse box over there,"

Tanner answered, pointing in that direction. The panel running ceiling to floor, they'd left swung open. The drawer remained pulled out a half foot.

"I've never ... I didn't know that was there," Sylvia said.

"I don't think anyone except Uncle J knew it was there," Cynthia said. "That's why he hid this stuff there."

"How'd you find it?" Sylvia asked. "I take it the wine press is involved."

"Once we figured out how to get to it without getting killed ..." Tanner started.

"Syl, the short answer is that it doesn't matter how but what we found," Cynthia said, cutting him off.

"But what does it mean? What's the long answer?"

"It means we can tell you the long answer since you're probably the one living member of this family we can trust."

"Okay, Cuz, I've got the time," Sylvia said, pouring more wine and mentally adjusting her schedule for the new day. With the top of the bottle, she pointed at Tanner's near empty glass. "You good?"

Tanner held his hand over his glass and smiled. "No thanks. Don't want you questioning my merits as a bodyguard again. Cynthia, we should go back to what happened when Joel fired you. You start, and I'll fill in where needed."

Cynthia chuckled, realizing that being blunt and commanding was just part of Tanner's well-intentioned nature. "Sure. Syl, some of this you know, some you don't. Some is going to hurt or shock, but it explains a lot of what's been going on this week, as well as since the time we were kids."

An hour more into the new day, Cynthia and Tanner finished. Sylvia, after a few questions, sat back and was silent. After a moment, she sat up, placed her elbows on the table and looked at Cynthia and then Tanner over hands clasped under her chin. "Then Uncle Joel, Danny and Clint are all in on it, in other words, suspects?" she asked and faced her cousin. "And, you and I are ..."

"Still family. Only, the lineup's changed – I think," Cynthia finished, as she put a hand on Sylvia's forearm and squeezed it lightly. "I'm still sorting it all, especially the Joel and Joan and Grandpa Moses and Tannerson relationships."

Sylvia nodded. "Cyn, this changes everything. It explains ..."

"I know. I know, but right now, today and quickly, I need you to do me a big favor."

"What?"

After explaining the arrangements for and purposes of the meetings with Clint, Danny, and the private investigator later that day, Cynthia said, "I need you to go through every one of your dad's journals, appointment calendars and any other record you have of his from a month before his death and around the time of the assault and trial."

"Including the copy that he made of Tannerson's Phase Four journal?"

"Especially," Cynthia replied, nodding.

"What am I looking for?" she asked, already organizing the task in her mind, evaluating its impact on the new day's schedule, and figuring roughly how and where they'd factor in this new reality and its fallout for the Martin family and GASMAX Industries.

Cynthia wrote on the back of one of the envelopes and pushed it in front of Tanner. "That everything?"

"That'll do it," he said and placed it in front of J Martin's eldest child.

"I can do that," she said after reading the list.

Driftwood Cove Quarry

SHIELDING HIS EYES against the morning sun, Clint looked up the trail to the parking lot where he'd left his truck. He smiled. *Good. Got here before Princess C and Strong*, he thought. *Want everything all set for my guests.*

"More like my victims," he said and closed the breaker inside a metal box mounted next to a large display case. The hum of the motor of the open-air elevator, that took climbers to the quarry pit floor, broke the morning silence. He glanced at the map of the Quarry Forest in the display case beneath its framed glass. His eyes were immediately drawn to the 'You-Are-Here' text box, marking the rock quarry climbing wall that claimed Justice Martin's life. After unlocking the door of the elevator, he cycled the chain and latticed entry open and shut. "Good."

He glanced at his watch, checked his phone for messages and scanned the trail to the parking lot. He looked at the map and shook his head, frowned and rapped the glass covering the map.

Though Joel insists his ultimate Plan B will likely not be required, he made Danny and me study this map until we could draw it from memory. He could now easily visualize what the locals dubbed the "Village Hole in the Ground." This included the abandoned quarry's deep and large excavation as well as its buildings and equipment that lay north of the GASMAX plant. The dense Quarry Forest separated it from the plant's north parking lot and tank farm. Due east, on the other side of Highway 733, was the GASMAX tidal hydraulic electric plant and its deep draft jetty.

With an index finger Clint traced the Quarry Forest. He paused briefly along its west boundary defined by the north-to-south flowing Rock River and the B&O Central rail bed. The rail line paralleled the river from Sand Dollar to the north and to Central City in the south. He swept his finger to the right and tapped the quarry building and its parking lot where he'd parked and soon would his guests. He continued the trace east on the lot access road. Before it reached where the road ended at Highway 733, he drew his finger down the access road that branched south on the east side of the woods. A few miles farther south he reached a split in the road. A slight left turn led to the plant's loading dock. He followed the sharper right turn at the split that went west past the tank farm to the GASMAX plant's north parking lot. *If I fail today and, despite Buck's claims, this route will be a factor. So, I can't screw this up. I gotta do what's necessary.*

Clint stepped back and crossed his arms. He sighed and eyed the map. *Though I have significant issues with Papa J, he was one brilliant, foresighted SOB. It was his vision that convinced Grandpa and Joel to buy the quarry and surrounding forest.* The larger initial GASMAX purchase, including the plant site, was bounded by the highway on the east, the river on the west and the Old Bridge Road, running east-west, south of the plant. Clint chuckled when he noted the map labeled the boundary road with its official name, 'GASMAX Road.' *Just one more acknowledgement by village leaders of how much Driftwood's well-being is wrapped up with the fortunes of GASMAX Industries.* GASMAX paved the road and made other changes to afford access to the plant's southern parking lot as well as a private gravel road to the Martin family cabin. With an eye to the future family good fortunes, J got his father and brother to pay extra to have southern land cleared for a family cabin, although making sure to leave a surrounding wood.

Guess my well-being is also wrapped up in the fortunes of GASMAX Industries now, Clint thought, recalling his beloved cabin's renovation that he longed to focus on. *Just hope I get to go back to it.*

He turned, surveyed the thick forest and reflected on the campgrounds J constructed within. Since the equipment was already on site for the plant's site clearing and construction, J easily lobbied for additional funds to clear five campground sites in Quarry Forest. This included blazing the trails to connect the sites as well as to clear paths along the river and the southern quarry pit boundary. J patterned the clearings and connecting trails on a baseball diamond. Clearly labeled on the map, was the east site dubbed First Base, the north site Second, the west site Third, the center site Pitcher's Mound and the south site Homeplate. Trails connected all campgrounds and provided access to the paths along the river and the quarry pit's south rim.

The river pathway ran from a junction with the border trail near the quarry rock wall and paralleled the train tracks and river to the GASMAX plant's south parking lot. Shorter trails from Home Plate and First led to the GASMAX plant north parking lot. A path, wide enough for his truck, ran from the Second Base site to the quarry building's lot. Though today he'd parked in the lot, he usually parked at Second Base and packed in his camping equipment to one of the other sites. *I'm want to live in these woods forever, but if this morning doesn't go well,* he thought, *later today I'll be parking at Second Base and pitching camp in this forest for the last time.*

Clint, recalling its part in Joel's next, but hopefully unnecessary, progression of Plan B, tapped the glass over the Third Base campsite. Though it was the smallest cleared area, it sat upon a small island formed by the Rock River flowing south on the west side and the equally deep and fast flowing Quarry Branch River on the other. The branch split off from Rock River north of the island. It carved the island's east shore before rejoining the river. Five wooden bridges forded the branch river to connect the campsite to the trail system. One bridge was out for repair. Clint cringed when he recalled the part that bridge played in Joel's ultimate Plan B. *If it's necessary.*

"Hello, Clint."

Cynthia's greeting broke Clint's reverie. He looked up the trail. Cynthia and Tanner approached him, walking through patches of light and shadow. He smiled and waved. *Can't screw this up. Do what's necessary.*

THE MORNING SUN had not yet found the quarry pit floor when Cynthia, Clint and Tanner stepped off the quarry elevator. After sliding the lift cage's chain-link door shut, Clint directed them to a broad and well-marked path skirting the pit floor some seventy feet below the rim of the quarry. Breaking the early morning silence of what promised to be a sunny warm day, the pea-sized, gray-tan gravel crunched beneath their feet. For a moment, caught up in the freshness of the new day, Clint forgot the purpose of this meeting. *Focus, boy*, he chided himself.

"It's about fifty yards this way to the rock-climbing wall," he announced, assessing Cynthia and Tanner silently. She wore tan slacks and a practical white shirt. Tanner was decked out in a flannel plaid shirt and jeans not too unlike what he wore. *They look no worse for the wear from Buck's bungled attempts on their lives. In fact, they look like they'd stepped out of the pages of one of those sporting goods catalogs. Nice hiking shoes. Wonder if they've been into Mom's and Dad's closet?*

"Clint, I knew J was working with the county to turn this into a park, but I didn't know they were this far along," she said, pointing at the railing and lights defining the walking path. "The path and elevator look new."

"Yeah, they are. Once all the permitting and liability issues were resolved, we poured a lot of time, money, and effort into this place. Most of it was devoted to making it safe for tourists and climbers," Clint replied with an edge of sadness, but also pride in his voice. "The hiking trails crisscrossing the quarry forest to and from and along the railroad tracks, the river, and the parking lots are all complete."

"Last I heard, J said something about the property still needing to be deeded over to the county parks and rec," Tanner injected. "This is from a brief conversation we had the last time I drove for him. He and Joel were going for lunch."

"Uh ... yes, the deed's been transferred," Clint said. "What did they talk about?"

"Don't know. They put the glass panel up, but the discussion looked heated."

Boy, I'd loved to have been a fly on the rear window, Clint thought, as he stopped and pointed up the vertical rock wall and then to the ground. The top edge towered seven stories over their heads. The nearly vertical wall of rock was etched in morning sunlight that would soon chase away the shadows about them. "This is the place. Here ... right here they found his body."

Cynthia knelt down and ran her hand through the loose gravel. Some traces of white chalk or paint could still be seen. "What was the cause of death?" she asked.

Clint crouched beside her and pointed above his shoulder. "He was about fifty feet up. He'd set a spike and tied off. From what I could surmise, the rope failed when he put his weight on it. The spike is still up there."

"What killed him, the fall?'

"No. He'd have survived the fall if he hadn't hit his head on the ammo box."

"Ammo box?"

"It was what he used to carry the marker spikes. It was right next to his backpack."

"Odd," Cynthia said, standing and wiping the dust from her hands. "He was an experienced climber and always had first-rate gear. And I thought his latest kick was free climbing. Why the harness and all anyway?"

"Dad laid out this entire wall to ensure the most challenging yet safest climbing possible," Clint replied, pointing back towards the elevator. "The north side of the quarry was the working side. This is the berm side. It has the steepest and most structurally sound slope, not quite vertical but close enough to provide something for beginners, as well as more advanced climbers, whether doing top rope, lead, or free solo."

Tanner nodded. "Looks like it, but pretty much bouldering, huh?"

"Yeah. Once we open, no real high free solo will be permitted. Just low height climbing to limit liability. Also, every five yards he made an assent and insured that there were adequate hand and footholds. If not, he'd set a spike and I'd install the man-made holds later."

"Who found the body?" his cousin asked.

"I did," Clint answered sadly.

"You find anything unusual?" Cynthia put a hand on his shoulder.

"What ... No," Clint lied. *Why'd she ask that?* he wondered.

"Nothing in his pockets or in the pack?"

"Well, the usual. Keys, cash and the typical pocket stuff. The pack just had some camping and climbing gear and a chalk bag," Clint replied and briefly grinned. "No suicide note, if that's what you're asking."

"Something like that."

"Dropping fifty feet and aiming to hit a metal box with your head doesn't sound like the way an engineer would kill himself."

"Yeah, I guess it doesn't." Cynthia sighed and pointed up. "What's at the top?"

Clint followed her extended arm. "Oh, there's a path like this one with a low railing. The rail can be used for rappelling."

"So, it is possible J completed the ascent, and he ..." Cynthia said.

"Fell?" Clint ventured.

"Or was pushed or was hit with something and fell."

"But what about the rope and harness?"

"The killer, or maybe killers, put it on him and attached the rope after," she countered.

"But I found them on him," Clint protested. "Unless you're suggesting I ..."

"Oh no, Clint, I don't suspect you of that!" Cynthia replied quickly, squeezing his shoulder.

"Yes. Of course not," Clint said sheepishly and studied his cousin's face. *At least not now you don't suspect me. God, Joel is right - she is too close to the truth to stay alive. This isn't going to be easy but hearing this makes it easier.*

"So, you figure that spike was a marker he set?" Tanner asked, studying the wall now fully lit by morning sun.

"Hmm, yeah," Clint answered, still wondering what else Cynthia knew.

"You or someone else checked it out?"

"For what, a suicide note?" Clint forced a brief smile. "But, yes. With Chief Smith's permission, and with one of his officers, I climbed up and looked. Just a marker spike and nothing else was there. Same as the ones found in the ammo box."

"Mind if I look?" Tanner asked as he set his left foot and both hands on the wall.

"What the ...?" Clint uttered when Tanner had already ascended above his head.

Cynthia placed a hand to her mouth. "Mr. Strong, it's just one surprise after another with you," she said as Tanner, with few pauses, quickly navigated hand and foot holds to the spike. After a stop to examine the spike, he completed the free climb to the top. "Clint, let's join him, but use the elevator."

They returned to it without speaking. After Clint pulled the elevator door shut and pressed the up button, Cynthia broke the silence. "You're involved in this up to your neck, aren't you?"

"What makes you say that?" he replied, unable to keep the surprise out of his voice. "I haven't done ... up to my neck in what?"

"All this, the quarry-to-park conversion as well as the cabin renovation. It's your thing, your passion. Just like J, you love to fix and tinker. It's admirable."

"Oh, I thought you meant something else," he said with a relaxed smile. "Yeah, I do love this. Kind of sorry Dad won't be around to see it completed. He had big plans. As you'll see, the quarry building renovation includes space for the county Parks and Rec offices and the village historical society, including room for a museum."

"Impressive," Cynthia said. "It's obvious to me that J didn't create the GASMAX Special Projects Assistant position for nepotism make-work."

"A rare Princess C compli...," Clint started. "No. I'm such a jerk at times. Thank you, Cynthia, for saying that."

Cynthia smiled and squeezed her cousin's shoulder. "But what did you mean when you said, 'I haven't done' – haven't done what?"

"That? Oh, after all that's gone on this week and your surprising number of near-death experiences, I'm more than a little jumpy and kind of defensive."

"Why so?"

"With Danny around and Buck Wilson on the loose after another assault in the same EOS room, and considering that my testimony at their trials helped to put them behind bars, I feel responsible in some way ... guilty and threatened. Doesn't make sense, does it?" he said looking at his shoes. "I thought you were accusing me of something."

"Hey, look at me," Cynthia said, nudging him to face her and gripping his shoulders briefly. "Don't forget that it was the charges J brought as well as my testimony. You've done nothing wrong. In fact, I'm impressed that you and Danny appear to have patched things up. When I got here, I thought you two only had called an uneasy truce for Aunt Joan's benefit. Now it seems as if you two are thick as thieves like you were when we were kids."

Thick as thieves,' you don't know how right you are, he thought as the elevator stopped and he slid the door open. He saw Tanner waiting up the path from the elevator landing. "Look, Wilson is still out there, and maybe he wants to settle scores with Dad, you and me. He got Dad, keeps missing you and he just hasn't gotten to me yet. In any case, Cuz, I appreciate what you said about Danny and me. It means a lot," he stated before he turned.

"Clint, wait. Before we join Tanner may I ask a favor, just between you and me?"

"Sure, anything," he replied instantly. *Won't matter,* he concluded to himself, thinking about what awaited her and Tanner in the quarry building.

"I need this as soon as you can get it," she said, handing him a piece of folded paper.

Clint flipped it open and nodded. "Sure. I'll have to make a call, but I can have it for you tonight."

Quarry Building

"CLINT THIS IS amazing," Cynthia said after the three toured the offices and museum space, all under construction. "When we were kids, I remember coming out here and throwing rocks to see how many windows we could break. But it was a metal building then. What did you all do, tear it down and put up a new one?"

Clint put his hand on one of two knobs of the double door at the rear of the museum space. "No. The original structure had good bones, steel-framed. We stripped it to the foundation and frame, and we rebuilt with new HVAC, plumbing, and electrical. We hope the brick and slate siding reflects the heritage and history of a rock quarry. We also did this," he said, pulling one door open and then the other. He motioned them through. "This is what's really cool."

"What the ..." Cynthia uttered, taking in the contents of a large open room easily over fifty yards long and thirty or so wide. Its peaked ceiling with exposed steel A-frames rose another ten feet above the two-story high walls. "Clint, this is incredible."

"Cool," Tanner exclaimed, stepping forward to get a better look at the rust-red box-like machine that dominated the center of the room. It sat upon a raised platform, a dozen feet wide and twenty feet long. The platform was supported by steel I-beams bolted and welded together to lift it fifteen feet above the smooth concrete floor. Metal steps on each side allowed access to the platform that held a large electric motor connected to the machine by a belt and pulley arrangement.

"This is one of the horizontal shaft impactors. It used to be out in the quarry pit," Clint stated, pleased by Cynthia's and Tanner's reaction. He walked toward the machine. "It's a rock crusher. It makes little ones out of big ones."

"I see," Cynthia said, pointing to a six-foot-wide conveyer belt running from floor level at one end of the room. "Large rocks put on that end and conveyed to ... what's that, the crusher input?"

Clint chuckled. "Close. It's called the liner plate assembly. In the quarry, a diesel mining shovel would fill one of those big-wheel haul trucks with large rocks blasted out of the north wall. The truck would dump the rocks onto a conveyer much longer and steeper than our display version."

"And after it crushed the rock, the small ones would drop onto a lower belt like that one, huh?" Tanner asked, pointing at the conveyer belt at the opposite end of the room. It was similar to the upper one, but it led to a wheeled, metal ore cart that sat on a narrow-gauge rail track that ran under an articulated metal door in the wall.

"Yes, but in the quarry the belt would run upwards and dump into a pile. Haul trucks would be loaded and, depending upon the end use, take their loads for further transport to make things like asphalt, concrete or decorative landscape rock."

"What happened to the haul trucks and the shovels," Cynthia asked.

"Dad sold all the trucks and shovels, but he saved one of each for static displays. They're in Vermont being refurbished. We should have them back next month. We're going to put them outside."

"But the crusher will be dynamic," Tanner asked, grinning. "I'd love to see that."

"Tanner, you impressed me as a gadget junky. So, you're in luck. Dad got this thing operational just before ... Well, I have some big rocks set on the belt to show you two how it works. Come," Clint commanded with a smile and obvious excitement. He led them to a set of metal stairs on wheels.

After giving them hard hats and donning one himself, he grabbed safety glasses, ear plugs and gauze mouth and nose masks from a bin. Then Clint led them up the stairs to a platform edged with metal stanchions and a double course of safety chain. "Eventually we'll have a permanent observation platform with Plexiglas, sound proofing and exhaust fans. So, all this won't be necessary," he said, gesturing to the glasses, plugs and masks. "Go ahead and put on the glasses and masks and put in the ear plugs. Sorry about the masks and the way they smell. Dad thought scented was the way to go. Give me thumbs up when I signal from below."

"Below? Where are you going?" Cynthia asked.

"Oh, I have to operate the crusher from over there," he replied, pointing to a panel on the side of the crusher. "Also, while you watch, I'm going to step out and make a follow-up call for you."

She nodded, putting on the glasses and mask and opening the pack with the yellow earplugs.

Tanner donned his glasses and made ready his plugs. "What call is that?" he whispered in her ear, briefly pulling the mask away. "He's right, these masks stink."

"Not bad. Lilac kind of," she said and smiled after pulling the mask aside. "The call's related to one of the entries in ..." she started, but stopped when she saw Clint motion. "It's show time."

I hate this, Clint thought and hesitated with his finger over the start button. "But, we're Martins," he said. "We do what's necessary. 'So, bro, you gotta do what you gotta do'." He snorted after parroting Danny's words when he expressed his reluctance to be a party to murder. With more force than necessary, he pressed the button when he saw their thumbs up.

The rock crusher came to noisy life and both belts rolled. When he saw his cousin and then her bodyguard raise their hands and flail to steady themselves, he stepped quickly to the open door. *The chloroform in their masks is working just like Wilson said it would.* He paused at the door and looked back in time to see the duo collapse onto the conveyer belt. *Perfect, but I don't want to watch this,* he concluded, as the belt transported their motionless bodies to the crusher's gaping entry. He stepped out.

CHAPTER 17

A Cheating Heart

Quarry Building

BY THE TIME THEY ASCENDED the steps to the demonstration observation platform, Tanner had concluded that there was something off with Clint Martin. *He's really lapping up how impressed we are*, he thought. *He needs too much positive stroking.*

We're not getting the whole story, and he's building up to something that has nothing to do with his daddy's park project. Yep, when he's talking nuts and bolts, I believe him, Tanner concluded silently, *but anything else involving Papa J is suspect.*

When Clint jokingly explained that the horizontal shaft impactor was a rock crusher that makes little ones out of big ones, Tanner added to himself, *or dead people out of live ones.* And he wondered, *Where'd that come from? Just thinking more like a bodyguard than a tourist, I guess.*

Clint's obvious heightened nervous excitement as he directed them into place for the demonstration prompted Tanner to seek Cynthia's eyes to see if she shared his concern. *Nope. She looks like she's just as eager to see the demo as Clint is to show it. It must be Martin DNA or she has a better poker face than I do.*

His uneasiness increased when Clint donned a hardhat and handed them their safety equipment. *Overkill*, he thought, instinctively keeping Cynthia behind him as Clint led them up onto the observation platform. *Despite these stanchions and safety chains, this feels like a set up.*

Strong's suspicions heightened when Clint directed them to don their safety gear and he apologized for the masks' scent. Likewise, before Tanner could, Cynthia questioned Clint's need to leave the platform. *I don't trust this guy where I can't see him. Maybe it bugs her too.*

"Oh, I have to operate the crusher from that panel," Clint replied, pointing to a section mounted on the crusher's side. "Also, I'm going to step out and make a follow-up call for you."

Tanner donned his glasses and readied his plugs. "What call is that?" he whispered in Cynthia's ear, briefly pulling the mask away. "He's right, these masks stink." He put the mask back in place but left it loose.

"Not bad. Lilac kind of," she smiled and said after pulling her mask aside. "The call's related to one of the entries in ..." she started, but stopped when he saw Clint motion. "It's show time."

Tanner's qualms didn't diminish any when he noted that Clint hesitated after he'd quickly closed a breaker, checked gauges and had thrown switches. With his finger poised over what he assumed was the start button, Tanner noted that Clint's excited features, obvious even with the hat, glasses and mask, had vanished. *He's struggling with something.*

After they gave Clint the thumbs-up signal, he punched the button with what looked to Tanner like more force than necessary. Despite the earplugs Tanner heard the rock crusher come to noisy life. Both belts rolled, adding their chorus to the crusher's cacophony. When the first large rock dropped into the crusher, the noise again increased with jolting punctuation and dust filled the air. Despite the sickly lilac odor, Tanner was glad he had the mask and glasses.

He looked at Cynthia when he felt her hand grip his arm and lean into him. Her other hand reached for the safety chain. *Must be the bump on the head*, he thought with alarm. He placed an arm around her waist. Suddenly he felt dizzy and grabbed for a chain. His vision blurred but he could see Clint point to his phone as he stepped through the open doors.

Tanner missed the chain and fell, pulling Cynthia into the fall. As they plunged onto the conveyor belt, with his last conscious effort, he rolled and pulled her tight so he'd land on his back with her on top. With his free hand he also managed to pull away his mask and glasses. Pausing only to get his breath, he wrapped Cynthia in his arms and rolled off the belt. The fall to the floor knocked him out. Before the darkness deepened, he clawed her mask off.

THE DARKNESS VANISHED and Tanner opened his eyes. He realized that the rock crusher was silent as he was greeted by the concerned faces of Cynthia and her cousin. Kneeling next to him, Cynthia stroked his face. Clint stood behind her with what Tanner quickly concluded was a mixture of relief, worry and disappointment. "What happened?" he asked as he sat up.

"Easy does it," she said, placing hands on his chest and shoulder to steady him. "It was the masks. There was something in them. You ripped yours off when we fell. You must have pulled mine off when you rolled us off the belt before we would've dropped into the crusher."

"So, just like the plane, huh," Tanner said getting to his feet. "But I saved your butt this time."

"Yes, you did," she replied and grinned before kissing him. "I found Clint unconscious in the museum, and we just now stopped the crusher."

Clint nodded.

He looks more worried than relieved about being alive, Tanner thought, locking eyes with the younger man before Clint quickly looked away. *There's someone or something he's more afraid of than death.*

Highway 733

"SO, SHE BOUGHT it?" Joel's question sounded clearly in Clint's earbuds, ending the long pause following the young man's recitation of the quarry building events.

"Completely," Clint replied, following Cynthia's and Tanner's truck south on the highway. "She believes that Wilson is the bad guy. He's out to get me as well as her,"

"Excellent, nephew," Joel sighed. "We've regrettably advanced to the next progression of the backup plan, but her thinking is properly aligned. So, now, Buck, you're up."

"Where are they?" Wilson's question cut short Clint's pleasure in hearing rare praise from Joel Martin. It also minimized his time to commiserate over the personally negative ramifications of the 'next progression.'

"They just turned off for the tavern," he answered tersely. "I'm on my way to the cabin. You all set, Wilson?"

"Yeah, I'm walking out on the beach now. The boat's in the cove. She'll have it beached in a minute."

"The PI there?" Joel injected.

"As best as I can tell. I had to beat feet to the tunnel so I could put this hokey disguise on in time."

"No chance she'll recognize you? The local cops are looking for you."

"Don't sweat it. I boosted the car, the tunnel is set and, at this distance, we'll both look the part," Buck replied with confidence, and after a pause added, "The red wig is a nice touch, kinda hot."

"Glad you approve," Joel said. "Just keep your focus on the task at hand."

"You sure Danny will play her part okay?" Clint ventured. "We had an argument last night. Her blood was up when I left, and she's still pissed about the missed shot at the bank."

"Let me worry about that, Clint," Joel chided. "I'll be seeing her later. She'll be focused. You just make sure you both are. This ends tonight, one way or another. Be on time this evening and as planned, clear?"

"No sweat," Buck replied with the swagger that Clint envied and irritated him greatly. "I got the boat loaded. It just needs to be topped off. With luck in the tunnel, there'll be less to do."

"Yes, sir," Clint said, forcing a confidence he didn't feel. "I pitched camp last night. I'm on my way to the cabin now to get what she wants. You still sure it's a good idea for her to get Grandpa's stuff?"

"As I said, Clint, let me worry about that," Joel shot back. "It won't matter after tonight anyway."

"Chances are it won't matter as much after this morning, boss," Buck bragged. "So, maybe we can skip all the gas plant stuff and just get out of Dodge."

"It's too late," Joel said. "There are more loose ends than we can eliminate with just Jones' death to maintain the status quo. Strong and most likely Simpson now know too much, and we have no idea who they've talked to. Simpson's tight with Chief Smith."

"Let's not forget Sylvia," Clint commented. "What about her?"

"She's harmless, Clint." Joel sighed. "Just like her dad, she's smart, disciplined and consistent. However, unlike J, she's not selfish enough, and, despite her keen affinity for word, math and logic puzzles, she lacks the imagination to quickly put these pieces together. By the time she does, if she ever does, we'll be well safe."

"Yes sir. That sounds about right. She's a real straight arrow," Clint said after a pause. "The Princess was always the real brains of the duo, but it's good to know there's an option."

"If that assessment changes, Clint, I'll let you know and you'll know what to do, right?"

"I do."

"Gentlemen, given our assassination track record to date, it proves conclusively that we needed the backup plan's next progression. Now get to work."

The call ended as Clint parked in front of the cabin. Looking over his shoulder at what was in the truck bed, he thought, *I need just a few extra things for the likely fireworks in the moonlight tonight to cancel the family sin debt. For sure they'll be more and very different pyrotechnics than Justice or Moses Martin would have imagined.*

Wilkes Tavern Parking Lot

"SO, YOU DON'T buy it?" Tanner asked, shifting into park and scanning the tavern's gravel parking lot. A blue, sun-worn sedan with out-of-state plates was the only other vehicle other than their own.

"Not completely," Cynthia said, sitting back and unfastening her seat belt. "It's not impossible that Wilson killed Uncle J and is now out to get Clint and me. But he's ..."

"... not smart enough," he finished, "at least not without some help and direction."

"Exactly. So, we have to keep pulling the threads until we find out who is and what's behind all this. There are lots of pieces like our letters from J and what I found in the safe deposit box that somehow makes better sense of what's going on."

"Like somebody keeps trying to kill you and me?" Tanner smiled grimly, unfastened his seatbelt and opened the door.

"Or somebodies," she added as he got out and she moved behind the wheel.

"Yeah, or somebodies. Then there are those dreams," Strong said, before shoving the door shut.

Cynthia rolled down the window and looked at her watch. "Julie Simpson has some information she gathered at my request. She said she'd be around the steps where we almost went flying off the cliff. I wish I could speak with her, but Sylvia said she found something at the house that I need to see right away. And, I have to meet up with Danny in a few hours."

"Go," he commanded with a smile quickly eclipsed by concern. "23-4."

"What?"

"Just something that a guy I flew with used to say before we went up," Tanner laughed but then frowned at the memory. "From the Bible, Psalm 23, verse 4, though I walk through the valley of death I will fear no evil for you are with me. '23-4' was kind of shorthand between us with a double meaning."

"Something bad happened to him, didn't it?"

"Yes," Strong answered sadly after a pause. He slapped the door. "Get going, I'll catch up later."

Cliff Overlooking Smugglers Cove

DESPITE THE WIND'S swirling and whistling amplified by the Smuggler Cove's rock walls, Julie Simpson heard Tanner before he found her. She was hunkered down prone between two boulders which sat atop the bluff overlooking the cove's beach. After a brief glance away from her binoculars and a silent hello, she motioned for him to join her. Once he had settled next to her, she offered him the binoculars. The surveillance point permitted an unobstructed view of the entire stretch of sand and water below.

"You're a trusting soul for a PI," he said.

"Mr. Strong, you look just like the photo that Cynthia attached to the text she sent saying you'd be filling in," she said with a tight smile. "Besides," she added, pulling her hand from beneath a floppy hat resting next to her shoulder. Her fingers gripped a small caliber pistol.

"I see," he said. "Can't say I'm surprised by your and Cynthia's thoroughness."

"She does impress," she said, realizing he was still sizing her up. Having followed his part in what the locals called 'The Perils of Cynthia,' she'd already concluded he lived up to Justice Martin's accolades. The late J Martin called her a week before he'd departed on his last solo hike. Martin made a point to tell her she could trust Strong with her life and why. "From what I've seen and what J Martin told me, you do too."

"He also said good things about you." Tanner chuckled. "Said I could trust you with my life and told me why. High praise. He didn't say that about many people. So, I'm impressed and confident in who, we hope, is our newest ally in the war for survival being waged in the wake of J's death. I understand you have something for me."

"Just like a Marine, straight to the point. I like that," Julie said, waving the pistol toward the beach below. "But I need to finish up here."

"Who are you surveilling?" he asked, pressing the binoculars to his eyes. "The couple on the beach?"

"Yes. She arrived in the beached outboard. He's a husband suspected of cheating. Got a call from his frantic wife last night right after Cynthia called."

He nodded. "They're obviously more than friends."

She put a camera with a long lens to her eye and brought the couple into focus. The pair, engaged in an animated conversation, punctuated with touching, caressing and kissing, filled the magnified view. He was attired in a denim shirt and jeans, a ball cap pulled down over long hair and dark glasses. She was casually dressed in shorts and a halter top that were appropriate for the sunny summer day now in full swing. Most of her face was hidden by large sunglasses and a shadow cast by a hat, similar to Julie's, and pressed down over long red hair.

"Who are they?"

"Sorry, but client-PI confidentiality and all," she said, working the shutter. "I know the guy's name, but I don't know the girlfriend. Maybe the photos will help. There's a unique tat on her shoulder."

Tanner lowered the binoculars. "The guy's height and build are similar to Buck Wilson's, but the redhead doesn't look like any of the other characters in our drama. Then again, I may be seeing Buck Wilson where he isn't."

"Yeah, he does look a little like that creep, but I handle two or three of these cheating heart cases each summer." Julie chuckled. "Even though 'The Perils of Cynthia' are the latest grist for the Driftwood rumor and gossip mill, our village's many annual pedestrian performances of domestic summer intrigues go on, and, fortunately for me, pay the bills."

"I guess you're right." Tanner laughed. "How'd you know he'd be here, from the wife?"

"Yep. The sedan in the parking lot matches the description she gave," Julie replied, pressing the shutter button as the couple again kissed and embraced. "That'll be a good one for the lawyer."

"Looks like they're leaving," he said, watching the woman walk to the water, get in the boat and motor off.

"That's odd."

"What?" he asked, shifting back to the man walking toward the entrance to the tunnel that Cynthia had described.

"Why's he going that way?" she wondered as he entered the tunnel. "It's the long way. Come on. We'll follow him. I want a closer look."

He handed the binoculars back to Simpson as they stood. "Why? I thought the photos were all you needed."

"I've been watching the Martin family for years, as a cop and more recently as a PI," she answered as she gathered her bag and surveillance gear. "Come on. This may be an act in your drama after all."

"Shouldn't we call the chief?" he asked as they walked.

"If it is Wilson," she replied. "Here. Before I forget." She handed him an envelope from her bag. "Cynthia hired me to do some records inquiries. These are the results. Most I got online. However, I had to call in a favor and drive to Sand Dollar early this morning to get the rest."

Okay, I'll get it to her," he said, shoving the envelope in his trousers pocket as they descended the steps to the beach. "Is there anything noteworthy or urgent in here?"

"Tanner, I'm a very good detective when I have enough information," she replied. "Though I can't see it, what the envelope contains may have something to do with J Martin's alleged accidental death and his wife's supposed suicide. My impression is that Cynthia, and maybe you now, are the only ones with all the pieces to the puzzling events of the last few days."

"You're right," Tanner agreed. "I just hope that Cynthia and I stay alive long enough to solve the puzzle."

"True," she agreed and added, "I hope so, too."

"You said you've been watching the Martins recently. For whom?"

"Can't say. Over here," she replied, pointing to a dark opening that would be missed if someone didn't know it was there.

"Or won't say for confidentiality reasons and your bills?"

Julie stopped and looked at Tanner. "Very astute, Mr. Strong, but fact is I don't know who. I'm not proud of this, but, yeah, about a month or so ago I got an envelope in the mail containing a stack of cash and a note engaging my services to loosely surveil the Martin clan and make periodic reports."

"No idea who sent it? How do you make the reports?"

"No idea. The note included an address with a PO box in Central City and an email address composed of random numbers and characters," Julie said thoughtfully. "With a little PI slash former cop sleuthing and my contacts, I could figure out who, but I don't want to kill the goose that lays the golden egg."

"How's that?"

"Every report, even if there's nothing noteworthy, was followed by another envelope with a generous payment for my time and expenses," Julie smiled. "Come on before the cheating heart gets away."

"Wait," Tanner said, grabbing her shoulder. "You see or hear anything that we should know? My experience is that those closest to the action can miss something important."

"Yeah, that's true. I can see why Cynthia trusts you and why J kept you around," Julie said, gently pushing Tanner's hand away. "I guess general impressions don't violate my anonymous client's confidentiality. Ever since Cynthia's assault and the subsequent trial, the Martin family has been a pressure cooker of dysfunction and familial tension. Since Danny's and Buck Wilson's release from prison the pressure has increased."

"For instance?"

"Well, you probably saw that Joel Martin was in town a lot more the month before his brother went missing."

"Not really," Tanner said thoughtfully. "But then I'd only know that if I'd been tasked to drive or fly him. And J Martin didn't say anything to me, but even though I saw and overheard things, he kept his personal affairs to himself especially when family was involved."

"J or Joel?"

"Both."

"Figures." Simpson snorted. "Well, a week before J went missing, he and Joel got into a very short but vocal argument at the coffee shop here in Driftwood. I wasn't there but the shop owner told me about it."

"What were they arguing about?"

"The loud part was short, but the owner said she heard only one word, a name really, Schwartz, Doctor Corbin Schwartz."

Tanner's eyes went wide. "What! Who?"

Julie nodded, pointing at the envelope he held. "Thought that would spark your interest. Chief Smith and I were the detectives assigned to Cynthia's assault case. As I recall he was the psychiatrist J Martin got for Cynthia's post-trauma counselling. From your reaction, you must be familiar with the good doctor."

"Yes," he replied and added softly, "very."

"So, am I."

"How so?"

"J Martin was a good man, let's just say he took in strays," Julie said warmly and then her face darkened. "After Danny's and Buck's trials I ...

The short version is I went off the rails for reasons best left unsaid. I quit the force, and ..."

"J hooked you up with Dr. Schwartz. Nuff said, Julie," Tanner said gently. "J did me a similar favor. From what I can see it helped ... worked for you."

"Yes, it did. Anyway, the doc's name and signature are on a document in there. Look, Tanner, the Martin pressure cooker is about to explode. J Martin's death and Joan Martin's may only be the relief valve lifting. I fear that Cynthia, you and now me by association, will be the next victims and soon."

"Why so?"

"That common link to Schwartz for one thing. Another is just my PI gut," she replied grimly, touching his shoulder.

"What's your gut telling you?"

"I hope this is one of those rare times it's wrong. But it seems this job of surveilling the Martins was intended to keep me in Driftwood Cove to play some part in 'The Perils of Cynthia'. And that may be very risky and soon."

He nodded. "All true."

"Now, let's go. I have bills to pay," she commanded with a tight smile and pointed to the tunnel entrance. The dank odor of seawater and wet sand assailed them as they entered the tunnel. Julie flipped on the flashlight she pulled from her bag, "You know about this place?"

"Never been inside before, but I often heard about it, especially when I flew J to Driftwood," Tanner answered, following her. "He loved telling its history and sharing his personal experiences. I know that the tavern was once a B&B, once a speakeasy and once a summer resort hotel. J especially relished the dark smuggler side of its history."

"I believe that," she said over her shoulder, shining the light on the opening to their right where a wooden frame had once mounted a door. "That's one of the smuggler hidey holes. He tell you about the hurricane parties?"

"Oh yeah." Tanner laughed and frowned. They turned toward the ladder at the tunnel's end. "I know they're a part of Martin family and GASMAX lore with a tragic side ... a Martin brother died during one of those parties. Jake?"

"Yeah, it was quite sad. Jacob Martin, Cynthia's father, died that night." Julie stopped, face Tanner and recited a brief account of Joel, Jacob, and J Martin's hurricane party. It included Jacob's heroic death and the shattered remains of the sailboat, the *Lucky Lindy* out of Sand Dollar and registered to a Niles Tannerson.

"Tannerson? I know that name. Cynthia ..." Tanner started. The sound of cracking timbers cut him off. Julie screamed as the tunnel roof collapsed. As the flashlight dropped from her hand, she felt Tanner's arms close around her as they fell.

CHAPTER 18

Deadly Opener

Smugglers Cove Beach

THE SOUND OF CRACKING TIMBERS and Julie's scream merged with the weight and sound of falling wet dirt. A brief whiff of fresh sawdust assailed Tanner's senses before the sudden darkness that followed when Julie's flashlight fell. In the split second that followed, he wrapped his arms around the PI. As the heavy dirt and broken timbers worked to trap and smother them, he held her tight and propelled their combined weight toward where he supposed was the nearest hidey hole. After they fell, he rolled on top of her.

As much as he could, anticipating that he'd be immobilized, he tented his arms over her head to create an air pocket. It proved unnecessary when he realized they'd landed in the hole; only his lower legs were pinned beneath the collapsed tunnel rubble just outside. Though trapped, he could feel Julie moving beneath him and heard her coughing. "Julie, you okay?"

"Yeah," she gasped once the crack and roar of the collapse had ended. "You?"

"My legs are pinned," he replied pushing himself up and off her. The flashlight cast a murky grey light. "I see the beam of your flashlight. See if you can crawl out."

"I think I can." She grunted.

He felt her move and, when she was free, he collapsed face down. The dirt where she'd lain felt warm against his cheek. "Can you get the flashlight?"

"Yes," she said, and the retrieved light broke the remaining darkness surrounding him. "Are you hurt, your legs?"

"No, I don't think so," he said, spitting out some sandy dirt. "They're just pinned. Can you see?" He sensed her crawl by and then felt her hand on his lower leg.

"It's a wood beam," she said and grunted. "I ... I got it. Move!"

The pressure on his lower limbs diminished. Taking a deep breath, he pulled his legs free. He sat up. Julie, pointing the light at him and holding her bag in her lap, kneeled next to him. "That's got it. Nothing's broke." He grinned, patting his prosthetic as well as the pocket with his gun and Cynthia's report.

"Thank God." She smiled and aimed the light's beam at the hidey hole's entrance, partially blocked by rubble. "Let's see if we can get out of here." The hidey hole went dark as she shone the light into the tunnel. "Looks like we can squeeze through. The tunnel's blocked to the ladder, but if we crawl, we can make it back to the beach."

"Let's go," he said, crouching before standing. "I'm good. Go."

"Okay," she replied. She pushed her bag out and followed it.

"I can stand," Julie announced a dozen feet short of the tunnel exit. She and Tanner walked onto the beach. Breathing deeply, she sat.

"You okay?" he asked and bent over, rubbing his lower legs.

She nodded. "Your legs?"

"Still good to go," he answered, offering her his hand. "Let's hurry. We might catch him in the parking lot."

"Gone," Julie announced breathlessly as they gained the parking lot after taking the steps two at a time. The pickup was nowhere to be seen. She pointed to the side of the building. "Come, my car is parked out of sight over there."

After they reached her black sedan, Tanner walked quickly around it. "No flats. He must have been in a hurry or didn't see it," he speculated.

"Or was sure he got us," Julie observed thoughtfully. "You smell the sawdust?"

"Yeah. I thought that was just some adrenalin ... oh, I see," Tanner said.

"Let's check out the tavern," she said. "Beating feet, he may have left something behind."

The tavern doors were ajar. Tanner kicked one open and, holding his gun above Julie's flashlight, stepped in. "Clear," he shouted after a quick look around.

Julie entered. "This way," she said, pointing to the back of the room and grabbing the flashlight. She led him to the basement.

"The trapdoor to the tunnel?" he asked, pointing at a busted padlock and the broken hasp on a square wooden door in the floor. Next to the lock lay a pair of large bolt cutters.

"Yeah," she said placing the light next to the door. "Give me a hand."

The trapdoor quickly opened. He took the flashlight. "Look," he said, kneeling and directing the light into the opening.

Julie knelt next to him. The light revealed a chainsaw with a bright yellow motor casing lying at the foot of the ladder. "Hold this," he commanded, handing her the light before climbing down the ladder. He took off his shirt and used it to grasp the saw's case. With difficulty, he navigated the first two rungs one-handed before Julie could grab hold.

"Look at this," she said, shining the light on the chainsaw and then the bolt cutters after they had laid them next to each other. Both were stenciled with 'Property of Waterman Construction.' "That's the construction outfit building the Starfish condos up the shore from the Martin beach house."

"I know the place," Tanner said, putting on his shirt. "GASMAX has some money invested in that project."

She snorted. "Like most everything else in Driftwood. And, oh by the way, my source reported that after prison Buck Wilson got a part-time job with Waterman."

"I drove J there for a couple of site visits. I met the project manager and both foremen. It might be worth a visit. You game?"

"I appreciate your enthusiasm, Tanner," she replied with a tight grin. "Though this is very likely a part of your drama, I now need to call Chief Smith. It's his call regarding follow up. Besides, he needs to get his guys out here to check the saw and cutters for prints."

"Right you are." He sighed, patting his pocket holding the envelope. "Besides I need to deliver your report to Cynthia."

"Let's get out of here," she said, nodding at her phone. "No coverage down here."

Eye of the Storm Beach House

"THAT'S IT," CYNTHIA said, closing the last folder Sylvia had presented and nodding at a bulky manila envelope sealed with packing tape, "except for that." She sat back in the dining room chair and briefly closed her eyes against the morning sun now finding that side of the house. The table where days ago she'd enjoyed a meal with her aunt and cousins was scattered with papers, folders, a banker box and some of J Martin's journals.

"More coffee," Sylvia asked, stepping into the kitchen through an arch separating the two rooms. "I'm getting some."

"Please." She sighed as she sat up and reached for the envelope. "I don't know which I needed more, the shower and change of clothes after the ride on the rock crusher or the first cup of joe."

"Maybe both," Sylvia said, setting a fresh white mug before her cousin seated at the head of the table. She sat next to her. "The clothes fit alright?"

"Perfect," Cynthia answered, pulling at the front of the white blouse and patting a pant leg of the khaki slacks. "Thanks."

"I'm not sure what's in that," she said, pointing at the thick envelope.

"But it had your birthdate on the outside, and it looks like it was deliberately and doubly sealed to prevent casual viewing."

"Well, let's see ..." Cynthia began when her phone rang. She pushed the envelope aside and answered the call. "It's Danny," she said and took the call.

Sylvia nodded, stood, and went to the window while sipping her coffee. Viewing the sunlit line where the ocean met the day's cloudless sky, she noted that the windows were dirty. *Must call the maid in next week*, she thought and returned to the table after Cynthia said, "Yes" three times, "See you at one," and "Bye."

"That was short and sweet."

"Just Danny confirming our meeting at the plant at one."

"Well, if you ask me, cousin, I'd ..."

"Hello." Tanner's shout and knock at the front screen door cut her off. Cynthia rose to let him in, but before she could, they heard the door open and his steps in the hall just before entering the room.

"Tanner!" Cynthia cried, seeing his face, arms and clothing soiled. "What happened? Are you okay?"

"I'm fine. Just a little mussed up." He smiled. "Julie and I had a little more excitement at the cove than anticipated."

Cynthia stepped toward him when her phone rang. Clint's caller ID appeared on the screen. She glanced at it and back at Tanner. "Just a moment. I got to take this, it's Clint," she said, holding up a finger and pressing the phone to her ear.

Sylvia guided Tanner to a seat at the table. "Coffee? A towel?" she whispered with a smile.

"Both," he mouthed, nodding. She went to the kitchen, but she caught scraps of Cynthia's conversation with her brother. "Yes, Clint, I know where you pitched camp. Just before sundown all three of us will be there," she heard her say with some impatience.

Sylvia grabbed a towel and wet it. As she poured the coffee Cynthia was silent. Then she said with warmth, "That's good news, Clint, and I appreciate you saying all that."

"Here you go," Sylvia said and smiled before putting the cup in front of Tanner. She handed him the towel and sat next to him.

"Thanks," he said as Cynthia ended the call with Clint.

"See you before sundown. Goodbye. Now, Tanner, what happened?" she asked, setting the phone on the table.

"What did Clint have to say?" he replied, wiping his face and arms with the towel.

"Uh, he has the stuff I asked for, and he confirmed our meeting. Oh, yes, and he over-apologized – again - for the rock crusher 'accident'."

"That's why I say you don't go out there tonight," Sylvia injected before Cynthia held up a hand.

"Before we settle that, Tanner, what happened?"

"I tend to agree with you, Sylvia," he said, and rubbed the back of his neck with the towel. "Anything else?"

"Also, something about finding out, as he put it, "what likely drew Dad to the quarry and make the fatal climb." Now tell us what happened."

Sylvia listened to Tanner's account and studied her cousin's reaction. *Something is going on between these two*, she thought, seeing more than just concern crease Cynthia's face. She shook her head. *He must know about Stan in Central City.*

"But you're ... you both are okay?" Cynthia asked when he finished and she briefly squeezed his forearm.

I wonder if she remembers Stan? Sylvia mused, standing and picking up the soiled towel and holding it at arm's length, but asked, "Yes, Tanner, you and Julie weren't injured, were you? Want another?"

"No thanks," he replied after a quick inventory of his clothing and arms. "I could use a shower and ... oh, here's Julie's report." He pulled the report out of his pocket and pushed it toward Cynthia.

"Any surprises?"

"I didn't have time to look. Besides, it's your report," he said. "However, she did mention that ..."

Julie Simpson's "Hello" and knock on the front door cut him off.

"I'll get it," Sylvia said. "But I want to hear what she mentioned."

Julie Simpson followed Sylvia into the dining room, and Sylvia waved her to the seat next to Tanner. There was a marked contrast between the two survivors of the collapsed tunnel. Whereas Tanner looked like he desperately needed a shower and a change of clothes, Julie's hair was shiny and groomed from a recent shampooing and brush work. She had applied makeup and was attired in slacks and a spotless beige top. Only her bag looked like it had been a part of the tunnel crawl.

"How come you don't look like you just crawled through twenty yards of dirt?" he asked finally.

Julie laughed. "I was a cop long enough to learn how to live on short naps and to clean up quickly before getting back in the game. You tell them what happened and what we found?"

"Yes." He said, pointed at the envelope in front of Cynthia. "I just gave her your report. I was about to mention the Dr. Schwartz connection."

"The shrink?" Sylvia asked. "The one Dad made us all see after the trial?"

Tanner looked at Julie and then at Cynthia. "More surprises, huh? The psychiatric connection gets bigger."

"More than you know," Sylvia said while Cynthia opened the envelope from Julie and examined the contents. She waved a hand at the other items on the table. "These records show that Dad, and sometimes with Uncle Joel and Grandpa Moses, met with the good doctor regularly after Cynthia's birth and Uncle Jake's death. And after the trial, Dad had Mom, Clint and me, as well as Cynthia, see him for post-trauma sessions. I think he even made a few house-calls on Danny in prison. Somewhere in here it says Uncle Joel was pretty insistent about that. Also, Dad had a final visit with him a few weeks before he went for the hike."

First Tanner and then Julie explained their time and circumstances as Dr. Schwartz's patients. "Did he hypnotize any of you?" Julie asked when she finished.

"Yes," Cynthia and Tanner said in unison.

"Me, too," Sylvia added after a pause. "Clint for sure, but Danny I don't know. Hey, let's not read too much into this. It helped me and Clint, and Mom and Dad said the same. And, given Dad's habit of taking in strays and rehab projects ... sorry, no offense."

"None taken," Julie smiled.

Tanner grinned. "Rehab project is not a bad way to put it."

"Given his habit of helping others, I'm not surprised he sent you two ..."

"Look at this though," Cynthia said, holding up one of the papers from the envelope. "Not sure how you got this, Julie, but this is a photocopy of a memo to J from Dr. Schwartz dated about the time of that last visit. It alludes to what Sylvia says, and it ends with this odd and ominous statement, "Given the contingency you suppose, there will immediately arise a very likely risk from within and without to Cynthia's life despite the memory triggers.""

"Memory triggers like those words in the envelopes?" Tanner said suddenly.

"Yes," Cynthia replied and explained about the words to the other two as well as her recurring dreams about the assault and Tanner's and her sudden knowledge like the clues leading to the letters in the wine press.

"Tanner, like I told you, you and Cynthia have the most complete picture required to sort this all out," Julie said, leaning forward and looking at him and then Cynthia. "The risks to your lives are obvious and most are public knowledge."

"That's for sure," Sylvia agreed. Let's see, a crash landing, a car explosion, the car wreck at Dead Man's curve, another assault right here in this house and let's not forget the 'accident' with Clint's rock crusher this morning." After making a fist and while recounting her cousin's near-death experiences she ticked off each example with her fingers. "That's five in all." Looking at Tanner, she raised her other hand's index finger and finished, "And if you hadn't taken her place at the cove, it would be six. She'd have been in that tunnel this morning."

"There may be a seventh instance," Julie said, breaking the silence in which they all considered Sylvia's observation. "When I spoke with Chief Smith, he told me that they dug a large caliber bullet out of the brick facing around the entrance to the bank."

"So, how's that fit in with all this?" Cynthia asked.

"Seems a young bank guard, who let's say was very taken with your big city styling, closely watched you exit the bank. While you were waiting for Mr. Strong to arrive, he heard what he thought was a car backfire, but, after you drove away, he noted a large hole in one of the bricks. He told the bank manager, who called the cops."

"So, maybe seven attempts on Cynthia's life," Sylvia said, raising the middle finger of her other hand. "But by who?"

"Or whom," Cynthia corrected. "Schwartz wrote "from within and without." I hate to go down that path, but if we assume that he meant from within and from outside the Martin family, we have all sorts of suspects. The obvious without is Buck Wilson, and the within ..."

"Don't, Cynthia," Sylvia cried. "It's your family!"

"Well, besides Danny's obvious ax to grind with me, there's what we found in the safe deposit box."

"How so?" Sylvia asked.

"For reasons I don't fully understand, those items must be considered in the context of Uncle Joel's love letters to Aunt Joan, including a reference to Grandpa Moses' affairs while Grandma was still alive. That is somehow linked to J's accidental death and Uncle Joel engineering my sudden exit from GASMAX."

"Then there is J's pirating Niles Tannerson's intellectual property," Tanner said. "Could Joel be complicit?"

"It's a certainty," Cynthia replied and sighed. "It somehow all adds up, in Joel's eyes at least, that I've gone from being a Martin family and GASMAX asset to a dangerous liability."

"What about Clint?" Sylvia asked.

"Given his part in the rock crusher accident, he's clearly suspect. So, I'd say one or all three of them along with Wilson could be out to finish me."

"What about me, Cuz?" Sylvia asked, standing and crossing her arms across her chest.

Cynthia shook her head, stood and placed a hand on her shoulder. "Not you. We have too much good history, and you are the most like your dad. You have his humanity but not his cunning. I can't say that about the rest of our family."

"Hmm, I take that as a compliment," Sylvia said, dropping her arms. "So, we're good?"

"Yes, come here." They hugged.

"I hate to break the moment," Julie said. "But, unless you want me to butt out, will you share what you've discovered?"

"Of course," Cynthia said, looking at Tanner and Sylvia, who both nodded. She and Sylvia sat down. "I'll start with Uncle Joel and my forced resignation from the GASMAX board. Sylvia and Tanner, jump in any time."

After she got to the part where Tanner extracted her from the Buck Wilson encounter at the banquet, he raised a hand and stood. "Look, since I know the rest from this point on, except for what Sylvia found, I'm going to excuse myself and get cleaned up. Unless you moved it, Sylvia, my grip is still upstairs in the hall. Can I use a shower?"

"The bag is still next to chair outside Cynthia's room. You can use the shower in that bathroom. The police took down the yellow crime scene tape."

When Tanner returned, Cynthia recapped what Sylvia had found as well as what was in Julie's report that confirmed her list of likely suspects, as well as the motive. "That being a cover up of the theft of intellectual property or some kind of jailhouse-hatched vengeance plot?" He asked.

"Maybe both," Cynthia said thoughtfully. "The latter focuses on me, but how is the former served by my death or yours? Except for this sealed envelope, nothing here or anything else we've learned, dreamed or real, explains it."

"Unless you left something out. Let me mull this over," Julie said. "In any case, I think you can safely meet with Danny alone, but I recommend that Mr. Strong and I accompany you for the meet with Clint. It smells like a trap."

"I agree," Tanner said. "We should bring Chief Smith in on this."

"You have," Julie said. "Chief Smith is shorthanded following other leads. He's got a team up on Harper Bluff looking for shell casings. He and his officers are following several other Buck Wilson sightings as well as leads in the Joan Martin disappearance. So, as he's done before, he's deputized me to follow up the construction site lead. I may be overstepping my deputized status, but I'd like you two to go with me to the construction site."

"To help or to keep an eye on us?" Tanner asked and smiled.

Julie snorted. "Maybe both."

"Since we agree the meet with Danny at the plant is minimal risk, may just Tanner go with you?" Cynthia asked,

"That should be okay," Julie agreed after a pause.

"Well, it's not okay with me. After that episode at the rock crusher, I don't trust Clint or his little sister," Tanner protested and looked at Sylvia. "No offense."

"None taken," Sylvia said quietly. "Blood is not as much an issue anymore. Besides, they're not high on my trust list either."

"I'll be safe at the plant," Cynthia assured him. "Go with her. We'll all join up before the meeting with Clint. Okay?"

"Okay," he said after a silence.

"What about me?" Sylvia asked.

"You stay here, Sylvia," Julie answered. "Although I'm going to phone the Chief with all you've shared, you need to stay here and guard this evidence. Is there some place you can lock it up?"

"It'll all fit in Dad's safe," she replied after surveying the items of the table.

"You have your gun close by?"

"Of course."

"Oh, that's right." Julie laughed. "J Martin kids all were trained in Kung Fu and small arms after the trial. Let's go, Tanner."

"I have some time before going to the plant," Cynthia said after they left. She picked up the sealed envelope. "So, let's look at this."

A ring tone sounded from the kitchen. "That's my phone," Sylvia's said and went to the kitchen. The caller ID showed 'Uncle Joel.' "Hello, Uncle," she said, watching Cynthia struggle to open the sealed envelope.

"Yes, she's here," she said. As she listened, Sylvia cautioned herself, *Just answer what he asks.*

"Dr. Schwartz was mentioned, but only in a passing comment," she lied and, listening to Joel, she leaned on the kitchen counter so she could see her cousin. Cynthia's animated difficulty in opening the envelope's seal made her smile.

"Yes, sir. I heard you," she said suddenly. The smile collapsed into serious and determined lines as she listened attentively. "I understand that the backup is warranted. I know what to do. Of course, I'll do it right away."

After her uncle's next few words, she turned and selected a long kitchen knife from the wood block on the counter offering a selection of black handled cutlery. "No, sir. I have no qualms. Yes, I'll do what's necessary," she said quietly and then, raising her voice, "I'll call you later. Goodbye."

Sylvia looked at the black screen for a moment before pressing the knife with the point down against her hip in the forward grip position as she returned to the dining room. Approaching from behind, she could see that Cynthia was focused solely on opening the envelope. Shifting the knife to her other hand to hold it in a reverse grip for stabbing, she stopped when Cynthia asked, "Sylvia, do you have something sharp?"

"Yes," she said, raising the knife. "I saw you struggling. I have just what you need right here."

Cynthia held her hand out. "Please let me have it."

"Well, here you go, Princess" Sylvia said with artificial respect, bringing the blade down.

CHAPTER 19

Troubled Waters

Eye of the Storm Beach House

CYNTHIA HEARD SYLVIA END THE call, and, after a pause, her footsteps on the kitchen tiles and dining room hardwoods. Little else registered, though, as she focused intently on opening the envelope with no success and growing frustration. *Come on*, she silently commanded before asking, "Sylvia, do you have something sharp?"

"Yes. I saw you struggling. I've got just what you need right here."

"Please let me have it," Cynthia said, holding out her hand.

"Well, here you go, Princess," Sylvia stated as she had done in jest and countless times over the many years, mimicking the younger Martin siblings' mock deference. As adult friends, they occasionally resurrected the titles.

Cynthia smiled, laughed and turned. Sylvia brought the knife down, twirled it in her hand and set it flat in front of her. "Try this."

"Thank you, Lady Sylvia." Her cousin chuckled. "You still do it too, huh?"

"Yes," she replied and sat down. "Don't remember much else from the knife-fighting lessons in Dad's mandated post-trial commando training. Every time I pick up a knife, any knife, I cycle it through forward and reverse grips."

"And end with the twirl laydown?" Cynthia asked, cutting through the tape. She opened the envelope. "I bet that startled a few first dates."

"Sure did, but I knew that if the guy called for a second date, he was serious relationship material."

"Or crazy." Cynthia laughed. "I do the knife thing, too. Who was on the phone?"

"Uncle Joel."

"What did he want?" Cynthia asked without mirth. She looked at Sylvia and stopped pulling papers out of the envelope.

"Wanted to know if you were here. Since Dad was found, Joel's phoned almost every day. The calls are mostly about GASMAX business, but he always asks about family."

"Makes sense, I guess. Including me?"

"Of course, once you got here, and more frequently after each of your ... unfortunate events. He's worried about you."

Cynthia snorted. "I bet. Anything else?"

"Yes. It was something strange. Out of the blue, he asked if any of us had mentioned, seen or heard from Dr. Schwartz."

"What did you say?" Cynthia inquired.

"Based on what we all talked about earlier, threats from within, and what was in those envelopes, I half lied. I told him that Dr. Schwartz was mentioned but only in a passing comment. He seemed pleased with that answer and quickly changed the topic to a routine and benign HR assignment he gave me yesterday. Odd though, he asked if I had any qualms about it. After I assured him that I didn't and I'd do what's necessary, he ended the call abruptly. That is the strangest call I've ever had with him. Weird, huh?"

"Yes, it's out of character," Cynthia said, pulling a stack of papers out of the envelope. Except for the top sheet, the rest were letter-size and yellowed by time. The top sheet was flimsier stock, smaller, a dull white, and one edge was torn. The other edges retained the faint remnants of gold gilding.

"Maybe losing J and the fallout of your termination are taking their toll," Sylvia suggested.

"Possible but not likely," Cynthia said. "Now let's first see what we've got here." She read the handwritten note on the top page. Her eyes narrowed, and she again read the last few sentences. She flipped through the remaining pages, pausing briefly to read the first few sentences on each before returning to the torn page. "Oh my God!"

Starfish Condominium Construction Site

THE SUN WAS in the western sky when Tanner and Julie reached the Starfish Condominiums. The construction site was roughly two miles down the coast from the GASMAX tidal hydroelectric plant. A trio of three-story buildings containing thirty condos each were arrayed in a crescent on a slight bluff above a beach-rimmed cove whose southern side extended farther seaward than the northern. The south side culminated in a rocky pinnacle, Parrot Point. The light atop the point marked the west end of what was labeled on navigation charts as 'Rocky Shoals.' These notorious stony shallows extended four hundred yards offshore.

Construction of the northern-most building was complete. Colorful flags in front flanked signs proclaiming 'Sales Office, Condos From the Low 400s' and 'Models Now Open.' A few cars were parked outside. The middle building appeared complete on the outside, but its sign declared 'Hard Hat Area' and 'Please Visit the Sales Office.' The southern building was obviously far from complete. It was framed but insulation and siding were more lacking than not. Julie parked between one of several pickup trucks and an electrical contractor's white van.

"Larry, hi," she hailed a passing youth in a soiled tee shirt, blue jeans, steel-toed boots and a yellow hard hat pushed on top of long, dark hair. "Where's Stiles?"

The young man stopped, tilted his hat back, smiled and pointed toward the building. "Hi ya, officer. Second floor."

"Thanks. You staying out of trouble?"

"You bet," he replied nervously and quickly walked away.

"DUI a few months before I quit the force," she said as they went up the wooden steps to the second floor. "Good kid. Single mom had some problems with him for a while."

"Sometimes I forget this is such a small town," Tanner commented.

"Sure is. More so, once you subtract all the tourists," she said, pointing to a thick-set man engaged in a conversation with a wiry Asian woman in blue coveralls and carrying a canvas tool bag in one hand and a spool of wire in the other. "It's kind of a ghost town in the winter."

"I've noticed that, too."

"That's Spencer Stiles, the head construction manager," Julie said as Stiles pointed the worker toward the stairs to the third floor.

"Spence, hi," Julie shouted.

"Julie Simpson," he said, extending a hand. "Been a long time. Who's this, another friend of yours who needs a job?"

"Tanner Strong," Tanner said shaking hands. Consistent with a man not a stranger to manual labor, Spencer Stiles' grip was firm. Both men sized each other up with favorable conclusions. "We met once before. I was here with J Martin. I was his driver."

"So, are you out of a job now?" Stiles asked.

"No, he's GASMAX security, Spence," Julie injected, hoping to get quickly to the heart of their visit. "Chief Smith deputized me to help out with the Cynthia Jones case. Mr. Strong is the company man assigned. You got time for a few questions?"

"Sure, but I don't know what I can tell you."

"We're looking for Buck Wilson. He's a person of interest."

"That's no big surprise," Stiles said and frowned. "I'm looking for him too."

"Why's that?"

"The last time I saw him was two days ago. He worked half a day and bolted, claiming he was sick."

"By the way you say that, I assume that wasn't unusual."

"You got that right, sister. If I hadn't hired him as a favor to Joel and J Martin, I would have fired his butt," Stiles declared harshly. "He plays that connection to the hilt, coming and going as he pleases. When he left, he even borrowed a chainsaw to chop up some firewood at the Martin cabin."

Julie and Tanner looked at each other before she asked, "Was that a chainsaw with a yellow housing?" She pulled out her phone and found the photograph she'd taken of the bolt cutters and the chainsaw. "This it?"

"Yeah. The bolt cutters are ours, too. Where are they?

"We found them at Wilkes Tavern this morning. They're being held by the police as evidence in a homicide investigation," she said and briefly explained the tunnel collapse and the tie to Wilson and the construction company property.

Stiles snorted. "So, Wilson's the prime suspect and on the run. Figures. Well, based on past experience, I didn't expect to see him anytime soon anyway. Good riddance, but I wish we could get the chainsaw. We need it to chop up some of the trees we knocked down for the south lot. Any chance of its return soon?"

"That depends on what Chief Smith's lab boys find," Julie explained. "I'll put in a word with the chief."

"Okay. Thanks."

"If Wilson shows up or contacts you ..."

"Wait a minute," Stiles said cutting her off, holding up his hand and pulling his cell phone from his pocket. "He called earlier but I let it go to voice mail. I had to talk to the electrician and get her going."

After he'd accessed his voice mail, Stiles enabled the speaker phone. "Spence, Buck. Look, I'll be out for the next few days. I'm driving some GASMAX big shot around in one of their boats. Just wanted you to know."

"What's the time of that call?" Tanner asked.

Stiles squinted at the luminous screen. "It was 3:15, just after I started talking with Shirley."

Julie looked at her watch. "Assuming he was at or on his way to the GASMAX boat dock when he called, it's a long shot, but we may catch him."

"Let's go," Tanner said, nodding at Stiles and nudging Julie's elbow.

"Thanks, Spence," Julie said over her shoulder.

"Don't forget about my saw," he shouted at her back.

She waved.

GASMAX Plant

OUT OF HABIT, Cynthia pulled into one of the GASMAX plant's VIP reserved parking stalls. After passing under the canvas canopy that covered the front walk, she entered the smoke-glass enclosed lobby. She smiled at Grant, the security guard who greeted her by name. As she went through security, they exchanged pleasantries. He offered her his condolences for the loss of her uncle. To her surprise her GASMAX plant access had not been pulled.

"Ms. Jones, Ms. Martin is expecting you. She's in the control room," Grant said once the green light on his console flashed as she placed the ID card on the electronic proximity pad. "Would you like an escort?"

"No, thank you, Grant," she replied, grateful he hadn't required her handbag containing the gun to pass through the x-ray machine. "I know the way."

As she walked to the doors opening into the plant proper, she remembered that her name and the times of her visits were electronically recorded in the remote log at the Central City corporate headquarters' security offices. *Hope that doesn't raise any security flags,* she thought.

Tall doors opened automatically once the ceiling mounted sensors detected her badge. *Good, no security alarm.* The sound of her shoes on the polished concrete floor of the two-story-high auxiliary room rose above the muted, low-frequency hum of large ventilation fans occupying most of the ground level. A large but silent emergency diesel generator filled the far end of the room. In the unlikely event that the public power electric grid failed, the diesel would start automatically, and its generator would pick up essential loads. The control room occupied half of the second-floor level. It was accessed via metal stairs and a broad metal catwalk. The open-lattice walkway spanned three large gas processing tanks and towers. Above its metal railing, it was open to the ground floor.

After Cynthia pushed a button in the door frame and looked up at the security camera in the overhead, the control room door lock buzzed. "Hello, Danny," she said after she opened the door.

Standing in front of a chair that was centered on three vertical panels with indicators and lit and unlit flow diagrams, her cousin raised her index finger. Using an electronic tablet, she quickly made entries as she scanned the panels and their sloping aprons. The latter were festooned with gun-handle and button controls for the valves, breakers, fans, pumps and other plant components. Some of this equipment was visible through the large rear window overlooking the larger plant spaces adjacent to the auxiliary room. Danny walked to one of two flat screens on either side of the window. These provided multi-viewed camera shots of key components as well as selectable data displays. "Just a minute, please," she said finally and smiled while touching the screen and recording entries as the display changed. "Got to finish the four o'clock rounds before the computer bitches at me."

Taking an office chair set near the circular escape hatch opposite the control panel, Cynthia rolled it next to Danny's. After wondering about the yellow banner stretched cross the escape hatch declaring it "Out of Service," she turned her attention to her cousin.

To her surprise Danny was smartly dressed in pressed tan slacks and a crisp blue GASMAX polo shirt. Her makeup was simple, and her black hair attractively arranged. *Almost didn't recognize her*, she thought, as Danny set the tablet on one of the panel aprons and sat. "Danny, you look great," Cynthia said with warmth, momentarily forgetting her suspicions.

"Why, thank you." She smiled. "Coming from Princess C, that means a lot."

Cynthia laughed. "Princess C. I guess I'm stuck with that."

"My turn," Danny said, waving a hand at the panels. "You did a great job on all this. I understand from my training and reading that you are largely responsible for implementation of the Phase Three automation and integration of AI. It's incredible that only a single control room operator is now required with no man-in-the-loop or safety degradation."

"Whoa," Cynthia commanded gently. "I appreciate the complement, but Uncle J and his team of mad scientists and engineers did all the hard parts. Sylvia and my team did the easy part of orchestrating installation and testing by the pros."

"Well, I find it all very impressive," Danny said, and proceeded to give an unsolicited explanation of plant operations, safety and security as well as their current status. "Phase Three Automation is such that, at night, the single operator is the only person required in the plant. This minimizes the loss of life in case of a major mishap. Once Phase Four completes testing, the sole nighttime operator can be on call, and, through password-protected apps, complete almost all operations with any smart device. Though the fourth phase of GASMAX's patented process means we are even more highly efficient and cost effective, risk for catastrophic explosions is higher but remains acceptable, and ..."

"Danny, excuse me, but you said "once Phase Four testing is complete." Your dad put that testing on hold just before he left on that last solo hike. It's still not going on, is it?"

"Uh, well, Uncle Joel restarted it a day later," Danny replied and shrugged. "Well above my paygrade, but I thought you knew that. Maybe it got lost in the ... you know, with Dad's death and your ... departure. But yeah, the night shift operator has been on call for the last week now. The AI works great."

"How so?"

"Well, I usually hang out in the break room out front, but as of two days ago we're allowed to go offsite."

"Very impressive, cousin," Cynthia said after Danny finished describing the testing and the results to date. "I can see now that your high marks on your last eval were well deserved and not just your supervisor sucking up to the boss by giving his kid a gold star."

"Cyn, thanks for saying that. I appreciate it coming from you. My super says you were his best and brightest trainee," Danny said and grinned. "You know, I believe that is the first time that I can recall you complimenting me."

"Danny, I ...," Cynthia started and paused when she realized that Danny was right. "If that's the first time, I owe you an apology. You sound like you really like this job and know what you're doing. To be honest, from the memorial on, I felt it was the same old Danny, but seeing you here ... You look great and sound like a new person."

"No apology necessary, Cuz," she said and laughed. "If the old Danny makes you feel better, I have figured out how the GASMAX plant could be made to blow up but still have enough time to hit the escape hatch. It's a wild slide ride to the river. You ever try it? We did it in training."

"A long time ago. Point is, I like the new you." Cynthia chuckled. "Speaking of the wild ride, how long has the hatch been out of service?"

"Oh, a tree or something fell and blocked the river exit and cracked the tube. It should be cleared and the tube repaired by the midnight shift," she said and swiveled in her chair to face the panel. "I'm not being rude, but, with the day shift AI setting, I have to keep an eye on my indicators. I promise, no explosions before midnight."

"That's good, I've had enough 'explosions' this week to last a lifetime."

"Yeah, the car bomb and the rest," Danny said, making a note on her tablet. "Though I heard in prison about how to make such things happen, I hope you believe me that I've had no part in any of it."

"The 'it' now includes a suspected sniper who shot at me at the bank."

Danny's finger paused above her tablet screen. "Do tell," she finally said and finished her note.

Cynthia explained the report from Chief Smith and added, "That is something you knew how to do before prison."

Danny chuckled and continued her notes without looking up. "For one thing, handling a firearm would violate my parole, and, most significantly, my marksmanship is so rusty I couldn't hit the ground with a rifle butt. Besides, I understand that Buck Wilson is back in town."

"He's being sought by the police as a suspect," Cynthia admitted, without going into detail.

"That ass ... jerk certainly knew how to do most of those things even before prison." Danny sighed. "Lockup must have been graduate education for him. But I'd be surprised if he was your man."

"Why's that?"

Danny put the tablet down and turned to Cynthia. "Uncle Joel visited me a few days before my release. He told me that Buck had gotten out the week before, and he and Dad met with him for a little man-to-man."

"Just Uncle Joel and J and Wilson? Where?"

"Yep, just the three of them. I don't know where. Most likely whatever rock Buck lives under. Anyway, the conversation was very one-sided. Uncle Joel said that he and Dad in no uncertain terms warned Wilson to stay away from the Martin family, especially you and me. He bragged to me that to convince Wilson how serious they were, they alluded to some past criminally liable acts in their own youth. How'd Uncle put it ...? Yeah, "you don't want to test our lethal ruthlessness and resolve." It scared me the way he said it. You know how Uncle Joel can be, the black-hat villain type when he wants to."

"Yes, I know," Cynthia said and frowned, remembering her last meeting with Joel and its aftermath. *Sounds like they didn't tell her the whole story*, she concluded.

"But I don't think they told me the whole story."

"Why's that?" Cynthia asked with a new and growing appreciation of Danny's maturity and insight.

"Just a gut feeling." Danny shrugged, wringing her hands before wiping a tear away. "And trust me, prison refines gut feeling. So, as Joel talked, I sensed there was something else about Joel's relationship with Wilson that made the whole tale sound off or incomplete. Does that make sense?"

"Yes, it does," Cynthia replied taking her cousin's hands in hers.

"You know, I have not seen or spoken with Wilson since his release from prison," Danny said and sobbed. "You gotta believe me. It's a condition of my parole, and I don't want to screw that up. I never ever want to go back to that horrible place. All I know is based on what Dad and Joel told me."

"Danny, what is it?" Cynthia asked startled by Danny's emotional break.

"It's ... it's these memories of Wilson's assault, how he hurt you, the impact on our family ... I hated you for the longest time," she said, weeping and grabbing Cynthia's shoulders. "But after the first year in prison I ... Cynthia I'm so, so sorry for everything. I was such an immature jerk for so long. You remember how Grandpa and Dad would always go on about how we Martins should always do what's necessary, love God and do good, bearing fruit in keeping with repentance?"

"Yes, it is a Martin family and GASMAX edict and motto all rolled into one, and mentioned often," Cynthia replied. Suddenly, recalling the last few days' events and her life's trajectory after the assault, she silently realized, *I've done a pretty good job with the first part, doing what's necessary, but have made a mess of the last.*

"Well," Danny said, "in prison I figured out that before I was busted that I was well schooled in how to do what was necessary, in paying lip service to loving God and 'acting' good but not really bearing any fruit in keeping with repentance. Before lockup, my only regret was I got caught. Prison opened my eyes to the fact that I was sorry for what I had done and how it hurt others - my family - and that I had to change direction. I had to ... Look, now I understand that regardless of what Dad put in that codicil, you'll do right by me. Please forgive me, please."

Stunned that the family black sheep had just articulated her own sudden moral revelation, Cynthia pulled Danny into a long hug and, then cupping her face and wiping away the tears, said warmly, "Trust me, you're not the only one of us who have fallen short of what Grandpa was saying. Of course, I forgive you. We're family after all."

"Yes … we are."

In more ways than you can imagine, Cynthia added silently as they let go of each other. "Danny, Julie Simpson, Tanner and I are meeting with Clint later at his campsite to hopefully put the last pieces of the puzzle in place and, as your brother claims, "make things right." Please join us."

"I'd love to." Danny sniffed, but frowned and pointed at the panels. "Can't, work. I've pulled a double shift to support Phase Four testing, but tonight I've got to stay onsite. I'll come by EOS after midnight."

"Great," Cynthia said. "I look forward to it." After a brief hug, she left.

ONCE OUTSIDE THE building she called Tanner.

"We're enroute to the Driftwood Bay boat docks," he stated after explaining what they had learned at the construction site.

"Then we'll all meet at Clint's camp site," she said, getting behind the wheel. "I want to get there before sundown."

"Sure. How'd it go with Danny?"

"Good. It was better than I'd thought, but I'm not one hundred percent sure yet," she answered and started the car. "Based on what Clint has, I'll know."

"Okay, but wait for us before you do anything."

"Yes, sir," Cynthia smiled. "Be safe, Tanner."

"You too. Bye."

ONCE THE DOOR had closed behind her cousin, Danny wiped the last of the forced tears from her cheek. Smiling, she pulled out her cell phone and dialed her uncle's number. Turning away from the security camera, she held it to her ear. "She's gone."

"Did she swallow it?" Joel asked.

"Hook, line and sinker."

R. NICHOLAS POHTOS

Driftwood Bay Boat Docks and Slips

BUCK WILSON KICKED the empty, red jerry can aside and set the third six-gallon container of gas in front of him. After fitting the nozzle in place, he continued to fuel the GASMAX Chris-Craft 27 launch. *What a pain*, he thought, looking at the GASMAX crates he'd stacked across the middle of the boat dock. Since he was fueling the seaward of the two corporate boats moored in tandem on the company dock's south side, the crates provided an effective barrier from anyone viewing the dock from the shore. This was necessary since the cops were looking for him, and the side benefit was that he was able to shed the hat, wig, and dark glasses used at the cove that morning. The barrier's only negatives, he realized, was it might draw attention to the dock. Also, the stack of boxes was a blind spot if someone investigated the odd arrangement.

Buck looked at the can and then his watch. *I can finish refueling both boats and still make Joel's delivery on time*, he calculated. "Come on," he said and shook the can gently. Its contents sloshed. *Thank God, this is the last can for this one*, he thought. *If that lazy, lying moron brother of Danny's had really done his job, both boats would already be topped off like Joel wanted, and I could have been at the hydroelectric plant jetty early.*

He heard before he felt the can go empty. He tossed it, and it skidded to a stop next to the others. After securing the fueling port, he double-checked the backpack containing his phone and Joel's special delivery items. Satisfied, he secured it behind the cockpit on the passenger area deck beneath a tarp. *After that miss at the tavern, I can't afford disappointing him again*, he reasoned. *Funny, he didn't seem upset when he got the word that Simpson and Strong had escaped the tunnel. Well, maybe he's finally figured out we just need to put a bullet in Jones and her pals the next chance we get. I hate all this pussyfooting around and the clever accident crap.*

Returning to the pier, Buck wiped his hands on his jeans, rolled up his denim shirt sleeves and grabbed two full gas cans. After making his way through the narrow opening left between the crates, he started to empty the first can into the second launch's eighty-five-gallon tank. *Two cans should do it for this one*, he estimated. As the gas began to flow, he realized he was visible to observers on shore. He scanned the boardwalk connecting the docks and running along the shops it fronted.

"Damn," he cursed, spotting Tanner Strong and Julie Simpson when they emerged onto the sidewalk alongside one of the dockside eateries. Though they were still a good thirty yards away when they descended the steps to the boardwalk, he saw Strong point in his direction. Simpson pulled a gun from her bag. Setting the can down, Buck felt the empty spot in his belt. *Crap, it's on the boat*, he cursed silently, remembering he'd left his gun and his phone in the other launch. His mind raced as he formulated an escape plan. Soon his face brightened. *I know.*

As Buck watched the detective and her companion, now both armed, approach in a crouched run, he quickly implemented his plan. Upending the open jerry can, he poured a liberal amount of gas on and around the unopened can of fuel. Then, backing slowly toward the opening between the crates he saturated a broad path on the wooden dock with gasoline. Before the crates obscured his view, he saw Strong and Simpson reach the dock and open the berth's shore side chain linked door.

"Good, it's not locked," Tanner said, lifting up the gate's latch and banging the gate open. "Where's he gone?"

"Behind those boxes," Julie gasped loudly, screwing up her face. "Gas! The creep has soaked the pier with gas."

Tanner nodded and pointed at the obviously full jerry can and the surrounding wet planks. Edging to the side of the dock, Strong closed the launch's fueling port. "Keep him busy," he whispered, motioning Julie to get onto the boat.

"Wilson, stop! Police!" Julie shouted as she climbed aboard. Tanner freed the nylon bow and stern lines and followed her onboard.

Buck heard Simpson's command as he finished emptying the jerry can on top of the remaining full ones before letting loose his boat's mooring lines. Certain that the smell of gas, or their conclusion that he was armed would delay them, he jumped into the launch. He retrieved his gun and flipped the safety off. "Can't do that, Simpson!" he shouted and fired a shot into the air.

The ebbing tide pulled Buck's boat away from its berth, instead of starting the engine, he pocketed his pistol and used the boat hook to push the vessel away from the head of the dock. "I ain't going back to prison!" he screamed, not able to think of anything better to say to buy time.

"Damn fool, he's going to set the whole dock on fire," Strong hissed, pushing their boat off the gas-soaked berth with his foot before joining the PI in the cockpit. He frowned when he saw that the ebbing tide retarded his impromptu shove off. Motioning for Julie to keep talking, he found the key in the boat's ignition.

"Look, we just want to talk," Julie claimed loudly without emotion.

Not believing anything you say, Buck declared silently, remembering Julie's part in his last arrest and the subsequent trial. As his twenty-seven-foot boat drifted another five yards from the dock, he took the flare gun from its bulkhead mount and loaded it from the bag hung next to its bracket.

As they awaited Wilson's reply, aided by a push with the boat hook, the twenty-seven-foot boat that Tanner piloted drifted further from the dock. "Will it be enough?" he worried, noting that the tide's flow pulled them more along the dock than away from it. "Damn," he said, shaking his head and inhaling air ladened with the strong odor of gas.

"About what?" Wilson finally shouted, aiming the flare gun at the head of the dock. Taking one last look to ensure he was well off, he pulled the trigger. The flare leaped across the water white, hot and true, smacking into the closest full jerry can. As the cans and dock erupted in flames, he dropped into the captain's chair and started the boat's Mercruiser engine. The Model 8.2 Mag EC 380-horsepower boat roared to life. The stern bit in quickly, and he spun the wheel to carve a high-speed arc toward Pelican Point and the channel from Driftwood Bay to the ocean.

Between the first explosion and the second when the fire found the jerry can on the other side of the crates, Buck heard Tanner cry, "My God, no! Get down!" and Simpson scream. Wilson smiled, steadying the boat on a straight course for the open sea and pushing the throttle forward. "I didn't miss this time," he declared happily. "Two down and one to go." *But Jones is Joel's problem now*, he reminded himself. *Besides, once he has his special delivery, I get paid off and I'm out of here and all but done with the Martin crazies.*

CHAPTER 20

A Rocky Finish

Driftwood Bay Boat Docks and Slips

I DON'T LIKE THIS, TANNER thought when Wilson initially failed to reply to Julie's request to talk. So, after using the boat hook, he took the seat behind the boat's wheel. His hand found the key again, but he didn't turn it, pausing when he heard Wilson cry out, "About what?" A second later Tanner saw the water in front of their boat reflect a burst of bright white light. Glancing sideways to where the flare gun was mounted on the bulkhead next to the captain's chair, he turned the key. As Wilson's end of the dock erupted in flames, their craft's Mercruiser engine rumbled to life.

Conscious of both the fire to the left that would only get worse when the initial blaze found the jerry cans on the landward end of the dock and their proximity to the adjacent dock, he only nudged the throttle but spun the wheel hard to the right. He swiveled toward Julie as the second blast occurred. "My God, no! Get down!" he cried, tackling her to the deck as she screamed.

Immediately after the second explosion's noise and heatwave subsided, Tanner opened his eyes and saw Julie's surprised face inches from his. "You okay?" he asked.

"Yeah," she said. "Get off me and drive."

"I guess you are." Tanner grinned briefly, settling into the captain's chair. He grabbed the wheel and realized his gut-driven engine start and maneuver had gotten them safely clear of the GASMAX dock now engulfed in flames. He turned the wheel to the left to pull them out of the circle away from the fire and eventually into the neighboring dock.

Seated in the other captain's chair, Julie pushed the hair out of her face. "That was close," she said. Before turning to Tanner, she looked back at the smoke and the fire that now included the fuel-soaked water where they'd had been berthed. "That was some quick thinking. How'd ... look! There he is!

Can't you go any faster?"

Tanner followed her extended arm and finger toward the mouth of the bay. The other Chris-Craft 27 was on a straight course to the open sea and nearly abreast of Pelican Point. "Let's see," he said, pushing the throttle all the way forward and steering to follow.

Eye of the Storm Beach House

"DONE," SYLVIA ANNOUNCED when she walked onto the deck.

Cynthia didn't respond. Her cousin stood in front of the Adirondack chairs and matching table. Arms crossed, she looked seaward. Sylvia noted a pistol, flashlight, cell phone and a folded newspaper on the round tabletop. Tapping the silent woman's shoulder, she repeated, "Cynthia, it's done. Everything fit in Dad's safe."

"And the combo?" Cynthia asked, glancing sideways. "You changed it?"

"Of course," Sylvia replied and tapped her forehead. "In addition to being up here, I sent it via secure email to your old EA, Connie. She still thinks your termination is temporary."

"Good, and I hope she's right," Cynthia said and smiled briefly before lapsing into another silent moment. The mention of Connie's name kindled memories of an existence that now seemed so radically different and full of a simpler though selfish innocence. She wondered if she would or could ever feel that way again. Considering the conversation with Danny in which Cynthia realized a personal moral failure shaped by a flawed Martin family and business code of ethics, she thought, *do I want to?* Shaking her head, she checked her watch.

"Are you ready?" Sylvia asked nodding toward the table.

"Locked and loaded as Tanner would say. The phone is fully charged. Paper says the moon won't rise until a half hour past sunset tonight. So, I took Uncle J's special flashlight. Hope you don't mind."

Sylvia picked up the long, black flashlight, and clicked it on. Its narrow high intensity beam split the shadow of the house cast by the sun low in the cloudless sky. "The hurricane party flashlight." She smiled, turned it off and set it next to the gun. "A family heirloom, but I'm sure he'd approve. Not sure he'd be okay with you going to this meeting alone, especially after dark."

"I won't be alone. Tanner and Julie will be with me."

"Last I heard, they were not going with you, but would meet you there, right?'

"Yes. They're following a lead on Wilson, but Tanner said it was a longshot and they'd be there in time."

"Humph." Sylvia snorted. "And if they're not and if this is a trap? Look, why don't we just turnover everything we have to Chief Smith and let him sleuth it out? Family thing or not, it's his job, not yours, Tanner's, Julie's or mine. Attempted murder is involved."

Cynthia looked at her cousin and pointed toward the ocean to her right. "About over there," she said. "It's summer. So, it'll rise over there."

"What are you ... oh, the moon. In the southern sky, that's about right. One of the many lessons from Dad's stargazing phase of our growing up. Or was it from Clint's spiritual summer?"

"Both. It's the July full moon tonight, the Thunder Moon." Cynthia laughed at the memory. "It's larger and has an almost blood color as it rises and before it bleaches out higher in the sky. I remember we could read by it out here when we were kids."

"Ah, yes, it is so named for all the storms of the season," Sylvia said. "You ... we are certainly in a storm, aren't we?"

"Yeah, it does have the rep as a bad omen. Remember that time Grandpa Moses visited? We were little, but what he said that night while we all watched the blood-red Thunder Moonrise scared me so much that it stuck. It was something from the Bible, Old Testament, I think. He roared, "The sun shall be turned into ... something ... and the moon to blood before the terrible days of the Lord almighty"."

"Close. It's actually, "The sun shall be turned into darkness, and the moon into blood, before the great and terrible day of the Lord come." It's from the Book of Joel, King James Version. Grandpa was a King James man. Oh, it is also in the New Testament, in Acts I believe."

"You're quite the Bible scholar, Cuz," Cynthia said. "When did this start?"

"Nothing like that. I have a photographic memory." Sylvia chuckled. "I took a comparative religion course in college, and the prof made us read the entire Bible. Don't ask me for a theological interpretation beyond the fact that a blood moon implies bad news for humans. And that brings us back to your solo trip into a likely trap. It could be a bad omen for you. Is that what you were driving at?"

"Perhaps it is a bad omen and you're right about a trap," Cynthia conceded and sat down, "but I have something else in mind. Have a seat."

Sylvia nodded and sat in the chair on the other side of the table.

"But I also remember Clint's astrology phase," Cynthia continued. "He talked a lot about full moons. Though I lack your precise memory, I do recall him saying something like a Thunder Moon marks a time and season for leveling up and shedding the old for the new person we're meant to be."

"You're into astrology now?"

"No, but I think there is a time element in all this." Cynthia shrugged. "I feel there is a window of opportunity to sort all this out, level up so to speak. If we bring Smith and the police in, we'll miss the chance while Smith gets up to speed. The fact that Uncle J was so insistent on fast-tracking the memorial and will-reading as well as considering all that has happened and what we've learned makes me think someone and something will slip through my ... our fingers if I don't go out there tonight. Also, I suspect Tanner, you, even Julie now, and I could end up dead if we don't face this tonight."

Sylvia sighed. "And we're Martins. As Grandpa Moses and our parents pounded into our heads, we boldly 'Do what's necessary, love God and do good, bearing fruit in keeping with repentance,' right?"

Cynthia sat on the edge of the chair and looked at her cousin. "No, Sylvia, that's not right. I ... they really sold us a bill of goods."

Sylvia sat up, faced Cynthia and touched her knee. "Whoa, girl. That's Martin family blasphemy." She smiled until she saw Cynthia's dark countenance. "What do you mean?"

"It's something very astute that Danny said today about our family ethics axiom."

"'Danny' and 'astute' are not two words often heard in the same sentence," Sylvia observed. "What did she say?"

"She said that she realizes that before she was arrested, she, like all us kids, was well schooled by parents and Grandpa in how to do what was necessary, but we were taught little about the rest. She's right, we only had lessons in and examples of paying lip service to loving God and in 'acting' good. However, it never really bore any fruit in keeping with repentance."

"Wow, my little sis said that?" Sylvia asked and nodded. "She's spot-on in that regard. Dad and Uncle Joel did some remarkable good for Central City and here in Driftwood, but I always felt it wasn't rooted in any repentance, that is, remorse, regret, sorrow or changing direction. Instead, it seemed that they were just trying to balance the books for some serious wrong they had done while doing what they saw as necessary. So, with a semi-clear conscience, they could do what they wanted."

"In retrospect, I'd agree with that," Cynthia said and smiled briefly. "Danny said that before she was locked up, she had no true remorse. She was only sorry she got caught, but in prison she realized true sorrow. She came to regret what she'd done and how it had hurt others – most of all her family. She realized that she had to change direction. Syl, we ... I, at least, have messed this up too. Fortunately, we have people around us who don't. Guys like Tanner and Julie get it right all the time."

"How so?"

"Where I've always 'done good' to get something out of it, they do it because it's just the right thing to do. I don't know if they care for or love God, but they actually, unselfishly care for – love – others. They do good without expecting something in return."

"Like, saving your butt?"

"Yes." Cynthia smiled. "And like Julie saving you from that falling paint can."

Sylvia nodded and frowned. "Cyn, you were right the first time. It is 'we' who have fallen short of the family motto. So, I go with you." She stood and picked up the gun. "I know how to take care of myself, and you saw what I could do with a kitchen knife."

Cynthia smiled, stood and took the gun from her. She slipped it in the side pocket of her slacks, and slid the phone in the other. It rested next to the folded, torn and gilt-edged page from the well-sealed envelope and Tanner's handwritten note from J. Then she hefted the flashlight and said, "No doubt about that, but, as we agreed, we need you to stay here in case this trip to the woods goes south. At least one of us has to survive to tell the truth."

Sylvia nodded.

"You have any questions? I've told you everything I know, as well as what I suspect."

"No. I've got it all, including the duress phrase," Sylvia sighed, tapping her forehead. "As I said, photographic."

"Remember, call Smith if you don't hear anything from me before nine o'clock."

Sylvia hugged her cousin. "Will do. And please call or text when Tanner and Julie show up."

Cynthia let go of her cousin and studied her worried face. "I'll call," she said and walked away.

Thunder Moon is also called a Full Buck Moon, Sylvia thought. Cynthia disappeared into the dark living room before Sylvia picked up the newspaper. She rolled it up and tapped the opposite palm with it. *But why bring that up? She has enough on her mind without an indirect reminder that Buck Wilson is still at large and likely out to kill her on sight.*

Martin Family Cabin

JOAN MARTIN SAT up, threw off the covers and swung her legs over the side of the bed. The side where Joel had lain was cool to the touch, confirming her memory that he'd left some hours ago with a brief goodbye and kiss. She turned on the lamp on the nightstand and looked around the family cabin's backroom. Her son was correct. It was livable but just barely. *At least there's still electricity in this room,* she observed silently.

Pushing off the bed with her left hand, she flinched when she stood. Lacking a proper nightgown, the tee shirt allowed her to examine the bruising and discoloration from where she'd drawn blood for the staged suicide. Though she'd been a blood bank phlebotomist for several years before she met J Martin at a blood drive, her skills were rusty and the task was complicated by having to draw her own blood on a rocking sailboat.

She glanced at the clock on the nightstand. *Still hours to go*, she thought as she entered the semi-functional bathroom. After a cold shower she dressed, slowed by the need to ease the blouse sleeve over the discolored forearm and the raw pain from where she'd flayed skin from her left index finger. She had pressed the shreds of skin onto the bloodied knife, making it look as if she'd slit her wrists.

She made the bed out of habit. *I'm slept out*, she concluded, despite a persistent form of fatigue rooted in raw nerves from the week's events, including the physically painful fabrication of her own death. Also, deep sleep eluded her due to the lingering doubts about Buck Wilson's reliability that resurfaced when he had rendezvoused with the sailboat.

Despite Joel's assurances and Wilson's silent, competent and respectful aid in dumping the anchor and coating the knife and gunnel with her blood and skin, she still didn't trust the ex-con. She had to admit that this young man, the central figure in events that had torn her family apart, had taken special care of her, treating her with deference while safely and covertly delivering her to the cabin.

Thoughts of Wilson recalled Joel's assurances that "today, tonight, we sever all ties with Buck Wilson, darling. We'll never have to set eyes on him again. I guarantee it."

'Tonight,' is just hours away, she reflected silently, noting the fading light coming in the cabin window, *and this will all be over*. She stepped to the window. The shadows in the forest beyond the clearing in the back were long and dark. She crossed to the door of the room and wheeled a small suitcase to the bed. *Besides no nightgown, I should see what else Clint didn't pack. I want to be ready to go when he comes for me.*

Offshore Abreast Smugglers Cove

BUCK WILSON GLANCED left at the opening into Smugglers Cove and noted the time on his watch. Despite the fireworks at the dock, he calculated that he would still arrive at the tidal hydroelectric plant jetty on time. He'd have to hug the coast closer than normal, but a few things were breaking his way. Visibility was unlimited, and there was no small-boat traffic ahead that might necessitate slowing or deviating course. He could safely proceed on the shortest track due north, having only to steer out to sea one time to avoid the shoal waters off Parrot Point near the new condominiums. In addition, a nearly flat sea only broken by the slightest swell permitted him to throttle up closer to the top end speed of over thirty knots, usually not possible on this run.

The setting sun warmed Buck's face, and the sea air invigorated him. Each breath eased another bit of tension and distress that had steadily mounted since the GASMAX banquet and his first encounter with Tanner Strong. Roasting him in the getaway from the GASMAX dock restored to Wilson a sense of ease, freedom and confidence shaken so badly when Strong had so easily laid him out on the banquet room floor.

Looking back to check the tarp was still secure over his cargo, all his newfound good feelings evaporated. "What the hell," he cursed bitterly, recognizing the other GASMAX Chris-Craft was in pursuit and closing. Recalling that the other boat was the faster of the two, he pushed forward on the throttle. It didn't move; it was already full open. "Damn, how'd they survive that?" He pulled his gun out of the cubby hole next to the empty flare gun bracket.

Dividing his attention between the water ahead and the approaching boat, Wilson realized the distance between him and his nemesis was shrinking. By the time they passed Whaler Cliffs near the Eye of the Storm beach, he could see that Julie Simpson was at the wheel. More alarming, Strong, aiming a handgun, was encouraging Simpson to close to firing range. *No, you don't*, he declared silently, quickly formulating a counterattack. He pulled the throttle back to idle the engine and spun the wheel. "Not if I shoot you first," he spit out as the distance between the two boats dropped quickly. The turn permitted him to easily put Tanner Strong in his sights. He pulled the trigger twice. With no little satisfaction, he saw his target clasp his left arm with his gun hand, and he heard Tanner's shot a split second before it only scarred the water between the two craft. *That should slow 'em down*, he concluded as he throttled up to full speed and turned north. The relative silence of an idling engine was promptly replaced by the Mercruiser's comforting roar.

The clearly visible rock-faced edifice of Parrot Point ahead reminded Wilson that he must turn seaward very soon to avoid its rocks and shoals. Accordingly, Buck concentrated on steering a safe course while evading his pursuers. He assumed Simpson had throttled back or steered away when Strong was wounded, so he settled on a course that would pass the shoals closer than he liked, but would serve to make his safe escape most likely. Looking back to confirm his assumption, he was surprised to see that the other boat was nearly alongside his and that Tanner had his gun lined up for another shot.

"Damn it!" Wilson shouted, suddenly turning the wheel to his right and throttling down. The boats collided. Tanner pulled the trigger, but he was thrown off balance. His shot missed Buck wide. Before Strong was thrown off his feet, Buck saw that the force of the collision had thrown the bigger man into Simpson, who surprisingly also dropped her speed. The collision put the two boats beside each other and nearly dead in the water.

As Buck fumbled to stand and grab his gun, he saw out of the corner of his eye Strong's move to gain his feet and leap into Wilson's boat. When Strong succeeded, Wilson suddenly swiveled up and out of the captain's chair, thwarting the attack. Tanner's momentum propelled him headfirst into the windshield, rendering him unconscious and bleeding. Having fallen back onto the port side captain's chair, Buck managed to point his gun at Strong. Standing and seeing no movement, he quickly shifted his aim to Julie. She was slumped over the wheel of the other boat.

"They're both out cold." Buck laughed, kicking Tanner before grabbing the boat hook and pulling the other craft fully alongside. He noted the proximity to the shoals and rocks off Parrot Point and saw that both boats were pointed at the deadly shallows. He pushed Tanner into the starboard captain's chair, and, after placing the rudder amidships, he locked the wheel. The cockpit gauges indicated the engine was still idling.

After grabbing the tarp and backpack from his boat, Wilson stepped into the other. He kept his gun pointed at Simpson until he was satisfied that she was truly unconscious. He pulled her into the back of the boat, found her bag and pulled out her handcuffs and binoculars. He cuffed her hands behind her and, using some of the mooring line, tied her feet. He tossed the binoculars onto the passenger captain's chair.

Wilson returned to the other boat. Tanner moaned and moved to sit. "No, you don't," Buck declared and struck his head with his gun butt. Strong again slumped over the locked wheel. "Perfect." After ensuring that he had his gun and anything else that could indicate he'd been onboard, he stepped back onto the other boat.

"Keep an eye on this, sweetheart," he chuckled, placing the backpack on the deck next to the motionless detective. He covered her and the backpack with the tarp. Taking the captain's seat, he used the boat hook to nudge the other boat's throttle forward, and then pushed his own to match speed. Eyeing the closing distance to the rocks and shoals, he again advanced both throttles forward, and he steered to stay alongside and point both vessels at the rocks and shoaling water now clearly visible. At twenty-five knots, Wilson shoved Tanner's throttle full open and pulled back on his own as he turned to the open sea and deeper water.

Once safely in deep water, and having heard the other boat crash upon the rocks, he idled his engine. Standing in the back of the boat and using Julie's binoculars, he surveyed the other GASMAX launch's broken remains. Even without the binoculars, he could see large pieces of broken fiberglass and some metal framing among the rocks. Despite the white water, an oily fuel slick was evident. He looked for Tanner's broken body but didn't see it.

Julie Simpson moaned. Wilson pulled the tarp back. She struggled against her restraints, managed to sit up and pushed her way onto the bench seat. Her eyes went wide when she saw the other Chris-Craft's shattered remnants.

"Wilson, what have you done? Where's Tanner?

"If you weren't a cop, you'd be over there broken and floating face down with him," he snarled and backhanded her with the binoculars. Knocked out, she collapsed on the deck. He covered her with the tarp and looked at his watch. After pulling the tarp over his cargo, he got the boat back on course. By the time he was at full speed, he could see the line of the tidal hydroelectric plant's long jetty. He looked at his watch and thought of Joel Martin impatiently waiting for him. *What's he going to do, fire me?* he thought sardonically.

CHAPTER 21

R.I.P. Tide

Waters off Parrot Point

TANNER REALIZED TOO LATE THAT he would miss Wilson when he leapt into the other launch. He collided headfirst with the boat's windshield. The collision gashed his forehead and quickly rendered him unconscious. Now - whenever 'now' was – he knew he must fight and claw his way out of this quagmire. The effort to awaken from this nightmare also roused a pounding pain in his skull. His stunned and dulled senses, the other fruits of his collision with the windshield, allowed only a moan for his feeble push to sit.

"No, you don't!" a shrill and deafening male voice sang the lyric of his pain's new lullaby. There was no time for a refrain before something blunt struck the back of his skull. Slipping and sliding back into quicksand darkness, he heard the same harsh voice croon the coda, "Perfect."

"Beth Togarmah. Wake up, Tanner," an imagined Cynthia commanded tenderly as darkness waned and he felt vibration and wind on his face. *Am I flying?* he wondered. His vision was blurred, but he sensed light, a bright, sun-like glare. He ran his hands along the steering wheel of the Chris-Craft 27 launch now speeding toward shoal water at well over twenty-five knots. *But this is a steering wheel. It's not a plane's yoke, and it won't move.* The boat hit some choppy water. The bow bucked up, throwing the semiconscious man upright in the captain's seat.

"Bailout, buddy!" Tanner's dead comrade ordered just before the darkness completely dissolved and his vision cleared. He gripped the wheel tightly, but it wouldn't turn.

The familiar look and feel of the GASMAX boat traveling at high speed aided in gathering his wits, completely clearing his senses and correctly orienting him in the present, rooted in recent events. The high-speed waterborne pursuit of Buck Wilson, including the gunfight and collision all aligned, but something was off. He shook his head, followed his pilot's instincts and scanned the boat's gauges. *Normal for high speed*, he observed. He looked left and aft. The back benches and the other captain's seat were empty. *Yeah, Julie's on the other boat.* He looked forward through the windshield streaked with his blood. *That's not normal!* he thought with alarm. *We weren't that close to land and ... damn, rocks!*

Strong wrenched the wheel right without effect, and after missing the lever, on the second try, he pulled back on the throttle. "It's locked," he cursed, banging the helm as the engine noise dropped. Before he could unlock the wheel and turn the boat, he estimated its momentum would smash it into the wet-black rocks now clearly dead ahead.

Getting to his feet, Tanner placed one hand on the windshield frame and the other on the right-side gunwale. Leading with his good leg, he pushed up and jumped overboard. The sudden effort and motion, coupled with the effects of two blows to the head made him dizzy. Although he had cleared the boat, his right hip had struck the gunwale just before he landed in the water. The collision and weight of his metal prosthetic violently cartwheeled him into the water. He sank quickly.

Quarry Forest Campsite

CLINT'S TEXT SAID he'd pitched camp in the Quarry Forest's south campsite, Homeplate. Cynthia turned left off Highway 733 on to the road to the quarry building parking lot. Not far from the lot, she took the left on to an access road on the forest's east edge that ran a few miles south to a split in the road. She steered right onto the branch that took her west past the plant's tank farm to its north parking lot.

As Cynthia parked near the north fence, she noted that the lot was nearly empty except for two cars. She reasoned that one likely belonged to Danny who was working the double shift for testing. *The other one looks like a GASMAX sedan.* She gathered her phone and the flashlight before putting the gun back in her pocket. After a quick and well-practiced application of insect repellant, she found the opening in the lot's chain linked fence.

Despite the lengthening shadows, Cynthia easily located the trail head for the trek into Homeplate. Circumstances aside, she enjoyed the hike. The trail ended abruptly in the south clearing where her cousin had pitched camp. The trailheads for the paths to three other campsites were visible. "Third Base, Pitcher's Mound and First Base," she recited and smiled. The Third Base island-site was her favorite. It's abandoned well and a spooky cave in a steep-sided rocky bluff also made for great adventures during childhood camping trips with her uncle and his family. Considering the bluff's elevation, she wasn't surprised when Clint said J had recently erected the high-end tower for zip lines to run from Third Base to First Base. Likewise, the bathhouse under construction at Third Base, though not centrally located for all campers, made sense given the island's proximity to the river and its existing well.

Nicely done, she thought, inspecting Clint's camp. Her cousin, however, was nowhere to be seen. "Clint," she shouted.

There was no reply. She checked her watch. *I'm early*, she concluded and smiled. *In this great outdoors stuff Clint comes closest to being like Sylvia and not Danny.* The tent was up and properly oriented for fire pit smoke consideration. The entrance flaps were neatly tied back. Through a zippered mosquito net opening she saw that a sleeping bag was neatly rolled out and a camper's backpack lay next to it. A shallow but efficient drainage trench surrounded the tent's base. The ice chest and food containers were sealed shut against animal scavengers. They sat next to two folding chairs with a table between them. An unlit lamp rested on the table. Kindling and logs were efficiently arranged in the stone-lined pit, anticipating the dark night's cool breezes that were still the norm for this time of year.

After helping herself to a water bottle, placing the gun and flashlight on the table and pulling out her phone, she sat. *No messages from Clint or from Julie and Tanner*, she determined quickly.

Clint's absence was nearly as worrisome as no word from the other two. Despite her familiarity with these woods from many summer camping trips, the lengthening shadows conspired with near-death events and the uncovered evidence to shake her nerves. *Everything suggests that this is a potentially lethal family meeting alone with one of the people likely trying to kill Tanner and me, for sure, and maybe even Sylvia and Julie*, she thought. The sudden crunch of gravel behind her broke her dark reverie. Grabbing the gun, she stood quickly and turned, bringing the barrel to bear on the intruder.

Waters off Parrot Point

WITH GREAT EFFORT, Tanner clawed his way to the surface. When he broke the surface, pieces of the GASMAX launch's fiberglass hull and frame were still falling. A two-foot fragment splashed next to him as his oxygen-starved lungs gulped in air. His breathing returned to normal, but the pain in his head, the sting of saltwater in his head-gash and in the torn flesh of his gunshot wound were grim reminders of his battle with Wilson. He spit saltwater and something else. "Oil ... gas!" he gasped. Common sense reinforced by military flight training drove him to take a deep breath, dive deep, and swim hard to get away from the crash site.

By the time he surfaced, several yards away in clear, deep water, he had sorted out what likely had happened. *That crafty bastard,* he thought, gasping for air and treading water. *Wilson swapped the boats. He's got Julie. And, somehow, he lashed things up so I'd crash on the rocks!* Tanner got his bearings before swimming toward shore. He estimated it was a few hundred yards or so to the beach at the condo construction site. *If Cynthia's right,* he reasoned as he swam as hard as he could despite the persistent head pain, *Wilson's on his way to the hydro plant to join Clint and whoever else is trying to kill us. I got to get there fast. It's Julie's and maybe Cynthia's only chance.*

Quarry Forest Campsite

"CLINT," CYNTHIA SAID when she recognized her cousin stepping into the clearing. She lowered the weapon.

"Whoa, Cuz," Clint said, raising a free hand without letting go of a wooden chest held firmly in place on his shoulder.

"Sorry. I'm just a little jumpy," she stated, sitting again and placing the gun next to the flashlight. "Got here early. I was lost in thought or something."

After setting the chest in front of her, Clint took a beer from the cooler and sat. "No problem." He smiled. "With all that's happened you're allowed." He popped the can and took a long drink. "Want one?"

"No, thanks," she replied, raising the water bottle before pointing at the chest. "That it?"

"Yeah. That's Grandpa Moses' treasure chest in all its glory." He laughed, gesturing with the beer can toward the wooden trunk with a rounded top. Rough black metal bands held even rougher planks in place. Matching iron hinges and a hasp held the top shut. An old fashion skeleton key padlock dangled open in the hasp. "You said it's what you wanted."

Cynthia ran her hand over the top of the chest. "Funny, I remember it was bigger than this."

Clint chuckled. "Me, too. I always thought it was a pirate's treasure chest. God, I loved those stories. Remember, even when we went camping, he schlepped it in. At night, he'd get us all round the fire, open the chest and pull out a souvenir or two from his travels."

"Yeah, and he'd tell some tall tale about them which we all believed." Cynthia laughed, remembering how the orange and yellow campfire light highlighted the lines in the old man's weather-beaten face. It made him appear even wiser and more fascinating than they already believed he was. "Yes, he could be bigger than life sometimes."

They both sat back and stared at the trunk silently. Finally, remembering why she was there, Cynthia studied Clint and concluded that her cousin was also caught up in treasured childhood memories so often elusive in adulthood. Even in the shadows cast across the campsite, she was taken with the thought that this wasn't the melancholy man she'd spoken with over coffee after the plane crash. Nor was he the bitter, angry and disheveled young man from the memorial and will reading. Even the agitated excitement during the quarry visit was gone. He appeared at ease and at home. Well-rested, he was nicely groomed in boots, jeans, a hiking vest and a plaid wool shirt. Like Danny, Cynthia saw him in a new light in the setting that he so often claimed was the source of his true passions. *Perhaps the 'threat within' didn't include him or Danny*, she thought hopefully, recalling the earlier visit with her cousin at the plant. *Wishful thinking?*

"What's in it?" she asked, sitting up and breaking the silence.

"Oh, just his souvenirs." He took another drink. "I'm not sure what you expected to find. Maybe after we get back from the rock wall, we can rummage through it. Speaking of which, we should get going while we have some light. I ..." Clint's phone rang, cutting him off. He looked at it. "Hey, I gotta take this."

"Sure."

"Hello," he said and listened. He looked at Cynthia and stood. "Yeah, that's correct. Hold on."

"Cyn, it's the contractors about the cabin. They're getting back to work tomorrow. Need my order forms." He pointed at the tent. "Be back. This may take a while."

"Take all the time you want," she said. "I'm going to poke around in the chest."

After he'd stepped away, Cynthia quickly pulled out the padlock, flipped the hasp and opened the chest. In two scoops she emptied the contents into its top. After looking over her shoulder, she reached in and rapped the bottom with her knuckles. It was hollow. *Just like J's journal said, and it's a false bottom*, she observed silently as she felt along the edges. *Should be an opening somewhere along here.* She smiled when her index finger found the half-moon hollow.

She removed the false bottom and looked inside. After another glance toward the tent, she lifted out a black leather-bound book with *Holy Bible* engraved in gold leaf on the cover. "Okay, goodbye," she heard Clint say. She quickly returned the Bible to the chest, put the false bottom in place and flipped the top toward her. This allowed her to scoop the souvenirs back in before Clint sat down.

"Sorry about that." He nodded toward the chest. "Any hidden treasure?"

"Not that I could tell ...," she said and finished to herself, *... yet.* "You get the contractors taken care of?"

"Almost." He sighed. "I hate to delay the visit to the rock wall, but we can still visit it in the dark. I need to hike back to my truck. It's parked at Second Base. I've got to square away one more thing with the contractors, and the necessary papers are in the truck. You can go with if you'd like."

"No, Clint, you go ahead. I'll wait here." She gestured to the table. "I'll take another pass at the chest. You have a match?"

"Sure." He fished a box of matches out of his shirt pocket and tossed it to her. "I'll be back as fast I can get the plumber on track."

"Thanks," she said, catching the box. She lifted the chimney and lit the lamp as Clint disappeared into the falling darkness.

Tidal Hydroelectric Plant

AS CYNTHIA INSPECTED Clint's campsite, Joel Martin eyed the sun now low in the sky behind the metal towers that supported the lines from transformers in the tidal hydroelectric plant's switch yard to the power company grid. Checking the time on his phone, he cursed, "He's late!" He once more scanned seaward for Buck Wilson and the GASMAX launch. Taking a short flight of metal steps from atop the turbine-generator building, he stepped onto the three-hundred-foot jetty that ran perpendicular into the estuary now nearly emptied by the ebbing tide.

Once he got halfway to the head of the jetty and still saw empty ocean, he called Wilson's cell again. No answer. The opening sound of the turbine generator building's ebb tide gate behind him drew his attention. He dialed Clint's phone as he watched the seawater, captured in the tidal basin during previous flood tide, rush out. The flow of the seawater spun the blades of two water turbines that turned generator rotors connected to the turbine shafts by articulated gearing.

GASMAX sold the resulting electricity to the local power company, and the sale more than offset the gas plant's monthly electric bill. It also generated income that easily paid for the power plant's operating cost and long-term maintenance. As his phone rang, Joel smiled at the memory of how his brother's engineering genius teamed with his own expert business acumen had crafted this commercial efficiency. *I miss that*, he thought, once more haunted by the ghosts of happier cooperative times.

"Hello," Clint said, his voice chasing away Joel's ghosts.

"Is she there?" Joel asked while scanning the darkening horizon to the south.

"Yeah, that's correct. Hold on." Clint replied, and after a stretch of silence, "I can talk now. She got here a few minutes ago. What's up?"

"Wilson isn't here yet."

"How about Danny?"

"She's all set up, but until I have Buck's special delivery we can't proceed. We need to stall."

"Should be no problem. She's seemed more eager to get into Grandpa Moses' story chest than visit the rock wall. Also, she's buying this cabin contractor story. I can play that, but I may have to leave her alone to sell it."

"Anything in that chest?" Joel asked. The mention of his father's name and that ridiculous wooden trunk made him uneasy.

"No," Clint answered. "I went through it thoroughly. It's just all those trinkets, odds and ends and other junk he collected in his travels."

"Hmm, well, okay. Do or say whatever you have to. I'll call or text when I'm ready."

"Roger that, but ..."

"But what?" Joel demanded sharply and then softened his tone. "Don't go weak on me, son. We're almost home free. Stay the course and do what's necessary."

"Yeah, I know, but ... murder. I ..."

"But nothing, boy. Buck up. Okay?" Joel said. *Damn, he fears or hates Buck Wilson*, he thought, suddenly realizing the irony of the terminology he used to encourage Clint.

"Okay. Goodbye," Clint nervously replied, confirming Joel's supposition.

Joel eyed the black screen. *It's still a tossup as to which one of those two will be the weak link in this operation. Until now I was sure it was Danny*, he thought as the glint of setting sunlight off a boat's windshield broke the gathering twilight.

"It's about time," Joel said as the GASMAX launch came clearly into view. Its white bow wake deeply scarred the dark blue water. "At least, he's pouring on the speed." By the time Joel reached the end of the jetty, Wilson had cut the power and turned the Chris-Craft to lay alongside the bottom rungs of the metal ladder that ran up one of the jetty's long black pilings.

Wilson tied the boat off to an upper ladder rung, anticipating the eventual flood tide and the water from the tidal basin filling the estuary. Hefting a backpack onto his shoulder, he climbed the ladder. "Hi, boss," he said with a smile.

"You're late," Joel said sharply, and then, taking the edge off, "You got the stuff?"

Buck handed him the backpack. "In here, safe and sound. You got something for me?"

Martin opened the backpack and examined the small leather case as well as the firearms and ammunition. He grinned briefly and pulled out his phone. "Check your account," he said after a few screen strokes. "That's half."

Wilson worked his phone. After a minute he smiled. "Excellent. What about the other half and the extra items?"

Joel unzipped his black windbreaker and took out a folded, letter-size manila envelope. "The 'extras' are all in here: passport, photo IDs and credit cards. You get the 'other half' at the rendezvous. Due to your tardiness we're behind schedule so ..."

"Whoa, boss." Buck held up a hand. "Not my fault and we've got a problem."

"What problem?"

"Come on I'll show you. It's on the boat."

Visibly impatient, Joel followed the other man down the jetty ladder and climbed aboard the bobbing launch. "Now what's the problem? I don't ..." Joel asked but stopped suddenly when Wilson pulled back the tarp in the back of the boat, revealing Julie Simpson's unconscious body. "What the hell happened?"

Buck quickly explained the encounter at the boat dock, the boat chase and Strong's demise. Sensing that he was generating little forgiveness for being late, he added, "Also, she's been snooping around the village inquiring about the Martin family history and, more recently, asking about you?"

"So, why didn't you just leave her onboard with Strong?"

"She's a cop."

"A PI," Joel corrected.

"Well, the way she was acting at the dock it sounded like she was a cop. I'm told that Chief Smith deputizes her when he's shorthanded." Buck eyed Joel to see if he was following his reasoning. As usual, he couldn't read the older man. "In any case, I didn't think killing a cop would be a good idea."

Joel sighed. "Normally, Buck, I'd agree with your reasoning." Wilson was visibly surprised by Joel's response, but before he could say anything, Martin continued, "After tonight it really doesn't matter if she dies. But it does need to look like an accident. So, here's what I want you to do."

AFTER LEAVING BUCK to complete the task of disposing of Simpson, Joel returned to his car. His personal black company sedan was almost swallowed up in the evening darkness surrounding the switchyard despite the security lights along the yard's chain-link fence. Before getting behind the wheel, he texted Clint's phone, 'Go.' After a brief pause, his phone screen lit up and the message notification displayed, 'Roger that.'

Prior to starting the car, Martin opened the backpack. He took out the two different-caliber pistols, loaded each from the appropriate box of ammunition, and slipped spare rounds into each front pocket of his windbreaker. After wrapping one pistol grip with black electrician's tape, he put a gun in each front pocket of his black cargo pants.

Martin started the car and took the hard leather black case from the backpack. It was not much bigger than his cell phone. He lifted the lid and smiled as he verified that the syringe and a glass vile containing a vibrant green fluid were intact.

AFTER JOEL DEPARTED, Buck implemented Martin's plan to kill Julie Simpson and make it look like an accident. *The man is pretty smart*, he thought as he uncuffed the detective. He rubbed her wrists to stimulate circulation to diminish the marks left by the cuffs. Likewise, he untied her feet and rubbed her ankles. After removing her long-sleeved blouse, he rolled it up and used it to tie her hands in front. Finally, he unbuckled her belt and removed the buckle and belt strap end from the front loops. Rolling her over, he buckled the belt behind her back.

The tide was coming in and the estuary was filling with water from the tidal basin. The boat was already riding even with the rung where he'd tied it off. Though the waning twilight made it difficult to see, Wilson stripped to his shorts and hoisted Julie over the side. He got into the water with her and felt her move as he wrapped his arms around her. She moaned when he unbuckled her belt. After placing the buckle and the other end around a wrung of the ladder, he cinched the belt as tightly as possible. He grabbed her by the shoulders and pulled. Satisfied that she was held secure enough for the rising tide to drown her, he climbed back into the boat, cast off and moved the boat up the jetty toward the beach.

After tying off the boat, he grabbed a towel and his clothes before making his way to the turbine generator building. He remembered from a prior visit that there was an unlocked employee restroom with a shower. He'd use that and dry out. Although the power plant was an unmanned facility, he also could keep an eye landward. The plant went silent as the ebb tide gate closed, allowing the estuary to fill. He looked at his watch before stepping into the shower. *In two to three hours, I can retrieve her body and dump it overboard off Parrot Point on the way to the rendezvous. As Martin said, it'll look like she and Strong both died in the same unfortunate boating accident. I hate the bastard, but I gotta admit he's a smart one.*

CHAPTER 22

A Shot in the Dark

Tidal Hydroelectric Plant

WHEN TANNER STAGGERED OFF THE beach, he was relieved that no one was at the Starfish Condominium construction site. Despite the ringing in his ears and occasional nausea, he had quickly found a truck, broke a window, and hotwired it.

The tidal hydroelectric plant was a few straight miles north off of Highway 733. In the growing darkness, he almost missed the turnoff for the short road to the plant's parking lot. As he slowed to make the right-hand turn, he recalled that the plant was fully automated and unmanned. *How do I open the lot's gate?* he wondered.

His headache was persistent now, and he felt a constant pressure in his head. He realized these were symptoms of concussion. Clouding his thinking, this made it difficult for him to solve the gate problem. The dilemma vanished and his thinking cleared when a black Mercedes sedan reached the intersection first. As he turned right, the sedan crossed the highway to take the road leading to the rock quarry. *Problem solved, the gate closing is greatly delayed*, he recalled. *Hey, I know that car ... that was Joel Martin!*

Shaking his head to fight off another bout of dizziness, he slowed. *I'd love to follow him, but the gate's open and Julie's here*, he reasoned. He turned off the headlights before entering the lot. *After I find her, we can get over to the quarry*, he decided as he parked near the sidewalk leading to the tidal basin.

He got out and opened the toolbox mounted forward of the truck's rear fender. Selecting a claw hammer and a six-inch awl, he pocketed both in his still damp pants. *No gun. So, these'll have to do.*

He stepped onto the walk and quickly hiked the gravel path skirting the tidal basin wall leading to the turbine generator building and the jetty beyond. He slowed his pace when he spotted the GASMAX launch tied off to a jetty piling near the generator building. *No one's onboard*, he observed, hefting the claw hammer. He stood still, looked, and listened.

Despite the ringing in his ears, he could tell that the plant was quiet. He recalled from a visit and plant tour with J Martin that silence meant the tide was changing. The only thing he noticed out of the ordinary were the lights on inside the employee restroom that included showers. The washroom and an adjacent rest area were built for periodic maintenance team visits. They sat atop the unmanned facility's generator structure that spanned the seaward end of the tidal basin, separating it from the estuary on the ocean side. "Wilson," he hissed, glancing again at the boat tied up at the jetty. He scooped up a hand full of gravel to augment his makeshift arsenal.

As quickly and quietly as he could, he ran to and up the steps, pausing at the top. A short walkway, with a handrail to prevent falling into the estuary, led to the restroom. Its left side ran past a dark opening into the break area containing a picnic table, benches and vending machines. Light shone out from the restroom door that was ajar as well as its narrow window near the ceiling. The clear sound of running water rose above the ringing in Tanner's ears. "I got you now," he declared as he advanced to the door with hammer raised and his fist tightly clenching the hand full of small rocks.

"No, I've got you," a voice behind him countered.

Tanner turned as Buck Wilson, barefooted and bare-chested and dressed only in jeans, stepped out of the break area shadows. Light from the restroom glistened off his wet skin. He leveled a gun at Tanner's chest. "Man, you do not die easy," he said, pushing aside the long, dark hair that was matted across his forehead. He took a step toward Tanner.

The sudden sound of the floodtide gates opening below them joined their discourse. As the turbine building rumbled into action, other mechanical and machine noises joined in.

"Wilson, where's Julie?" Strong shouted, ignoring Wilson's advantage in weapons, raising the hammer and stepping toward Buck.

"None of that. Drop the hammer and freeze," Buck ordered. Tanner dropped the hammer and raised his empty hand. "By the sounds of those gates, I'd say she'll soon be breathing her last."

"What have you done to her?"

"She's trussed up to a piling at the end of the jetty," Wilson laughed.

"What?" Tanner cried taking a half-step closer.

Without crediting Joel Martin, Wilson enthusiastically described Julie's dilemma. He chuckled and concluded, "Now I'll have two bodies to dump."

Fury welled up in Strong and his head pounded with pain. "You sadistic bastard!" he screamed, throwing the handful of gravel into Wilson's face and lunging to tackle him. The gravel hit Wilson in the forehead and eyes, and he jerked the trigger. The shot went wide as Wilson instinctively raised both hands to his face. He dropped the pistol when Tanner collided with him, knocking him into the wall. Strong swung, and his right fist connected with

Wilson's jaw. Before he could follow with his left, the exertion of the first punch initiated a wave of dizziness. He stumbled back against the rail.

Wilson, having cleared the gravel from his eyes and realizing an opportunity to strike back, instantly sprang. Towering over Tanner, he threw a right cross punch that stunned his opponent. Wilson closed his hands around the larger man's neck and pressed. They rolled along the railing before Tanner weakened and Wilson gained the advantage. He leaned into him, bending his foe backwards over the rail while pressing his thumbs into his neck.

Both men could hear the flood tide swirling around the turbine gate below. Tanner flailed his arms and legs, trying without success to break the chokehold and to get traction with his feet.

"It's all over, Strong," Wilson hissed, his face within an inch of Tanner's. He pressed harder with both thumbs to end the struggle.

Tanner frantically sought an action to respond. *Focus, it can't be all... all...*, he thought desperately, laboring to breath. *That's it, awl!* With his right hand he grasped the carpenter's awl in his pocket and pulled it free. *One shot at this. I'm blacking out,* he coached himself, raising his arm.

The awl sank into Wilson's left shoulder up to the hilt. He immediately released his grip, rolling off Tanner to his opponent's right side and lying against the rail. Before he could grasp the awl to pull it out, Tanner, gasping for breath, got to his feet and swung his right arm hard to his right. The backhanded blow caught Wilson in the chest propelling him over the rail. Tanner rolled to his right, grasped the upper rail, and peered into the estuary. Wilson hit the surface and disappeared in the swirling water above the floodtide gates.

"Good riddance," Tanner grunted when Wilson didn't surface. He sank to the ground as a wave of dizziness and nausea came and went. His breathing returned to normal as the headache retreated to a low-grade pain accompanied by slight pressure behind his forehead. "Julie!" he cried, jumping to his feet and scooping up Wilson's gun. He ran down the steps and to the end of the jetty. Pausing only to drop the gun, he dove in.

Strong swam back to the piling ladder and followed it under the surface. He soon found Julie, and the top of her head was only a few inches below the surface. Remembering Wilson's description of how he'd bound her, Tanner put his arms around her and pushed up to raise her head above the water's surface, but it wasn't enough. The upward motion was abruptly stopped by the belt that was buckled and wrapped around the ladder rung. He felt her legs moving. *She's still kicking to keep her head above water,* he thought. By feel, he found the belt buckle, but he was unable to free her.

Damn, he thought, growing desperate for air. *That's it!* He unbuttoned and unzipped her pants, and, wrapping his arms around her, he succeeded with a firm push to raise their heads above the water. She was limp in his arms. "Come on, Julie, breathe," he ordered, hooking one arm on a ladder rung and the other around her waist and sharply pulling her close. "Breathe, damn it!"

Julie convulsed in his arm and coughed up water as her eyes opened. She smiled weakly. "About time you got here."

"Thank God," he gasped. After he freed her hands, they climbed up onto the jetty.

"What happened?" Julie asked as they sat to catch their breath. She shivered, now fully aware that her blouse and pants were gone.

"Come on," Tanner said, standing and helping her up. He swayed on his feet.

She guided his arm around her shoulders, and he leaned on her. "Easy does it," she cautioned with concern. "Based on that cut, you've been hit in the head and have a concussion."

"Yeah, and more than once." He forced a laugh. "Help me back to the turbine generator building over there. There may be a phone and some dry clothes. I'll get you caught up before we go."

"Go where?"

"Quarry Forest to help Cynthia." They took a few unsteady steps and soon made slow but steady progress. When they got to the walkway to the restroom, he stopped and pointed over the rail. "That's where Wilson went in," he said before motioning towards the picnic table. "Now let me rest while you find Wilson's phone. I think there are some coveralls in there."

She helped him sit, shivering as she stood. "Normally a man has at least bought me dinner before he's undressed me," she said and smiled. "You okay?"

"I've been better, but good enough," he replied and forced a smile. "It's a date, dinner and a movie when this is all over. Now go!"

She returned wearing a set of blue GASMAX coveralls and carrying Wilson's phone and the envelope with his 'extra items.' "Found them," she said and smiled. She tugged the collar. "And the coveralls are a perfect fit." She frowned when she saws that Tanner was flat on his back.

Tanner raised his head, "Great, help me up. We gotta get ... get ... to Cynthia." His head sank back to the table.

"The only thing we 'gotta' do is get you to a hospital," she said, dialing 911. "You have one bad concussion." After talking with the operator, she called Chief Smith. As they waited for the ambulance. She checked Tanner's breathing and pulse every few minutes. She stroked Tanner's arm and whispered, "That's it. Sleep. You need lots of it.".

Tanner stirred. "Cynthia," he said before falling back to sleep.

Julie patted his hand and checked his pulse again. "Cynthia's on her own, big man," she said. "Besides, my PI gut tells me this is a Martin family affair tonight and it is members only. We'd just be in the way. I just hope she survives it."

The ambulance soon arrived. Before she got in the back for the ride to the hospital, she noted that the moon was low in the southeastern sky. Larger than normal size, its blood red-orange color reflected faintly in the dark mirror-smooth ocean water. *That's right, it's a Thunder Moon tonight*, she recalled. The ambulance doors slammed shut and the siren wailed.

Quarry Forest Home Plate Campsite

MOSES MARTIN'S KING James Bible lay open next to Cynthia's phone and gun on the camp table. A bell tone announced the text message, 'Still arguing with plumber. Clint.' He had been gone more than an hour.

She frowned, having mixed feelings about his prolonged absence. The sun was well down, and she wasn't looking forward to the trek to the rock wall in a dark, dense wood that hid who knows what danger. On the other hand, she appreciated the extra time to study Grandpa Moses' Bible to see if she could make sense of the message, 'Beth Togarmah.'

The trunk and its contents were staged next to her chair so she could quickly hide the Bible in the false bottom beneath Moses' junk when Clint returned. If she could believe what he had said about the trunk, he had no idea that the book was there.

Using the gilt-edge page from her pocket, she confirmed it was a flyleaf page ripped from her grandfather's Bible. In its handwritten note he confessed that his iniquity and deceit directly precipitated the fall of the Tannerson house and that family's demise. In addition to confirming a close connection to Niles and Melody Tannerson, he also speculated that his moral failings dumped retribution for his sins into the 'laps of my children and of theirs after them.' *How true that may be*, Cynthia thought, considering the recent deadly Martin family travails. Mulling over the recently discovered evidence, she speculated who had torn out Moses Martin's handwritten, remorse filled note. *J or Moses, maybe*, she thought. *Joel is a less likely a candidate.*

"What about Beth Togarmah?" she wondered, recalling Tanner's envelope in her pocket and its two-word, handwritten text. Further online search of 'Beth Togarmah' told her that Togarmah was mentioned in Chapter 10 of the Book of Genesis in what scholars call the table of nations. The text tabulated how Noah's descendants through his three sons, Shem, Ham, and Japheth, populated the nations of the Earth after they left the ark.

Togarmah was one of Japheth's three grandsons through his son, Gomer. His descendants became the people of what is today southeast Turkey. *Really awful names*, Cynthia thought and smiled briefly, recalling the laugh she'd shared with Sylvia when they simultaneously said the same thing.

From the internet, they'd also discovered that the house of Togarmah was mentioned twice by an Old Testament prophet, Ezekiel. In both instances, he prophesized that horses and soldiers would come from these northern people to join God's holy war against an offending nation south of Turkey. Also, and of the most interest to their investigation, 'house,' they discovered, is 'beth' in Hebrew, the Old Testament's original language. So, 'house of Togarmah' is equivalent to 'Beth Togarmah.' *So ... so what?* Cynthia thought again. *But then Syl had found that note in J's study. On a day-by-day calendar page, a few weeks before his final hike, he wrote 'Dad's Bible in old trunk false bottom – in cabin.'* They both remembered the trunk as well as the Bible, but they didn't remember Moses keeping anything but his story props in the chest. Sylvia recalled the trunk was stored at the cabin. At the quarry in response to her request, Clint said he'd put it into storage with the other items cleared out for cabin renovation and would have to arrange to get it. *So, it's worth a shot*, she concluded, thumbing through the gilt-edge pages. *A missing piece or pieces may be in here.*

It's obvious that Grandpa read his Bible, she thought, noting that many pages were worn and smudged with several margin notes in black ink in his tight handwriting. Most of the notes were dated thirty years ago. A few entries were cross-references but most were questions for God. *He seemed to be looking for loopholes more than answers, like a man struggling with some lifelong dilemma*, she concluded after reading several of the notes. The margin note dated the day before her birthday and concerning his assessment of his sons' potential for a part in some kind of family redemption strategy was telling and confirming.

Not surprising, the note was prefaced with the elder Martin's ethical edict to 'Do what's necessary, love God and do good, bearing fruit in keeping with repentance.' He'd underlined each word separately. She frowned. Notably and not unexpectedly, 'Do what's necessary' was double-underlined. She grinned briefly, recalling the events and discoveries in the wine cellar, when she read the rest of the preface note, 'The parents have eaten sour grapes, and the children's teeth are set on edge – Jeremiah 31:29.' "The grandchildren's too," she said softly and flipped the page.

Consistent with Moses Martin's love for family traditions, he had meticulously and neatly filled in the Bible's front page that recorded family genealogy names, births, deaths and marriages. These were also in his handwriting but oddly written in pencil rather than black ink. She drew her finger down the list, recognizing relatives' names and noting that the record started with 'Moses Japheth Martin' and not his or Grandma's parents. *That's a bit peculiar*, she thought.

"Hmm, let's see if he wrote anything about Togarmah," she said, flipping to the Book of Ezekiel. The pages of the two chapters that mentioned it did not have notes or other annotation. They revealed nothing more than what she and Sylvia had gathered online. However, in Genesis 10 she discovered three annotated verses:

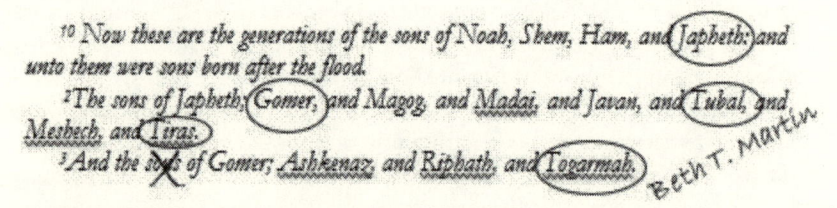

> ¹⁰ *Now these are the generations of the sons of Noah, Shem, Ham, and Japheth: and unto them were sons born after the flood.*
> ²*The sons of Japheth; Gomer, and Magog, and Madai, and Javan, and Tubal, and Meshech, and Tiras.*
> ³*And the sons of Gomer; Ashkenaz, and Riphath, and Togarmah.* — Beth T. Martin

"Beth T. Martin ... Beth Togarmah Martin," Cynthia said slowly, holding the Bible closer to the lamp to make sure she had read the name right. "Wait a minute!" Closing the book on her hand, she read her grandfather's name engraved on the leather binding, 'Moses Japheth Martin.' Flipping to the genealogy page, she placed her finger on Moses' name and went down the list. *There's Grandma with 'MET 1964' written next to her name. When they met, I guess. There are the three sons: Justice Tubal Martin, Jacob Gomer Martin and Joel Tiras ... the sons of Japheth!* she realized and flipped back to Genesis.

No wonder they never used their full names that I can remember. Father died before I was born and Mom never said anything about his middle name. And all I remember is that J and Joel used middle initials. Even at GASMAX in any document I ever saw it was just an initial. Tubal and Tiras — can't say I blame them.

"Grandpa and Grandma, what were you thinking?" she said, shook her head and found a pen. On the already greatly annotated first page of Genesis 10 she wrote, 'Moses' above 'Japheth,' 'Jacob' above 'Gomer,' 'J' above 'Tubal' and 'Joel' above 'Tiras.'

She tapped the page with the pen and wondered aloud, "But my father, Gomer, didn't have a son ... maybe that's why 'sons' is x'd out. But, by this construct, my original name should have been Cynthia Togarmah Martin. Instead, my given middle name is Martha."

She wrote 'Martha' under 'Togarmah' and sat back. *If I drop the 'g' and 'o' in Togarmah, the remaining letters can be arranged to spell 'Martha,'* she figured. *But, I'm not a Beth or even an Elizabeth. So, this is likely just coincidence or overreaching hope. Unless ...* "One of the certificates in the safe deposit box was a death certificate," she remarked suddenly. "The baby's name was Elizabeth T. Tannerson, Beth Togarmah Tannerson ... Niles Tannerson's daughter? If so, what's she doing in the Martin genealogy where I should be? Unless ..."

Flipping back to the Martin family tree page, she found her penciled entry. "It's Grandpa's handwriting all right," she observed softly. Holding the book closer to the lamplight, she saw that he had erased and written over an original entry. In the angled light the original impression made by the pencil revealed his first entry, 'Elizabeth Togarmah Martin.' She once more read Moses Martin's note on the flyleaf before she sank back into the chair and stared at the Bible. "Oh my God! Somehow, I'm not a Martin but a Tannerson," she said finally and considered what that could mean. *Worst of all, if MET are initials ... My God, could I be both? In any case, I can see now why Joel, and some of or all of the other Martins want me out of the way.*

Cynthia's phone's message ring tone broke the stunned silence of her revelation. The text from Clint read, 'Almost there.' She quickly closed the Bible, returned it to the chest, hiding it beneath the false bottom and Moses Martin's story props. She swung the top shut just as Clint returned.

There was no time for her to call Sylvia or attempt to contact Tanner and Julie before he walked into the campsite. "Okay, Cuz, let's get going," he ordered cheerfully when he appeared, rapping a dimly lit flashlight against his open empty palm. "Gotta replace this. Batteries are about dead. We'll need flashlights for a while, but the moon should be up soon and it'll be a full one. So, there'll be plenty of light to make good time."

"Yeah, it's a Thunder Moon tonight," she responded and smiled to hide a rising anxiety. She stood and gathered her flashlight and phone before putting her gun in her pocket. "Clint, couldn't we just do all this in the morning?"

"Uh, no ... Look, I have to be at the cabin super early to meet contractors. They're being real butt heads about ..." he said with some surprise. "That doesn't matter. Look, I just think you really, really need to see this as soon as possible."

"What is it?"

"I can't ... you have to see it. I can't put it into words, but Dad wrote some kind of message on the rock wall. Please, I think it's important. Tomorrow may be too late."

Cynthia knew that Clint struggled with being deceptive, because for the most part he was an open book. Unlike Danny, he couldn't pitch the bull, but he tried at times. From the years of shared big sister duty with Sylvia, Cynthia concluded this wasn't one of those times. And too, something about J Martin and his message was truly making Clint uneasy. There may be something sinister still to fear, but it would be something he wasn't directly or fully involved in nor have direct responsibility. Clint had a conscience still capable of being guilt ridden, an attribute she was coming to realize very much lacking in the other Martin sons – and daughters - of Japheth. *We've all fallen short in the loving God, doing good and bearing fruit in keeping with repentance department*, she thought sadly, seeing that Clint looked nervously away as he pleaded for the nocturnal visit to the wall. *Hell, I'm not sure any of us even loved each other the way we should.*

Though she would feel safer if Tanner and Julie were with her, she felt secure enough given her assessment that Clint still posed only a minimum direct threat. Also, she agreed there was some urgency for going with him but likely not for the same reasons he imagined or professed. *Going back to the GASMAX parking lot may be no safer than hiking deeper into the woods with Clint*, she reasoned, considering the new understanding of her identity in the context of the week's events and recent revelations. "Okay, Clint," she said and sighed. "Let's go."

"Great. Let me get another flashlight," he said and headed for the tent. "We'll be back before you know it. The sooner the better, right?"

You don't know how right you are, my cousin or maybe nephew, she thought while sending a text to Sylvia.

Quarry Forest

FINALLY, DANNY THOUGHT when she saw the 'Go' text from Joel. She rolled onto her stomach and pulled the sniper rifle toward her. Before putting her eye to the shooter's spotting scope, she tugged flat the thin dark grey mat she'd laid atop the deer stand. Though moonrise was some minutes away, the night-vision-equipped scope plainly revealed an empty clearing that Martin family members had long ago dubbed the Pitcher's Mound campsite. *Tonight,* she mused with pleasure, *it will serve the family in a new and lethal way.*

J Martin had built the deer stand decades earlier, and the rough wooden platform could accommodate three hunters. It was situated twelve feet up in a tall oak tree ten yards down the blazed trail from the Pitcher's Mound to the Third Base campsite. Originally, when they were young, it also served as a tree house for J's children and their cousin, Cynthia. For J and Joel, in those years and since, it doubled as a deer blind in hunting season. *And, when we were teens,* she recalled fondly, *it also suited our purposes for activities Mom and Dad would not approve of.*

There was no guitar case with ironic anti-gun stickers or casual hiking attire tonight. Like Joel, she was dressed in black jeans, boots, tee, jacket and ball cap. Having left her car in the GASMAX north lot and, after setting the plant in the full-AI-controlled mode for tonight's scheduled Phase Four test, Danny parked the car Buck had 'borrowed' in the quarry lot. Slinging the rifle over her shoulder, she quickly trekked to the dear stand. She carried supporting gear and an extra handgun in a black tactical backpack. She twisted the cap backwards on her head before running her hand along the sniper rifle's stock. *All set,* she asserted silently.

She pulled the rifle into the prone firing position. Using the telescopic sight with the night-vision capability, she confirmed in greater detail what the spotter scope revealed. The green luminous clearing was empty except for her black pack. Before abandoning it in the clearing, she'd emptied it, except for the handgun and spare ammo. She snorted. "Uncle may be overplaying it. However, with Clint playing the unknowing Judas goat, it'll keep the Princess in the clearing long enough."

Danny checked her watch. *Moonrise soon,* she observed. *No wind, a clear field of fire and just thirty yards. I won't miss this time,* she concluded and grinned briefly. *And won't Uncle and Bro be surprised when I go off script. It'll work out better this way.*

The moon, more white than orange, was above the eastern tree line when Cynthia and Clint entered the campsite. Danny followed them with the spotter scope. As she anticipated, Princess was in the lead, and, as expected, she motioned Clint to halt. She pulled out a gun before cautiously approaching the backpack. "Not cautious enough, Princess," Danny hissed softly and took up the rifle.

When Danny centered the crosshairs on Cynthia, her target had knelt to inspect the pack's contents. Clint, visible at the edge of the scope, was well clear. Taking in a breath, Danny slipped her finger inside the trigger guard, and she squeezed the trigger to the first pull position. Cynthia said something to Clint over her shoulder but remained centered in the crosshairs. Slowly exhaling, Danny paused, pulled the trigger and smiled. Cynthia clutched at her chest and fell backwards. "That's for me and Buck, Princess" she said, working the bolt action to load a second round. She placed the crosshairs on Clint. He was crouched down and immobilized, but, as she squeezed the trigger, he suddenly threw himself to the ground. She worked the bolt a third time, but when she aimed only Cynthia's body remained in the clearing. She was certain that she saw movement behind a tree at the clearing's edge.

"Damn!" she cursed, standing up. "Clint, you ... I knew it." Slinging the rifle over her shoulder, she descended the wooden ladder quickly and quietly. *I'm completely off script now,* she thought. *I gotta take care of Bro before Joel steps in.*

CHAPTER 23

Fireworks and Moonlight

Quarry Forest Pitcher Mound Campsite

"Thereʼs just a gun in here, and ..." Cynthia said over her shoulder before the bullet ripped through her blouse. However, the slug only sliced open the flesh over her ribcage before burrowing into the ground. Grimacing, she clutched her right side and fell. Despite the pain and desire to seek cover, she realized that standing would just make her a bigger and better target for a second shot.

A second explosion split the night. The bullet missed Clint, its obvious target, and validated her assumption. *Now itʼs time to move*, she concluded quickly. She heard before she saw Clint crawling toward a tree at the clearingʼs edge. She scrambled to her feet and ran after him.

They reached the tree simultaneously. She pressed her back against the treeʼs side away from the clearing. He threw himself flat and pressed his face into the ground. A third bullet struck the tree. A piece of coarse black bark burst from the impact and smacked his jaw. "Iʼm hit!" he cried, clutching his cheek.

Cynthia, pressing her back harder against the tree, lowered herself to sit next to her cringing companion. "Youʼre not hit," she savagely observed and pressed her hand against her wound. Sheʼd somehow managed to hold on to her gun and laid it in her lap.

Clint looked at her. Shadowed by moonlight, his eyes widened as she pulled open her blouse. One side was torn and, the moonlight revealed that both sides were black with blood. Her dark blue eyes were narrow slits as she examined the gash in the flesh just below her breast. Her face, contorted with anger and pain, was framed by wildly disarrayed hair.

Cynthiaʼs eyes found Clintʼs. He quickly shoved his face back into the ground. *Guilty conscience*, she thought. *But he probably didnʼt expect to be a target.*

Despite their dilemma and her anger, she was able to smile briefly at her terrified cousin. She minimized the extent of her injury, saying as calmly and evenly as possible, "Clint, I'm not badly hurt. It's only a flesh wound. It missed the ribs." Inhaling deeply, she moved her right arm up and down. "See? You okay?"

He didn't reply.

Picking up the gun, she looked at him. "Hey, are you okay?" Burning pain radiated from her wound. *He's scared*, she thought.

His face, under wet and matted hair, was distorted by fear. Eyes wide, he looked up. Finally, he nodded, giving a silent thumbs up.

He's never been shot at. In J's mandated self-defense, small arms and tactics training, she recalled, *we were all taught that most people are scared to almost immobilization the first time a shot comes their way.* He had had the same training, and tonight he proved the point. All the great outdoorsman bravado and confidence dissolved with the first shot. *He's a wreck, but I need him if we're going to get out of this alive,* she concluded, and her gun hand trembled despite her best efforts to hold it steady. *Hell, I'm not much better off.*

As if sensing her critical scrutiny, Clint propped himself up on one elbow and patted his cheek. His eyes went wide when he saw blood. "I'm hit! See, I'm hit!" he hissed, extending his hand toward her.

"No, you're not, Clint," she corrected. She rubbed his cheek and showed him her hand. Realizing she needed him to master his fear and follow orders, she took most of the impatient disdain she felt out of her voice before adding, "It's a scratch. Some bark flew off the tree. It hit your cheek."

"Oh," his mouth silently formed the word. He eased his face to the ground. When he heard her move, he quickly looked up and cried, "Where … Where are you going?"

Cynthia suppressed the desire to slap him. There wasn't time or swinging room for shock therapy. *It'd probably have the opposite effect anyway*, she thought as she considered her cowering cousin.

Leaning forward and looking around the tree, she examined the dirt trail that she knew led to the Third Base campsite. As she recalled, it was fifty plus yards to the western campsite and an equal distance from that site to the narrow walkway along the river. Considering where she had stood when she was hit and the side of the tree that had been hit by the third round, she estimated that the shooter was up that trail. *The deer stand, of course. Not getting out of here that way*, she concluded, *unless the shooter moves.*

The northbound trail entrance was also visible in the moonlight. It led to the Second Base campsite and the quarry wall path beyond. *That way maybe*, she speculated. *Clint's truck's parked there.*

In one of the shadows cast by trees along the westward trail, something metallic twinkled in the moonlight and a bright flash erupted. Once more, the early Thunder Moon night's staccato chorus of crickets and tree frogs was joined by the crack of rifle fire.

"Down!" Cynthia shouted as the ground near her left leg exploded. Dirt, pine needles, and twigs pelted her and Clint. She pulled her knees to her chest and leaned hard against the tree. The sudden move spiked the pain from her wound.

"No!" Clint choked. Covering his head with his hands, he pressed his face to the ground. "This wasn't supposed to ... This can't be happening."

"Shut up," she barked and grabbed his hair. She pulled his face within an inch of hers and shifted her grip to his neck. "You're all right, but you won't be unless you get a grip. We need to move now. We've been seen. The shooter's down the trail to Third Base and is on the move. The next shot won't hit the ground."

Clint, near panicked, stared at her silently. She felt knots in his neck muscles. Softening her voice, she relaxed her grip. "We need to get up and try for the north trail and fast. Can you do that?"

Gentle words had the desired effect. Some of the tension in his neck lessened. Clint blinked. "Yes ... I can do that," he replied without emotion.

Cynthia removed her hand and smiled briefly. "Good. Now we need some more firepower. There's a gun in that bag. Stay put and I'll get it."

He nodded.

Despite recent events and his likely complicity in all this, something about her cousin still warranted guarded trust. Turning her attention to escaping in one piece, her eyes darted from Clint to the dark backpack that lay where the shooter had abandoned it. *No doubt it was meant to slow us down and set up the shot*, she reasoned. *Yep, he led me into a trap, but something didn't go the way he thought it would. So, his survival is linked to mine ... for now.*

The extra gun, she figured, gave them a better chance, but getting it was dangerous, and the risk increased with each passing second. Glancing up the west trail and assuming the shooter was still repositioning for another shot, she crawled to the backpack, pulled out the pistol and threw it to Clint. She patted the bag until she found the spare clips of bullets.

Clint instinctively rose to his knees and caught the gun. The move was smooth, a reflex reaction to Cynthia's toss. Realizing what he'd caught and that she had abandoned him, he sat back quickly. He held the gun at arm's length as if he had caught a rattlesnake.

Cynthia crawled back to him. A bullet struck the ground that she had just vacated. She impatiently planted the pistol grip in Clint's palm. "Come on, Clint, you know how to use this. You're a crack shot. Snap out of it. I'm scared, too."

"Yeah." He nodded, not taking his eyes off the blue-black pistol. Gripping it correctly, he examined the gun and ejected the clip. He checked it full, replaced it and chambered a round. "Ready," he said.

"Good. Safety up to shoot and down to safe," she instructed quickly with a smile. "Shoot when you have a target, but not in my direction. Got it?"

"Yeah. Up to shoot and ... and not you," he replied and managed a brief smile.

"That's it," she said. "Eight shots and then empty. Count them." She put spare clips in his shirt pocket. "Here are some clips." Patting his arm and glancing over her shoulder at the north trail entrance, she pulled him onto his knees.

"What ...," he blustered. From his tone, Cynthia was confident that her tutorial had revived his fear-suppressed ability to proficiently handle the pistol and had restored a large measure of self-confidence.

"Let's move," she jerked her head to the right. "We're taking the trail to Second Base. If we make it, we have a chance with your truck."

"Okay," he whispered and followed her as she crouched and led him in the undergrowth of the clearing's perimeter to the north trail's entrance.

Another rifle shot fragmented the night, briefly driving them flat on the ground. "The shooter's moving to head us off," Cynthia hissed and scrambled to her feet. "Move."

Clint followed and saw the patch of earth he had so lovingly hugged blow up.

"Move!" Cynthia repeated through clenched teeth. They reached the trailhead and ran down the trail. Clint's labored but even breath told her that he had controlled his fear. *We might make it out of this alive*, she thought.

Cynthia considered the cloudless sky and full white moon both a blessing and curse. Running down the narrow path, she could clearly see while dodging or pushing aside the sharp branches and thick bunches of leaves crisscrossing the trail. Unfortunately, moonlight also made it easy for the shooter to set his or her sights. They were easy targets amongst the foliage especially if the sniper had reached the clearing they had just left. They were leaving a trail that anyone could easily follow. *A blind man could track us*, she cursed silently, pushing another branch aside.

Emergency Room Moses Martin Memorial Hospital

THE HOSPITAL ER'S small waiting room was empty except for Julie Simpson and a worried parent sitting next to a sunburnt boy holding his right forearm. She sat in the chair nearest the examination room glass doors through which Tanner had been wheeled when they arrived an hour earlier. Nearby the mother and her son sat across a desk from an admissions nurse with a practiced but effective smile. She watched the animated exchange between the three, but her thoughts were on the other side of the doors. It was so much so that she wasn't aware that Sylvia Martin had entered the emergency room until she sat down next to her.

"Julie, how is he?" she asked.

"Sylvia," Julie replied, startled out of her thoughts. "When did you get here?"

"Just walked in. You looked lost in thought, and, no offense, you look like hell. Are you injured?"

Julie tugged at her blue coveralls and pushed a hand through her dry and matted hair. "Guess I was a little, but it's no more than a bump and bruise thanks to Tanner," she said and grinned briefly. "And, yeah, I've looked better. Tanner and I have had quite the time. The man is fearless. By my count, he's saved my life three times."

"Yeah, he's heroic to a fault," Sylvia said and sighed, recalling Cynthia's accolades for Strong delivered in a similar adoring voice. "How's he doing?"

"They're doing a head MRI. He has a severe concussion, a grade three, I think they called it. They're concerned about a brain bleed."

"You sure you're okay? They check you?"

"They did. I'm fine." She laughed. "Just a little less for the wear, but it's nothing like a couple of near-death experiences to mess your makeup and hair."

"When I called Chief Smith, he told me Tanner was injured and brought here. He also said you were with him, but he didn't say much else," Sylvia said, raising a hand to the ceiling in exasperation. "I take this is all tied in with you and Tanner following up that Buck Wilson lead?"

"That's an understatement, Sylvia," Julie replied, sitting back. She suddenly sat up and grabbed Sylvia's arm. "But have you heard from Cynthia? Tanner was convinced she was ... is in trouble. He saw Joel Martin, or at least his car, heading to the quarry and Clint Martin is ... well, you know your brother."

"It's okay, the cavalry is on the way," Sylvia said with a smile, gently breaking her grip.

"Cavalry?"

"Cyn texted me our prearranged code word, 'cavalry,' to call in the cops. Chief Smith is sending an officer to the quarry."

"Thank God." Julie sighed, sat back, and looked at her watch. "I just hope that he gets there in ..." She stopped when the ER's glass entry doors opened and a stocky man walked through. His gray flecked hair and close-cropped beard outlined a square face with a blunt nose and black-rimmed glasses that magnified brown eyes. He went to the admissions desk, and he interrupted the mother and nurse. The nurse pointed to where Julie and Sylvia were sitting.

Both women rose when he approached. "Ms. Martin and Detective Simpson," he said extending a hand. "I don't know if you remember me. I'm ..."

"... Dr. Corbin Schwartz," they finished.

Quarry Forest Second Base Campsite

A FAINT SMILE creased Cynthia's face when they reached the opening into the Second Base clearing and saw Clint's truck. "Clint, we made it," she announced and paused before crossing the circular clearing. Assuming they'd eluded the shooter, she ran to the truck. "Get in and drive!" she ordered.

"Okay," he grunted, climbing behind the wheel. "Where?"

"To Home Plate," she barked, slamming the door shut.

"What? Why not ..." he asked as the engine roared to life.

"Go! The shooter followed us up here."

Clint spun the wheel, stomped the accelerator and flipped on the headlights. As they entered the southbound trail, the headlights revealed a figure carrying a rifle. Clint pressed the accelerator. "Danny!" he hissed bitterly.

Cynthia recognized Danny's surprised face just before her cousin dove off the trail to avoid being hit.

Branches scratched the sides of the truck as the trail narrowed. Clint slowed as they entered the Pitcher's Mound clearing. He aimed for and ran over the backpack as if it would serve as a kind of consolation prize for not hitting his sister. Frustration and fraternal hatred contorted his face.

Can this family be any more dysfunctional? Cynthia wondered briefly before their escape demanded her full attention. "Kill the lights and turn right," she commanded, pulling the wheel. "Head to Third Base. It's our only chance."

"What? Why?" he asked, glancing sideways. He shrugged. "Well, you've been right so far," he said, applying the brakes. When he turned off the headlights, the moonlight still clearly illuminated the entrance for the trail to the small island. "But we can get to the north lot."

"True, but there's a fence. We can only get through it on foot, and the trail is too narrow for the truck," she replied. "Besides, she expects us to go south. She'll pick us off before we get to my car. Also, you said the zip lines were working. We can use them to get from Third Base to First."

Clint nodded, turned right and accelerated down the trail to western campsite. "You're right," he admitted just before the rear window shattered. The bullet missed them and passed through the windshield, leaving a spider web of cracks surrounding a quarter-dollar-size hole. "Can't see to make the bridge!" he cried.

"Lights!" Cynthia screamed, rolling down her window. The lights illuminated the trail and the entrance of the wooden span across the Quarry Branch River to the Third Base island's east side. "Clint, the bridge ..."

"Is out!" he finished loudly, standing on the brakes. The large truck

SINS OF OUR BLOOD THUNDER MOON

slowed but did not stop before it slammed through the wooden sign declaring the outage. The pickup flew out over the river, before it plunged into the water front bumper down and well short of the opposite shore. The force of the collision threw them forward. The truck settled on the bottom, and water flooded the cab.

R. NICHOLAS POHTOS

CHAPTER 24

Deadly Tough Love

Quarry Branch River

BEFORE SHE MADE HER WAY across the rope bridge spanning the branch river, Danny Martin observed with some delight as her brother's truck nosedived into the river. In the bright moonlight, she could see that the roof of the truck remained above water after it settled on the bottom.

"No, you don't get off that easy," she declared as she unslung the rifle and set it down. She scuttled down the steep bank to the narrow flat shore and waded to the truck. Working quickly, using the hilt of a hunting knife, she smashed away windshield remnants, and, using the blade's business end, deflated airbags. Pushing Cynthia and then Clint upright, she put their heads above water. "Didn't buckle up." She chuckled, returning the knife to its sheath.

Starting with Cynthia, she pulled them free of the truck. "You better not be dead," she said, laying her brother next to her cousin on the narrow sandy shore.

Clint moaned and Cynthia coughed. "Good," Danny said and slapped each of them before retrieving the rifle.

"Ow!" Clint cried, pushing himself up.

"What the ..." Cynthia managed to say before spitting out water and pressing her hand against her cheek.

"On your feet," Danny ordered, motioning with the rifle muzzle.

"Danny, what are you ..." Cynthia started as Clint helped her up.

"Shut it and walk!" she ordered, pointing left. "Hands where I can see 'em. There's a path up the bank near the bridge. Move!"

The trio made their way to the island's Third Base campsite clearing. The west side was crowded by the bathhouse still under construction. The north side was truncated by the base of the rocky bluff and the entrance path to steps ascending to the zip line tower. In the moonlight, Cynthia clearly saw the metal tower, topped with a covered platform. Equally visible were the parallel zip lines disappearing in the eastern sky to where they terminated at a lower platform tower at First Base. The cave in the bluff and the old well were concealed in shadows.

"Stop! This'll do," Danny barked. "Turn around." She walked around her captives. "You look like a couple of drowned rats."

Clint and Cynthia exchanged glances at the wet clothing and hair clinging to their bodies.

"I see I didn't miss you completely, Princess."

"No, you didn't," Cynthia said. She nodded at her blood-stained blouse opened to the waist. "Just a flesh wound. May I?"

"Yeah, sure." Danny chuckled.

Cynthia flinched as she gradually lowered her hands and slowly buttoned the wet garment. *Got to buy some time*, she thought, studying Danny and the surroundings. Danny's face, framed by silver-black shadows and an explosion of hair made silver by moonlight, hid little of her fury and menace. A cruel narrow smile twisted her lips, and perspiration glistened on her cheeks. Her eyes were sunk in dark pools, each broken by a tight point of light. Moon shadows made her chin appear more pointed than round. A black denim jacket, trousers and boots as well as a hunting knife in an ankle sheath completed her merciless, menacing, and mercenary appearance.

Moving her head slightly as she fastened the last two buttons, Cynthia judged the distance to the bathhouse, the path up the bluff and Danny and Clint. Tucking the blouse into her slacks, she realized that her gun still rested in a pocket. With exaggerated effort and reaction due to the pain from her wound, she ran her hands through her hair.

"That must really smart." Danny grinned and brought the rifle barrel to point at the wounded woman's chest. "Your gun." She gestured with the rifle at the ground.

Cynthia pulled it out, set it at her feet and kicked it toward Danny.

"You too, brother dear."

Cynthia heard Clint's pistol hit the ground. *Fewer advantages now*, she thought. "Danny, you can't get away with this," she said in a steady voice. Cynthia judged the distance to her cousin and realized that she didn't have a chance of getting her gun without being shot. "Too many people know Clint and I are here."

"Both of you, on your knees. Lock your hands behind your head!" Danny snapped.

Cynthia and Clint sank to their knees.

"There'll be none of that, Cuz. Besides, you're blowing smoke. Anyone who'd help is otherwise occupied or disposed of, and no one else knows you're here except for me and dear old Uncle Joel. And he hasn't told a soul. Your boyfriend or bodyguard or whatever he is, and the PI are noticeably absent."

"What's been done to him ... them?" Cynthia asked with alarm. She took a breath and added, "But you're forgetting Sylvia."

"So, you are sweet on the thickheaded Tanner." Danny snorted and smiled. "If I know Buck, he ... they're all dead."

"Why you little ..." Cynthia cried out before Danny backhanded her. The blow staggered her backwards, but she remained kneeling, grasping her chin. Clint leaned back and held his hands in front of his face.

"Now that felt good." Danny laughed. "I always wanted to do that, Princess." She scooped up Clint's gun and pointed it at him. She motioned for him to raise his hands.

"What are you going to do?" Clint stammered, raising his hands higher than before.

Cynthia heard panic in his voice and saw Danny's dark eyes sparkle. *Delight or loathing or both*, she thought. *Her blood is up. That may help.* Still rubbing her cheek to make the long shot shorter, she concluded there was a reasonable chance to disarm the sister if the brother did something foolish to provoke her. *It's always been a love-hate thing between them, especially after the trial. If she first vents hate and abuses before shooting him, there's a good chance I can get to her before she gets off a shot.*

Danny's fury left her face. She smiled and walked behind them. She pressed the rifle's barrel against Clint's back and pushed. An animal-like cry escaped him. "It's payback time. First, you, Bro, and then the Princess here. Oh, I'm not forgetting sis. Don't worry, Lady Silvia is already taken care of."

Out of the corner of her eye, Cynthia could see her pistol half covered in leaves lying about three feet to her right. *Yeah, it's now a longer shot, but that's all we have left*, she silently calculated as Danny regained a devious edge to her cruel and murderous intentions to violently settle Martin family issues. *Keep her talking.*

"Don't do it, Danny," Cynthia said and stood slowly. When Danny didn't stop her, Cynthia took a short step toward her. She could clearly see Clint and his sister in the moonlight. He was frozen with fear, and Danny caressed the trigger with a slow up and down motion. "Please, Danny, this won't fix anything or make things right. Don't make it worse and go back to prison." Danny took her eyes off her brother and looked at Cynthia. Her finger slipped outside the trigger guard.

"You're ... you may be right," she said with the same sad repentant voice she used when they had talked at the GASMAX plant. "I just don't know any other way."

"Sure, you do. You showed me at the plant. Don't ruin your life," Cynthia pressed gently. "Don't ruin mine."

"Yours?"

"I just got my little sister back. You ... we're a family again. Please,"

Cynthia pleaded, spreading her open hands.

The barrel of the rifle lowered.

Martin Family Cabin

JOAN MARTIN, NO longer able to lay on the bed and stare at the ceiling, got up and paced the cabin's sole bedroom. *I wouldn't be surprised. He always said I wasn't any good at waiting.* She smiled briefly. He was gone, but that truth was slow to take full root in her new reality.

Joel satisfied and sparked her passions in ways his older brother never did, and his spontaneous and risk-taking style was a flame that drew her like a moth. However, the logical J, more loving and compassionate than passionate, took a moderate and deliberate approach that was the source of great comfort and security. *But, now that the nest is empty that wasn't enough,* she reminded herself. Then again, J's sudden demise and the drastic and hurried actions of Joel's plan for their new life weighed upon her. *Maybe Joel is too much the other way for me.*

She looked at her cell phone and sighed. *The great backup plan is underway,* she concluded, noting the time and considering the moonlight that flooded the room through its one window. *There's no turning back now. Or is there?*

She touched the phone's black surface and dialed a number from memory. As it rang, she looked out the window and marveled at how much the moonlight lit up the backyard and the woods beyond. *How J ... we loved this place,* she recalled before a familiar voice answered.

"Hello, Louis ... Yes, yes, it's me, Joan." She listened to a string of questions that a lawyer would naturally ask a missing client and close friend. "I'll explain everything, but later. Right now, I desperately need your help."

The unconditional positive response brought a brief smile. "Thank you. I'm at the family cabin. Please come get me and call the police. My family is in trouble." She nodded as the family lawyer asked the logical questions.

"In the quarry forest right now," she replied. "Yes, all the kids and maybe J's bodyguard. It's ..." Another question cut her off before she finished. "It's Joel. Yes, he's there now. At least he should be."

Joan nodded as Louis Belmont talked.

"No time for that. I'll explain later. I'll call Sylvia. Please hurry," she said and ended the call. "Sorry, Joel my love. Now there's really no turning back."

Quarry Forest Third Base Campsite

WHEN HER COUSIN lowered the rifle, before she could react, Cynthia lunged and wrapped her arms around her. The collision knocked the rifle from Danny's hands and took both of them to the ground. After slapping her back, side and leg, Cynthia found and pulled Danny's knife from its sheath.

Danny rolled right and sprang to her feet. She faced her cousin with a defensive posture while quickly calculating a path of attack. She shifted her weight as Cynthia passed the knife from one hand to the other to thwart a quick counterattack.

"Danny, enough," Cynthia declared firmly, anticipating Clint would seize the opportunity to grab his gun or hers to end the fight. "It's over."

Danny smiled, looking beyond Cynthia.

Cynthia glanced sideways. Her face fell when she saw that Clint was face down. She briefly lowered the knife.

Seizing the advantage offered by the impact of her cowardly brother's inaction on behalf of her opponent, Danny kicked out. The knife flew from Cynthia's hand as Danny dove, scooped up the rifle and rolled to stand. She pointed the barrel at Cynthia who was holding her hand. "That's gotta hurt too, Princess." She laughed. "Clint, get up."

Cynthia helped him to his feet.

"Now back on your knees."

"Nice try playing the family card, Cuz," Danny said as they sank to their knees and put their hands behind their heads, "But we both know this 'family' is wrecked by unresolved anger issues and a bent moral compass, mine especially. Can't do much about anyone else's but mine."

She pushed the rifle barrel into Clint's back and her finger found the trigger. Her brother sobbed.

"For once in your life, Clint, man up." His sister's voice dropped to a ragged whisper. "You're going to hell, brother," she finished, sliding her finger up and down the trigger before taking a breath.

"Danny, no!" Cynthia screamed, moving right to try for the rifle. She twisted and stood, but she lost her balance and fell back facing Danny and her brother.

Before Danny squeezed the trigger a sudden noise in the bushes behind her startled her. Ignoring her brother, she swung the rifle toward the noise. A man's dark form launched from the undergrowth and crashed into her, causing the rifle to fly from her hands. The blow threw her onto her brother, and the two tumbled along the ground, ending in a heap of tangled arms and legs.

Cynthia rolled to her left and scooped up her pistol. Coming out of the move in a crouch, she pointed the gun at where she thought Danny's assailant should be. He was gone! She saw that Clint and Danny had pulled themselves apart, but they appeared disoriented. She sensed motion to the left and swung her weapon towards the danger.

A man's form towered over Cynthia briefly. She had time to pull the trigger just before a boot clad foot shot out and kicked the gun from her hand. The shot went wide of the dark figure. The stranger's kick also threw her to the ground next to Clint and Danny. She landed flat on her back. The impact momentarily stunned her. Despite the pain that shot up her wounded side, she pushed herself up onto her elbows. Her eyes widened as Joel Martin emerged from the shadows. He held a pistol in one hand and Danny's sniper rifle in the other. *Same black commando outfit as Danny's. It figures, but this ...* Cynthia wondered, glancing left at her cousins who were still down.

Joel grinned briefly and took two steps towards the fallen trio. He hefted the rifle to point the barrel at Cynthia, while aiming the pistol at the other two. He walked to Danny. She blinked, and her dark eyes were void of rage. Surprise and something else had replaced it. Martin flipped Danny's rifle around and struck her chin with the butt.

"Sorry, sweetheart. This is the end of the line for you," he told her as she fell back moaning before unconsciousness claimed her. He patted her hips and pulled a set of keys from one pocket, her GASMAX ID badge and rifle rounds from two others. He stood, looked at his fallen niece and sighed. "Breaks my heart to do this," he said finally and pointed the pistol at her chest. "You're just too much like your dad." He pulled the trigger. Danny's body convulsed and then was still.

"No!" Cynthia cried, pushing herself up to lunge at Martin, but he swung around quickly and held the handgun between them.

"Freeze," he ordered in an even voice, pressing the barrel into her chest. She took a step back and raised her arms.

"Good girl." He said before ordering, "Clint, on your feet. Stand next to her."

"My God, Joel! What have you done?" Clint cried, staring wide-eyed at his sister's body before finding his voice to also spit out, "I ... I thought we had an understanding."

"The key word is 'had,' son," Joel said. He dropped the gun next to Danny's body and pointed the rifle at them. "Now, you two, start moving. We're going for a walk down to the river. It is beautiful in the moonlight. Move, and keep your hands where I can see them."

The trio started down the trail. "Why'd ... why'd you do that to Danny, Joel?" Clint persisted. "And you can't just leave her there."

"Good question, Clint. Cynthia, do you care to tell my less than brilliant nephew the answer?"

Cynthia looked over her shoulder. Joel face was devoid of emotion but Clint's wasn't. "She knows too much, Clint. Just like we do, and Uncle doesn't like loose ends."

"Well put. To be precise, she knows something that jeopardizes my future plans. And, you two know too much about the past and present as well as the future," Joel added.

They followed the trail that ran back to the bridge that was out. They stepped off the trail onto what was left of the bridge on the island side. Two sawhorses were arrayed across the bridge, providing a barrier and warning of the drop into the fast-moving water below. "Clint, move the sawhorses, and, you two, stand on the edge."

"But why did you leave Danny back there?" Cynthia asked after Clint pushed the sawhorses aside and they stood with their backs to the river and their arms raised. "That's a significant loose end."

"Not really," Joel replied, raising his voice to be heard above the sound of the roaring river. "She's not going anywhere. I'll clean up that mess shortly."

"I see," Cynthia said after a pause. "No stone left unturned, right? Besides, even if you don't, another dead Martin would keep Chief Smith and his officers chasing a lot of dead ends related to her criminal past."

"Very good. So much like your father."

"Stop it!" Clint shouted and shook his head. Clint gestured again toward Cynthia. "Look, Joel, I don't care what you did to Danny or do to Cynthia, but we had a deal. I kept my end of the bargain until you ... until Cynthia, Strong and that PI started poking around and Danny ... went crazy."

Joel silently studied him. "You're such a disappointment, Clint. Too much like my brother, Jacob. Now Danny is like I was at her age. She acted just as I predicted. If you'd asked me, Clint, I would have told you everything was going according to plan. I was satisfied with our arrangement, but you got spooked. What a pity Danny went off script and you lost your nerve, boy. Danny and you would have been protected and come out of this okay."

"But ... I thought we'd go back to ..." Clint's face was a study in dazed confusion.

Cynthia frowned as Joel's words knocked a hole in her conclusions based on recent events, evidence and what she'd found in Moses Martin's Bible. Certain parts now didn't fit, and ones she'd glossed over as not essential started to make more sense.

"Did you really think we could go back to things as before, just without brother J? After Cynthia and Simpson, aided and abetted by you, dug up all those skeletons, there's no going back. That's delusional. You should have known better, son. Just like J, eventually for nothing more than a clear conscience you'd kill the goose that lays the golden egg. I'm a survivor, Clint. I told you it was time for the next progression of Plan B."

"Plan B, right. Look, Joel, we can work something out," Clint pleaded. "I understand now. I can do some damage control. I'm good at that. You can trust me."

The older Martin smiled sadly and rested the butt of Danny's rifle on the ground and, squatting, leaned the barrel against one of the sawhorses.

As he quickly stood, he pulled a revolver from an ankle holster and brought it level with his nephew's chest. "There's no damage to control, kid," he said and pulled the trigger twice. The bullets caught Clint in the chest. Clutching his chest, he staggered backward and fell off the bridge. His scream rose above the sound of the flowing river water, but it faded as he disappeared from sight. Joel holstered the still smoking pistol and retrieved the rifle.

CHAPTER 25

A Fall Doesn't Kill – a Sudden Stop Does

Quarry Forest Third Base Campsite Bridge

"NO!" CYNTHIA SCREAMED, REACHING FOR Clint. With a foot on the bridge's jagged edge, she grasped empty air and fell.

Joel quickly slipped his arm around her waist and pulled her back. "No, not yet," he said, his breath warm on her neck and his voice thick with menace. "I'm not through with you."

Cynthia broke free when he relaxed his grip. She backed away and faced him. His face was lost in shadow except for the moonlit trace of a thin frown. "You're crazy!" she raged. "You're so weighed down by three decades of lies and deceptions that you've lost your soul. That was your son! Danny is your daughter, family!"

Martin leveled Danny's rifle at her. He grasped her arm and pushed her toward the trail. "Walk," he commanded flatly, pressing the barrel into the small of her back.

She shook off his grip but raised her hands and stepped away. *The same hardhearted but sad determination he had when he fired me*, she thought, looking briefly over her shoulder.

They walked in silence to the Third Base clearing. He tapped her shoulder with the rifle barrel and then waved it to the left. "South trail to Home Plate," he ordered.

"Where are we going?" she asked, turning toward the opening to the path that crossed another wooden bridge spanning the branch of the river.

"The plant," he answered. "We've got to have a final chat."

Their pace slowed as the trail narrowed. After they crossed the bridge, the path narrowed further and the overhang grew denser, blocking out nearly all moonlight. Cynthia used her sense of touch to push more and longer branches aside. *Usually, the Quarry Forest fall and overgrowth is cleared and cut back by this time of year. They either missed this trail or haven't gotten to it yet*, she figured.

"Hold up," Joel ordered. He slung the rifle across his back, and then pulled the handgun from the ankle holster.

Too much overhang for the rifle, Cynthia thought.

"That's better. Move!" he barked.

The snub barrel, pressed briefly in her back, confirmed Cynthia's assumption. *This may work*, she calculated, slowing her stride, and feigning greater effort to push aside the tangle of branches and leaves. Judging how closely Joel followed, she assessed each branch. She found one at head level and long and thick enough to forcibly snap back at her captor. She pushed it to near breaking. "Ugh." She grunted, released the branch and fell forward.

"Damn!" Martin cried.

Sounded like he fell, she thought. *Good.* She rose and ran back up the trail toward the bridge. After the first full step, she stumbled over Joel. She extended her hands and broke her fall. Remaining upright, her right hand closed on the handgun. Before Joel could react, she wrenched it from his grip and continued up the trail. After she crossed the bridge, the Third Base clearing, bathed in unobstructed moonlight, was clearly visible. *I may make it if I don't get a bullet in the back*, she estimated, eyeing the partially completed bathhouse and the bluff behind it that was topped with the zipline tower.

Quarry Branch River and Rock River Junction

THE WEIGHT OF wet clothing and water-filled boots permitted Clint to only keep his head above water as the river's current swept him along. The rapidly moving and swirling water carried him south and then west. He rolled around and off large rocks in midstream where the branch of the river widened before joining Rock River. The slackening current finally allowed him to gain the shore. He staggered up the flat stretch of rocky beach just short of where moon shadows were cast by the railroad bridge spanning the mouth of the Quarry Branch River.

He lay on his back for several minutes. When his heart ceased racing and he regained his breath, he assessed his physical well-being. "Nothing broken," he eventually said, sitting up. In the moonlight, he easily fixed his location when he recognized the bridge's unique steel lattice frame.

"I made it." He laughed, unbuttoning his hiking vest and flannel shirt. Peeling them off, he unbuckled and removed the bullet proof vest. With some effort he pried loose the two slugs embedded in the vest. "That crazy old man was serious. He really shot me." He pocketed the two misshapen bullets and probed his chest beneath the vest where it had prevented lethal injury. He flinched, thinking, *That probably left a mark.*

Lying back, he looked at the moon now in the western sky and at the bridge. He knew what his next steps would be, but he wanted to relish the moment. "I can be smarter than Dad after all," he shouted at the Thunder Moon. *See Papa J, the Princess can be outsmarted, and you won't be there to save her this time.*

Third Base Campsite

JOEL MARTIN, AFTER hastily unslinging the rifle and roughly aiming down the trail, pulled its trigger. *Maybe that'll give her something to think about and slow her down,* he thought, getting up. After rubbing where the branch had smacked his forehead, he pulled a small flashlight from his vest and scanned around his feet. "Damn, she's got the gun," he fumed. With the rifle at the ready, he elbowed his way through the branches to follow her. *Should have known she was up to something when she slowed down.*

He stopped at the bridge and, using the rifle's night vision scope, scanned up and down the branch river. *Most likely going back to the campsite*, he concluded silently, checking his watch. *Gun or no, I gotta hustle. There's a schedule to keep, and if she's figured a way ...* "Of course, the zip lines!" he said and broke into a run down the broader, clearer and unobstructed moonlit trail into Third Base.

Joel entered the clearing as Cynthia approached the bathhouse. "Cynthia, stop!" he shouted. With the practiced reflex of a former biathlete, he raised the rifle, aimed to just miss her, and fired.

Cynthia stopped and ducked when a corner of a concrete block in the bathhouse wall above her head shattered. Instead of freezing, she calmly turned, crouched, and pulled the handgun into a shooting stance.

Martin dove and rolled right as the pistol barked twice. He quickly sat up, worked the bolt action and brought the scope to his eye. Cynthia jumped through the open bathhouse door just before his next round hit the its steel frame. *Good, she's run to ground,* he thought as he closed the short distance to the incomplete structure. He pressed his back to the wall next to the door.

What did Clint say? Yeah, walls and roof are up, but windows and doors ae only framed. And piping is plumbed and shower and toilet partitions are installed, but ... boxes of faucets, toilets, sinks and windows and doors are stacked everywhere. Some block the other door! There's no way out. She's trapped!

Pitcher's Mound Campsite

TWO DISTANT GUNSHOTS pulled Danny to full consciousness. *They're gone,* she thought, opening one eye. She slowly sat up and rubbed her jaw, looking around to confirm that she was alone. "God, that hurts," she hissed and stood.

She quickly realized that the rifle was gone, but the handgun Joel had fired at her lay where he'd dropped it. *I knew he wouldn't really shoot me, but it sure sounded that way,* she thought, picking up the gun. She verified it was loaded and placed it her pants waistband. *The way Clint and the Princess carried on, they sure bought it. Guess the body convulsion and playing possum bit before I passed out really sold it.*

She found her hat and studied the moon and stars to get her bearings and then checked her watch. She rubbed her jaw again and winced. "Plan B, my butt. That hurt," she said before entering the southbound trail to Home Plate at a jog.

Third Base Campsite Bathhouse

"CYNTHIA, YOU'RE TRAPPED," Joel shouted before peering around the door frame. "Toss out the gun and come out. We'll talk. It doesn't have to end like this."

A gunshot rang out. The bullet missed his head. He spun back, taking refuge outside the door. "How else, Joel, except with me dead?" she said. "Sure, you need me alive - at least long enough to get what you want, but your revised Plan B or whatever's is getting more screwed up with every delay."

Right you are, Joel thought, glancing at his watch. "Maybe, but perhaps the value of what you know has dropped to zero."

"If so, I'd be dead. You're too good a shot to have missed twice."

"Perhaps, but your situation remains hopeless," he countered. "I counted three shots, and, with the two I used on Clint, that means you have one left and no reloads. Come out and we'll talk."

"What I know you still desperately need it," Cynthia said.

"How do you figure?" Martin asked, crouched, and edged around the door jam. *Sounds like she's retreated to the far end. So,* s*he can't see me or she's saving her last shot. Keep talking.*

"I'd be dead already. Your Plan B has undergone several revisions since the banquet when Tanner stepped in. As you told Clint, it no longer supports some status quo sans Uncle J. You've gone full circle. Again, you need me alive for some purpose that involves what I now know or what I knew when Buck Wilson tried to drug me."

Joel skirted boxes stacked inside the door and entered first stall. He pressed his back against the stall wall. He listened. *She's still moving,* he thought. "Do tell," he said.

"Uncle J's death was no accident. He was too expert of a climber. You caught up to him at the quarry wall. You two fought. It got physical, and you pushed him," she said.

Joel flinched at her assertion that he'd murdered his brother. "My God," he whispered.

"What you don't know is if I found evidence and, if so, who else has it."

She's right, he thought, *but J's death was a terrible – necessary – accident.* "That's nuts," he countered. *She's moving, but where? Using a rifle in these tight quarters is problematic.* As he removed rifle's telescopic sight, he said, "J and I were partners as well as brothers. We turned your grandfather's struggling and failing gas company into a multibillion-dollar giant. Why would I want to kill him or risk that?"

"It was a billion-dollar house of cards," she replied, "built on the theft of intellectual property and probable murder. The truth of Niles Tannerson's work was about to leak out, or something about the fourth phase transition had gone very wrong. You and Uncle J no doubt differed about how to handle that. He still had a conscience and, as we know, you can be ruthless."

"It's called being practical," Joel asserted and stepped out of the stall. He put the detached night-vision scope to his eye. "But do go on."

"Your relationship with Uncle J changed drastically. But you hadn't changed, he did. Silvia, Clint, and Danny all said that in the year before his death, he was uncharacteristically moody, melancholy and ... acted guilty about something. That something goes back thirty years, doesn't it?"

"Go ... Go on," Joel said, lowering the scope. His reality was built on the confidence that he had successfully hidden the actual events in the Wilkes Tavern basement and on Smugglers Cove beach. *She was right. J was the only one who could shatter my reality. Even the old man didn't know the whole story, or did he?*

"You had to assume that Joan knew what J knew, or, as it turned out, that he made a provision for me to find out. What was in the safe deposit box makes sense. What Uncle J knew for sure was that the truth of the past had to come out. I'd like to think he found some peace in that even though it would mean a deathblow to GASMAX as well as for you and him personally and professionally."

"This is all sentimental and moralistic fantasy," Joel said. "J was a business man who understood that you had to do what was…"

"No! You're wrong. J finally realized that, after decades of doing what's necessary, despite all the good that the Martin family had done, it was all selfish and self-serving. J figured out that Grandpa's loving God wasn't enough. You had to love – serve – others to bear fruit. So, he was content to let the chips fall where they may, but you … well you're a heartless, selfish and self-serving Plan B guy."

"My God, girl, you do have a creative imagination," Joel said. "Your mother, Mary, was like that until she drank herself ... senseless."

"Leave Mom out of this!" Cynthia shouted. "The point is you needed Uncle J out of the way because after all these years he was going to queer the deal. The collusion in the theft of Tannerson's intellectual property had kept you in mutual check. But you lost your grip on him. And it was due to something more than just a guilty conscience. It was something personal, right?"

"You're fishing," Martin said and chuckled. *That bit about Mary rattled her. Good*, he thought. He abandoned the rifle, and sidestepped a crate and into the next stall.

"Your love letters to Aunt Joan," she said. "J found them. Your affair with her and Clint's and Danny's true paternity must have made the fight on the quarry wall even more contentious. I bet that, when you or Joan admitted that you were their biological father, he was always a few steps away from wanting you dead."

"How'd ... that's not ...," Joel choked out and froze. It as if she'd been there. As his argument with J verged on the physical, his brother's every move became animated by a swelling murderous wrath. "Well figured, Cynthia, but if I hadn't pushed him, he'd have tossed me off that wall. But why then would I kill my own children?" He moved to the next stall.

"As I said, Joel, you're selfish and self-serving - you've lost your soul," Cynthia said. "I realized this when you torpedoed my GASMAX career, willing to besmirch my mother's memory with your blackmail photographs and all. You and Uncle J along with Grandpa Moses likely drove her to drink and killed her slowly over many alcohol-soaked years. She no doubt figured out the truth about your house of cards. She realized that she, my father and her second marriage were just three more casualties of the lies and deception which you three used to build fortune and fame on another man's genius."

"That's not true!" Joel protested before finishing weakly. "About Jake and his fool-hearted bravery ..." Before stepping into the last stall, he used the scope again and saw her. *She's under the windows, using the wheelbarrow as cover*, he observed silently. *I can clear that.*

"Is it a lie?" Cynthia said. "Given your willingness to commit fratricide, I'm not surprised you shot Danny and Clint. Joel, you trap, use, and chew people up and, when you're through, spit them out. J knew this, and that's why he planted all the clues. I wouldn't be surprised if you had something to do with Aunt Joan's supposed suicide. Did you spit her out too?"

"Now, you're way off base. I love your aunt," he said, calculating the final distance to close and the best attack angle and tactic. "If all you say is true, why didn't I shoot you along with your cousins? I assume by now you've figured out that I have been behind the several attempts on your life and Strong's. By your reasoning, you should have joined them back there. Oh, by the way, I am truly amazed you eluded the many 'accidents' I arranged."

"Really? You're surprised? You and J made sure I was trained to swim in shark-infested waters."

"Right, you were," he said and laughed. "Even with the lost job, lost boyfriend and hangover, it would have been more prudent to assume you'd have more lives than a cat. If you'd stayed out of Driftwood Cove, I'm now convinced you would have somehow got back on the board and eventually ousted me. I'll give you that."

Silence followed before she said, "You figured after each failed attempt that Tanner, Julie Simpson and I had gathered more information and incriminating evidence. It changed the circumstances and, therefore, the Plan B you always talk about. So, we're back to where you need something from me before I die. And it's no longer just me you have to account for, is it?"

Martin chuckled. "Can't say you're entirely wrong, but it's now just you. Danny and Clint are off the board, and Buck Wilson eliminated your remaining allies earlier today. It was an unfortunate boating accident."

"Tanner ... no," Cynthia sobbed. A long silence followed as, he assumed, she regained her composure. "What about Sylvia?"

"A fire at EOS," Martin said and set the scope on a box. "You are right that the current circumstances have changed Plan B and what you know may warrant its final tweak. So, we need to have a last chat regarding those clues J left you." He stepped out of the stall and crouched.

"But that's still a last chat before I meet an accidental end," she finished. "What clues?"

"Oh, like the rest of the contents of the safe deposit box," he replied, setting his feet to spring over the wheelbarrow, "and whatever else you found in Dad's treasure chest."

"So, that's ..." Cynthia started.

Joel lunged up and over the wheelbarrow. "Got you now!" he shouted as his hands closed on her neck. He felt her fall back and beneath him as he used his momentum and weight to secure his grip and press with both thumbs.

Moses Martin Memorial Hospital Parking Lot

CHIEF SMITH EXHALED the smoke from the last drag on his cigarette. His radio crackled to life as he crushed the butt into the no smoking sign next to his patrol car. "Chief, this is Harper."

Pulling the mike from under the dashboard, putting it to his mouth and pushing a red side button, he said, "Go ahead, Charley."

"I'm out here at the quarry."

"Find her or the Martin boy?"

"No, no sign of Jones or Clint Martin. Been all up and down the walk above the rock-climbing wall. Other than what sounds like campers firing off a few firecrackers, it's pretty quiet out here. There's only a few fireflies and an occasional cricket. You sure this is the place? Should I hike down to the south campsite? You said that's where Martin pitched his tent."

"Sylvia Martin said they were going to the wall," Smith answered finally after considering Harper's reference to firecrackers. He looked back toward the hospital ER entrance. The brief face-to-face with Sylvia and Julie Simpson had changed priorities and added new ones for his limited force. From what he understood, Strong was completely out of action and Simpson wasn't going anywhere until she knew he was out of danger. At least Wilson was no longer a concern. "No, we'll assume Jones is okay for now. I'll visit the GASMAX plant and search the campgrounds. I need you to get over to the Martin place."

"The one off GASMAX Road?"

"Yeah, the cabin. Pick up Joan Martin. She's waiting there." The radio was silent. "Charley, you copy?"

"Yeah, Chief, but I thought she was dead ... suicide."

"She's very much alive. Arrest her."

"On what charge?"

Smith shook his head. "Faking a suicide. Doesn't matter. Make something up. She may be complicit in whatever Joel Martin is up to. In any case, I want her in custody until we sort this out."

"Roger, Chief. I'm on my way. Out."

Smith looked at the microphone before flipping it onto the seat and starting the engine. *Hell of a night*, he thought, mulling over what Sylvia Martin and Julie Simpson had told him. He glanced briefly at Moses Martin's name on the hospital sign illuminated by bright electric lights. In smaller raised letters below was inscribed the Martin patriarch's motto, 'Do what's necessary, love God and do good in keeping with repentance.' "Just empty words, old man, unless you love people too." He snorted and shook his head as he drove out of the parking lot.

Third Base Campsite Bathhouse

"NO!" CYNTHIA CHOKED out despite Joel's stranglehold. Having assumed that he wanted her alive and would not shoot, she'd positioned herself in the only open area between the back wall and the wheelbarrow. Close to the long narrow open window frame, she stood so he'd have to clear the wheelbarrow to attack. When she felt his hands close on her neck, she dropped back and down. As he tightened his grip on her neck, she brought both hands up to his chest and forcefully pushed up. Leveraging off his momentum and timing her fall, she flipped him up, over and behind her.

Joel released his hold to break the fall. It was to no avail. He slammed flat on his backside. Cynthia heard a cross between a gasp and grunt when he landed. Though the exertion spiked the pain from her wound, she jumped to her feet. She pulled herself up and rolled out sideways through the window frame. The gun in her waistband caught on the metal border. It fell out and back into the bathhouse. "Damn," she cursed, grabbing for it without success. She dropped to the ground. "Only one shot left anyway."

She paused to get her bearings in the silver moon light before she raced up the bluff's double switchback trail to the base of the zip line tower. The metal and wood structure rose another twenty-five feet above the bluff's forty-foot peak. Holding her injured side and catching her breath, she looked down at the bathhouse. There was no sign of Joel.

With any luck the fall knocked him out. If not, he won't fit through that window, and he'll retrieve the rifle before coming out the other end. If Clint told me right, I should make it, she reasoned optimistically. Ignoring the posted danger sign, she climbed the three flights of steps that zig-zagged up within the metal tower enclosed with wooden walls to the zip line launch platform.

Cynthia smiled and stepped around the 'Closed-Certification Testing In Progress' sign. Test weights were stacked on one side of the platform's metal grating. *Good, Clint was right. Both zip lines are installed and anchored into the back wall. The safety netting is gone and the guywires are in place. They finished testing,* she thought. As she inspected the zip line trolleys and seats, she noticed the cable conduit tracing a line from an opening in the roof down the side wall to disappear through an opening in the platform floor. *I bet the cell tower antennas are even installed ... My phone!* She patted the pocket that held it. It was empty.

She grimaced when she realized both zip lines were configured with hornet trolleys that are equipped with handlebars and the big-boy rectangular seats. *I'd prefer a harness,* she complained silently and untied the trolley restraint, *but beggars can't be choosers.*

Glancing down as she slid the trolley to the edge of the platform, she saw Martin. Standing at the bluff's base he aimed the rifle at her. She grasped both rubber-gripped handlebars of the dual-wheeled trolley and swung her legs to mount the seat suspended by a thick nylon rope from the trolley's underside.

With the sudden weight, the trolley slid down the sloping multi-strand wire cable, and she quickly picked up speed. She heard the rifle shot a split instant before the bullet struck the trolley. She had cleared the Third Base campsite when she opened her eyes and saw as well as felt that the trolley was damaged. The tops of the trees and silver-black flashes of reflected lunar light raced below her feet. A twenty or so mile per hour wind kept the hair out of her face. Despite these heralds of an increasing speed of escape, she frowned. The nut and lock washer of the bolt holding the two sides of the trolley together had been hit. It was deformed but appeared to still be secure. The vibration through the trolley's handlebars felt abnormal. Since she'd never used this particular zip line and trolley before, she had no real idea what was normal. *Just hold together long enough*, she prayed, sighting both the break in the trees denoting the west side of the First Base campsite and the landing tower on the clearing's far side.

Recalling that Clint had said it was a three-hundred-foot zip line with a bungee cord brake block and spring assembly, she knew this permitted a greater slope and more speed. *But if that bolt is too loose*, she thought, eyeing it anxiously, *the whole thing could fly apart during the braking and I might not reach the platform.*

The platform's edge and the black-square end of the bungee cord brake block, through which the zip line passed, came clearly into view. She looked up and thought, *Perhaps it's apprehension or tricks of the moonlight, or both, but the trolley looks and feels like it's vibrating more.*

When the trolley hit the brake block, Cynthia estimated her speed to be about thirty miles per hours. It slowed the trolley as the dual bungee cords, anchored to a post below, stretched and pulled. *Not good*, she thought when she felt the increased vibration in the handlebars. She was slowing, but still closing the edge of the platform quickly. "Hang in there!" she shouted at the trolley now shaking violently up, down, and sideways against the block.

If the trolley had not fallen apart, it would have driven the block into the spring assembly through which the zip line also passed before ending at its landing tower back wall anchor. If the testing and final adjustments had been made as Clint had claimed, the trolley would have stopped well inside the tower, and she would have safely dismounted. Instead, short of the platform's edge, the trolley flew apart. Casting aside the broken pieces attached to the handlebars, she fell. *Odd*, she thought and frowned, *no Tanner to catch me this time.*

CHAPTER 26

The Fatal Shot

―

First Base Campsite Zip Line Tower

UNLIKE THE THIRD BASE TOWER, the construction safety net was still suspended below the First Base tower's platform edge. Although the black nylon mesh broke Cynthia's fall, she tumbled and rolled. She stopped short of the net's edge but not before she entangled her hand and ankle, trapping her like a fly caught in a spider's web. As her racing heart slowed, she struggled to liberate her hand and foot. She smiled and said, "No new injuries."

When Joel Martin, rifle slung across his back, glided into view on the other zip line. Cynthia abruptly stopped trying to free herself. As he disappeared above onto the platform, she resumed her efforts. After freeing her hand, she sat and tackled the nylon line about her ankle. Bootsteps sounded on the steps to the landing that allowed access to the net. She pulled harder, but she froze when Martin stepped on the landing.

"Go on, Cynthia," he said, pointing the pistol that she'd lost. A coil of bright yellow nylon rope was looped over each shoulder.

She freed her ankle and looked below.

"Don't think about it," he cautioned. "The drop to the ground would break your neck. Get over here."

Cynthia complied, rolling, and then stepping off the net. Standing opposite him, she raised her hands. "Okay, now ..."

His backhand blow cut her off. "Shut up!" he commanded. "Down the steps and no more monkey business."

He stopped her when they reached the ground. Roughly he pulled her hands behind her, then tied her wrists with a nylon rope.

"Ow!" Cynthia complained as he jerked the knot tight.

Ignoring her cry, he pressed the gun into her back and shoved her shoulder. "Walk. South trail!" he barked. As he followed, Joel reflected on what she had said in the bathhouse. *Does she know the whole truth? If so, who else?* he wondered. *She knows the truth about J's death and Joan's infidelity, but does she know the truth of her own identity? The entire Plan B exit strategy could be compromised. I've got to know if there are any other loose ends.*

At the trailhead, Cynthia bolted right. Martin kicked out and tripped her. She fell on her side. "I thought you'd try something," he said and used a foot to roll her on to her back. "So, we gotta do this the hard way, huh? Stay put." He knelt, bound her ankles with the remaining strand of rope and shoved the gun in his waistband. Bending over her, he grabbed a handful of her blouse in each hand and pulled her upright. She hung like a limp rag doll in his grip before he set her on her feet.

She defiantly looked him in the eyes. "So, you going to beat it out of me?"

He shook his head before stepping back and walking behind her.

"Got to admire your fighting spirit," he said. "Cynthia, I'm not happy about having to kill you. You know too much for me not to, but you know something I need."

"And I'll just tell you because I see the hopelessness of my situation? Why would I help the one man most responsible for robbing me of everything I value? I'd rather die."

"Said like a true Martin. Your father would be proud. But I promise you that before you die, I will know all you know ... and don't," he said. "You will tell me." He drew the pistol back over his shoulder and, with no satisfaction, swung down hard.

"What do you think ...," Cynthia started, but the blow from the pistol butt cut her off. She fell.

Martin sighed and shifted the rifle slung over his shoulder. He picked up the unconscious woman and threw her over his shoulder. Despite the added weight, he jogged down the trail.

Third Base Campsite

"THAT'S CLINT MARTIN'S pickup all right," Chief Smith said, shining his flashlight on the soggy registration form he'd retrieved from the partially submerged truck cab, "with a bullet hole in what little's left of the windshield." After checking the rest of the truck as best that he could, he waded ashore.

He buckled his pistol belt over his wet trousers and shrugged back into his uniform jacket. Then he followed his flashlight to the place where he'd discovered three sets of footsteps and a pair of drag marks. *The shooter causes the crash, he drags Martin and his cousin from the cab and they come to, and they ...,* he thought before his phone, clipped to the pistol belt, rang.

"Yeah, Charley," he said, pressing the phone to his ear after seeing Harper's caller ID.

"Chief, hi. I picked up Joan Martin."

"Where's she?"

"I booked her on suspicion of conspiracy to commit murder and locked her up."

Smith smiled as he used his free hand to climb up the riverbank. "Conspiracy to murder who? I told you to make something up, but something believable."

"Well, she kept saying she'd helped Joel Martin kill her husband. So, I thought ..."

"Okay. You're right," Smith said, walking to the campsite clearing. "She say anything else?"

"Yes. She said her children and her niece, Cynthia, were in great danger from Joel Martin and someone named Wilson."

"Buck Wilson?"

"Yeah, that's right, the guy we've been looking for. She said Wilson set some kind of explosive, booby-trap at her beach house and that Joel Martin was doing something at the plant."

Smith entered the Third Base clearing and plunged his free hand into his jacket pocket. "That's believable. There's been some gunplay in the campground north of the plant," he said, confirming that the plastic bag containing shell casings was still in his pocket. He'd recovered them at the campsite before finding the trail of broken branches and skid marks on the trail from the Pitcher's Mound site to the branch river bridge. "I found Clint Martin's truck crashed into the branch river with a bullet hole in the windshield."

Smith pulled the phone from his ear when Harper whistled. "Wow, any bodies?"

"Not yet, but I'm still looking around," Smith replied, running his finger over the jagged corner of the concrete block that had been made by Joel's warning shot over Cynthia's head. "Look, you get over to the hospital ER ASAP. Keep Sylvia Martin there. If you can, get Detective Simpson to join me at the plant. I'm going there right after I take a look at one more thing out here."

"Roger that, Chief," Harper answered smartly. "Err, Chief ..."

"What?"

"You want me to call the on-watch plant operator and give em a heads up?"

Smith exhaled a sigh. "Do that," he ordered. "Good thinking, Harper."

"Thanks, Chief. Out."

Retirement next month can't come soon enough, he thought, turning on the flashlight and entering the bath house.

GASMAX Plant Control Room

A STING IN her arm pierced Cynthia's unconscious slumber. She swung her right hand. Her arm moved but halted abruptly. She opened her eyes. Bright light forced her eyelids shut. Drawing a deep breath, she slowly opened her eyes while inventorying what hurt. The sting in her left arm took a backseat to an intense burning pain in her side, and the throbbing in her head. *Yeah, the flesh wound from Danny*, she recalled. Her mouth was dry. She licked her lips. *Blood ... Mine*, she remembered when her tongue found where she'd bitten her lip when Joel hit her.

I know this place, she thought, discovering what restrained her right hand. Her wrists were bound with rope to the arms of a straight-back chair which faced the GASMAX operator's panel. Her ankles felt similarly bound to the chair's front legs.

"What the ... Joel," she stammered through parched lips, straining against the ropes.

Joel Martin placed an empty syringe in an open black case set on the panel's apron. "Good, I was beginning to think I'd hit you too hard," he crooned, flipping the case shut.

This sounds like the loving uncle and smooth-talking corporate Joel Martin I know, she thought. He used the same soothing, concerned, and assured voice as he always had during her growing up and later. It was the voice he used during their many corporate encounters.

Picking up a cloth, he knelt beside her. Tilting her chin gently, he applied a damp, cool rag to her face and the back of her neck. Despite a pungent soap odor, most of the tension left her body. She relaxed against the restraints. He held a glass of water to her lips. Despite a desire not to cooperate, she drank eagerly. "That's a good girl. Relax and drink slowly. Not so fast."

Logic cautioned her to be wary and resist, but whatever was in the syringe, and his soft familiar tone, brought serenity and well-being at odds with her likely lethal circumstances. The pulsating pain in her head and side and the discomfort of bondage were all but gone. "Drugs?" a voice, sounding detached from her body, asked.

Joel laughed softly, pulling a chair next to hers. He loosened her bonds and patted her knee, as he sat down. His touch was firm and surprisingly gentle. "Yes, Cynthia, it's a drug, but nothing harsh. A little concoction that Danny's friend, Buck, provided. Don't fight it. It'll help you relax. It heightens the senses, and, best of all, it loosens the tongue."

Cynthia rolled her head to look at Joel, and, as anger and fear evaporated, she smiled. Feeling serene, she completely surrendered to Buck Wilson's chemical cocktail. Her last grasp on reality spawned one last distressing articulation. "Something like truth serum? So, I'll tell ... feel ... anything you want. That's what you want ... isn't it?" she said, her voice trailing off into a whisper.

"Precisely," Martin hissed softly in tones that she now hungered. He smiled and gave her knee an assuring squeeze. He brushed an errant strand of blonde hair from off her face and ran a finger down her cheek. Her skin tingled beneath his touch. He found her hand and intertwined his fingers in hers.

Cynthia closed her eyes. The universe, at least the part that mattered, was now in Joel's touch and voice. She knew that she should care how she got from the campground, and she should shrug out of the loose ropes, but she no longer cared to. The drug coursing through her veins forced a capitulation to the present with no concern for the past or future. Rationally, she knew that Joel wanted her like this and that she should resist, but the drug destroyed reason's grip and the will to battle. His voice was a siren song she couldn't deny. All that mattered was that she was here, and he was talking and touching. "Now, dear Cynthia, let's talk. Let's talk about family history and other such things."

Cynthia perceived her voice as if heard through the thin wall of a cheap hotel room. Her speech was initially slow, reflecting some residual reluctance to cooperate. The combination of chemicals from the syringe, Joel's voice and his hand in hers, however, quickened her recital into a hurried flood of information. Like a desperate lover, eager to do or say anything to please a soul mate, she willingly surrendered all she knew and suspected about Moses, Joel and J Martin and their treachery, family skeletons and moral failures.

Joel winced as she cataloged the victims of what she called the Martin family ambitions, lust and greed. Her list of fatalities started with her father, Jacob Martin, who, due to Joel's contrivance, lost his life the night they found Professor Niles Tannerson's body and brief case. "You could have tried harder to stop Daddy from going to look for survivors you knew didn't exist, she said. "But Grandpa told you to make it look real to Uncle J and my father. It just got a little too real too fast."

Sorrow clouded Joel's face as Cynthia explained the link between her mother's slow alcoholic death and her husband's unnecessary demise, the death of her baby and Cynthia's true identity. Long suppressed remorse surfaced briefly as Joel heard her correctly explain how Moses, J and he had extorted Mary to keep the secret of Cynthia's true parentage from her daughter. "You three were responsible for Mom's failed second marriage and death. Every drink she took was poured as much by you three as by her own hand," she said, with drug induced bluntness.

Not wanting her to omit anything, Joel remained silent as she repeated or told him things he already knew. He suppressed anger and jealously when her chemically prompted recitation again revealed that his equally guilty brother, but not him, had retained a measure of her respect and affection. "J really manned up in the end, Joel," she said with warmth. "He showed more than a shred of integrity. He was going to admit the truth regardless of the consequences to himself and his family. He was going to do what was necessary to truly do good, bearing fruit in keeping with repentance."

Joel nodded when she once more asserted that he couldn't permit J's soul-cleansing confession and, so, Joel had formulated the original Plan B. She correctly suspected, however, that his strategy had to change frequently as the truth's details and evidence emerged as J's beyond-the-grave plan played out. "Your options became fewer when Tanner, Julie and I, the key players in J's plan, survived one murder attempt after another. So, your Plan B is now some kind of exit strategy. You disappear, leaving Tanner, Julie, Sylvia, Clint, Danny and me as the latest additions to the long list of victims of Martin greed and lust fueled ambitions," she said and broke eye contact with Joel. "We're here, no doubt, so you can distance yourself from GASMAX wrongdoing. Perhaps pin it all on J and Grandpa. And Me?"

A smile briefly creased Joel's face. "Well figured," he said softly. "J backed your meteoric rise at GASMAX to salve that conscience you admired so much. I on the other hand always believed that you keep your friends close and ..."

"... your enemies closer," she finished in a dreamy voice tinged with distress. "Uncle, or should I say brother, I was never your enemy. Yeah, you're not my uncle, are you?"

"No, you're not my enemy," he said. "Now tell me about how I'm not your uncle, how you escaped so many of my traps and what else you've discovered."

Cynthia held nothing back. She detailed, clearly and concisely, all the events, the evidence and the deductive logic since her meeting with Joel Martin in his office days ago. She covered it all up to the present night's shoot out and carnage in the campgrounds north of the GASMAX plant.

Joel sat back when she explained how J had, just before his ill-fated solo hike, aroused her suspicions regarding the safety and reliability of the Phase Four process implementation well underway. "I assume the plant is in full Phase Four AI mode now for conveniently scheduled testing, permitting Danny to be present in the Quarry Forest tonight."

"Well figured."

"Now, answer my question. You're not my uncle, are you?"

"How's that?"

Cynthia explained what she had found in Moses' Bible and said, "So, you see, 'uncle' you're really my half-brother, by my daddy Moses' mistress or ...

My God, my birthmother was ..."

"Yes, Moses Martin's other wife, Melody Ellaine Tannerson. A student-loan strapped medical intern named Corbin Schwartz delivered and swapped the babies at birth. That's a ghastly family secret I alone shared with Papa Moses. So, I'm not your uncle. I'm your brother, half-brother, little sister."

Cynthia turned and stared at him. "Moses' note!" she gasped and strained against the restraints. "He wrote that 'Niles and Melody Tannerson and their house have been second family, home and haven to me.' My God, 'MET 1964' ... is Melody Ellaine Tannerson!" She slumped in the chair. "Grandpa ... Moses Martin was not only guilty of adultery but also bigamy."

Joel leaned in. "Here's a nasty little secret that I alone kept. Niles Tannerson wasn't killed in the storm. I killed him. He wasn't washed ashore in Smugglers Cove. He sailed there and met me at daybreak the morning of the hurricane party. Per a secret deal with his new son in-law, Moses, he was supposed to deliver the journals. Instead, he told me he was going to renege, saying something about his grandbaby's inheritance. The fool thought that he could sail back to Sand Dollar in time for your birth. But ..."

"You couldn't permit that," Cynthia sat up and said, "So, you did what was necessary and came up with the first of many Joel Martin Plan Bs. You staged the shipwreck and body. And I bet Grandpa didn't know."

"About the murder, no, he didn't. He didn't need to," Joel answered. "Though he told me that the shipwreck and drowning were providential, I think he suspected the truth, because after that, he always called on me to do ..."

"What was necessary," she finished, her voice laced with disgust. "And you become CEO and President instead of J, losing your soul in the process. You know, Joel, I discovered one very important thing over the last few days."

"That is?"

"Witnessing the selfless Mr. Strong's heroics and learning the truth about you, J, and Grandpa made me realize I was becoming like you, ruthlessly doing what's necessary and believing that a public benefactor persona would pay for the sins of Martin ... our blood. If I survive this night that will change." Her heart raced and her skin glistened with perspiration before she suddenly sagged in the chair.

"That's a big if. In any case, we're done, dear sister," Martin assured her as he sat up, smiled and put a hand on her arm. "Extracting the truth with this drug has a nasty and exhausting side effect. The fatigue will wear off soon. I understand, though, that sounds may be distorted for a while after, but no matter."

"Good," she managed and pulled away from his touch.

"You've proven to be a very good detective. Better than the unfortunate Julie Simpson. You've a sharp eye for detail and a power of deduction that is most impressive. You'd have been a worthy successor to me. It's a pity ..."

"That you have to kill me. I've heard that once too often tonight," she shot back. "Seems like I've been in someone's cross hairs ever since our last meeting in your office, huh?"

"I see that Mr. Wilson's serum has lost its hold," Joel stated. He stood, took out his phone and tapped the text message icon. "Though you are skeptical, I do sincerely regret that your death is necessary." After slipping the phone in a pocket, he pulled the gun from his waistband and held it loosely at his side.

"That the gun you used to shoot Clint?" she asked. "And I bet you saved the last bullet for me. I'm going to be another notch on the old Joel Martin's six-shooter and another nasty family secret, huh?" She raised her arms. Her eyes darted from her wrists to Joel.

"I admire your fighting spirit and sense of survival, my dear. I always have. You learned well from me. However, I didn't loosen the ropes that much." He studied her through narrow eyes, and raised the gun.

Martin Family Cabin

SOMETHING'S WRONG, CLINT thought, his face bathed in soft incandescent yellow light from the cabin and silver-white light from the moon low in the western sky. From the clearing's edge behind the family cabin, he could see lights on in all the cabin's rooms. *That shouldn't be,* he thought. "Or that," he whispered when he saw that a police cruiser was parked so that the vehicle's frontend was just visible beyond the cabin's nearside.

He walked backwards and hid behind a tree. *Mommy dearest has gone off script or been found out,* he reasoned. *Maybe she bailed on the whole damn scheme. Wouldn't be the first time, and ... I can't say I blame her.* Though unintelligible, one side of a police radio conversation interrupted his speculation.

Now what? he wondered, gazing at the moon before stepping deeper into the shadows. Pressing against a tree, he patted his pockets. "Yeah, it's time for plan B's plan B," he whispered to himself, pulling a plastic pouch containing his cell phone from a pocket. He squeezed a button and, as the home screen appeared, he softly recited Joel's orders aloud, "If anything goes wrong, make the call anyway and go to the alternate meet-up site. Buck will be there with the boat."

He opened the phone contact list and selected the one titled 'K.A. Boom,' but paused, holding his finger over the white handset image. Knowing that placing this call would initiate the device that Buck Wilson had planted at the beach house, his last conversation with Sylvia came to mind. *Screw you, Dad,* he thought bitterly and frowned. *With any luck she won't be home and they'll still find enough evidence to nail dear old Dad anyway. Maybe I'm more like Papa J than I thought.* He touched the screen icon as he retreated into the woods.

GASMAX Plant Control Room

JOEL LOOKED AT his watch. "It's time." He sighed and turned to face the control panel.

"Let's see," he said and threw two switches on the control panel. "Yes, with Phase Four enabled that's right." Two green lights at the top of the panel now pulsated red. After pulling a notebook from his pant pocket, he thumbed through a few pages. "Here. Got to get the sequence right," he announced. Flipping the pistol to hold it by the barrel, he smashed a glass safety plate of a locked cover of a box on the panel's side. "Open both valves," he read.

With some effort he broke a lock wire and turned two small red valve handles within the box. A sharp hiss sounded outside the room and three more green lights turned red and flashed in unison with the other two.

Martin turned and smiled at Cynthia. "Perfect. Just like J warned about Phase Four."

"Joel, are you crazy? Don't ..." Cynthia challenged and strained against the ropes. They were too tight for a quick escape.

"I see you know what this means," he commented with some delight in his eyes.

"I'm not going to be shot, but something worse," she whispered.

He chuckled. "I would say the tables have very much turned from when you marched triumphantly into my office to show me the door." He smashed the two red valve handles with the butt of the gun.

"They're now impossible to turn," she said, stopped struggling against the restraints and stared at the flashing lights.

"Yes, that's correct. You do see where this will end, don't you?"

"From what I recall of my training and J's concerns about Phase Four, you're going to cause an explosion in the plant."

"That's almost correct. To be precise, I've disabled five safety circuits and overridden two interlocks. The Phase Three configuration would have made this impossible. The result will not just be an explosion in the plant, but of the entire building," he said with pride, grinned and swept his free hand back and forth across the control panel. He hefted the gun again, and with three blows he destroyed the switches he had thrown. "With the amount of combustible gas in this plant and out in the tank farm it will burn very hot and for a very long time. Hot enough to destroy almost any trace of a body."

"I see," Cynthia said and sighed. "The plant blows and the only evidence of who died here tonight will be in the safety log at corporate. I imagine that your name is in that log."

"'Very good," Joel said, "and there's one other name in that book."

"Mine," Cynthia hissed, "but what about the plant operator?"

"Good question, little sis." Joel smiled and pointed the gun at the ceiling. He twirled the barrel and dropped her and Danny's plant IDs on the floor.

"My ID! How …," Cynthia started. "It was in my purse …"

"That Buck Wilson obtained in yet another failed attempt on your life. So, yours, mine, and Danny's names are recorded but there's an entry showing she logged out after initiating the Phase Four AI test. I used her badge to log her in as I did yours. I've also planted enough evidence at the home office that makes you out to be a disgruntled employee, and I, the valiant CEO and loving uncle, rushed here to stop you, but …"

"We both … no, all three of us die in your failed heroic effort," she finished. "But Danny's body … Oh, you said you'd cleanup that mess later. And Clint's body in the river is just another mysterious Martin death or one that's …"

"Easily pinned on Buck Wilson. Very good, my dear, and?"

"And you no doubt left some evidence that I was in cahoots with J in covering up the problems with Phase Four."

"Correct."

"But how do you …" she started. "Oh, I see. You said you love Aunt Joan. She's alive and I bet your personal fortune, boosted by advance Phase Four license sales, and most of J's wealth is legally sheltered where you and Joan can get to it but with new identities. That's why Joan took the terms of the will so calmly."

"And, even if we're ever found out, you, as the sole surviving Tannerson, will not be around to lay claim to any of it through civil suits. The company, of course goes belly up, and …"

"You're remembered as a great and honorable man and not the adulterous, murdering bastard you really are," Cynthia cried out, straining against the ropes. "I just can't believe Aunt Joan could love you, let alone go along with murdering her children."

"Believe it. She took some persuasion, but she finally realized she wanted out of her miserable life in the Martin family as much as I now want out of mine. Only I understand how completely unhappy she was in that loveless marriage to J. I'm giving her a way out."

"No! That's just not possible," Cynthia raged, clenching her fists.

Martin took a step back. His smile shrank to a tight-lipped frown. "No, she's better off fake dead," he said and pointed the pistol at her. "I'd like to continue our family chat, but we only have about ten minutes. This will be quicker than burning to death."

"You're too good to me," Cynthia snapped.

"I do regret this, my dear sister. I've known many people in my life. You stand out among the best. The world will pale a little without your fighting spirit." He sighed. Her drug-compelled recital had filled him with a modicum of regret and sorrow. It stayed his hand briefly. *But no time for that* ..., Joel cautioned silently, and, glancing at his watch, he frowned. He raised the barrel, aimed and his finger found the trigger.

CHAPTER 27

Heart Attack and Heartbreak

GASMAX Plant Control Room

THE CONTROL ROOM DOOR SLAMMED open. "No!" Danny cried as she briefly filled the doorway before lunging at Joel across the few paces separating them.

Turning to face the threat, Joel pulled the trigger. The shot went wide, and the pistol flew from his hand, past Cynthia's face. She strained against the ropes to see past Martin. "Danny!" she screamed.

Danny tackled Joel and fell on him. They rolled on the floor behind Cynthia's chair. Danny jabbed a fist at Joel's throat, but he blocked the thrust with his free hand. He counter-punched at her stomach. Anticipating him, Danny grabbed his wrist and, with her free forearm, slammed him back onto the floor. The impact stunned Joel long enough for Danny to stand and draw the handgun with which Joel had shot her. "But you're dead," Joel protested, grasping the wrist of her gun hand.

"Unlike my idiot brother, I wore a vest," Danny said with anger. "Thanks for leaving the gun."

"Danny, what's happening?" Cynthia asked.

"I'm saving your butt, Princess," she replied, struggling to aim the gun at Joel. "I'll untie you once I ..."

Joel kicked at Danny's legs. He connected, and, as she fell on him, she shot but missed. Cynthia worked to get free of the ropes.

"Danny, stop!" Joel roared. He grabbed her wrists and rolled on top of her. The motion sent the struggling couple into the side of Cynthia's chair, knocking it over.

Cynthia freed one hand in time to break her fall. She landed with her back to Joel and Danny. Lying on her side, she struggled to free her other arm and feet.

Danny and Joel wrestled on the floor behind her. Danny rolled on top and, by luck more than plan, straddled his left leg before shoving her knee into his crotch. Joel cried out and released her wrists. Seizing the opportunity Danny brought the gun to bear. Despite the pain, Joel surprised her and again grabbed the wrist of her gun hand and rolled on top of her pressing the gun barrel into her chest. "You double-crossing SOB," Danny hissed as Joel pressed her finger to pull the trigger.

Danny's eyes went wide when the gun fired and Joel said, "Sorry, baby girl."

The shot ending the sounds of the struggle behind her made Cynthia freeze briefly before she freed her feet. *What the ...*, she wondered when she found that Joel had used her belt to bind her feet to one leg of the chair. *That gunshot sounded funny. It must be the drug*, she thought. She dropped the belt and awkwardly pulled and pushed herself to stand. She shook her head and turned to counter what she anticipated would likely be an angry, murderous and armed Joel Martin.

Confirming her fear, he towered over her, eyes blazing, as he brought Danny's pistol to bear.

Eye of the Storm Beach House

LEAVING THE HOSPITAL vigil to Julie Simpson, Sylvia Martin drove to the beach house. Tanner's MRI results were pending, but he was stable and asleep. She and the detective agreed that since Dr. Schwartz had joined them, her time and talents could be better applied elsewhere. This arrangement allowed her to address what she considered larger concerns. The fact that they had no contact with Cynthia by now was extremely worrisome, and there were company business concerns that she alone appreciated. *Considering what we concluded from the material in the safe*, she reasoned, turning onto the house's driveway, *and that Joel is suspect, I'm the GASMAX representative on site. I need the computers and phones in the study to handle what's coming and what needs to be done.*

She parked the car and entered the house. Moonlight gave her home's exterior a gothic cast akin to her growing anxiety. Her calls at the hospital and in the car to the GASMAX plant control room had not been answered. For the fourth time, she dialed the number. "Pick up," she ordered as she took the stairs. After the tenth ring, she gave up and dialed the backup plant operator.

"Hello, Ms. Martin," a fresh young voice answered.

"Hello. Something's terribly wrong at the plant. The on-duty operator doesn't answer. Go there and investigate. But wait for security before entering."

"Yes, ma'am. You want me to call them?"

"No, I will," Sylvia replied, noting the time. "Call this number when you get there. Questions?"

"The OPS Chief too?"

"No, me first. I'll call Carson. The Ops Boss is the next call after the security chief. Any other questions?"

"No ma'am."

"Great. Get going and be safe. Goodbye."

She entered the study and sat at the desk as the call went through to the security chief, a GASMAX veteran named Thomas Blair. "Code Red, Tom," she said firmly. After detailing the facts regarding Joel Martin's transgressions and Danny's and Clint's likely complicity, she and the chief had agreed on the modifications to the standard response. Those changes factored in her family dysfunction and that the police were already in route to the plant. At Blair's insistence, the alterations also allowed for the possibility of the CEO being innocent of misconduct.

"I got it," Blair said. "I'm on it, Sylvia. Anything else?"

"No. Thanks."

"I assume you'll call Carson."

"Next up. Goodbye," She answered flatly and hung up.

"Bye," she heard before the call ended.

The call with Fred Carson, the chief of plant operations, was equally short. However, as he spoke, Sylvia sat back stunned and shocked. The long-time ops chief calmly stated the likely explanation as to why the on-duty operator didn't answer the control room phone. He informed her that Joel Martin had resumed the Phase Four AI testing the day after J's body was discovered.

More disturbing than this fact had been kept from her as J Martin's executive assistant was that Carson told her that she had been cut out of the loop at Joel Martin's direction. Equally troubling was operation chief's report that her sister, Danny, was tonight's on-duty plant operator, and, since testing was underway, she was presently absent from the building and on-call. He placed Sylvia on hold while he called Danny's on-call number and Joel's cell phone. She wasn't surprised when he eventually reported that her sister and uncle didn't answer.

After detailing her suspicions regarding Joel Martin's and Danny's possible wrong doing, she said, "Fred, I may be over reacting, but I've deployed the backup plant operator and the security team. Please follow up with them and keep me informed."

"Will do," he replied. "Have you notified the Board?"

"My next call, but it would be better to know something more before further sounding the alarm at headquarters."

"That's true," he agreed. "Recommend you make at least a heads-up call while I get you some more information. I'm on it, Sylvia. Bye."

After the call ended, Sylvia pulled the desktop computer's keyboard in front of her. *Normally, I'd call the CEO, but he's likely gone off the reservation and isn't taking calls. So, who's in charge?* She wondered. She logged on to the GASMAX intranet to access company email. She finally reasoned, *With Dad dead, Cynthia fired and Joel gone rogue, I'll call the Secretary-Treasurer.* He was Hogan Garfield, a longtime board member recruited by her father. *By default, he's the man in charge.*

After a short heads-up conversation with Garfield, she looked at the time and sniffed. *Nothing more to be done until I know something. Should be time to freshen up and step up from casual to business-casual.*

Because Cynthia was using her room, she left the study and entered the adjacent master bedroom. She fingered the change of work clothes she'd laid out on the bed before the unanticipated sleuthing in the wine cellar. Entering the bathroom, she turned on the shower and unbuttoned her blouse. *Should be time. Got a feeling it may be some time before I can do this again*, she thought after stepping beneath the needles of hot water.

In the study, inside the credenza set beneath the wall safe behind the desk, a cell phone answered the mobile call Clint had placed to the contact 'K.A. Boom.' The hidden phone, in silent mode, lit up and displayed Clint's caller ID as 'UNKNOWN.' The identity screen vanished immediately replaced by a digital hour-minutes-second timer display.

Three green lights atop a box connected by a wire to the phone began to flash. Three wires, red, white and blue, ran from the box to three detonator caps plunged into a tubular run of dull white plastic explosive, spanning the entire back of the credenza shelf.

On the day Buck Wilson had upended and searched Cynthia's room, he'd first concealed the explosive device behind three locked opaque plastic boxes he set behind the credenza's sliding doors. A can of gasoline sealed in plastic rested in each box to complete what Wilson dubbed "Joel Martin's Plan B" device."

As Sylvia soaped her arms, the green lights stopped flashing. One light went red when '01-60-60' appeared briefly. It then flashed red as the seconds counted down, and the middle light joined in the synchronous red pulsations after the minutes display showed '59.' When she'd washed her neck and shoulders, the display reached '57.'

As Sylvia wrapped a towel about herself, the minutes display reached '48.' She glanced at her cell phone. *No calls and no news. Tanner and Cynthia are still not out of the woods*, she observed with a frown, smiling briefly at her play on words. She pulled a clean blouse on over fresh undergarments, smoothed her skirt into place and walked quickly to the study. She sat at the desk as the minutes display, just few feet behind her, reached '44.' *At least Tanner and Julie are relatively safe at the hospital, but Cynthia could still be in grave danger.* She sighed and said, "It just feels so wrong being the only one completely out of the danger zone."

GASMAX Plant Control Room

"JOEL, NO, WAIT," Cynthia pleaded, raising her hands and eyeing Danny's fallen body.

Martin lowered the gun, cocked his head and froze. His eyes went wide as the light left them. He dropped the pistol, grasped his abdomen and toppled forward, falling on Danny.

The impact roused Danny. Rolling onto her side, she climbed free. She rose, looking at Cynthia and then at Joel. She knelt next to his body, picked up the gun and felt under his chin for a pulse. "He's dead. He's finally dead," she said in a breathless voice shaped by adrenaline, and laced with triumphant disbelief. She began to shake when the fear induced fight-over-flight compulsion suddenly evaporated. With great effort and an ashen face, she stood.

"Danny," Cynthia said, extending her hand. "Here." She grasped her cousin's forearm to hold her upright.

"Cynthia, I ... I couldn't let him kill you," Danny managed to say after several deep breaths. She dropped the gun and fell toward her cousin.

Cynthia caught her by the shoulders before the younger woman collapsed into her embrace. Danny cried and her body shook with sobs.

"Danny," Cynthia said, fighting to speak calmly and gently pushing her to arms-length. Pointing at the control panel, she declared firmly, "We've got to get out of here."

Danny's eyes followed Cynthia's extended arm, and stared at the red flashing lights. She squinted, assessing the ramification of the lights and other indicators, and her eyes widened. "My God! What ... what did he do?"

"He ..." Cynthia started.

Danny held a hand up. Then, with the same confidence she had shown during their earlier control room meeting, she attacked the damaged controls. She threw two intact switches and twisted the two broken red valve handles without success. "It's no use!" she cried, pounding the panel apron with her fists. She looked at Cynthia. "We've got about five minutes before this whole place blows apart."

Cynthia nodded. "That's what Joel said."

Danny examined a gauge and tapped its glass face. She opened a plastic cover and pressed a red button. Her face tightened as she glanced at another gauge. "Damn! He's disabled the entire halogen system. It's going to burn like the sun." She turned to her cousin. "Cynthia, I can't stop this!" An explosion shook the floor below them. They both grabbed the bar fronting the control panel.

"Let's go!" Cynthia ordered as she scooped up the pistol. Danny swayed as she stepped from the panel. Cynthia took her by the elbow. "You okay? Can you walk?"

She nodded. "Just a little shaky from the fight," she said flatly, gesturing toward Joel's body. "Considering all this, I could run." She smiled despite their peril. "Besides, I got here in time to save your ass, didn't I?"

"Good point," Cynthia said and chuckled before pushing her companion toward the emergency exit slide. "You're going to have to. Now down the chute. Let's go!"

"No!" Danny cried, digging in her heels. She pointed at the yellow tape stretched across the entry and flipped over the sign declaring 'Out of Service'. "The tube's still out - collapsed. We've got to go out the door."

When they were outside the room, their footsteps on the catwalk were suddenly drowned out by what seemed like a cross between the roar of a hurricane and an explosion. Danny pivoted and pushed Cynthia hard against the railing.

"What the hell!" Cynthia screamed above the howling blast of hot wind and shoved her cousin back. Reading fear in Danny's eyes, she stopped struggling.

"A pressure safety lifted!" Danny shouted after pressing her mouth close to Cynthia's ear. "It relieves just above us, and the pipe hanger's broke free." Cynthia searched the ceiling shadows and saw a dark green pipe whipping back and forth like a pressurized and unattended garden hose. It savagely beat the space above the railing, effectively blocking their passage.

"On your stomach," Cynthia shouted, pulling the other woman flat on to the metal walkway. She crawled past Danny and led the way. After they passed the swinging pipe, she pulled Danny to her feet.

A low rumble followed by a loud crack joined the safety relief's angry bang and wail. The catwalk shook and swayed. Both women grabbed the railing and looked behind them. A cloud of white gas rose from below them and swallowed the door to the operating station. The metal walk lurched.

"I can't! I got to go back!" Danny screamed and turned to return to the control room.

"No, you fool!" Cynthia cried, grabbing Danny's arm. "Go!" she yelled, pushing her toward the stairs at the end of the catwalk.

They staggered to the head of the metal steps like two sailors crossing a heaving deck in a storm-ravaged sea. Danny, reaching the stairs first, froze. "They're gone!" she screamed at Cynthia and pointed.

Cynthia elbowed her aside and stared across the twenty-five-foot drop at the twisted pile of metal steps on the concrete floor below. Another explosion roared to their right and the pressure in the vast auxiliary room rose sharply. "Ow!" Cynthia cried, covering her ears.

"We gotta jump!" Danny screeched. "Or go back to the control room.

Maybe ..."

Cynthia shook her head, realizing that the fall would kill them or cause injuries that would make subsequent exiting and getting clear impossible. "No! We won't survive either way. Give me your belt," she mouthed the words, pulling at the dark leather belt in Danny's black denim pants.

"What the hell ..." Danny complained before realizing what Cynthia had in mind. She tore at the dull metal buckle and removed the belt.

Cynthia reached to remove hers before she recalled that she had left it in the control room. *One will have to do.* Taking the leather strap and shouldering Danny aside, she swung the belt at the chains and control box power cable for the small overhead crane that traversed the length of the room. The belt wrapped about the chains and cable before the loose end swung back towards her. She lunged for it, missed and lost her grip on the rail. She fell. Danny grabbed a handful of her blouse and pulled her back up onto the catwalk.

Giving her a thankful nod, Cynthia once more swung the belt. This time she caught the free end and pulled. With Danny's help, they heaved the crane's control box up onto the catwalk. Cynthia hugged the chains and gave a hurried nod toward the box.

Danny pressed the up button, but nothing happened. Their faces filled with despair as another explosion rocked the building. The catwalk lurched once more. Cynthia released the useless chains and grasped the railing. She looked over the side and saw smoke rise and flames lick the catwalk from the floor below. *It doesn't matter about the crane now*, she concluded silently, recalling the tanks of gas on the ground floor. *No way out down there anyway.* She searched the walls and ceiling for another escape route.

Danny stared over the side. "It's not supposed to end this way!" she cried, eying the control room door, and climbed the rail. "Got to jump! It's the only chance." Chucking the control box aside, she steadied herself to leap and embrace a fiery fate.

Moses Martin Memorial Hospital

"UGH," TANNER STRONG murmured. His eyes flickered briefly as he looked down his right arm. A tube stretched from a needle in the back of his hand up to a plastic bag half-full of clear fluid. It felt like wires were stuck to his chest. A rhythmic beep softly sounded from somewhere above. Unseen by him, three luminous green lines spiked safely with each beep.

Rolling his head left, he found his hand locked firmly in Julie Simpson's. She was slumped forward in a chair, her head resting on her arm and her eyes closed. Softly snoring, her hand gently squeezed his with each breath. *I owe her dinner*, he supposed, unable to form any other thought he could relate to, *because I've seen her in her bra and panties.*

Beyond her, in a recliner, a vaguely familiar man of stocky build was silently studying a cell phone. "Dr. Schwartz?" Strong asked. His tongue and lips felt thick. *Is this another session?* he wondered. *Man, my head hurts.* Due to desire or reflex, he returned Julie's next hand squeeze and smiled.

"Tanner," she cried, raising her head, sitting up and pushing hair out of her face. A smile creased her face as she grabbed his arm. "Thank God. Doctor, he's awake."

Strong pushed himself up. "Julie, how'd I ..." he started, raising a hand to his head.

Corbin Schwartz put a hand on his shoulder. "No, lie back down, Tanner." He surveyed the monitor next to the bed. "Your pulse is racing and I ... oh no!"

Tanner fell back. His eyes went shut and a monitor alarm sounded as the three lines of regular spikes went flat.

"What ... what's happening?" Julie cried as the doctor pushed her aside.

"Code Blue!" he shouted over his shoulder and placed his hands on Strong's chest. "Get some help in here!"

CHAPTER 28

Bombs and Bullets

―

GASMAX Plant

"No!" CYNTHIA SHOUTED, HEFTING THE control box, pulling Danny down off the rail.

"What the ..." Danny sputtered, as Cynthia pulled her close.

"The window! We can swing out of here," she shouted into Danny's ear. "It's our only chance. Come on!"

"You're insane," Danny protested, eyeing the control box's thick power cable and the six-foot windows arrayed side-by-side, with the windowsill seven feet below the roof. "We can't ... won't clear the sill!"

Ignoring the protests, Cynthia pushed her cousin farther along the catwalk until the control box cable was taut.

"Up on the rail!" she commanded loudly, shoving Danny.

Danny blinked and shrugged. "Okay," she mouthed as they pulled themselves hand-over-hand up the control box power cable to stand on the rail. "We're going to die anyway."

They leaned back and steadied themselves atop the railing. Facing one another, one sweaty hand at a time, they worked to secure a better grip. "On three," Cynthia ordered.

Danny nodded.

"One ...," Cynthia started when another explosion lifted the catwalk and their perch swayed. "Three!" Their weight shifted to the cable. It held.

"No!" Danny moaned and hesitated briefly. Though Cynthia pulled her off the railing, her slight delay spun them into space.

Though they swung only a few seconds toward the opposite wall, to Cynthia it seemed like minutes.

"Noooooo!" Danny wailed, squeezing her eyes shut.

Checking their swing to point their feet at the approaching wall, Cynthia realized that Danny was on the edge of panic. Sensing their upswing and counting a second, she raised her feet and shouted, "Let go!" She released her hold. She quickly struck Danny's hands, breaking her death grip, before grabbing the top of her cousin's pants. Cynthia pulled her as close as possible.

Danny cried something unintelligible.

Cynthia closed her eyes and pressed her heels together. *Hope I estimated the swing right,* she thought and prayed, *Lord, please let it be glass and not concrete.* As a partial answer to her prayer, Danny embraced her tightly, compacting their weight just before impact.

The collision shattered glass, sending pain shooting up Cynthia's legs. A shard ripped her blouse. Two others stabbed her arms before cool night air washed over her body as she fell. Clinging to Danny, they hit the awning. It collapsed but broke their fall as they dropped onto the grass beyond the sidewalk that ran beneath the canopy. The drop onto the canopy broke her grasp on Danny just before they hit the ground. She rolled and stopped flat on her back. With relief she felt Danny roll up against her.

Though the fall was arrested, it still knocked the wind out of Cynthia. She lay still for a moment, regained her breath and got her bearings. Ignoring the pain from the cuts and the two-story drop, she pushed herself up to sit. The hard landing had put them a short walk from the nearly empty parking lot. A GASMAX pickup and another car were visible, both parked under one of the lot's several lampposts.

An explosion rocked the plant. On shaky legs Cynthia got to her feet. "We've got to get moving, Danny," she said, looking at the building and realizing that the fire might soon reach the tank farm.

"Danny, we ... damn!" she cursed, recognizing that her cousin was unconscious. She knelt and examined a nasty cut on Danny's forehead. "She'll live," she concluded after determining that she was breathing evenly.

The pistol Danny had used to kill Joel Martin lay on the ground next to the her. Another rumble from the plant and her memory of Joel Martin's words about the magnitude of the inevitable explosion drove her to stand. Sticking the pistol in her waistband, she hefted the unconscious woman into a fireman's carry and staggered towards the parking lot. A fireball exploded from the plant behind her.

Moses Martin Memorial Hospital

AFTER SHE WAS unceremoniously shoved out of Tanner's room, Julie Simpson had been escorted under protest to an empty waiting area. From there she'd watched Tanner and the team around his gurney disappear through swinging double doors emblazoned with red letters declaring

SINS OF OUR BLOOD THUNDER MOON

'SURGERY.' Dr. Schwartz appeared shortly thereafter and gave her a guarded but positive update. He then offered to get coffee and she readily accepted. Taking the hallway next to the entrance to surgery, he'd gone to the hospital cafeteria.

Although only twenty minutes had passed since Dr. Schwartz's departure, the waiting and not knowing made it feel longer. Julie paced back and forth, ignoring the two rows of seating, set perpendicular to the walls and each other, bounding the waiting area. She finally sat when she concluded that pacing and staring at double doors would not make them open and divulge how Tanner was doing. *What about this guy makes me all ...? Come on, girl, pull it together*, she chastised herself. *Besides, there's something going on between him and Cynthia Jones*. Surprised and disappointed with herself, she sniffed and wiped away a tear. As she dabbed the other eye, her phone rang. The caller ID showed 'Sylvia Martin.'

After a curt exchange of greetings, Sylvia asked in a gentler voice, "How is he?"

"His heart stopped," Julie sobbed before she could catch herself. She inhaled deeply and regained her PI's indifference before finishing, "But they got it going."

"My God," Sylvia gasped. "Is ... is he going to be okay?"

"I ... don't know," Julie replied, anxiously glancing at the double doors. "He's in surgery now."

"Surgery?" Sylvia paused. "I thought he just had a concussion."

"But it's a bad one. The MRI shows a cerebral edema," Simpson answered calmly, finding that dealing with particulars and facts excluded an emotional response.

"A what?"

"One of those blows to his head from that bastard Wilson caused brain injury, bleeding," Julie said with calculated anger. "That's building up pressure in his skull. Intracranial pressure, ICP or something like that."

"I've heard of that. But will he be okay?"

Sylvia's concern strengthened Julie's newfound calm. "The surgery is to relieve the pressure. It's called a ventriculostomy."

"Brain surgery then. That's serious, isn't it?"

"Sounds worse than it is. They drill a hole in the skull and insert a tube to drain the excess blood, relieving the pressure. In severe cases they remove a chunk of skull. Dr. Schwartz said that as surgeries go, it's fairly routine."

"Should I come back and give you a break?"

"No. The doc is here translating the medical jargon. He's stepped away to get us coffee and check on the surgery," Julie answered with more confidence than she felt.

"You sure? I put a bunch of stuff in motion, but until I get some reports, I'm at loose ends."

"I'm sure, Sylvia. All we can do now is wait and see how the surgery goes. We've got this covered. You need to be where you are. With your father's death and Joel Martin's suspect behavior you're GASMAX in Driftwood Cove."

Sylvia chuckled. "You figured that out, too. That's how I'm proceeding."

"Speaking of Joel Martin, have you heard anything about or from Cynthia?" Thoughts of why she and Tanner had ended up at the hospital further focused her on something other than the unsettling but pleasing emotions for Tanner that had been sparked by their brief acquaintance and adventures.

"No, not a word from anyone. In addition to several unanswered calls to the plant control room, I've tried her number several times as well as Danny's and Clint's. No one answers. Oh, by the way, Danny is the on-duty operator tonight, but she's on-call."

"How's that?"

"The plant is in Phase Four AI testing tonight."

"AI?"

"Oh, AI is artificial intelligence. The plant is in full auto, unmanned. The on-duty operator can be offsite with phone on-call. Danny could be anywhere."

"You mean like in the Quarry Forest with Joel, Clint and Cynthia?"

"Yes. So, I've deployed the backup plant operator and the GASMAX security team. Even though the security squad is local, they're on phone standby. So, it'll take a while for the team to assemble and get to the plant. Also, Chief Smith is sending officers to the campgrounds and the plant. I've done pretty much all I can until we hear something from the plant or the chief. Has he or anyone else called you?"

"No, but one of his officers came by asking me to help chase down leads."

"Are you?"

"No. I'm not going anywhere until I know Tanner is okay," Julie replied with more emotion than she'd intended."

"I see," Sylvia said softly. "You okay?"

Julie cleared her throat before replying calmly, "I'm fine. Today just reminded me why I quit being a cop."

"Okay. I'll stay put, but if ... hey, there's another call. Stay on the line."

"Roger that." Julie, tapping her foot, again looked at the doors to surgery.

"Julie, that was the chief," Sylvia said. "There's been an explosion at the plant. I ..."

"Go! As soon as Tanner is out of the woods, I'll get over there. I'll call as soon as I know something. Bye."

"Bye."

As Julie lowered the phone, the doors to surgery opened. A man in scrubs and a surgical mask slung about his neck stepped through. Dr. Schwartz, stepping out of the hallway to the cafeteria and carrying two cups, intercepted him. *No smiles or frowns*, she observed, standing. She left the waiting area to join them. *Damn, their poker faces.*

Eye of the Storm Beach House

WHEN SYLVIA ENDED the call with Julie, she'd already taken the first step to the widow's walk atop the house. Hidden from sight in the credenza, '00-35-00' glowed briefly on the bomb's time dsiplay. When she reached the platform, it read '00-33-00.'

She looked to the west above the circular drive below and the tree tops beyond. Her father had always claimed that the GASMAX plant was just visible from atop the house. *I never could see it*, she thought, *but he was a head taller*. In addition to family gatherings on the widow's walk, he'd claimed that he greatly enjoyed the solidary time "above it all" as he put it, to sort things out. *Well, maybe he's right*, she hoped. *There's some sorting out needed for sure. If I can't see flames or the sky all aglow, it may not be too bad. Damn, is that fire or just the moon setting below the tree line?*

She looked at her phone, wishing she could will someone with information to call. The sound of tires on the round drive and a police cruiser's flashing lights interrupted her fruitless mental effort. A uniformed officer got out, put on a hat and strode to the front door.

Maybe the Chief has sent some news, Sylvia thought as she made her way to the ground floor and front porch. The silhouette of a tall man filled the screen door. Flipping a light switch, yellow light illuminated the familiar face of a young man who had once been her classmate in the Driftwood school system. "Charles Harper, what are you doing here? I hope Chief Smith sent you with some news."

"Good evening, Sylvia. No news from the chief," he said, removing his hat, "but I'm here on police business."

"I see. What may I do for you?"

"Ms. Martin, you need to come with me right now," he replied and put his hat back on.

"What? This is not a good time, Charley. There's been an explosion at the plant. This is now a command center and I'm representing GASMAX in Driftwood for reasons I don't have time to explain."

"I know about the plant. The chief just called it in. There's also been some gunplay in the campgrounds north of the plant."

"Then I need to get upstairs. My backup operator is enroute to the plant and so is the security team. My cousin is in those woods. They all expect to reach me here. Not to mention my board of directors. If you're here to stand guard," she said, opening the door, "you may join me in the study."

"That's not it," he said, placing a hand on her forearm. "We can't. There's a bomb in your house."

"A bomb! Says who?" She shook off his hand and looked over her shoulder before stepping onto the porch.

"Your brother. He's in the car in cuffs," Harper replied, pointing at his car. "He turned himself in. We picked him up in the woods near your family cabin."

Sylvia could see that someone was in the backseat. "What about Cynthia ... Jones? Was she with him?"

"He says she went off with your uncle and sister, but we've got to clear out of here. Clint said it's some kind of incendiary device." He looked at his watch. "The bomb disposal unit is coming from Central City."

"So, it'll be hours before I can get back in there, and ... okay," Sylvia agreed suddenly, "but I've got to get something out of the safe."

"I can't let you do that," Harper insisted. "Your brother says there's no time. Look, we gotta go!"

"Look, Charley, he would say that. Cynthia suspects he's thrown in with my Uncle Joel and my sister Danny. They're behind all these supposed accidents you and the chief have been investigating," Sylvia stated, gripping his shoulder. "What's in that safe proves it. Of course, they and Joel want to blow it up to destroy the evidence. Hey. They probably set the explosion at the plant ... Phase Four testing. My God, Cyn was right."

"Let go, Sylvia," Harper ordered, pulling her hand free and grasping her arm. "Don't make me put cuffs on you too."

Sylvia looked at her former classmate. His dead serious countenance and the feel of the gun handle when she put her phone in her pocket compelled her to agree. "Okay. Let's go." She smiled briefly. "You lead."

"No, ladies first," he said, and, taking her by the elbow, escorted her to the car's back door. Turning his back to her, he pulled his key ring out to unlock the door.

Sylvia quickly pulled her gun, stepped forward and pressed it into his back. "Hands up, Charley," she ordered firmly and pulled his cuffs from his belt. "Get behind the wheel."

"What ... Sylvia, what are you doing?" Harper sputtered as he complied.

She cuffed his hands to the steering wheel. "There you go. You'll be able to drive out of the blast area." She unlocked and opened the back door. "Clint, get out!"

"Sylvia, have you gone nuts!" Clint shouted. "That ... that bomb is going off in minutes."

"Then move!" she ordered, pulling him out onto the ground with a strength that surprised him. "We need to stop it. Now stay put while I send Officer Harper on his way."

After starting the cruiser and watching Harper drive off, she pulled Clint to his feet. "Where is it, brother?" she asked, pushing him up onto the porch.

"In the credenza, in the study where Buck put it," he answered. "I'm not going up there."

Sylvia pointed the gun aside and pulled the trigger. The slug ripped open Clint's shirt sleeve and the skin below. "The next one will go through muscle but no bone, I promise. Now upstairs," she commanded, opening the door.

Clint moaned and glared at his sister.

She pointed the gun at his forearm.

He nodded, clutching his wound as best he could with handcuffs on, and lurched into the house and up the stairs before Sylvia shoved him into the study. She pushed him into the chair next to the desk. She removed his belt and tied his ankles together.

"Sylvia, this is crazy. We've got to go!" he pleaded. "We're going to die!"

Ignoring his warning, Sylvia slid open the credenza doors. The luminous red indication of '00-21-09' captured her attention immediately. "21 minutes. Not much time," she said. "The black boxes, what's in them?"

"Gas cans."

"Nasty. Can I move them?"

"What? Yes, but you can't move or quickly deactivate the bomb. Buck said it's got a motion trigger and there's only one way to deactivate it."

Sylvia pulled the boxes out and set them next to Clint's chair before pulling a Swiss Army knife from the desk drawer. "So, how's it deactivated?" she asked unfolding one of the smaller of many blades. "Cut one or all of those wires to the detonators, I assume?"

"Yes, yes, all three wires," Clint replied frantically, "but that clever bastard set it up so you have to cut them in the right sequence or it goes off. Come on, Syl, it's useless. Let's get out of here!"

Hmm, red, white and blue wires," Sylvia said, noting that fifteen minutes remained on the timer. She sat at the desk and pulled sheets of paper from the top drawer. "Wilson was always a clever little sneak, but he was never that bright, and certainly not an original thinker. He'd probably used a memory aid."

"What are you doing?" Clint asked as Sylvia wrote. "This isn't one of your silly puzzles. Come on, let's go!"

"It's just one of a finite number of possible sequences. There's six ways. So that gives us a roughly sixteen percent probability of getting it right," she calculated and tapped the pen before writing again. "You see it's RWB – Red, White, Blue - or RBW, WRB, WBR, BRW or BWR. If we assume the white wire or W is his last name, Wilson, then we're down to RBW or BRW. That's it BRW – Buck, his middle initial for whatever and Wilson."

"No!" Clint shouted and slumped in his chair. "I can't believe I'm participating in this insanity. His name is Reginal Buchanan Wilson – RBW."

"How do you know that?" Sylvia said, looking up. "Are you sure?"

"Trust me, I know," Clint sighed. "When we were kids, he showed off his driver's license and I saw it on there. I called him Reginald once and made fun of him. And, not for the first time, he beat the crap beat out of me." He locked eyes with his sister and shook his head. "It's **RBW** if your assumption is right. And, Syl ..."

"Yeah," she replied, kneeling and putting the blade to the red wire.

"That's a big, big if."

"Yeah, it is," she agreed and cut the wire, noting the indicator declared '00-01-02.'

GASMAX Road

CYNTHIA LEANED AGAINST the rear fender of a police cruiser, took a sip of coffee and exhaled into the cup. The steam from the black liquid cleared but returned quickly. The vaporous activity captivated her attention until she looked once more at Danny's pistol. It lay in a clear plastic evidence bag on the open tailgate of the chief's pickup truck. Despite the row of trees flanking the entry drive to the plant's south parking lot, light from the gas plant blaze danced with the shadows across the bag. The truck was one of many law enforcement and fire vehicles as well as GASMAX cars and vans arrayed around the entrance. She'd been told that the fire and rescue vehicles from Sand Dollar had been deployed to the approaches to the north parking lot and tank farm.

Cynthia pushed herself off the fender and walked toward the gun. *It's the sound*, she concluded silently. *That drug Joel gave me made things sound funny or off for a while, but that sound – the gunshots - were really off.* A gray blanket with 'Property of Police' stamped on it fell from her shoulders. As she moved, she felt the pain from her gunshot wound as well as the various cuts, bruises and scratches. Early morning air cooled her back where her blouse had been ripped apart. She stepped gingerly over the several hoses snaked up the road toward the burning aftermath of the explosion that had nearly claimed Danny's life and hers.

The thought of her cousin made her glance sideways down the line of vehicles to where Danny still sat on a paramedic's gurney. Beside her were a medic, Chief Smith, and a uniformed police officer who had earlier draped the blanket over Cynthia's shoulders before he had quickly tagged and bagged the pistol. The resigned expression on Danny's face told her what her cousin clearly understood. Despite her heroics in the control room, Danny knew that she was going back to prison. The litany of charges she faced included several attempts on Cynthia's life. *Still, I gotta love her. She saved my butt. There's some good in her,* she thought as she recalled her rescue.

Another explosion lit up the early morning sky. Cynthia jumped and nervously glanced toward the plant. *That should be the last one,* she thought, recalling Joel Martin's prophecy of the fire and magnitude of the devastation. A heroic effort by the Sand Dollar, Driftwood and Central City fire and rescues squads, aided and directed by the GASMAX casualty response team, had contained the fire to the plant. It would not reach the tank farm.

The current blast sounded slightly muffled. However, it was a clear explosion despite the lingering effect of Joel's injection that had compromised her hearing when the shots were fired in the struggle that killed him. Her ears still rang from the explosions that had occurred during their escape, but she was certain something was not right about the sounds of those gunshots.

In the aftermath of their escape, after carrying Danny to the end of the drive, Cynthia had collapsed unconscious. Smelling salts administered by a worried-faced fireman yanked her back to the memory and reality of her recent brush with death. Danny was revived and sitting on the gurney when she found her. They sat side by side and watched the firemen battle the blaze until Danny's injuries again forced her to lie down on the gurney. Soon after, Cynthia was escorted to the police car and offered coffee.

That was over two hours and two cups ago, and they had spoken little while they were together. Cynthia gathered her wits by recounting to herself all that had happened that night. She figured it would help later when she gave the police her statement and it would keep her mind focused, despite the fatigue, aches and pains. She still worried about having no direct contact with Julie, Tanner or Sylvia. Chief Smith brushed her off with a short "They're okay" but he gave no specifics or an explanation of why they weren't present.

She'd momentarily lost sight of the gun in the bag when a fireman with a walkie-talkie stepped in front of her and hurriedly spoke into his radio. "Excuse me," she said absently and nudged the man aside.

He grunted as he gave way. Her eyes once more fixed on the bag, and her mind raced as she picked it up. "I heard the gunshots. I saw the body but ..." she said and broke the evidence seal and pulled the pistol out. She verified that it was empty and inspected the clip. Her eyes went wide. "Son of a ..." she sputtered, loading the clip. She flipped the safety off and walked to Danny's gurney.

Chief Smith looked up and started to smile until he saw the gun. "Cynthia, what the hell are you doing? No!" Smith shouted and swung at the barrel as she pointed it at Danny's chest and pulled the trigger.

CHAPTER 29

Head Fake

Eye of the Storm Beach House

WHEN SYLVIA CUT THE BLUE wire, the indicator read '00-00-23.' *Still no boom*, she thought, putting the blade to the white wire. She inhaled deeply at '00-00-18.'

Her hand perspired. *No time to wipe it*, she thought at '00-00-14,' exhaling and applying pressure. The blade snagged. "Damn," she hissed and pressed harder at '00-00-08.' Having cut the wire, she closed her eyes and sat back.

Sylvia slowly opened her eyes. No longer changing, '00-00-01' blazed forth on the display within the dim credenza interior. "No boom!" She cried joyfully, laughing and weeping in quick succession before standing.

"What happened?" Clint asked, uncurling from the ball he'd contorted himself into despite the constraints.

"My, oh my," Sylvia said as she leaned on the desk and looked at her brother. Her hands shook. "Clint, we did it! We got it right!"

"It's deactivated?" Clint asked, eyes wide and staring at Sylvia. "You did it … and you cuffed a cop and shot me. How …" A siren sounded.

"No doubt Officer Harper called in the cavalry," she said, removing Clint's belt, freeing his ankles. She tapped the cuffs with the buckle and placed the strap on his lap. "They'll have a key for those. Let's get you bandaged up."

"Thanks," Clint managed.

Sylvia's phone on the desk rang. "Yes." she said after pressing the speaker phone icon and motioning Clint to wait.

He nodded as she pulled a first aid kit from the bottom desk drawer.

"I'm at the plant," the backup operator reported, "but the police stopped me at the entry road. Ms. Martin, there's been an explosion. The whole plant is …"

"I know. What else? Do we know anything about the operator?" Sylvia asked, rolling up Clint's sleeve to uncover the flesh wound.

"Your cousin, Ms. Jones, carried her out. The paramedics and firemen are with them now."

"Very, good," Sylvia said with relief. She cleaned the wound, and, as she pressed the bandage into place, the study door opened. Two officers entered with guns drawn. "Look, I've got to go. The police are here. When Chief Smith shows up, tell him we found the bomb and it's deactivated."

Sylvia grabbed the phone, but she didn't hear "Yes ma'am" as she stood and raised her hands, the phone in one and a strip of gauze in the other.

Moses Martin Memorial Hospital

"SYLVIA, WHAT'S GOING on?" Julie whispered on the phone. Though the waiting area was empty, she spoke quietly. "I've called a half dozen times."

"How'd Tanner's surgery go?"

"Good. They relieved the pressure in time. He's on some meds for the bleeding."

"Have you been able to talk with him?"

"No, he hasn't regained consciousness yet. Corbin and I are taking turns in the room," she answered, stifling a yawn.

"Well, when he comes to, tell him Cynthia's okay."

"Great news!" Julie said brightly. "Did they catch Joel Martin? What about Danny?"

"Just got off a long phone call with Chief Smith. He reported what Danny and Cynthia told him," Sylvia said before explaining what happened in the forest and in the plant.

"So, Joan, Danny and Clint Martin came down on the good side, kind of?"

"Kind of." Sylvia sighed. "At least I hope so. Oh, please mention to Dr. Schwartz that the police want a statement from him."

"Then you, Tanner, Cynthia and I get a crack at him, right? I've got more than a few questions."

"Indeed," Sylvia replied.

GASMAX Road

"HE'S NOT DEAD," Cynthia declared as hands pinned her arms and the chief picked up the gun. "Chief, Joel Martin is still alive!"

"Cynthia, that's nuts," Danny protested, pulling herself upright with the chief's assistance. "I shot him. We fought and I shot him."

"With that gun," Cynthia said, nodding at the weapon in Smith's hand. "Chief, it's loaded with blanks. Check the clip."

Smith handed Danny off to one of the officers who had appeared when the shot was fired. "Hold her," he barked and inspected the weapon. "My God ... let Jones go."

"Ow," Cynthia cried and winced as she was released. The wounds were still there.

"So, what really happened in there?"

"They're blanks, Chief. Despite the distortion caused by Joel's injection, something was not right about the sounds of the two gunshots from that pistol. She's still in on it with Joel Martin," she said, pointing at Danny and facing Smith. "It was all an act for my benefit. A very dangerous, well-timed act, but an act nonetheless. I was to be the witness who would corroborate Danny's story that she'd shot and killed Martin to save my life. A dead Martin whose body was consumed in the fire and who killed J Martin would leave no loose ends for you to tie up. Case closed, right? But the truth is that Danny, Clint and Wilson were and still are all in league with Joel Martin."

"And Joan Martin?" Smith asked. "As I mentioned, we picked her up very much alive at the cabin after she turned herself in."

"Sadly, Joan too."

"But where's Martin? How could he survive that?" Smith asked, pointing over his shoulder at the still burning remains of the GASMAX plant. "You said that you left him in the control room. Are you saying he committed suicide to put Danny in the clear?"

"No, it's not in Joel Martin's nature to sacrifice himself. He takes other lives. He didn't stay there did he, Danny?" Cynthia challenged the woman standing between them.

Danny glared sullenly at Cynthia.

"Fess up, Danny. It's not just the blanks, your own words betrayed your charade."

"What?"

"When you were fighting with Joel in the control room he said, "But you're dead." And you said that, unlike Clint, "I wore a vest." It may have been the drugs at the time, but now I realize that means you were aware that Joel would shoot Clint."

"So?"

"Clint was shot after your staged death. So, you knew what was the next scene in Joel's act. You overplayed your hand, Danny" Cynthia said. "Besides, if you had a vest on, I would have felt it when I tackled you and took your knife. I didn't."

"Well, I ...," Danny started weakly, but fell silent.

"Also, Clint didn't really freeze with fear when I disarmed you. He knew you had to have us at gunpoint when Joel stepped on stage."

"You don't …"

So, Joel didn't stay in the control room did he, Danny?"

"No, … he … didn't." The words came slowly as she glanced at Cynthia and the chief before hanging her head.

"If he didn't die, where is he?" Smith asked again.

"Tell him, Danny," Cynthia commanded and touched her relative's arm. "You're not as good a liar as you think you are. Tell them where Joel went."

Danny looked at Chief Smith and whispered, "He went out the escape chute."

"But you both said that the escape chute wasn't functional."

"We were wrong. It was functional. Wasn't it, Danny?" Cynthia replied for her. "That's why you wanted back in the control room when you thought our way out was blocked."

Danny nodded and looked at the ground between her legs.

"You and Martin cleared it earlier today, right? And, I bet the maintenance records still show it's out of service."

Danny nodded again. "Yes."

"Chief, if you have the river searched west of the plant, you'll find the exit for the safety chute. Joel can't have gone too far. He's probably hiking north on the train tracks. I imagine he's in no hurry since he figures no one is looking for him. He probably has transportation staged up north."

Smith nodded. "Cuff her," he ordered a uniformed policeman, pointing to Danny. He pulled the radio off his hip and barked commands.

"What about Clint?" Smith asked. "You said that Joel had used a different gun to shoot him. My officer reported that he'd seen a vest and slugs."

"All part of the act, Chief. Joel needed a gun with live ammo for the unexpected. He knew Clint had a vest on, and they picked a spot where it was a drop into fast water. It's odd that he didn't pitch the vest and slugs in the river, but … well, it's Clint."

"Yes, but though he may have been in on it, he, along with Danny and their mother, have come forward to help us. Joan Martin told us about Joel, and Clint warned us about the bomb at the house. That makes no sense."

"Chief, that's the beauty of the plan. With Joel presumed dead, I suspect they were banking on a lenient sentencing for the repentant widow and her remorseful children who were beguiled by her husband's and their father's murderer and who had no real blood on their hands. Wilson and Joel Martin would be blamed for all the attempts on my life and others'. Sometime later, after the dust settled, I suspect the grieving widow and her two youngest surviving kids would have gone on extended holiday and disappeared into a plush new life arranged by Joel Martin. That's about it, isn't it, Danny?"

Danny nodded and added, "And, in the subsequent investigation, the planted evidence would have been found showing that you were a disgruntled former employee. So, I'd truthfully testify that I didn't actually see Joel sabotage the plant and that you might have done it."

"If the house had been destroyed with or without Sylvia inside, the evidence would be gone. So, even if Tanner Strong, Julie Simpson, or I survived, nothing could be proven," Cynthia added. "Even though Grandpa's Bible is likely still in the forest, it alone doesn't prove anything conclusively. By itself it only reveals Moses Martin's flawed scriptural search for the root causes of and solution for his family's generational dysfunction - the sins of our blood."

"That aside, Cyn, you've got to admit Joel had a beaut of a Plan B," Danny said, shrugging her shoulders. "It evolved and adapted as you escaped one trap after another. In the end it was better that you lived for some blame taking." Before an officer took her away, she added, "But, as usual, Princess, you were too smart for us."

"Yes, Danny, it was a beaut of a plan." Cynthia sighed, mourning the demise of the last warm feelings she had for Danny, her brother and their mom, "but sometimes I wish I wasn't so smart."

Chief Smith's radio crackled to life. "Chief, we got Joel Martin. He was in an RV that the chopper pilot spotted upriver at the end of a forest fire lane." He grinned at Cynthia.

She smiled back, but frowned as she watched Danny being pushed into the back of a police car. Only Sylvia remained as the sole survivor of the wreckage of her life-long extended Martin family. But, in addition to Sylvia, she now had a new family of sorts including her real birthright as a Tannerson to explore as well as new friendships with Tanner and Julie.

She placed a hand on the chief's shoulder and smiled. "Now, Chief, please, some details about Sylvia and the bomb at the house and Tanner Strong and Julie Simpson at the hospital."

EPILOGUE

2019

'Love the Lord your God with all your heart and with all your soul and with all your mind.' This is the first and greatest commandment. And the second is like it: 'Love your neighbor as yourself.'

Matthew 22:37-39
New International Version Bible

Driftwood Cove Chapel

TANNER STRONG CONSIDERED HIS REFLECTION in a mirror and ran his hand over his scalp, pushing a stray black hair back into place. His hair had completely grown back six months after the surgery. Even a year later, a habit persisted that had formed following the operation. He still felt a need occasionally to pause and press briefly and gently where the hole had been drilled for the ventriculostomy drain. Only a slight indentation remained. *More proof that I have, or at least had, a hole in my head*, he thought smiling. *But, next to a prosthetic leg, it's no big deal.*

Satisfied with his hair, he checked to make sure that his bow tie was straight, and, once a Marine always a Marine, he made sure that his gig line was straight, even though it was hidden behind a cummerbund. Finally, he inspected the spit shine on his formal shoes. *Nothing else to do now but wait for Collector to come get me*, he thought. He glanced at the door through which his best man, Colonel John Stamp, had disappeared minutes before. The Marine colonel was his former fighter squadron commanding officer, and his call sign was Collector. The colonel had gone to see if they were ready for the groom. *Am I ready? What's the hold up?*

He paced the small room off the chapel sanctuary. The Corps had taught him how to sit, wait and stay cool, but today he couldn't keep still or his hands dry. *Come on, Strong, you're just getting married, not flying into combat*, he chastised himself. *It was like Collector said, the clock on the wall and the time on the wedding invitations are meaningless. "We're all on bride time, so get used to it, buddy. It's a lot like wife time."*

He was very grateful that Sylvia had prompted, even nagged, him to seek out Collector. She correctly recognized his relationship with John Stamp was more than professional and one worth salvaging. To no avail, it had been Colonel Stamp who had stood by Captain Strong's assertion that it wasn't pilot error that had caused him to crash and burn and loose a leg. Despite such loyalty, by the time J Martin had rescued him from that bar, Tanner had cut even that last solid link to his past life and friendships.

Cynthia Jones helped too. She used the GASMAX political connections to prompt the Corps, via a congressional inquiry, to reopen the crash investigation. Though the wheels were turning slowly, she had recently been informed by a Senate friend of GASMAX that it was likely Tanner's record would be cleared. This was a great wedding gift. And, Julie Simpson, using her Driftwood Cove Police Department clout, provided Colonel Stamp a police escort from the airport. *Collector was really impressed*, he recalled and smiled.

He paused at the room's sole window and took in the view of Driftwood Bay below. Summer sun danced on the bay's waters rippled by an offshore breeze. *Wow, Sylvia Martin, Cynthia Jones and Julie Simpson are my best friends*, he realized suddenly. *Never thought I'd call a woman my best friend, let alone three of them. Considering how we were thrown together last summer, it's really not too surprising. Fortunately, subsequent events wouldn't let us go our separate ways.*

He pushed a drawn curtain further aside to watch a sailboat enter the bay and drop its sails. His nerves steadied as he recalled the aftermath of the plant explosion. During his stay in the hospital, the three women had taken turns to ensure him a daily hospital visit. Cynthia had insisted that GASMAX pay every medical bill that insurance didn't cover. Julie put her PI work on hold to stay in Driftwood and help the chief and to spend time with him at the hospital. Sylvia, despite the turmoil in her family, insisted that he recuperate at Eye of the Storm. There was plenty of room.

Joel, Joan, Danny and Clint Martin were all considered flight risks and were not able to post bail. *And today, EOS still has room because all the Martins except Sylvia are serving time.* He frowned. *How sad for her. It's tragic to lose family, but to also have all good memories tainted and crushed is heartbreaking.* That made Sylvia's compassion and grace towards him all the more amazing and endearing. It and her sense of family were a few of her many attractive qualities. She had recently reconciled with her mother but the rest of her immediate family were still lost to her. *Knowing her, maybe not forever.*

"Maybe Grandpa Moses had been right," Tanner said, recalling when

Sylvia had shown him the family Bible and Moses Martin's spiritual margin notes. "One of his grandchildren did break the cycle, getting the repentance thing right."

During that few months before he fully got back on his feet, he and Sylvia spent many an evening on the Eye of the Storm deck talking well into the night. Among the numerous things about her that impressed him was that she found time for him even while dealing with lawyers and multiple GASMAX travails. Cynthia or Julie occasionally joined their nighttime conversations, but, with their respective obligations, it wasn't until the rehearsal dinner last night that all three women had been with him at one time.

Cynthia, to no one's surprise, not only got back on the GASMAX board, but she was promptly elected CEO. Her first two acts were to have Sylvia appointed president and Tanner promoted to head of security. This was all part of quickly cleaning the corporate house. Tanner smiled when he recalled her saying, "The first step in a good Plan B is firing everyone responsible for Plan A." And she did. There were lots of new and younger faces at the Central City offices.

She and Sylvia labored long and hard, saving the company from the ruin and corporate culture Joel Martin had engineered. Much to the relief of the Driftwood Village leaders, the plant was being rebuilt to revised Phase Four standards and GASMAX remained committed to the investments Justice Martin had made in the community. Similarly, even before the company lawyers confirmed that Cynthia was the sole beneficiary of the Niles Tannerson estate, GASMAX publicly credited the late professor for the improved process. With no board objection, the new CEO announced that GASMAX had committed the amount that the lawyers and accountants estimated would have been Tannerson's financial gain to funding the Tannerson Foundation.

The foundation was formed to finance and conduct chemical engineering research and to fund a generous scholarship program at Niles Tannerson's alma mater. The foundation's offices were located in the rock quarry building with its laboratories replacing the rock crusher dynamic display.

Cynthia and her cousin, who was in reality her niece, persuasively hammered out a financial settlement with all licensees who had paid upfront fees for Phase Four. There would be some lean years, but they had kept the corporate ship from sinking.

Once he was cleared medically, Tanner, in addition to his new duties as security head, gladly provided pilot services, flying the new company airplane. He usually piloted the company plane when Cynthia shuttled back and forth between Central City and Driftwood Cove. That meant that he saw less of her and more of Sylvia at EOS, but he had frequent one-on-one time with her in the air. During these flights their relationship deepened. He discovered there was now something special about her beyond good looks and brains. The life-and-death events of last summer had changed her like carbon under great pressure becomes diamonds. She was now possessed of a selfless and compassionate courage distinctly absent before they crash landed. So, it was not just some PR fluff for public consumption when she revised Martin Moses' maxim wherever it appeared to declare, 'Love God and Others. Do what's right and necessary. Do good in keeping with repentance.'

Once Tanner was able to assume his GASMAX head of security duties, he joined in the business meetings Sylvia and Cynthia held at EOS. "Having cheated death together, I knew Cynthia and Sylvia were strong, tough, brave and smart. In those business meetings, I got to see just how much," he recalled aloud, glancing again at the door and wiping his hands on his trousers. *Just like Julie,* he added silently and grinned.

Julie Simpson was now the chief of police of Driftwood Cove. Some of the things that had happened at the hydroelectric plant over a year ago were still a little fuzzy in his concussion impaired memory. *But I clearly remember Julie, wearing nothing but her bra and panties, making a date for dinner and a movie,* he reflected with a broad smile. So, when he was finally able to leave the beach house, they had that date and several thereafter. Some dates were impromptu affairs, late night calls and meetings for drinks after hours. One was immediately after she'd been offered the chief's job. They had several long conversations regarding that topic. She claimed that his advice and faith in her were the key to her having accepted the job. Similarly, her counsel and advice were essential in crafting new GASMAX security strategies and measures. *Just like Syl and Cyn, I knew from that week last summer she was tough and smart,* he thought, *but, on those dates and later when she took the job, I got to see just how smart, how wise and just how beautiful she ....*

The door banged open, yanking Tanner into the present. A wiry, solidly built man with short cropped gray hair and in a dress uniform entered. "Rawhide, you're on,' Collector said and smiled. "You ready, Marine?"

"Oorah, Skipper," Tanner said and grinned nervously as he stepped past his best man.

"You'll do just fine. It's okay to have the jitters," the colonel whispered, placing a hand on Tanner's shoulder and steering him into the sanctuary and to the altar.

The bride processional music started. All the guests rose, and, as everyone watched his bride walk to the alter, Tanner glanced briefly at the front row pew. He smiled. Cynthia's left hand rested on Stan Carter's arm. The diamond engagement ring he had recently given her glistened in the chapel lights. Next to them, Sylvia's left hand was at work, straightening the sleeve of the new suit she had selected for Officer Charley Harper.

"Your bride is a hell of a woman," Collector said as she took her final steps. "You're obviously marrying your best friend. You made a great choice, Captain, and so did she."

Tanner nodded, but it was only when he lifted Julie's veil, looked into her eyes, saw her smile and joined hands that the universe disappeared except for the two of them in this singular moment. Time stood still and he whole-heartily agreed. *One of God's good works, she is a hell of a woman and my best friend to boot. I did make a great choice, and I vow to devote the rest of my life to proving she did too.*

ABOUT THE AUTHOR

Robert Pohtos, writing as R. Nicholas Pohtos, goes by Bob. After a twenty-six-year career in the US Navy submarine service and a second fifteen-year career as a not-for-profit executive, he retired and earned a master degree in history. During the course of his studies, he discovered the movie sound serial histography. As time permitted and for enjoyment, as well as a break from scholarly writing, he resumed writing fiction, incorporating the sound serial story structure; the result is this book.

His published works include *Most Deadly, My Darling*, (Bloomington, IN: 1st Books Library, 2000), a police procedural, mystery novel, and *In Our Own Eyes*, (Meadville, PA: Christian Faith Publishing, 2019), a Christian action thriller. For the latter he was one of ten writers, who, in rotation, wrote the chapters. *What is Right in His Eyes*, (publication pending) is a spinoff of *In Our Own Eyes*, written in rotation by some of the same writers.

Bob resides in Northern Virginia with his wife, Samantha, a retired United Airlines flight attendant. His daughter, Jennifer, is grown and has a family of her own.

SINS OF OUR BLOOD THUNDER MOON

Made in the USA
Middletown, DE
13 November 2022